Tinners & ̲̲̲̲̲̲

Andrew Ferris

*For Phil + Silly
with best wishes
Andrew*

MOORHEN PUBLISHING

First published in Great Britain in 2011 by
Moorhen Publishing
1 Hazelwood Close, Windmill Hill,
Brixham, Devon, TQ5 9SE
www.moorhenpublishing.co.uk

ISBN   978-1-905856-09-1

Cover design by Tammie Doe

Printed and bound in Great Britain by
SRP Limited, Exeter, Devon

Dedication

This novel is dedicated to my wife Sheila
who has been a constant source of inspiration
and encouragement.

Author's Notes

This is a work of fiction. Although some of the characters mentioned really existed, their actions and most of the events described are entirely fictitious. I would especially draw attention to Sir William Lemon; Sir Francis Basset; Doctor Hector Bull; Rev Cardew; Mr Clutterbuck; Doctor Luke (who married a member of the Vyvyan family). They were all men of their time who made a significant contribution to Cornish life. I hope that by mentioning them in this novel I give no offence to their descendants. Mrs Rosewarne is an entirely fictitious character and not linked to any member of the Vyvyan family past or present.

I am indebted to several of my friends for reading this novel during the development stages and offering advice and proofreading.

Thanks are also due to Marie Bird for her kindness in creating the map.

I have drawn freely from the following publications:
The Cornish Miner by A. K. Hamilton Jenkin
The First Cornish Hospital by Dr C. E. Andrews
Devoran. A different Cornish Village and *Mining History in Restronguet Creek* both by Barry Simpson.

Barry Burton of Moorhen Publishing is deserving of my special thanks. Without his knowledge of the publishing industry, which he generously shared with me, I would not have attempted to finish the work or bring it to publication.

Andrew Ferris

Glossary

Bob: The end of the beam (of a beam engine) that protruded beyond the 'bob wall' of the engine house: the only part visible to the outside world. It was the business end that bobbed up and down whose movement could be translated into pumping, winding, stamping (crushing ore) and other operations depending on what was attached to it.

Buddle: A settling tank. Used to concentrate the ore by sedimentation where water washed the lighter fractions from the heavy tin ore, which sank to the bottom. These could be mechanically operated or worked by hand.

Caffer : Nickname of someone who lived in the small hamlet of Coombe, a creek off the river Fal, north of King Harry Ferry.

Catspaw: On days when the water is glassy smooth, small puffs of wind are betrayed by small ripples that spread out as they progress, resembling a cat's paw.

Chill: a small earthenware lamp which burned fish oil (see Train below).

Core: time spent working at the mine – a work shift of eight hours.

Croust: silent 't', a meal break usually mid-morning but could be the main meal of the shift. In other parts of Cornwall it is called crib.

Fiddler's Green: a mythical place where a dead sailor found a paradise of wine, women and song.

Gurries: hand barrows, either with flat slats or a fashioned butt.

Hoggins: pastry, baked to carry to work. The pastry may be plain or have some filling.

Kibble: an iron bucket used to raise ore or rock to the surface.

Oggin: variation of hoggin (see above).

Pares: a regular gang of men working together.

Phthisis: a lung disease brought on by fine, airborne particulate matter (mineral dust and gunpowder).

Piggal: a beat axe; an axe with a cutting edge backed by a hammer surface.

Slimes: refined tin ore ready for the blowing house (smelter).

Slyph, The: a novel by Georgiana, Duchess of Devonshire, wife of the 5th Duke of Devonshire. The novel has been described as a witty exposé of the corrupt morals of the aristocracy (The Ton; see below) of 18th century England.

Talfat: a loft in a house; a stage of boards constructed beneath the rafters supported by poles; an open bedroom, having an area less than the ground floor and reached by a ladder.

Teel: cultivate a piece of land; dig over for sowing or planting.

Ton, The: Social set in 18th century England (said to be the top 10,000) who set the fashion, directed cultural life and lived in the public eye.

Trade; Traade: something of little or no value.

Train: fish oil – pilchard oil, used in lamps.

Tributer: a miner who took a share by contract of the ore raised. One who undertook to raise ore from a lode at an agreed percentage of the value 'brought to grass'.

Tutworker: a miner who was paid at a rate per fathom; e.g for sinking shafts, driving adits; work that did not produce any ore but was essential for the mine operation.

Visgey: a double-headed pick with an axe-like blade at one end and a flat mattock-like blade at the other.

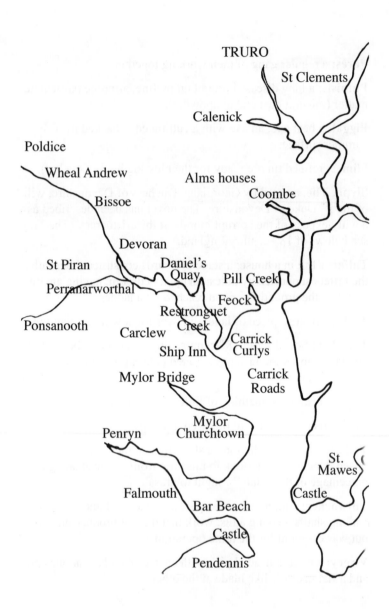

Chapter 1

February 1799

Dr Richard Maddern turned his face towards the sun enjoying the unseasonably warm weather and the gentle southerly that was blowing the *Sweet Union* barge towards Devoran, a small collection of dwellings and buildings connected with tin mining. Elijah, one of the two bargees, stood close by Richard looking out over the calm waters. He typified the look of a seaman – thickset, well-muscled with a broad, deep chest, his hair caught in a pigtail. His feet were bare, accustomed to the feel of the deck.

The light winds just gave enough way for the helm to answer and Elijah worked the tiller while Ginger, his mate, tended the sheets of the headsails to catch every catspaw. Even so, their progress depended as much on the flooding tide and, despite their efforts, the *Sweet Union* seemed drawn to one of His Majesty's sloops at anchor in Carrick Roads. This created a tension that changed the mood on board; Elijah's banter ceased and his eyes never left the sloop.

'Impressment Service,' he said.

Richard was about to raise his telescope to have a closer look when the bargee hissed a warning.

'No. Not yet.'

As they passed within pistol range, two others joined an officer at the rail.

'Ahoy!' the officer shouted to attract their attention. Elijah looked dead ahead, keeping the barge as far as possible from the sloop. Ginger looked back anxiously then turned back to his sail trimming. Slowly they left the sloop astern. Elijah looked over his shoulder.

'You can have a look now,' he said to Richard, 'but be careful.'

'There's something going on,' Richard said.

Elijah hid below the bulwarks and opened his telescope.

'Lowering a boat,' he said quietly. He got up quickly and whistled to Ginger. Taking the corner of a sail lying on the deck, with a swift movement he uncovered two swivel guns.

'Take the tiller, sir, while we beat to quarters.' He smiled sardonically. Elijah mounted the guns on the gunwales, one each side of the barge.

'Canister shot,' he said as he loaded the weapons.

'Are you sure taking on the navy is the right course of action?' Richard asked, bemused, as the seriousness of the situation unfolded. 'The ship might fire on us!'

Elijah shook his head. 'She's facing out to sea – tide rode. None of her guns will bear.'

Richard swallowed hard, unconvinced, and began to sweat.

Ginger emerged from the fo'c'sle with a large box from which he extracted six pistols and began to load them.

The boat from the sloop was catching them quickly; six seamen rowing in pairs and a young midshipman, perhaps twelve years old, in the stern sheets, steering. The gap closed and the midshipman put a glass to his eye and looked directly at them. Elijah responded by aiming the gun at the boat leaving no doubt of their intentions. The rowing eased and the boat stood off from the barge about thirty yards. In those quiet conditions, quietly spoken words carried over the distance.

'I am boarding to inspect your cargo,' the midshipman said.

To Richard's amazement, Ginger, who had not spoken a word until now, answered in clear ringing tones.

'You have no right – you exceed your duty. You may only inspect the crew and you can see from where you are that there are just two.'

'I can see three.'

'Doctor Maddern is a passenger.'

Silence across the glassy water increased the tension. The young man looked to his crew and muttered in a low voice. He was unsure. Then he called again across the water.

'What ship were you on?'

10

'Purser on the *Neptune*,' Ginger replied.

The midshipman nodded; pursers were mess deck sea-lawyers. He ordered 'Give way!' and steered back to the sloop.

Elijah breathed a sigh of relief and smiled at Ginger.

'Near thing,' he said to Richard and took the tiller again.

'Have you been pressed, Elijah?'

'Twice. First time I was just married with a young boy – few months like. Two years away before I got home. Both dead. They had nothing.' Elijah's expression saddened as he remembered. 'Pressing a man is a bad business – no questions asked. Beat, clapped in irons and then fighting for your life. Nothing you can do about it – legal they say. Legal my ass!' he added bitterly, turning away and gazing into the distance. 'Last time it was my own fault. After I found out me missus and boy died I went on the grog in Falmouth,' he shook his head despondently. 'The gangs look for drunks in the inns. Never again though.'

He patted the swivel gun affectionately. 'All ready! Flintlock. I'd kill the bloody lot – swing for it – all the way to Fiddler's Green, but they won't take me again!'

They sailed on in silence.

The entrance to Restronguet Creek was not readily discernible until very close. The sloop disappeared as they changed course and a happier atmosphere returned.

'Here's Tensy looking for his shilling,' Elijah said. 'See they iron poles – marking the Carrick Curyls rocks? We have to pay Mylor parish every time the mast passes.'

A small pulling boat was approaching, the boatman glancing over his shoulder from time to time, gauging coming alongside. He was a small, neat man dressed in a heavy dark Guernsey and black breeches, shiny with wear. His eyes, the colour of blue smoke, twinkled with amusement. Richard listened intently trying to grasp the local accent and learned they were speaking of the press gang.

Then, louder so that Richard might hear, Tensy said, 'We shall have a smother of wind from the sou'west 'fore night come, I'm thinking. Glass is falling fast – we shall have a guts-full of rain, no doubt.'

Elijah nodded his agreement.

'Well, I'll be casting off,' said Tensy. 'See you in the Ship going home along, Lij!'

'No bloody fear – loading slimes for Clenink.'

Tensy laughed and without another word pushed off and smoothly pulled for the shore.

Richard was already aware that the dialect would be a difficulty. Moreover, he thought that his lack of comprehension might be compounded by the taciturn nature of the native Cornish. Although that trait could have been heightened due to their not understanding him, as much as his not understanding them.

Overriding that issue were weightier concerns. Leaving Bristol was lifting the heavy emotional burden he had been enduring. His marriage had failed utterly and miserably. His two sons had been banished to boarding schools by their mother and he saw little of them. Now, unfettered, he found he could breathe more easily. However, when introspection caught him off-guard, guilt pressed on his shoulders. He was running away. When he fell into melancholy he admitted to cowardice. When he tried to rationalise his action the best interpretation he could put on it was that in fleeing to Cornwall he acted out of everyone's best interest, but especially his own. His self-imposed exile would bring loneliness; there would be few friends to make here. These thoughts added to his anxiety about his new life, an anxiety not allayed by this brilliant, sunny day. Somewhere, deep inside his being, there was a wish not to arrive, to go on, hoping all his problems would resolve themselves. But, like it or not, he was approaching his new home.

The two shores formed a narrow gut where the currents were powerful and the barge lifted on the flood tide.

'Poling once we're past the pool,' Elijah said quietly to Ginger who nodded and picked up a heavy long pole, one end of which he dropped over the side into the water as he walked forward.

'Now, sir, if you take the tiller, we'll do the poling.' Seeing doubt in Richard's face, he winked. 'I'll keep an eye on you. Tide's coming home so we shan't be long. Keep close to this shore, past the Ship and then alongside Gunna Woods.'

12

The Ship Inn was tucked away at the base of the hillside at the water's edge. Its thatched roof frowned over the windows placed high on the walls. A long-ago lime-wash had mostly flaked exposing the stone construction. The door was black, grimed over and weathered. The place did not welcome, but sat brooding and watchful. Beyond the narrows of the gut, the creek area increased considerably: hundreds of yards wide and extending over a mile with no visible end. Both men dug their poles into the creek's bottom and, placing the ends into their shoulders, walked the side decks towards Richard and then took the poles to the bow again to repeat the process.

Tregunwith Woods loomed, bare and gaunt in its winter deciduousness. Stunted oaks serried the shore, growing right to the water's edge where all their intertwining branches ended universally at the high water mark.

There was silence except for the regular splash of the poles, but Elijah had something to say each time he reached Richard. It was a way of pausing and recovering without having to show that it was the effect of the work that demanded the rest.

'That's Daniels Quay. The stack is a lead smelter.'

Richard saw a low quay ahead and to his right. A barge was alongside, discharging coals and adding to the large piles covering most of the quay. There was also a contrasting heap of brilliantly white material glistening in the sunshine.

'Lime,' Elijah explained following Richard's gaze, his breathing heavy from his exertions. A kiln was visible at the back of the quay.

The creek was narrowing and the way ahead was no longer clear. A great barrier, more than a hundred yards long stretched almost across the creek. Elijah explained there was a deepwater channel each side of the dam and that they must take the channel to the Devoran quays. Two large embankments ran upstream from the cross-river dam as far as could be seen. The dam and embankments held back the tide allowing tinners to remove the overburden and expose the tin in the riverbed. On the far embankment, large engines worked sending a rattling noise echoing across the water.

'Rag and chain pumps. Taking away water coming from streams and springs inside the diggings.'

The tide was not yet sufficiently high to see over the embankment so Richard's interest was taken on the right bank where a small farm nestled in a bare copse of beech and elm. Richard saw a figure walking along a path heading in the same direction: a young woman. He put his glass to his eye just as she looked straight at him. She continued to look in his direction until she stumbled and became a heap of clothes struggling to regain its stance.

'Don't go in there – Tallack's creek is full o'mud,' Elijah warned of the mud flats beyond which the girl had regained her feet.

She brushed down her cloak and dress and retrieved a wicker basket before stealing another glance in his direction. Through the glass he saw her smile.

'Keep her up!' Elijah's voice was sharp and urgent, awakening Richard to his tiller duty. Elijah made some comment to Ginger who responded with a hearty laugh.

Quays now began on his right, but instead of the expected bustle of dockers and merchants, they were empty except for oddments of unloaded cargo. Next was a timber pond and after that a row of low buildings set back from the wharves.

'Hutches,' Elijah said breathily. 'That's where the tin ore is kept waiting to be loaded. Ginger says you haven't passed your master's ticket on account of your navigation.'

Ginger had his head slightly to one side, not sure how Richard would react to his leg-pull whereas Elijah was grinning widely and retreated behind Ginger's back to hide his mirth. Ginger's expression showed that his worst fears might have been realised. Stepping one pace forward he removed his cap, revealing a completely bald head and knuckled his forehead.

'No offence meant, sir, begging your pardon.'

'No offence at all Mr...'

'Parker's the name, sir. Nicholas Parker.'

'You're not from these parts, Mr Parker?'

'Nicholas if you please, sir. No, sir. I am originally from London, a lawyer's clerk in the City.'

He saw Richard waited to hear more. 'Not all the work lawyers do is above the law and, due to circumstances, I became embroiled in a situation that could have seen me in the

Marshalsea. So to avoid the tipstaff I went to sea.'

'I am amazed.'

'Oh, it gets more amazing. I became Purser on the *Neptune* under Captain Freemantle – '

Elijah stepped nearer and touched Ginger's arm by way of entering the conversation.

'Ginger was the only honest purser in the fleet.'

Ginger, embarrassed by his friend's praise, altered tack.

'We were shipmates, Lij and me, and after a successful sailing we decided to swallow the anchor and set up business together. Lij is a first-class seaman and I am able to look after the business matters.'

The barge had drifted alongside the quay. Elijah jumped onto the dockside with a rope and took a couple of turns around a bollard to take the way off the barge which bumped gently against the wooden docks. The rope groaned and tightened – journey's end. In very short time Richard's possessions were unloaded – four large sea trunks, five large wooden packing cases and several pieces of furniture too large for either method of packing.

'Heavy stuff, sir.'

'Indeed – and how to get it to the house? The quays are deserted.'

Ginger heard Richard's concern. 'We have some other material in the hold for a mining agent and also we have to load slimes, so we are expecting someone soon.'

'I must settle with you,' Richard addressed both men, 'before I leave.'

Ginger handed him a headed invoice with the amount of one guinea already made out.

'Well thank you, Mr Parker. I hope the *slimes* don't prove too difficult to load and you have a safe journey to wherever it is.'

Ginger smiled. 'You'll soon pick up the local speech. Slimes are the refined tin ore, which we take to a blowing house – a smelter. We are going to one at Calenick, near Truro. Is that clearer, Doctor? If the Agent does not arrive soon, I will introduce you to a captain of the tinners who will be able to help you. They might appear to be a rough lot, but that belies a generous nature. The work they do would break most men in a week. All winds and weathers they are exposed for long hours, but they bear it with great good humour and fortitude. They work for a pittance and live in the most appalling conditions – far worse than being at sea. They make a fortune for the landowners who treat them little better, and sometimes worse, than their animals.'

'A word of caution, Mr Parker. In these days, such talk can easily be misconstrued as being seditious. It's best to weigh your words carefully.'

'Yes, sir, you are right. To speak of Tom Paine would be enough to ensure one saw the inside of Bodmin Gaol. Yet one who writes that every man has the right to the pursuit of happiness has much to commend him. Napoleon seems set to invade these shores. The navy will defend us and we have great confidence after the victory of the Nile last year, but we must be mindful that in 1797 there were mutinies at Spithead and the Nore, purely over the conditions sailors are subjected to. If the navy fails us we are at Napoleon's mercy. Difficult times, indeed.'

*

The path leading to his newly-taken house was wide and muddied, but an overnight frost and a dry day made the going relatively easy. Shortly it crossed a wider lane, which was the route used to bring ore down to the quays and equipment and coals up to the mines much further up the valley. Where the two paths crossed, he took the steeper direction up a hill. A row of cottages to his right ran parallel to the creek and some fifty yards back from it. The poorly-built dwellings had at their backs a deeply-rutted track filled with stagnant water. He stopped and looked more closely. He did not expect to be called upon by those within.

A woman emerged from one of the cottages and to his surprise he saw that it was she he had seen from the barge. She bade someone in the cottage goodbye and began to tread the lane carefully, her eyes cast to the ground to avoid the potholes. So intent was she on her footsteps that she was almost upon him before she looked up.

'Be careful, miss,' he said holding out his hand to assist her over the last large rut.

She stopped and blushed, but because of his position she was obliged to take his hand. He took her arm as she came closer and they finished the manoeuvre exactly as he wanted – very close to each other. The hood of her cloak reached his eye level and, despite her blushes, she tilted her head and looked him fully in the face – he perceived no real sense of embarrassment in her expression. Large blue eyes looked confidently into his with no sign of alarm or fear, taking in his features that he hoped pleased her as much as she was pleasing him. Her high cheeks were coloured pleasantly by the fresh air and her whole complexion was luminous and pure. Her lips were full, fleshy, glowing with a natural redness; he had an impulse to touch them. Light smiles flickered across her face, waxing and waning with her thoughts. Her blonde hair had winter's tints of auburn and fell from under her hood further than her shoulders; he thought that the summer sun would bleach it golden.

'Thank you. I aren't going to fall down again, so you can let me be.' The same speech cadence as Elijah's, but her voice was soft and almost musical. He didn't let her hand go as she suggested. Instead, he assisted her further onto the path.

'Dr Maddern at your service, miss,' he introduced himself. 'I'm sorry about the mishap earlier – my attention caused your foot to slip. No harm done I trust?'

'Only to me pride, and vanity is a sin.'

Richard reluctantly let her hand fall and they began to walk slowly up the hill, side by side. 'Do you live in the cottages?'

'No! God help us.' She looked at him to emphasise her words. Richard walked on hoping for more information but none came.

'Where do you live?'

'Why, I live just where you seen me.'

He stopped by his house. 'Since we are to be neighbours perhaps you will tell me your name?'

'Are you the gent taking up here?'

'Yes. Umm...what shall I call you?' he persisted.

'Nancy!' she laughed and skipped quickly up the hill, turning just once more to look at him before disappearing behind a high hedge. He smiled to himself, greatly pleased with the short encounter. His steps felt lighter as he approached the house and some of his earlier apprehension vanished. A low hawthorn hedge bordered his property and a gate, in need of repair, opened onto a neglected vegetable garden. A path of white spar stones led to the front door, set in the middle of the building, under a small porch. A small woman opened the door. Her face was long and added to the general mien of sadness or apprehension – he was not sure which. Her hair, gathered in a bow, hung down her back, but several wayward wisps that she constantly brushed aside like a nervous tic, spoilt the careful preparation. Her colour was that of a clean potato skin washed with winter's greyness; doleful eyes moved fitfully alerting Richard to some anxiety.

'Mrs Endean. You got my letter to expect me?'

'Yes, sir. Thank you, sir, and welcome to your home. Begging your pardon, sir, but the tradesman is here,' she informed him and Richard sensed this was expected to anger him. She led him towards the dining room where a large man in a smock was using a smoothing plane on a rough board.

'This here's Mr Williams the carpenter,' said Mrs Endean and then she stood back still expecting some words.

Mr Williams stopped and turned around at the sound of her voice. Richard looked around the room and saw the ceiling-to-floor oak panelling was almost finished and the workmanship he judged to be of the highest calibre.

'Splendid work, Mr Williams. It's all I had hoped for.'

'Thank you kindly, sir. The fact is, sir, I should've finished a week ago, but things haven't worked out like.'

'How long before you will be finished?'

'Oh, I only got to finish here and that's that. Gone afore the week's out if me timber's here with Lij.'

'I do believe it is on the docks right now.'

Mr Williams was relieved, but there was something else. 'Beg pardon, sir, there is another matter. Mr Trethowan only give me three guineas,' and he held up three fingers. 'Christmas gone, and I had to give it to the merchant. I couldn't make ends meet so I had to take on other work over to Carclew and that threw me out here.'

The speech came in a rush and Richard's ear for the local accent deserted him.

'You hadn't enough money to live off so you took some other work?' he ventured.

Mr Williams nodded.

'And now you would like a further advance I take it?'

'I was hoping for five guineas, sir,' and one hand was held up with all fingers and thumb spread.

Richard made out a receipt and handed it to Mr Williams to sign while he counted out the coins from his purse. Mr Williams hesitated.

'Now you'll need to sign your name just here.'

'Iss,' he said and took hold of the quill. 'Put your finger on the place, if you please.'

Richard placed a finger on the paper and Mr Williams, with a very shaky hand, made an awkward cross, the two lines not meeting symmetrically.

'Very good. Now, I must go back and see about getting the trunks and furniture here before nightfall.'

Except for the *Sweet Union,* the quay was deserted. His possessions were there along with the timber Mr Williams needed and some heavy ironwork for the mines. What took his attention most was an amazingly large bundle of candles. It stood perhaps five feet tall and as much around.

'Dr Maddern?'

He turned to see a man wearing a high pole hat.

'Yes.'

'Cappen James, sir. I understand that you would like your stuff moved to the house?'

'Indeed yes, Captain James.' He didn't look like a seafarer, but Richard addressed him by the title given. Behind the captain were six young men all dressed alike in mud-orange coloured smocks and dark breeches tucked inside leather boots. They waited patiently, shy and unsmiling.

'These boys will shift it for you.'

'Very well, Captain. I'm much obliged. How will you manage it?'

'Oh 'tiss no big job, sir – they'll do it on gurries,' he explained, and motioned to three handbarrows the youths were standing beside. Two shafts of wood, about five feet long with carved ends shaped for easier gripping, fastened together by short boards about eighteen inches long.

'I see,' Richard said harbouring serious doubts. 'Some of the chests are very heavy, Captain James – do you think they will be able to lift them without straining themselves?'

Captain James walked to the largest chest and tested its weight.

'Iss, they'll manage they all right.' He waved an arm at the youths who laid their smocks aside leaving them in thin shirts and braces holding up their breeches. Richard observed the tallest was a full three inches shorter than his own five feet ten. Their build was the outstanding feature; massively broad shoulders, thick necks and muscular arms. They began to load the trunks; the first pair gripped the shafts and gave a shout to co-ordinate their movements. The load lifted and they were away, quickly followed by the second and third pair.

'Steady!' Captain James roared after them but they took no notice and it was clear some competition was taking place as the speed gathered.

Captain James smiled to himself. 'Buggers they be – I told them no hank but I can't stop them.'

'How old are they, Captain?'

'Why, sixteen or seventeen I reckon. Strong boys. 'Tiss the work – tin streaming is hard but healthy.'

'Now, Captain James, how much shall I pay for the removal?'

'Aw, don't bother with that. Half hour will do it. If we need you in a hurry one day, I expect you'll help out, Doctor.'

'Yes indeed. Surely.'

'If you make your way slowly back now, sir, you'll be in time for the last load.'

On the way, he met the boys returning, full of merriment, speaking among themselves with shy glances in his direction. Before he reached the front door, he heard them coming from behind panting with the exertion. He stood aside and they passed in almost silence and unloaded in the kitchen. Mrs Endean was trying to manoeuvre the boxes and trunks to keep a clear area. Mr Williams was pulling the heavy loads into the hall

20

using round timber as rollers. The luggage kept coming and then the furniture and lastly the timber.

'No candles, boys?' Richard joked.

'That's for the mines,' one of the boys answered.

'And you are?'

'Joshua, sir.'

'What in heaven's name do they do with so many?'

The boys sniggered and whispered to each other. 'We believe they eat them, sir,' Joshua offered.

'Do they indeed? Well, my thanks to you all for bringing my belongings home safely. I have a florin to be divided equally – that's fourpence each. To whom shall I give it?'

'Joshua,' someone suggested and Richard duly obliged.

'A shilling is as much as us gets in a day, sir. Thank you kindly.' And with that they left, glad to get away before any embarrassment might occur.

A busy hour and the trunks and boxes were stowed in less inconvenient places allowing passage through the house.

'Would you like a dish o' tay, sir?' Mrs Endean asked. 'You must be chackun. I got a pasty in the oven; ready now if you like.'

Richard consulted his fob; half-past four and he had neither eaten nor drunk anything since that morning.

'A pasty, Mrs Endean! I don't believe I've had a pasty before now. And some tea – that will be splendid.'

Chapter 2

He awoke with an urgent need to pee and searched frantically under the bed for the chamber pot, but the welcoming touch of china did not come to hand. In desperation, he threw up the lower sash window and relieved himself onto the garden below. It took what seemed an eternity and in the growing light, he scanned the world looking for anyone who might catch him in his predicament. The sashes rattled in the wind like the clapping of hands to attract attention. The sleet-laden wind froze him while taking his steaming stream clear across the front of the house. Richard had a strong feeling that someone lurked in the lane below. Looking carefully he saw a figure moving behind the deciduous hedge.

A gentle knock at his door galvanised him into unnecessarily violent action shutting the window with a slam that reverberated through the house. Mrs Endean shrieked with alarm outside the door.

He crossed the room and opened the door. 'Ha! Mrs Endean,' he said as calmly as he could.

'Lord Help us, Doctor! Is something the matter?' She was trembling holding a large jug of hot water in a washbasin.

'Calm yourself, Mrs Endean! Here let me take the basin before any harm is done.' She handed the bowl over which he took to a marble-topped washstand.

'Thank you, Mrs Endean.'

Mrs Endean was already retreating shaking her head as folks do who harbour a suspicion. 'Breakfast is nearly ready, sir,' she said, that he understood to mean, 'don't be long'.

Breakfast in the kitchen, the only warm room in the house, was a feast of bacon, eggs, and some leftover pasty.

'The house is cold, Mrs Endean. I think we should light fires in the drawing and dining rooms to take the chill off.'

'Iss if you like, only Mr Williams might sweat a bit.'

'Ah yes. Well, perhaps in the rooms he is not working in?'

He made the normal morning enquiries for the post and newspaper.

'Post! My life and soul,' she exclaimed. 'Post is up from Truro seven in morning and down at seven in evening. *Mercury* is fortnightly – that'll be week next Thursday.' Her expression was serious and she waited for a reply to her information.

Richard did not understand completely what she said and decided to investigate papers when he went into Truro.

'Tell me, Mrs Endean,' and he paused with deliberation to get her attention, 'what do you know of a person, I mean a young woman, by the name of Nancy?'

'Oooow! How do you know our maid Nancy?' she was gleefully intrigued. Without waiting for an answer, she rushed on. 'You only been here a day and you're asking about maid Nancy! Pretty as a picture she is and handsome with it.'

'Good natured?' he ventured.

'Iss. Somebody will have her 'fore long – I'm amazed nobody's had her already; they tinners aren't fussy what they get up to. Mind, Billy won't let nobody near her!' Her voice rose to a pitch.

'Surely no-one would take advantage of her while out and about on her business?'

'Huh! Many's the maid that had to get married after running the lanes late at night – iss, most of them, I dare say.'

'But this Billy and she have an understanding?'

She scoffed. 'Billy thinks so sure enough. But Nancy won't have him. "No!" she says to me, "I don't want him Ruth," that's what she do say.' Her arms waved in the air and she brushed in quick movements at her hair with her hands. 'Time she was married,' she said in a quieter voice to the table. 'Two and twenty and no chick nor cheeld.

'Where did you see her?' she asked with sudden seriousness.

'In the lane, coming out of one of the cottages close by.'

'Oh iss,' she saddened quickly. 'The cheeld in the Raw is very sick. Nancy was helping out. She was here first thing.'

'What here? Where?'

'Why in the Raw!'

'What is the raw?'

'Why, the raw of cottages here.' She was exasperated by his slowness.

Richard let the subject drop; too much probing might arouse too much interest.

*

Mr Williams said he made about two guineas a month clear of his expenses, assuring Richard this was a good wage, and compared well with that of the hard-rock miners. Carpenters at the mines make less than this and their work was no more dependable.

Richard made out the bill for Trethowan, the lawyer. Mrs Endean knew a boy who would take the letters to catch the post for Truro on payment of a ha'penny.

He moved his instruments, in a magnificent mahogany chest, and his medicine cabinet into the surgery. This bare room, formally used for ore sampling, had slate benches on three walls and a slate floor. It was a cold and comfortless place, but behind an adjoining door there was a water closet; a handsome single-holed, polished mahogany board extended the full width of the small room topping a glazed porcelain bowl of pure white. The cistern bore the mark "Chas Fox Perran Foundry 1785". One large crate remained containing a hipbath and he wondered, briefly, about installing it in there. He spread his books over the floor and sorted them by subject: medicine, natural philosophy, literature and poetry. Remembering his conversation of yesterday, *The Age of Reason* and *The Rights of Man,* would be hidden from sight, keeping company with his private thoughts.

All through the morning, one thought kept intruding. Who was it in the bushes earlier? Could it have been Nancy? How to find out? Maybe he could meet her if she came to the sick child again. He would deduce from her demeanour if she were the one – she was just a simple country girl and questioning would draw out the answers. Doctors, like priests, could ask questions and expect to get answers. He could easily visit the child and make enquiries – some would argue it was his duty.

'Mrs Endean, what time will we dine?'

She was preparing vegetables and on the table was a plucked

pheasant. She faced him, brushing her hair back from her eyes and sighed. 'Depends.'

'On what?'

'On whether you want to eat at dinner time or tonight.'

He determined the best way forward would be to explain his plans rather than ask questions.

'I plan to visit the sick child in the Row now, but if this is not in accord with your meal arrangements then I will postpone it.' She stared at him vacantly. 'You understand me, Mrs Endean?'

'Why iss,' she said quietly. ''Tiss just you say s'many words me mind can't take it all in at once.'

Richard waited then raised an eyebrow to prompt a further answer.

'She haven't any money for you.' She had a forlorn expression.

'I'm not going to make a charge, Mrs Endean.'

'Ohh! Well,' she brightened and busily wiped her hands on her pinafore. 'I got plenty of cold meat if you want to push away,' and she interpreted for him, 'make do like – after you been. And the bird will be ready later.' She was eager, and did not want an act of kindness to a poor neighbour delayed.

Dressed warmly in a greatcoat, hat and scarf to ward off the damp sleet, and high leather boots to keep his feet dry, he splashed through the many puddles in the Row. It was not rain alone that filled the puddles and he saw where the night soil was thrown. A dead rat was propped against a wall, its eyes open, its fur formed into spikes by the wet, exposing pink flesh. He knew the face of penury and all it brought. He was not immune to its effects – his head would reel and his stomach churn but he knew worse was possible and steeled himself. Before knocking at the door, which only partly blocked the doorway, he looked down the Row at the other cottages. Built of rough stonework and held together by earth, they had a common appearance of destitution and filth. He rapped on the door.

'Who's that?' The voice was gentle enough.

'Dr Maddern, Mrs...' And he realised he didn't know whom he was visiting. Someone struggled at the door that opened a crack. A face appeared – a weary dirty face, but overlaid with curiosity. Richard touched his hat. 'Good morning, ma'am. It's Mrs...?'

'Trezise.'

'I am Dr Maddern, your new neighbour. I believe you have a sick child?'

She thought about the question for a while before replying. 'I haven't asked for no doctor.'

'Don't worry, Mrs Trezise. I just want to make sure the child is all right.'

She struggled with the door again and eventually it fell into the room. He stepped down into the darkness as Mrs Trezise struggled to put the door back. He helped her to close off the howling wind whose pitch changed to a shriek as the draught squeezed through the narrowing cracks about the ill-fitting door. An indescribable stench assaulted his senses; excrement and stale urine he expected, but overlaying this was an unrecognisable foul odour. He put a handkerchief to his nose and coughed.

'Slight cold,' he said. He hoped that given a short time his sense of smell would dull and the stench become tolerable. The beaten earth floor had no cover of reeds or straw. Light from a small window showed the only furniture was a small table and two chairs. A rough board across two blocks of stone raised a few pieces of crockery and pots off the ground. The far end of the room was barely distinguishable – boards almost entirely blocked off the window. There was an upper level, about half the area of the room, consisting of boards supported by roughly hewn poles. There was no fire in the hearth despite the house being desperately cold.

'No fire, Mrs Trezise?'

'No,' she replied guardedly. 'We wait until me man is here. 'Is clothes won't dry 'fore the morning else.'

Richard nodded. 'And where is the sick child?'

She walked towards the middle of the room where there was a small box. Rough hessian covered a child lying on a hessian sack filled with straw.

'Can you bring a light, Mrs Trezise?'

She fumbled in a pot and brought out a lamp. The tinder struck and the lamp gave a dim light, but it was also the source

26

of the awful odour that filled the cottage. His stomach heaved. He quickly found two candles in his bag, lit them from her lamp, and then asked her to extinguish it.

The child slept in a pitiable state. Clothed in a short vest, not reaching her navel, her body was marked with fleabites and her head crawled with lice. Thick mucus ran from each nostril like green wax. Her feet were cold yet her forehead registered a fever. He wiped away the mucus and she stirred.

'What is her name? How old?'

'Molly. Three this coming May.'

'How long has she been like this?'

'Three days.'

'Has she taken any nourishment – something to eat?'

'Some milk Nancy brought this morning.'

Richard continued to examine the child, but the conditions made it difficult.

'When was Nancy here? What time?'

'Early – afore light.'

Just as he feared.

'She won't last, will she?' It wasn't a question but a prediction. 'She'll be gone 'fore evening.'

He looked at the woman at his elbow. He could not come to a firm conclusion about her age. Her hard life would have added many more years than had actually passed. She was thin and dark circles of tiredness surrounded each eye; the skin on her cheekbones was drawn tight. Her clothes were threadbare and the apron she wore was stiff with filth.

'Where do you fetch water?'

She moved slightly, uncomfortable with the question. 'Down the lane. Something to put it in is what's wanted.'

'No buckets?'

She shook her head. The uncharitable thoughts he had a few minutes ago evaporated. These people were desperate.

'How old are you?'

'Two and twenty come spring.'

'Where are your other children?'

She pointed to the upper level and he raised his candle to get a better view. Three faces stared back at him from the gloom.

'They're quiet.'

'Hungry.'

A rough ladder was the only access to the loft and the three children moved back into the darkness as he reached their level. The little clothing they wore left no doubt they were all boys.

'Come here and tell me your names,' he encouraged, but the boys shrank further into the gloom. There were two hessian sacks filled with straw upon which they slept. The conditions here were no better than below and the cold was equally as penetrating. He descended carefully and faced Mrs Trezise.

'Will Nancy be bringing some more milk?' He asked the question with genuine concern, not to elicit further information about the girl.

'No.'

'I should like to take Molly to my surgery where I can examine her properly. I think she has no more than a cold, but I cannot be sure. Would you allow me to do that, Mrs Trezise?'

She nodded and a tear trickled down her face. 'It isn't the first we lost, Doctor – nor the last I speck.'

He picked up the box with the child and went to the entrance where Mrs Trezise struggled until the door opened. He paused at the threshold.

'Try not to worry, Mrs Trezise. You can visit whenever you wish.'

Mild panic set in when he arrived and told Mrs Endean what he carried. She rushed around the kitchen table, her hands held close to her head.

'Oh my dear soul. Whatever shall us do? Oh the poor little cheeld.'

Richard placed the box on the kitchen table, which brought a rebuke, so he put it on a chair before the warm range.

'Now, Mrs Endean, a jug of warm water and a washbasin if you please, then we can give little Molly a clean.'

He cut the small vest from Molly and disposed of it in the range. Her body was too thin and her extended belly was a sign of malnourishment. Molly didn't make a sound and Richard found this disconcerting. A healthy two-year-old in a strange house with strangers should be howling. She must be in some discomfort or perhaps hungry or most likely both. Mrs Endean put a basin of water on the table and stood by ready for action.

'You see the state of her hair? Yes? The easiest solution is to cut it off do you agree?'

She nodded and they set to work, burning the lice-ridden hair.

'Poor little thing; bald as a coot. Ne'er mine. It'll grow again, me 'andsome.'

'I wish she would cry – not *too* much you understand. Now I'll lift her carefully into the basin and if you can support her for a while...' Molly made a whimper and tried to open her crusted eyes. A few drops of oil of wintergreen and camphor generated a steamy aromatic atmosphere. 'That may help to clear her nose and make her breathing easier.'

Richard began to wipe her eyes free of the yellow matter. Molly gasped, cried, and tried to knock his hands away. It took a while, but when her blue eyes were clear she looked around and fear stood on her brow. Tears welled up and her bottom lip trembled.

'Trouble coming, Mrs Endean. Hello, Molly,' Richard said, but it did not pacify the child. Now she began to cry properly and Mrs Endean lifted her out of the basin, placed her over her shoulder, and rocked her gently while drying her.

'I expect she'll have trouble clunkun if her throat is bad,' Mrs Endean ventured an opinion.

Richard paused hoping for an explanation, but none was forthcoming. 'Keep her steady and I'll look down her throat. If there is an obstruction then swallowing could be a problem.'

Mrs Endean greeted this with an exasperated sigh.

'Just a little inflammation – no more than can be expected with a cold. No diphtheria. If I hold her in the towel could you get some warm milk with sugar, Mrs Endean?'

She set off then stopped. 'I think 'tiss better to call me Ruth, Doctor – 'tiss quicker.'

'Yes, thank you, Ruth.'

Molly settled as he dried her in front of the fire, closing her eyes and sucking her thumb contentedly.

Mr Williams was at the door and approached almost reverentially. 'Begging your pardon, sir, but how's the little maid?'

'Come in and see. Needs a wig, but I think more comfortable

and she'll be better still when she takes some milk.'

'Poor little devil – hardly any flesh on her bones.'

'She'll be all right soon. Mr Williams, I would consider it a favour if you could fix the door at Mrs Trezise's cottage. It's off its hangings. I'll pay you for the work as soon as you've finished.'

Without hesitation he agreed. 'Iss. I'll have a look 'fore the light goes.'

Molly took some milk, but not being able to breathe through her nose she often gasped and looked distressed.

'We must clear her nose, Ruth. If you hold her I'll mix some menthol in lanolin and rub it on her chest – the vapours may help.'

Ruth made a dish o' tay and they drank it watching Molly as she slept in a makeshift bed made from a small crate.

Chapter 3

Three days later the day dawned cold with a brisk wind. Ruth called it a "black easterly" as she scuttled about the house making up the fires. 'All you want for is a fire in this weather.'

Later in the morning, Ruth announced, in her usual fashion of running about the kitchen shouting, that post had arrived.

'The clerk is here, and he has post!' she pointed rigidly towards the back door.

There, Richard found a man shaking from the cold and looking as though he had been left in mid-sentence.

'Doctor Maddern?' he enquired.

'Yes, indeed.'

'Burley,' he introduced himself, 'clerk to Mr Trethowan, sir.'

Burley didn't suit him. He was a stick-like person stiff from head to toe in tightly-fitting black apparel, topped with a tall, narrow black hat that he raised in greeting. He eagerly accepted refreshment beside the kitchen range before they proceeded to business.

Burley set three envelopes and a purse on the table in the drawing room. The business was quickly dealt with: settlement of Mr Williams' account, a banker's draft for the purchase of a horse from Sir William Lemon and another draft for future expenditure and some cash.

'There is the matter of your housekeeper, Mrs Endean. Since engaging her we have paid her monies for running the household and her wages to the end of January. I visited once a month for these purposes.'

There was a knock at the door and Ruth entered. 'Begging pardon, but the groom is here. Sir William's man,' she explained, 'about the 'oss.'

'Ha! Good. Please ask him to wait, Mrs Endean.' He turned

back to Burley. 'How much are her wages?'

'A shilling a week with all found.'

A shilling a week – not even two pence a day. Burley was uncomfortable with Richard's silence.

'That is the usual rate, Doctor. The remoteness of the place left us with few choices of housekeeper. Mrs Endean comes with good references from her previous employer where she worked with the cook.' He paused still concerned about Richard's unresponsiveness. 'I'm sure you can adjust her wages to a more satisfactory level now she is used to her living. I dare say she would take sixpence a week without any dissent. Erm, is something troubling you, Doctor?'

'Not at all, Mr Burley. Thank you for your clarity and briefness.'

Burley smiled. 'Mr Trethowan would appreciate a visit from you at your earliest convenience to settle your account.'

'It's a pity you didn't bring it for my perusal...'

'I anticipated such a request, Doctor, and I have made up the accounts. They do not show the detail of course.'

Richard slit at the seal and looked at the last page and almost to the last line. 'A princely sum, Mr Burley! Just remind me – you did say that you had made up the bill?'

'Yes, sir.'

'And has Mr Trethowan approved it?'

Burley flushed. 'Mr Trethowan does not always need to see an account, but since you ask I will make sure he approves the figures.'

'Thank you, Mr Burley. Have a safe journey home. I look forward to our next meeting.'

Burley left the house and was speaking with the groom when Richard stepped outside the back door, but quickly departed. Richard immediately appreciated the meaning of "black easterly". The air was penetrating and chilling to the marrow.

'Morning, sir. Peters, Sir William's groom, sir.'

Peters was short and roundly robust, his body pushed against his smart riding gear at all points.

'Sir William invites you to Carclew to see the horse, sir.'

'I should like that very much, Mr Peters.'

It was a short distance along the lane to a junction with an earth embankment that gave access across the Carnon River. The causeway, ten feet above the riverbed and one hundred yards in length, held back the Carnon River and the outfall from the County Adit. They passed a vile-smelling vitriol works. Half way across the causeway, they could glimpse the tinners in the distance working in a huge bowl in the creek bed, three hundred yards wide and half a mile or more in length. At the end of the causeway, they crossed the small Trewedna River. At Perranwharf, there was a surprisingly large vessel with its cargo of timber strewn over the quays. Not far from the quay was a rough tavern that Peters informed was nicknamed the Norway, because of the trade with that country in pit props for the mines. At Perranarworthal, there were several weatherboard houses beside the lane and further along Charles Fox's foundry, one of the biggest in the world, Peters informed him.

'We have to cross the river at this point.'

The mansion was still some distance along a gravelled drive and even further to the stables. There, Richard looked over a smart chestnut gelding called Jake that he was to purchase, subject to his approval. The mansion was in the Palladian style. A majestic granite portico set on colonnades reaching fifty feet and grand granite staircases to either side gave access to a balcony with an iron balustrade. Symmetrically disposed ornamental loggias stretched to each side of the portico ending with garden temples. Fit for almost any man of substance in England, but clearly it didn't suit Sir William. Building work on a massive scale was going on and numerous workers busied themselves with granite blocks and timber.

Richard mounted the steps and the door opened before he knocked. He recognised Mr Charles Scott, Sir William's steward, a tall middle-aged man, in a black frock coat.

'Allow me to take your cloak, Doctor – the maid is tending to Sir William,' he explained.

Scott returned with two glasses of wine on a silver tray.

'A fine house, Mr Scott.'

'It is indeed, but as you can see from the activities outside, changes are being made. Sir William has asked to meet you and, if you don't mind Doctor, I shall deal with the business of the horse while you attend on him.'

Sir William Lemon was in a small study waiting for Richard. He rose cheerfully; his eyes twinkled in amusement as they shook hands. He was not tall but thickly-built with greying, thinning hair; middle-aged and dressed severely in black, alleviated by a white shirt glimpsed at his throat.

'Good morning, Doctor Maddern. I'm so glad to meet you,' and he indicated a mahogany chair at a small marble-topped table where Richard should seat himself.

'Scott will see to the business while we get to know one another.' He spoke with no hint of superiority or condescension. 'Doctor Bull speaks well of you. I gather you studied together at university.'

Richard was on his guard – Sir William had a reputation for having a sharp and perceptive mind. Educated at Oxford, matriculating at seventeen, he did the Grand Tour three years later. He was President of the General Cornwall Infirmary and had been MP for Cornwall for twenty-five years: someone so powerful needed careful treatment.

'We were not at university together, Sir. We met when I was walking the wards at the London Hospitals. Dr Bull was an assistant surgeon at that time.'

'Ah! And where did you read medicine?'

'Oxford.'

'Ah, my old alma mater. Christ Church.'

'Balliol.'

'And walking the wards means what exactly?'

Richard smiled. 'It means one has paid to follow in the footsteps of the great masters thus gaining access to the best minds and the most up-to-date medical techniques. Or you might say, money fills the pockets of the great and even if the walker's mind remains empty he shall be forever given the accolade of walking the wards with this or that eminent physician and acquires some of that man's reputation.'

Sir William relaxed into his chair with a wry smile. 'You sound somewhat cynical, Doctor.' He did not wait for an answer. 'Doctor Bull is of the same age as yourself?'

'I have never questioned Dr Bull as to his age.' He paused leaving the real question in the air before informing, 'I am thirty-two.'

'Touché, Doctor! I should mind my own business,' he laughed lightly. 'Dr Bull's age was a problem for a while, but he was so highly recommended we felt we must take the chance. Appointing younger men shows our faith in the future does it not?'

Richard nodded his agreement.

'What made you come here to work when you obviously could have a practice in London or any of the big cities? And you're not joining the staff at our hospital I understand?'

Richard laughed at the sudden flurry of questions. 'Hector is well named, Sir. His persistence finally persuaded me to come here. I did practise in Bristol for two years, but not in London – that period was finishing off my qualifications.'

'And Bristol didn't suit?'

'I confess to having an aversion to socialising – I always seemed to be in the suffocating presence of the pretentious and affected.'

'Or the parsimonious and the bigoted. I know what you mean. I think we have something in common there, Doctor. Would you join me for a cold collation?' Sir William wanted to learn more.

As he crossed the hall, a handsome Broadwood grand piano distracted Richard. Rather than displayed in the centre of this wide space, inviting to be played, it was tucked away under the overhanging balcony.

'You play the piano?' Sir William asked.

'Yes. My father imported one at great expense for my mother and she taught me to play. When her talents had been exhausted she hired a teacher for us both.'

Sir William lifted the lid and looked at the neglected keys. 'No one plays which is a shame since I paid far too much for it and even more getting it here.' He stood back inviting Richard to play, who winced at the distorted sound.

'Needs tuning, Sir.'

'Umm,' he said without further explanation, but the meaning was clear. 'Come!' he invited with an open gesture at the door of the parlour. 'What does your father do?'

'He was a member of the Court of Directors of the East Indian Company.'

'Court of Directors!' Sir William was clearly impressed.

'Yes. People tell me he was especially lucky with his timing when he inherited from his father – the company was at the beginning of an upsurge in business.'

'Envious people always claim luck when a person succeeds. Your grandfather was a director also?'

'Yes, he was the source of our wealth.'

'Mine too! Yes, 'tis true. My grandfather, the Great Sir William as he was called, started with little. He was born in Germoe into a poor mining family. The tale was he started as a bal boy and went on to amass a fortune. You speak of your father in the past tense?'

'When I was at Oxford my father rightly assumed I was of an age when parental supervision was no longer required. He joined a ship going to India, but his real mission was to join Lord Macartney's Embassy to China as an attaché to advise on commercial matters. He took my mother with him. Unfortunately, in India they both succumbed to disease. It was a dreadful shock.'

'And are your interests still with that company?'

'Yes. I was for a short while a member of the Court of Directors as long as I was a pliant tool to whichever faction was in the ascendancy. But I did not take to that situation and resigned to the Court of Proprietors.'

'Yes,' Sir William murmured thoughtfully, but did not pursue the topic. 'And where is the family seat?' he asked becoming aware the young man before him had the assurance that education and private means brought. The baronet became more attentive and studied his guest closely.

'My father bought a town house in the Inns of Court. It was convenient for the City and Leadenhall Street was within walking distance.'

They sat opposite each other at a small circular table. The maid brought a salver of fowl and then another with meat – enough for a dozen people. She poured claret from a pewter jug.

'You didn't follow the family tradition?'

'No. I could not make up my mind whether to study music or medicine. My mother would have chosen music and I always tried to please her, but in the end medicine won.'

As Sir William leaned forward to examine the fare Richard asked where all the game came from.

'Out of the biggest larder in the district – my woods, my rivers, my fields!'

'You claim rights over rivers?'

'Until there is someone big enough to challenge me, I do.'

'How big do they have to be?'

'Viscounts, earls and so on,' and he laughed.

Conversation ceased as they began to eat. In a pause, Sir William set off on another tack.

'You will discover that the Cornish worker has an innate sense of self-preservation and puts no man, not even people like myself, above him. He is usually civil, but not too subservient. He teels his garden – '

'Teels?'

'Ah yes, the dialect – it means to cultivate. He keeps a pig when he can afford it. If the employment doesn't suit then he tries to make his own way – fishing sometimes, but more especially smuggling. I'm speaking of the miners of course and not my estate workers. I always have a sneaking admiration for the freer spirit of the miner. He does not rebel for better wages or improved working conditions – he holds himself responsible for that and is very self-sufficient in that respect. But he does revolt when hungry – twice within my memory – and when he does, it is very ugly. On the last occasion, the militia was called out and ordered to fire upon the crowd.' Sir William went into a reverie.

'They – the militia – refused. Bonaparte would have rejoiced at that news. Do you fear Bonaparte, Doctor?' he asked with a degree of gravity.

'He's not after my head, Sir.'

'No. But mine!'

Sir William became thoughtful before going on. 'Some measures have been taken since the uprisings to ensure bread can be had at a reasonable price. I buy barley at seventeen shillings a bushel and sell it to the estate workers at fourteen shillings a bushel. I say this, not to flatter my own ego, but as an example of what landowners can do. Basset provides soup at some of his mines before they go underground.'

Richard was surprised at these revelations, which resonated with his own thoughts.

'More wine, Doctor.'

The wine flowed freely, loosening tongues and relaxing minds.

'You'll never make a living here you know, even as a bal surgeon, there aren't enough patients.'

He smiled again and Richard sensed something else was coming. 'I would like to retain your services for myself and Lady Lemon and other members of the family – in an emergency I could have first class treatment within an hour – is that amenable to you?'

'Yes, of course, Sir, nothing would please me more. As to the few patients – that's exactly as I wish it.' Richard leaned conspiratorially across the table. 'Medicine is in an unhealthy state and the science is not able to meet the challenges. I can tell you what you are suffering from and if it will kill you and when, within limits. I can do nothing to cure you – or little at any rate. Diagnosis without cure is not a happy state. The days when an individual could make a major contribution are fast approaching their end: the Edward Jenners of this world are limited.'

Sir William stared at his glass absently while the maid filled it. 'That is not what we want to hear. Yet you argue against your own state, Doctor. You are alone, therefore, from your own reasoning, you can achieve little.'

'That is my dilemma and why I have secluded myself in this part of the world to allow myself time to study and think. Often we do not ask ourselves the right questions before deciding on a course of action. We tend to treat the symptoms of a disease as if they were the cause. Some of the treatments are quite incomprehensible – a person with a cold is kept in the cold when you and I know what we want more than anything is a warm fire or bed!'

They fell silent each thinking about what the other had said.

'No doubt you have been studying me since we have met? What is your prognosis?'

Richard was used to this sort of question; one that had to be deflected to avoid harming a burgeoning relationship.

'Full of health, Sir,' and he raised his glass.

'And what if I were to say that is not so?' he spoke quietly and in a graver tone.

'I can only see what you present and to my eye you look perfectly healthy. But you have put your finger on one of the great problems – we have no way of measuring the body's vital functions.' He reached and took Sir William's arm and felt the pulse. It was an impulsive act that startled the older man and had Richard been looking into his face he would have seen a quick disturbance flicker across it that showed Sir William to be wondering whether his guest was enthusiastic to an uncommon degree, over-confident or could not hold his liquor.

'This speaks to me about your heart, but I do not understand the language. I can count the beats and I deduce nothing amiss. Then if you run up and down the stairs several times, the rate quickens, but again nothing amiss. In a fever sometimes the rate is quick and at other times slower. Therefore, is a fast pulse good or bad? If one of your mighty engines performed like that you would want to know why.'

Sir William considered the question. 'We measure the efficiency of an engine by the amount of water raised from a ton of coal. But, the efficiency increases with increasing pressure. How you would translate that to the human body I know not,' he said, shaking his head.

Richard let go of his wrist and sat back into his chair. 'It is an interesting comparison – an attempt to measure the blood pressure of a horse was made years ago by a reverend gentleman. It was a clumsy instrument and would be a threat to life.'

'That's surely the reason for the new hospital?' Sir William ventured.

'No. It is not a teaching hospital. It will serve the poor as best it can. But consider – twenty beds for ten thousand miners, beside patients from other occupations.'

A longer silence ensued before Sir William opened another avenue of discussion. 'How do you intend to put your talents to use?'

'My only patient so far is a young girl from a row of cottages close to where I live. The door to the house was off its hinges. It had a beaten earth floor and there was no warming fire in the hearth and no food for the sick child. The place stank unbelievably from a lamp the woman lit so – '

'Train – it's called train. Fish oil in an earthen vessel called a chill.'

'Ah! The little girl had a fever, but her extremities were cold. Imagine the hopelessness the mother had to bear. Yet I discovered three other children over my head in a kind of loft supported by poles...'

'It's called a talfat. These things are common place.'

'But the squalor, Sir! What sort of landlord condones these awful conditions?'

'I know the houses you speak of – I am the landlord.' He held up a hand as a startled Richard was about to apologise. 'No, no. I understand how you feel, but let me explain. It is a common practice for miners and the like to approach a landowner for permission to raise a house on his land. It suits landowners to have workers close by and the houses cost very little; three guineas may cover it. The landowner leases the property to the builder, for three lives – most usually the couple and their eldest child. When the lease expires, the landowner takes the property back. During the time of the lease they pay rent of course.' He paused and a crooked finger touched his lips. 'Now in the particular case of which you speak, six tinners came to me with a proposition to build six adjoining properties. I agreed. Now because of their straightened circumstances, I as landlord am taken to task. Is that fair I ask you, Doctor?'

Richard found himself in an embarrassment of his own making; too much wine had dulled his thinking and weakened his defences.

'Come along, Doctor, deliver the coup de grace. *Conscience doth make cowards of us all*! ' He chuckled and waited with a twinkle in his eye.

Richard lowered his head. 'I must beg pardon, Sir, for being so rash – '

'Stuff! Out with it or I'll think you a lesser man.'

'Very well, Sir. You are making costly alterations to an already splendid mansion. Just the sort of activity the French aristocracy are losing their heads over. However, suppose the spoil from your work here gave a hard standing at the back of

40

the houses, which would improve their sanitation and therefore the lives of the inhabitants? You would be able to apply conditions: for example, they must have a privy in the garden to dispose of the night soil.'

'Do it, Doctor. I shall provide the rubble and you shall give the conditions and supervise the privies – this falls neatly into our respective roles don't you think? The benevolent landlord and the caring doctor. Do you agree?'

'Gladly, Sir!'

Sir William rose and accompanied Richard to the door. 'Just one more thing: I have a distant relative, Captain Tremayne, living in a grace-and-favour cottage on the estate. I would be much obliged if you would call on him. He's a rascally fellow who has seen much – too much. But I am very fond of him.'

'I consider it a pleasure, Sir, and may I say how much I have enjoyed your company and table.'

'You are welcome, Doctor. I expect Scott is ready for you.'

*

'Did you find Sir William in good form, Doctor?' It was clear Scott had anticipated some sort of encounter.

Richard laughed, took his cloak and threw it over one arm. 'I did, Mr Scott. You might have warned me!'

'Oh, that would have detracted from the enjoyment. Here is a retainer for your services to Sir William and Lady Lemon,' and he handed over a letter addressed to Doctor Maddern and a small purse containing five guineas.

Scott escorted Richard through gardens in-the-making, passing by a pond close to the cottage he was to visit. A maid answered the door and showed him into the parlour where, much to his surprise, there was Nancy. She blushed and he felt his own colour rising. Richard introduced himself and explained why he had come.

Captain Tremayne shook his hand, but did not get up. Richard looked appreciatively at Nancy now he could see more of her. She was a beauty in all respects. She met his stare fully and he sensed she approved of him as well.

'Umm! I see you two know each other. Don't worry, Doctor, she has the same effect on me I can tell you.'

41

The situation was becoming desperately awkward for Richard, but his medical profession came to the rescue. 'I've come to see if I can be of any assistance, sir.'

The old seaman laughed. 'You're not as pretty as Nancy and I'd rather have her tending to my needs – best loblolly I've come across in all my years at sea.'

'Loblolly?'

He smiled wickedly and winked, 'Surgeon's mate.'

Richard flushed even more and the old man took pity. 'Surgeon's assistant, Doctor.'

'If I am interrupting I can call another day.'

'Not at all, Doctor.' Nancy looked to the Captain and he nodded for her to continue. She rolled up the right leg of his drawers to reveal a heavily-bandaged leg. She began to remove the dressing very carefully. The bandage had not been secured well.

Suppurating ulcers covered the old man's leg and the smell of decay was most noticeable. The old salt stirred uneasily as the last few windings of the bandage came off and pulled at the flesh. Nancy discarded the soiled dressing and began to redress the leg without treating the sores; the fresh dressing was not clean.

'Excuse me, Miss Nancy, can I show you a better way of putting the bandage on?'

He showed her how to apply the dressing more firmly and produced a pleasing herringbone pattern and tied it off. She bundled the soiled material and was about to exit hastily when Richard asked her where she was taking them.

'The housemaid, Lucy, washes them ready for the next time.'

'I will come with you. I need to give her some instruction as to how they should be washed.'

He was surprised when she bobbed a short curtsy. He followed Nancy to the kitchen where the girl who answered the door was busy at the range. She was about Nancy's age, but of coarser appearance and less well presented.

'This here is Lucy,' Nancy said. Lucy was overawed, but quickly recovered herself.

'Lucy these dressings need to be soaked in carbolic and then

42

boiled in a copper until they are perfectly clean. Are you able to do this?'

She brushed loose hair from her eyes. 'Iss, we got a copper outside in the shed, sir.'

'May I see it?'

'Iss if you like,' and she led the way.

Nancy followed; she was not listening to what Richard was saying, but looking and admiring the man. He seemed perfect: articulate, handsome and intelligent. She liked the way his dark hair swept back from a high forehead and tumbled in close curls to the nape of his neck. His eyes were clear blue and his features sharp and clean cut. He had a noble upright bearing. She had never seen anyone so well groomed. And his clothes!

'Do you understand, Lucy?' he said, but when he turned to Nancy for affirmation, she was looking directly at him with a far away expression.

She started and again blushed. In desperation, she looked to Lucy, who was grinning in a knowing way.

Caught between the two girls it was Richard's turn to be speechless.

'Please excuse me,' he said 'I must see to Captain Tremayne.' Hotly, he turned and left as composed as he could. As he closed the door, he heard the beginning of an interesting conversation.

'How much did he offer you?'

'A guinea.' It was an unenthusiastic reply.

'A guinea! Old sod only gives me a shilling.'

Richard returned to Tremayne.

'Well, Doctor, having dragged yourself away from our two beauties, what more do you have to tell me?'

Richard examined the Captain seeing blackened gums, and feeling loose teeth. The bony part of his nose was soft and not firmly attached. Under his wig, the hair was thin and the scalp ulcerated and scabby. These observations and the condition of the leg left Richard in no doubt on his diagnosis.

'Are you in any pain, sir?'

The twinkle disappeared from the sailor's eyes and without his wig he looked old and worn. 'Yes, yes, I am.'

'Have you a prescription?'

'Rum at night, though I need more of late. What ails me, Doctor? You must be frank.'

Richard paced the room before coming back close to the sailor.

'When you were young, sir, did you contract the pox?'

Tremayne laughed as he replaced his wig. 'Pox, you say! Yes, I had the pox – what sailor didn't? Jack-ashore is a fool who buys liquor and the pox. I was a young lieutenant on the *Dragon* in sixty-nine in Port Mahon. The mercury treatment – it was terrible! Nevertheless, it cured me. The gleets disappeared and the rashes. I never had any trouble since. I was more cautious after that, but it didn't stop me whenever we were in port.'

Richard waited for the merriment to fade and then spoke in a quiet voice. 'It never goes away. The great pox, syphilis, is a master at hiding in the body. The treatment you had banishes the symptoms from view, but finally it comes back.'

'Finally! That has a death knell tone to it, Doctor.'

Richard nodded slowly and then for emphasis said, 'Yes,' quietly.

A silence fell between them while Captain Tremayne absorbed the terrible truth.

'I think a glass of rum, Doctor, if you have nothing else to prescribe. I've seen brave men die a cruel death with the pox – I don't want to suffer that.' He took the glass, drained it, and asked for another.

'I will make sure you do not suffer.'

Tremayne sipped the second glass and looked a little more at ease.

'Bathing will help also – do you have a bath?'

The captain smiled. 'I stand naked before this fire weekly and Lucy washes me. Then I wash her!' he added and laughed.

That accounted for the shilling Richard thought, and wondered how far the adventures went.

'How long have I got, Doctor?'

Richard knew the question was coming, but it did not make it easier to answer. In truth, he didn't know – a few months, but not a year.

'You should put all your affairs in order, Captain.'

'All my affairs,' he repeated sadly. 'I have willed everything to Sir William. I sometimes think that's why he invited me here.' He thought for a while and then brightened again. 'Lucy should have something.' He thought again. 'And what about Nancy? I should like to do more for her. She's such a sweet girl, it's a great pity she has no education. I could leave her some money – enough to make a difference. How much would that be I wonder? A hundred pounds? Two? She could do something with that. What do you think? No, I have it! I have a small bundle of shares William covets. He covets them but, as a member of the Government, they could cause him some embarrassment.' Tremayne did not explain and Richard saw fit not to enquire.

'I shall imagine the day when he learns they have gone elsewhere. I need to speak to a lawyer – not Trethowan. Not only is he a thief, but he's an informer – Sir William's informer.'

'A thief?'

'A legal thief! I always pay half what he demands and he never comes back to me. Clutterbuck! I'll get a letter to Clutterbuck. Would you fetch pen and paper for me? On the bureau.'

Five minutes later the letter was ready for posting.

*

It was late in the afternoon when Richard rode through the great gates again. The light was still good being seventy days or so since the shortest day. The east wind blew cold and the descending icy dew made it more penetrating. As he reached the Kennal River, Nancy was fording the stream now swollen by the coming tide. Uncontrollably, his spirits rose and he arrived at her side in midstream. She was negotiating the large stepping-stones, but she knew he was there and halted on one of the bigger stones, smiling as he approached.

'I aren't going to make a fool of myself again, 'specially in this here predicament.'

He laughed and was pleased she was her former cheeky self. 'If you are going home I can offer you a ride on Jake.'

'Then you'll have to walk.'

'No.'

She peered from under her hood and then threw it off and shook her long hair free. Still she looked, questioning his short answer, so full of meaning.

'Get up there with you?'

'Why not? Third class riding is better than first class walking. And I think Jake will take the strain.'

She scoffed at this jibe. Richard leant down towards her and whispered. 'There's no payment of any kind expected,' and laughed quietly.

'All right then.'

Richard slipped back off the saddle and, leaning towards her, gripped her around the waist and hoisted her up to sit side-saddle. He gathered the reins and encompassed her in his arms. Jake forded the river and mounted the short slope onto the carriageway.

'Nancy?'

'Umm?'

'I have a letter to post.'

'See they wood houses? The one in the middle takes the post.'

Richard dismounted and led Jake. An old woman peered from the bow window as he entered, ringing a bell attached to the door. The woman scurried behind a wooden counter and waited, closely scrutinising him in silence.

'Good afternoon, ma'am. I have a letter to post to Truro.' She was a small skinny woman with a mournful expression shrouded by thin grey hair. She took the letter and scanned the address.

'Thrupence.'

As Richard hunted for the postage in his purse, he saw her bending and dodging to get a view of Nancy. Richard offered the pence that she took without a word.

'Thank you, ma'am, and good day.' The bell tinkled and he was outside again amused by the almost wordless encounter. He climbed up beside Nancy and noticed the old woman was at the window again consumed with curiosity and nosiness.

'Talkative lady!'

Nancy laughed. 'Mizz Jack don't miss nothing. She wants to

know who I'm with that's all.'

As they crossed the wharves in front of the tavern, they were greeted with catcalls from the men who obviously knew Nancy. He asked her what they were shouting. She revelled in the attention tossing her head and swaying her lovely hair and laughing with the men, but not returning any words. They passed onto the quiet lane leading to Devoran and Richard asked again, 'What were they calling?'

'Nothing.' She looked past him back to the quays and then directly into his eyes. 'I aren't telling you,' she teased, then sniggered, and looked away. She was very close and they brushed against each other from time to time as Jake swayed in his motion.

'You must visit Perranarworthal often to be so well known.'

'We come to St Piran's most Sundays. Then I shops at Mizz Jack's. Course, I sees to the Cappen twice a week so they do see me coming and going a lot.'

'When do you next tend to Captain Tremayne?'

'Today's Tuesday and if I can judge the tides right I shall go again on Friday.'

'Good, I have to give Captain Tremayne some medication.'

Nancy was still in a deep study and did not take in what he had said much to his frustration.

'I have to study the tides see. They're coming home at the minute and if this easterly keeps up, crossing the river will be a problem.'

'Jake will take us over and back without any problem.'

Her hand went to her mouth to cover a smile. 'Oo, my gore you'll have a scandal 'fore long at this rate.'

'Does that bother you, Nancy?' he asked smiling. She did not answer and he could not see her face.

'I have a promise from Sir William of ballast – stones and the like, to make the lane in the Row drier and firmer to stand on. I need to talk to the tenants all together. How can I best do that? Do you know all the people living there?'

'Everyone,' she said in a quiet, wistful tone. 'They're all in a sad way – poor and hungry most times. Some worse than others.'

'None can be as bad as Mrs Trezise.'

'Lucy is.'

'Lucy lives in the Row?'

'In the end house. Two young children and no father. Pressed we believe.' She continued in a forlorn voice, 'Gone these two years and she hardly got a penny from the parish.'

'How does she live?'

'Washing and scrubbing; three days a week over to Carclew, and walking two mile each way! She has to leave her children next door and pay a penny for each. Whoring as well.'

This revelation shocked Richard.

'Mazed Monday is when she earns her living.'

'Mazed?'

'Mad Monday. The tributers are paid monthly and the share-out is usually in the pubs. If 'tiss on a Monday they stays in the pubs with plenty of money. Two men in the day bring her as much as a tradesman earns. She gets visitors at night as well.'

The conversation had taken an astonishing turn – astonishing, that is, to learn it from Nancy and the casual manner in which she related it.

'I'll ask them when they can see you, all together.'

Richard had turned Jake up the hill when she suddenly asked about Molly.

'Molly is doing fine. Would you like to see her?'

'Can I sneak in by the back way?'

Richard looked around and was about to say no one was about when he saw a man standing opposite the postern to his house.

'Oh, there's someone waiting for me,' he said.

Nancy looked up the hill. 'Not you – 'tiss me he wants.' Her voice had an ominous tone. ''Tiss Billy Uddy.'

Richard saw a handsome man several years younger than himself and slightly shorter. He had a round, open face, weathered from an open-air life that also bleached his short fair curls. Massive shoulders and a broad powerful chest told of the underlying strength. His sunny attributes contrasted sharply with his expression of smouldering fury.

'Will you be all right? Should I take you home?'

'I'll be all right, Doctor. Billy's tough, but he's no match for Daddy. I'll see Molly another day.'

Chapter 4

'Truro's crowded with military,' Richard observed to Hector Bull.

'Has been for some time. Bonaparte threatens daily and we have to be ready. You've read the latest news in the *Sherborne*?'

Richard nodded in reply to Hector's question.

'Half the marriages in the town are to soldiers,' Hector informed him cheerfully.

'And more than half the births, no doubt!'

Hector laughed. 'Keeps the surgeons and midwives in business that's for certain.'

They were in Hector's office in the almost completed General Infirmary.

'It's good to see you here, Richard. To know that you are close at hand is a great comfort to me. You won't miss grand society, that I do know; glad to see the back of it, I suspect – and of Kathrine, no doubt.'

Richard nodded, not wishing to engage in a conversation about his wife.

'How did you find Sir William?' Hector asked, moving quickly on.

'I hadn't met him previously, and I found him pleasantly devoid of pretentiousness. Of course, I was somewhat wary.'

'A generous subscriber and my immediate superior.'

'His whimsical mien can be disarming to the unwary,' Richard said, remembering his faux pas of the previous day.

Hector looked thoughtful and toyed with a quill. 'You are in a much better position than I, in those situations. I would like to press harder for funds, but the consequences of overstepping the boundary are...well, bounty is a fickle mistress!'

'Lemon is outwardly receptive to ideas, and he wants to be seen as a benefactor, as long as it doesn't torture his purse too much. He cited two occasions when the miners, from want, had risen against the price of bread. The price of grain, of course, is a direct result of the Corn Laws that keep prices high to protect the interests of the landed gentry like Lemon. He said he sells barley at a subsidised price to his workers – claiming an act of benevolence. However, upon enquiry, his steward, Mr Scott, informs me that Lemon mills the barley and takes a share of the grain in doing so. He is not as benevolent as he would have us believe.'

The shape of Hector's face was one conducive to lugubriousness and Richard's gloomy recital caused his jaw to sink, and incipient jowls make their presence known.

'I'm a doctor, and one that shuns politics,' he sighed. 'I see want and waste often in close company with each other. The Reverend Cornelius Cardew is chaplain to the infirmary, and draws a salary of fifteen guineas per annum. A nurse is paid seven guineas per annum. It is not difficult to imagine which I would prefer. My salary is one hundred and fifty guineas, and there will undoubtedly be opportunities for gratuities. My accommodation here is free as are my provisions. That is a comfortable living. There are restrictions of course; I cannot stay overnight away from the premises without permission. But if I should be outspoken,' and he looked fixedly at Richard, 'my resignation would be called for. I should be pilloried, and the likelihood of finding another position, such as this, would be impossible.'

Richard clapped his friend on the shoulder, 'Come, put our time to a more useful purpose by showing me around your wonderful hospital.'

The building was ready to receive the sick and lame poor, but the opening was being delayed. Hector wryly explained, 'The birthday of our royal patron, the Prince of Wales, is on 12th August, so the deserving patients have to be patient and not expire in the meantime.'

The first floor was for female patients, the second for males.

'Each will have ten beds laid-out parallel to the walls. The nurses have their sleeping quarters off the main wards. Each ward has its own kitchen where the nurses will prepare and cook the patients' meals.'

Their footfalls resounded on the bare boards and echoed from the plainly plastered and lime-washed walls. The wards were spacious, airy, with high ceilings; large windows threw cheerful daylight into the room even on that winter day.

'The other staff are all professionals – there are six surgeons, drawn from the town practices, and two physicians, John Gould and Stephen Luke, both excellent men and well connected.'

'Meaning?'

'Gould, who is fifty-nine, married into the Rashleighs. Luke is thirty-six and married a daughter of Lord Vyvyan. Luke studied in Paris. And he has been the Mayor of Falmouth. Marrying well is a great boon.'

An uncomfortable silence fell between them, and Hector covered his embarrassment by hurrying to his quarters.

'As House Surgeon, I have to see to all the administration of the hospital down to the meanest detail – even looking after the pigs, fowls and horses.'

'Is it the case that the nurses take no part in the dressing of wounds and so on?' Richard asked.

'Yes of course – attention to the patients is the main concern of the doctors and surgeons. You are not suggesting nurses get involved at such a level are you?' Hector was somewhat incredulous.

Richard's thoughts went back to the previous day where, with a little training and encouragement, Nancy could have been of great service. Men liked the female touch, and anything that added to the well-being of a patient usually aided recovery.

'Water from a well is pumped to the kitchens in each ward,' Hector moved on.

'There is no connection to a main water supply?' asked Richard.

'Unfortunately not. Nor is there a main sewer – the infirmary has its own drainage. If you look out of the window, you can see the men at work. Drainage, I recall, is one of your specialities.'

Richard grinned. 'It's very important in my estimation. Pure water and good drainage will keep disease at bay. One only has to look to...'

'See here!' Hector pointed to a small aperture in the wall. 'For my cats to come and go. They are less confined than I am.'

After an hour, Richard suggested Hector join him for a meal at the Red Lion. 'And then you shall help me buy some clothing for a young lady.'

'Lady?' Hector stopped abruptly in his steps.

'She's nearly three years old.'

In the busy town Hector continued to explain the changes taking place, as though it were an extension of his hospital. As they approached the Red Lion, Hector pointed to a new wide street where fine houses swept up a steep hill out of the town.

'Lemon Street,' Hector announced. 'When finished, it will be one of the finest examples of modern development in the country.' He wagged a finger at Richard for emphasis, and repeated, 'In the country!'

They dined handsomely on game accompanied by a burgundy. Richard, somewhat in his cups, ordered a bottle of port.

'A good day, Hector. I paid Trethowan just half his bill before visiting Clutterbuck and transferring my affairs to his firm. Then I visited the Miners Bank in Princes Street where I found everything in a very satisfactory state. Then on to my good friend, in his very own, newly-finished, hospital. What more can a man want? Health, wealth and happiness!' Richard raised his port glass.

Hector beamed back a broad, alcohol-induced, smile. Neither was drunk, but jocund and happy with the world. Happy thoughts turned Richard's mind, to his surprise, to Nancy – also not a subject for discussion. By association, Captain Tremayne also came to mind.

'You must indulge me with another opinion, Hector. Apart from my young lady, I have another patient. This one is in the final stages of syphilis, and suffering from suppurating sores on his leg. Is there a dusting that can be applied to dry-up the sores?'

'Syphilis you say? That is classed as an improper disease by the management, and those presenting with it will not be admitted, along with cholera, smallpox, pregnancy, tuberculosis, lunacy and so on – the list is long, and I believe uncaring. No child under ten years or anyone over sixty is admitted.'

'Who makes such rules as these? Should not a pregnant

woman be confined in the surroundings of the best care?'

'Ah! The rich are also not admitted,' Hector resumed. 'They must seek comfort in their own homes.'

'Dusting?' Richard reminded him.

'Magnesium sulphate is the usual treatment to draw the poison out. Applied as a paste. I think other forms of desiccant would be too powerful.'

The last of the port drained. Richard glanced at his watch, and was alarmed at the time.

'Hector, we have clothes to buy and the hour is already late!'

They visited a shop in King Street, where, for the best part of an hour, they viewed almost everything the owner indulgently showed them. Richard bought far more than was necessary, and left with a large brown paper parcel. At Boscawen Street they bade each other farewell. In a pleasant alcoholic haze, Richard retrieved Jake from the Red Lion stables and began his homeward journey.

A mile from the town he paused at Calenick where he looked at the blowing house. The afternoon was spent and the light fading as evening approached. All was quiet along the deserted road; nothing and nobody ventured abroad. Richard was lost in his thoughts, going back over the day. One recurring worry was Nancy and Uddy. Uddy was unpleasant, and he had seen fear in Nancy's eyes as he lifted her from Jake. How well he remembered that moment.

'Whoa!' A loud shout; someone grabbed the reins. Jake reared, and Richard jolted back to sensibility, but dropped the parcel. His first thought was that a footpad was holding him up and he was unarmed. He pulled the reins to calm Jake.

'Steady boy – steady.'

He could not see who was accosting him, but whoever it was had a firm grip of the reins.

'Give him his head damn you!' he shouted into the darkness. His crop lashed out and found its mark. A yelp, the reins were freed and Richard regained control.

'Who the devil are you?' he shouted at the disappearing shadowy figure. He retrieved the parcel, and stared into the darkness. He was close to Devoran, his house was a few hundred yards away – Uddy! He had a sudden conviction.

After stabling and feeding Jake, Richard strode into the kitchen where Ruth was waiting.

'I didn't know what to have ready, Doctor, so I got cold meat if you'd like some?'

He checked the time: half past eight. It was later than he thought.

'I've dined in town, Ruth. I shall be in the dining room. Come and unwrap this parcel.'

He poured a large brandy, drank it off and poured another. Then he sat before the blazing fire to think. Ruth arrived and he pointed to the parcel.

'Take a look, Ruth – clothes for Molly.'

Ruth became excited, pulled at the knots, freed the strings and then carefully unwrapped the paper – it would do for another day.

'Aw, my dear life! 'Tiss handsome. Aw, the little maid will look a treat in them, Doctor.'

'After her bath in the morning, Ruth, you shall have the pleasure of choosing what she shall wear.'

'Pity, we had visitors today.'

'Oh, who? And why a pity?'

'Why, Nancy called to see Molly, and she had Missus with her.'

'Missus?'

'Trezise!' she exclaimed. 'Mrs Trezise couldn't get over her, – how well she was looking.'

Nancy had been there! That made it more certain that it was Uddy.

Chapter 5

The temperature was forty degrees, the weather dull, with overcast skies. Dressed warmly, and wearing a great cape, he made his way towards the causeway where access to the tinners' embankment was easy. As he walked one embankment he saw the other, on the far shore of the creek, hundreds of yards away.

After walking for half a mile, he came upon an astonishing sight: perhaps two hundred men and boys inside the enclosure were shifting mud from the creek to the embankments. He continued to walk towards Devoran and, when almost opposite his house, he reached the main centre of activity. Someone close-to was smoking a clay pipe, and appeared to be writing.

'Good morning. Richard Maddern,' he introduced himself. 'I am new to these parts and wish to get acquainted with the streaming operation.'

The man got up slowly, straightened carefully, grunting as nervous twinges in his back came to life. He wore a heavy, mud-stained oilskin that enveloped him from neck to ankles. Under an oilskin hat was a face full of character, where myriads of fine cracks had flowed into each other producing deep fissures. Blue eyes peered from beneath half-open lids, and a smile, below thick grey-streaked moustaches, gave a cheerful welcome.

'Redevers Collins, Doctor, if you please – clerk to Mr Williams. Mr John Williams is Sir William Lemon's agent, who looks after all his mining business hereabouts. People call me Brother.' Mr Collins spoke clearly with a strong Cornish accent. He surprised Richard by knowing that he was a doctor.

'Brother?'

'Aw, we all got names – when young, my nearest sister had trouble with my name, so she just called me "Brother".'

Richard gazed upon the scene for a moment. 'How do they

manage to extract tin from this hell-hole, Brother?'

The clerk chuckled quietly, and sat again on a small three-legged stool.

''Tiss difficult to work it out I know, but let's see if I can make it a bit clearer.' He lit his pipe, and when it was going to his satisfaction, he blew a large cloud of smoke across the workings.

'This method of winning tin is the oldest, and the most profitable. When the Romans and Phoenicians came here thousands of years ago, they bought tin washed from rivers, not from deep, hard rock mining, like as up the valley.' He waved his pipe further up the river. 'Not only is it easier to win, but 'tiss almost pure tin ore – why, they only have to wash the mud out of it.' Then he got up again, firmed the tobacco in the pipe, made smoke and continued.

'Further up the valley, the banks of the stream were pulled into the water which washed the soil away leaving the heavy tin. They work in pares – that's usually two men and two boys, often from the same family. There might be twenty pares of men all told working the same stream, each having their own "set" – that's an agreed length of bank to work, usually for a year. Now, what we have here is different. This isn't a stream, 'tiss a creek, with several rivers running through. This is too big a job to manage by the pares system. They had to all teel in together. The rivers are diverted to each side – one behind us and the other on that side over there,' and he pointed his pipe stem clear across the creek. 'The dam on the seaward side, has to be kept tight, and 'tiss a job for everybody.' He turned to Richard, and pointed again with the stem of his pipe, to nowhere in particular.

'That isn't zackly right but 'twill do for the minute.' He sucked the cold pipe and decided not to relight it.

'Mother Nature has done the most part of the separation of the tin here. The rivers wash the tin ore into the creek bed over hundreds of years. Unfortunately, she made a mess of it after that. She covered it all over with mud and the like, and that's what we got to get rid of. First come the tin, then oysters, then thick mud. Mr Williams do call it overburden – I call it something else – 'tiss a burden all right, no doubt about that. Sometimes 'tiss thirty feet before the black tin is spied. And that's what you see all around us. Overburden. Mind, to keep the tide out we need it – if it weren't here we should have to bring it in somehow – perhaps the good Lord knew what he was doing after all,' he chuckled again. 'Iss perhaps he did. Now, how to go about it? They take the tin for washing; over there be the stream where you see the pump working. Then 'tiss ready for the blowing house.'

'Smelter?'

'Iss! See, once the overburden is gone, the rest is pure tin, black and handsome; some lumps as big as your fist – iss! Some of the tin levels are a fathom or more deep! Iss, a fathom! I never heard tell of tin that deep.'

'The men look healthy considering the conditions they work under.'

Brother drew a knife from his pocket and then a brown hard object that Richard likened to a dried turd. Brother was aware he was being scrutinised, and glanced occasionally in Richard's direction. He carved a small portion from the lump, placed it in the palm of one hand, and ground it with the heel of the other. When he deemed all was satisfactory, he loaded the bowl of his pipe and lit it.

'Drawing handsome,' he said and blew smoke to prove it. 'Never seen a prick of baccy before?' he asked slyly from beneath his heavy eyebrows.

'Each pare got their own pile of slimes,' and he pointed behind him. 'At the end of the month, more agents arrive and buy the tin. Then 'tiss shipped out to a blowing house where the tin is released. And the boys have a bit of a blow out themselves, in the winks – you know what a kiddlywink is?' Again the askance look.

'A public house – tavern. Mazed Monday!'

'You got it! As to being healthy – well 'tiss that sort of life.' He picked up again on an earlier question. 'Anybody out in the open air all day, using a piggal and visgey builds a fine body. These boys are the best wrasslers by far; bigger than the hard rock miner – broader in the shoulder.' And he shrugged his shoulders to emphasise the size. 'Wheeling a barrow all day is a terrible hard job – there aren't many that can stick it.'

'What are the men wearing – it all seems alike?'

'Iss 'tiss. Smocks made special, from a blanketing material. And the boots are of leather plated with iron – broogs, they call them.'

The men gathered and walked towards the embankment.

'Croust!'

Richard looked at his watch and saw the time was approaching ten. Brother observed his every move.

'They been at it since six this morning – and a good many walk five miles to get here, some even more,' he said. Then, as if answering a criticism, 'Aw, they don't mind that.' He became studious. 'They should work until the light fades, but looking at the weather we shall have rain shortly and that'll be that!'

'Can't say I blame them – it must be terrible working in the mud in heavy rain.'

'Iss, but that isn't always the reason why – they got other things to do. They aren't like the miners up the valley, underground. They don't know whether 'tiss Christmas or Easter down the mines, or day or night come to that!' and he laughed. 'Most of these boys got a small field or do a bit o' fishing and...' he touched the side of his nose, 'smuggling. That's the best trade of the lot! I know where there's several ankers of brandy hid away right this minute!'

'Ankers?'

'Barrels!'

The men sat on the embankment in groups and began their meals.

'Am I keeping you from your meal, Brother?'

'No, Doctor, I'll have something later.'

'Tell me – do you know a man by the name of Trezise?'

Brother twisted on his stool to face him and became serious.

'Edward Trezise – iss I know him. As good a soul as you're likely to meet in a day's march.' He pointed the stem of his pipe in the general direction of the seated men. 'He's over there – slight fellow with dark hair. Suffers a lot from his chest – always coughing up black trade. I well remember his first day; by the afternoon his arms was so tired he couldn't grip the handles to lift the barrow any more. He's tough, but most days he goes home tired as a 'oss. He got a job to breathe – he never works a full week and that keeps him poor. He started down the

58

mines as a boy and was good at it. He collected what he calls specimens – different ores, all sorts. They nicknamed him Specy. And he's always the first to see gold!'

'Gold? There's gold here?'

'Iss. Not much. Little grains mostly. They all carry a quill, and if they see a glint in the tin – in they go. Edward do laugh at them sometimes – what they pick up. But he knows, and from time to time he gets enough to buy a few things.'

*

The sound of merriment greeted him at his door. But as soon as they heard him, it ceased completely, like children when caught in some forbidden activity. In the kitchen he saw Ruth, looking expectantly, Mrs Trezise, dressed in a clean apron and, much to his surprise, Nancy, smiling happily.

'Morning ladies – nice to see you, Mrs Trezise, and Nancy as well. And who's this pretty little girl?' He gathered Molly into his arms and hugged her closely. He then displayed her for all to see.

'Looking much better, Mrs Trezise, don't you think? But you can't have her yet!' he said in mock covetousness. Unfortunately, the joke missed its mark, and Mrs Trezise began to weep.

'Oh here, here! I was speaking only in fun! You can take her whenever you wish.'

Ruth touched her arm in sympathy and Nancy offered a handkerchief.

'I ain't crying because I can't have her back, Doctor – 'tiss that I'm so happy to see her like she is. She never had such clothes. I thought the Lord was taking her home, but you brought her back.'

'Nothing as dramatic as that, Mrs Trezise. A bad cold, that's all. Just a bit of warmth and nourishment to keep the Grim Reaper at bay – can't have him taking pretty girls before their time!'

'How much longer before she can come home, Doctor?'

'I want to see her gain a little more weight first, and to tell the truth, Mrs Trezise, I would like the weather to turn warmer. I don't want the cold to get to her again until she is quite well.'

'Edward's been cutting more wood and furze when he can, to keep the place warmer, but he's having trouble with his chest again and he gets so tired...' She crawled back into her black abyss of despair, and the mood of the group took on a shared pity.

'So I believe, Mrs Trezise. If I get an opportunity, I'll take a look at him. Perhaps some tea for everyone, Ruth,' he said, mainly to get away from the close-to-maudlin femininity, and maintain some professional dignity. 'I'll take mine in the drawing room.' As he took his leave, he caught Nancy's sparkling eyes. 'Nancy, before you go I'd like a word with you please.'

A soft knock at the door, and Nancy coyly entered a few minutes later.

'Come in, Nancy, please and sit down.' He got up, and pulled a chair so she had to sit close, and opposite. 'Is that a new dress you are wearing?'

'Iss. I wore it to church for the first time last Sunday.'

'Nancy, I wanted to speak with you because I was concerned about leaving you the other evening with Billy Uddy. He seemed to be in a bad mood and I thought you might come to some harm.'

She blushed and looked at her hands.

'Did he see you home?'

She nodded. 'He sees me home quite often.'

He was about to tread on private matters, but his position as doctor would be able to rescue him if he placed himself in an embarrassing position.

'Do you have an understanding with Billy?'

She looked up with a bewildered expression.

'Has he asked you to marry him?'

She now looked boldly at him, and just as he decided to stop his line of questioning the words rushed from her in a torrent.

'He asks me to marry him every time I see him. I keep telling him he's the last person I'd marry. But he won't take no for an answer.' The "no" she said firmly, probably how she pronounced it to Uddy. 'He just keeps saying that if he can't have me nobody else will. I think he'll kill me one day – if he gets in drink he'll do it. He carries a knife all the time – not in

60

his belt like anyone else ready to use for working but behind his neck in a sheath – ready like! But what shall us do? I can't stay home all the time just in case I meet him, can I?' She spoke with emphasis then she relaxed a little, remembering something. 'When I was seventeen, there was a nice boy who paid attention to me. Martin Daniels, a tinner – tough enough, but gentle. Billy caught him one night and beat him nearly to death. He never got over it – he can't speak or do hardly anything. His mother and father look after him because he can't do nothing for himself. I visit him sometimes, but he doesn't know who I am. And Billy would do the same again! I'm too frightened sometimes, to make friends with a boy or man – 'tiss like signing his death warrant.' At this point, she stopped and looked directly at Richard. Her expression was clear.

Richard quietly fumed, but knew that anger would solve nothing – thinking would.

'Have you told anyone else about this? The vicar?'

'No. Just you.'

The confident woman of just a few minutes ago, laughing, and enjoying the companionship of the others, had crumbled to a terrified girl. Gone were the teasing eyes and smiling mouth; her courage had wilted. Yet Richard found that even in this mood her striking beauty still shone through, though with a different cast.

'When you arrive at your home with Uddy what happens?'

'He leaves me before we get to the gate – he never comes in because Daddy won't have it.'

'Do they ask if you see Uddy?'

She looked away – this was another subject that had bad connotations. Tears welled up but she was still sufficiently in control to stop them.

'I lie – I says I never sees him. 'Tiss almost the worst part – lying to Daddy and Mummy.'

Tears trickled down her face and Richard offered his handkerchief.

'Never mind, Nancy – you keep all these things to yourself for the best possible reasons; so as not to burden others with them. No-one will hold that against you – especially not your nearest and dearest.'

'I'm surprised they haven't noticed. When Billy takes me home, I go straight to bed – hardly saying goodnight. I goes up and reads until I'm too tired...I shouldn't be like this, Doctor. I got things to do!' She began to rise, and Richard motioned her to stay.

'We have to sort this matter out, Nancy. You cannot continue either to be in fear of your life or be restricted from seeing whomever you choose.'

More relaxed, she listened attentively, occasionally fidgeting with the handkerchief.

'We can do one of two things neither of which you will find pleasant – but difficult choices never are.' She was looking into his eyes and he sensed a trust developing between them. 'I can speak with Uddy, and ask him to leave you alone.' She shook her head. 'Or you must tell your parents what is happening.' She was about to interrupt him but he went on. 'They of all people must know. Just imagine if something awful happened to you and they only then discover you have been living in the shadow of Uddy's violence, and not asked for their help.'

Tears came again as he expected, but a solution would only follow after all the facts were known.

'I can't do it – I don't have the words to say it properly.' Frustration now heated her cheeks and tightened her jaw.

'Should I speak with your parents?'

'Oh yes. You have such wonderful ways of putting things that make it sound better.' The smiles returned and Richard was flattered.

'Now, Nancy,' he said, in a more cheerful manner, 'before we go to your home we have to speak with the residents of the Row? Yes?'

Her hands flew to her mouth, and her eyes widened. 'What time is it?'

'It's nearly noon.'

She jumped to her feet alarmed. 'They be there! They be waiting.'

Richard, uncharacteristically, leapt to his feet following her example – then he calmed down. 'It's alright, Nancy – we'll get our cloaks and be on our way.'

The weather was quickly deteriorating and a thin drizzle was coating everything with small beads of water. Each family was waiting in their respective doorways, peering in their direction as they approached. The row of six houses stretched further than his voice would carry.

'See that big tree down the far end?'

'Good idea Nancy – Can you all crowd under the tree to keep out of the worst of the rain?' he called, and waved his arm in the direction for them to follow.

The dreary trail of human wretchedness came to a halt under the dripping branches and Richard knew he had to be brief. He backed close to the trunk of the tree, and Nancy managed to stand close behind him.

'I have been speaking with Sir William Lemon about ways of improving the conditions in your homes and the surroundings. This lane is used for the disposal of night soil.'

The crowd, squinted against the increasing rain, huddled together for shelter. He did not have their full attention and needed to be more direct.

'You must stop emptying your pots in the lane. You bring disease into your houses by treading in your waste and taking it into your homes.'

He saw several mutter to each other seeking clarification. A man, with a ruddy face, at the edge of the crowd raised his arms to speak.

'Horace Gay, he has two boys, both tinners – there besides him. He does a bit of fishing, shoots ducks, and traps rabbits in the day, and by night, he poaches. He keeps Lucy in meat – and he and the boys visit Lucy in turns.' Nancy spoke quickly, with no expression or emphasis. She never failed to astonish him in the manner in which she delivered information of a shocking nature without any hint of embarrassment or shame.

'Don't throw your shit out in the lane – that's what he's saying,' Gay explained.

'Put it in the garden or the privy,' Richard shouted to the crowd.

'I aren't sharing with that filthy old bitch!' called a woman in her family group of four children standing and one in her arms.

'That's the Heard family – he's a tinner – in his father's pare but he's the one that runs it. They'm talking about Everlidia Clemo – she lives next to Lucy and looks after her children. Husband died last year; children all gone but pay her rent. They won't have her – she's too beastly.'

Everlidia was a coarse woman, overweight and past middle age. She had a face accustomed to misery. From the creases in her brow to a heavy hanging mouth, all features sloped downward. Her lower jaw was loose, and two large teeth pointed out and up, like boar's tusks. She chewed constantly, and cupped a hand to her ear. Thin hair hung in filthy strands, wet from the rain. Her apron was a sack, tied around her middle.

'Thank you, Mr Gay, for giving a clearer meaning to my words. As to sharing, I hope you will all have your own privy in each of your gardens – I shall provide some timber.' The wood from the crates was still in the stable.

'I can't build a shithouse,' Everlidia complained.

Horace Gay laughed; his face turned a lively colour. No one else took any interest – they were still listening to Richard.

'Sir William has promised he will deliver stone ballast, free of charge, to make the lane a firm standing – with a good firm lane and privies in the garden, he promises more will follow.'

Edward Trezise raised an arm to speak. Close too, Richard saw dark rings around each eye and a tangible weariness in his face.

'There's plenty of spar stone to be had in the workings – 'tiss better than rubble from Carclew. What us need is a plough to get it here.'

'Nancy?'

'Iss, spar stone is the white stones,' came his interpreter's voice. 'A plough is a wagon.'

'Thank you, Mr Trezise, I'll see Sir William tomorrow and ask.'

'Best not tell him, Doctor,' said a strong healthy-looking man surrounded by his wife and five children.

'That's Robert Hooper, Captain James's first mate – biggest pare in the works.'

'Let him deliver the rubble and we'll use the plough while 'tiss here. We can lay the rubble first and put the spars on top – make a proper job.'

64

There was general agreement to this plan.

'And the privies?'

Hooper spoke again. 'If you supply the timber and nails we'll put them up.'

Again, a murmur of consent.

'Excellent. Thank you, ladies and gentlemen. Just one more thing before we can all get out of this weather. Do try to keep your drinking water in a separate pail. Don't put anything else in that pail – bucket?'

'Kibble,' someone shouted, and they all laughed. 'Don't shit in kibble as you drink from,' another shouted.

'Where in hell can I git a bucket?' Everlidia complained again.

They were about to disperse when Lucy asked a question.

'Doctor, can us pay a penny a week for you to see to the babies?'

'If any of the children are sick call for me or bring them to the surgery at once – don't wait until you have the money. If I can see them as soon as they are unwell they have a better chance of being cured.'

A further mutter of approval and they moved away.

*

Written under the lid of the wooden box was "W.H. Mortimer. Purveyors of firearms to His Majesty the King". In the box was a pair of the finest duelling flintlock pistols. He placed them in a leather saddle holster and strode purposefully to where Nancy was waiting. She was blowing gently into Jake's nostrils, and whispering softly. The horse's flanks shivered, and Richard knew he would react in exactly the same way. He helped her into the saddle and climbed up behind. The weather had improved and the sun shone warmly. They took the lane at the top of the hill, turned right, and soon arrived at a sharp bend where a group of houses stood.

'Mr Jennings lives in there – 'tiss a wink really.' Nancy resumed her role as guide. The lane curved steeply down towards some docks, and a large timber pond. Jake slipped on the uneven surface throwing Nancy back, into Richard. He held her tighter, and she rested against his chest, her head just under his chin. He expected her to move away when Jake regained his footing but she did not. The motion of the horse caused her body to brush against his hands. They were both aware of it, and a silence fell between them: the silence enlarged its value. Although Richard's mind affirmed its pure intentions, other parts of his anatomy told of the truth. An uncomfortable firmness was making riding difficult, and Jake's motion compounded the rising to a rigidity of maximum proportions. He needed to get a hand into his breeches to ease his pressing problem. But Nancy was so close she would feel exactly what he was doing and that could be open to misinterpretation.

'Nancy.'

'Umm?' and he felt her laughing silently.

'Nancy.'

She turned abruptly to face him, grinning broadly; white teeth and flashing eyes so close – almost too close to focus.

'What?'

'Nancy,' he repeated softly.

'You've said that three times – now, what do you want?' she challenged. He had to disappoint her and himself and break the spell.

'Your name, your surname, what is it?'

She made a knowing grin. 'Is that all? Rosewarne.'

She flirted with admirable skill. Not only had she made him physically uncomfortable she had put him mentally at bay as well.

'Rosewarne – that's a pretty name.'

'What do you think it means? Rosewarne?'

'Someone who delights in the colour and soft velvety texture of the fleshy petals, and feels heady from the heavy fragrance.' It was his time to flirt and she was captivated by his words and voice. She slumped, ever so slightly, and he felt a sigh in her bosom.

'That's just like a poem, what you said.'

'Do you like poetry, Nancy?'

'Mummy has a Book of Common Prayer she had when a child – she was called Florence Vyvyan then,' she said, remembering the inscription inside the front cover. 'And when I reads that, it...' and she stopped, searching for words.

The passing reference to Vyvyan aroused Richard's interest but he did not want to be sidetracked from his purpose. 'Seems like poetry?' he prompted.

'Iss. What poems do you know?' She faced him and looked directly into his eyes. 'Well?'

'What?'

'Do you know any poems?' she asserted firmly.

'Oh, many, Nancy. Would you like to hear one?'

She nodded and looked away in anticipation.

'Since we were speaking of roses I know a poem that Andrew Marvell wrote to his mistress. It is addressed to a rose – what I mean is he speaks to the rose he is sending her telling of...Oh! You tell me what you think it's about.

> *Go lovely Rose*
> *Tell her that wastes her time and me,*
> *That now she knows*
> *When I resemble her to thee,*
> *How sweet and fair she seems to be.*
>
> *Tell her that's young,*
> *And shuns to have her Graces spy'd*
> *That hadst thou sprung*
> *In desarts, where no man abide,*
> *Thou must have uncommended dy'd.*
>
> *Small is the worth*
> *Of beauty from the light retir'd*
> *Bid her come forth,*
> *Suffer her self to be desir'd*
> *And not blush so to be admir'd.*
>
> *Then die, that she,*
> *The common fate of all things rare,*
> *May read in thee*
> *How small a part of time they share,*
> *That are so wondrous sweet and fair.*

'Did you like that Nancy?'

'It was beautiful, and you said it so...You speak...How do you remember so much?'

The path took a steep dip towards a small but fast-running stream. Jake felt his way down the slope, carefully forded the brook, and then surged up the far slope back onto the even path again. Nancy was thrown heavily back into Richard. Instinctively, he held her tighter in his arms, pulling her hard against his body. He felt the softness of her breasts, his mind reeled, and that spot in the body where sense and emotion tussle was in turmoil.

'The next gate is the farm. Mummy is sure to be looking,' and she moved very deliberately away from him. She knew exactly what she was doing.

He dismounted, adjusted his breeches discreetly, knowing her eyes were following all his actions. When he looked again she was hiding a smile. He led Jake, lifted the latch and opened the five-barred gate that swung open and came to rest with a sharp crack against a stout post. The path had a dressing of fine, sharp beach shingle keeping it free of weeds. The high Cornish hedge that ran fully the length of the path on his right side was topped with mighty elms. On the opposite side an orchard fronted the farmhouse. A gaggle of geese began to chatter to each other, soon gathered volume and rose to an out-of-unison honking. A collie appeared from the outhouses and bounded down the path to greet the visitors but was halted by a sharp call from the house. Mrs Rosewarne, Richard assumed, stood in the doorway shielding the low-angled sun with a raised hand.

The house was old. Four small-paned windows were not symmetrically disposed in the façade, as the new Georgian architecture demanded. The two windows in the upper storey were positioned high on the walls where the thatch eyebrowed over the tops. The two ground-floor windows were also not equally disposed about the heavy oak door. The fresh lime wash had taken on a rosy tint as the sun headed towards its setting. As they neared the house, Nancy waved, and called to allay any anxieties. Her mother remained at the door, smoothing her hair into place. She had a pleasant appearance and, at forty or so years, she did not have the careworn, unkempt appearance of her contemporaries in the Row. Richard reached up to help

Nancy. Her eyes were daring him as his hands closed around her waist. Her mouth had a shadow of a smile as she placed her arms around his neck. In such a position, she could afford to flirt outrageously, knowing he could not accept the challenge.

In the parlour, Nancy introduced Richard. The room was warmed by a black range upon and in which an evening meal was cooking. A large, scrubbed, pine table and four chairs filled the centre of the rectangular space. Deep beams carried the upper floors but still allowed ample space for Richard to stand comfortably. The walls were lime washed, and the golden light that entered the prettily curtained window, facing the creek, cast a warm glow, even on the slate slabs of the floor.

'Rest easy, Mrs Rosewarne, Nancy positively blooms with good health – you need have no concern about that. I come on another matter I think you and Mr Rosewarne should be acquainted with.'

She gave a curt nod. 'Will you take some cider, Doctor?'

'I will indeed, ma'am. Gladly.' She gave a quick smile of acknowledgement and excused herself. Nancy breathed as though she had held her breath for the last few minutes.

'Don't worry so, Nancy, it will be all right once we acquaint them of the reason for my visit – they still believe you are ill.'

Whispers at the door pre-empted the arrival of Mrs Rosewarne, bearing two mugs of cider, followed by a very large man, with two more mugs. He ducked under the doorframe and then straightened between the beams in a well-practised motion. Mr Rosewarne's large muscular frame carrying no surplus bulk lent a commanding presence. Sleek blond hair swept back on each side of his head and tied in the fashion of seamen. He had fine angular features set in a broad face. He looked to Richard and smiled. 'Bob Rosewarne,' he said and Richard grasped the huge hand and felt the strength of the man.

'Richard Maddern.'

'Pleased to meet you, Doctor.'

Mrs Rosewarne offered a mug of cider to Richard, and then gave another to her husband.

'To put you at your ease, there is nothing wrong with Nancy – my reason for being here is not medical.'

'You'd better be seated, Doctor,' Mrs Rosewarne said

quietly, pronouncing each word correctly, and obviously in her usual manner. Relief was almost palpable but the couple were attentive as Richard related the events leading to his visit. When he finished, there was a brief moment of silence.

'Well, you should have told me my sweetheart,' Mr Rosewarne said, with more than a hint of compassion. Nancy sucked at her lower lip and tears welled in her eyes.

'Come here,' he spoke gently, and she went to his arms.

'I wanted to, Daddy...'

Mrs Rosewarne got up and comforted her as well. Nancy said she was sorry. Richard now felt like an intruder but knew there was no quick and easy escape route.

'Please excuse us, Doctor,' Mrs Rosewarne said, and smiled. Immediately, a strong resemblance with Nancy was apparent – a quick, expressive, readily happy mouth with even white teeth.

'Bob!' she called. It was time to pay the guest attention. Mr Rosewarne placed Nancy on his knee and faced Richard. Nancy had a wet face but an altogether more cheerful countenance. She smiled broadly at Richard while still hugging her father closely.

'We must thank you for telling us about all this. 'Tiss mostly of our own making really. When they was children together, we use to encourage it – they playing and all. But as they grew up, Nancy did not like him s'much. But I didn't know it got this bad.'

'You'll have to speak to Billy, and make sure he understands he is to mend his ways.' Mrs Rosewarne scolded mildly.

He nodded and bowed his head slightly – there was no doubt who ruled.

'You be careful, Daddy; he's got a knife widun...'

'With him,' Mrs Rosewarne gently corrected.

'With him, all the time.'

He nodded again. 'I know that my handsome. Billy isn't the best when he's in drink. I'll see him in the morning – that's best. And don't you worry about me. I can handle Billy all right.'

Richard had no doubt that Mr Rosewarne was fit and very able in a fair fight, but Uddy may not see it that way. Having been the cause of the situation, he felt under a certain obligation.

'Would you like me to come with you, Mr Rosewarne, as a witness, in case Uddy does not see reason?'

Mr Rosewarne chuckled cheerfully, and shook his head, slowly. 'Don't you worry either, Doctor. I've known Billy and his father for a long time. Knife or no, I can always best both of them.' Then he added quietly. 'And I shall have my old gun handy,' and he winked.

Richard's worry increased as he drained the mug and stood.

'I have overstayed my time and I beg your leave. Thank you for the refreshment, Mrs Rosewarne. Mr Rosewarne, good day.'

Nancy freed herself quickly. 'I'll go to the gate wiv...with you, Doctor,' she said, which did not allow for any other alternatives.

Richard led Jake to the gate and Nancy walked beside him. 'Thank you for commun.'

'Commun?'

She smirked at the correction. 'Coming.'

'I hope your father doesn't get into trouble with Uddy. I would feel better if I were present.'

She laughed again. 'What would you do against Billy?'

It was his turn to smile wryly. 'I'll see you tomorrow at Carclew, Miss Nancy. What time will you be there?'

'Late in the morning,' she said as she opened the gate and walked a little further – out of sight from the house. 'The spring tides will flood the path. ''T'will be nearly eleven before I can get across the stones.'

''T'will it indeed!'

She pushed him away in fun. It was the first occasion she had touched him deliberately.

He caught her at her wrist and pulled her to him.

'Thank you,' she said looking up and into his face.

'Mummy's watching, Nancy!' he teased.

'I don't care.'

'Well I do. I don't want Daddy coming at me with his blunderbuss. I'll wait to see what happens to Uddy first.'

He mounted Jake and took another look at a lovely face that was beginning to show signs of adoration.

'Good day, Maid Nancy,' and he spurred Jake on.

The sun, still perceptibly warm on his face, was comforting and the late wistful song of a robin close to hand and the far-off haunting cry of curlews changed his mood. Loneliness he banished by his constant work, but it crept insidiously back. How easy it would have been to speak the words she wanted to hear, run his fingers through her hair, and kiss her upon the lips.

He didn't know her well enough. She had no learning; when the lust was over what then?

> *Enjoyed no sooner but despised straight*
> *Past reason hunted; and no sooner had,*
> *Past reason hated, as a swallowed bait.*

A rustle above him beyond the steep bank with its thick gorse brake disturbed his reverie. He looked carefully and, just as he decided it was of no consequence, it happened again. He reined Jake in and stood still. A distinct thump came from the high bank. Jake shivered and snorted softly. Richard felt a shiver in his own spine.

'Steady, Jake!' he whispered. 'Whoa boy.'

He got Jake moving which calmed both horse and rider. Barely a few paces further and the rustling started again. The watcher was human, and most likely Billy Uddy. He reached for the pistol at his right side, and cocked the hammer. Jake walked on, and the noises followed close-at-hand – nothing showed, but the relentless dogging continued. Ahead, a sharp bend to the right, afforded no view of what might lie around it. There was an obvious place to lay an ambush. He spurred Jake into a trot and rounded the bend. As soon as the path straightened, he reined Jake back and turned to face the way he came. The rustle in the bank was now louder, as though the chaser was caught off guard, and had abandoned all notions of covertness. Billy Uddy tumbled down the bank and onto the path. Richard decided his best course of action was to take on his adversary and dug his spurs into Jake, yelling encouragement. Jake needed none and reared slightly before picking up a good canter. Uddy heard the hooves, got up quickly, and charged back into the hedgerow that bristled with ancient thick brambles and spiny gorse, and scrambled to the top of the bank.

Richard fired. Uddy leapt into the thickest undergrowth and out of sight. The shot echoed around the creek rousing all the birds, which flew in every direction, filling the natural amphitheatre with sudden raucous alarm calls. Richard drew the second pistol and cocked the hammer. 'The next ball will find your brains if you have any, Uddy!'

It seemed an age before quiet returned and, by that time, Richard could no longer hear any noise from the bank. He turned Jake and made for home.

Chapter 6

Richard held a small brown ribbed bottle an inch above the tabletop and let it fall. Captain Tremayne was sleeping an old man's sleep – head back and mouth wide open. He startled, not comprehending what had caused a rapid return to the land of the quick. Slowly he turned and seeing Richard, smiled.

'Ha! Doctor Maddern,' he spoke quietly then broke into a rasping cough. It was some time before he regained his composure. 'Please excuse me, Doctor. I caught a chill and it has left me with a cough.'

Richard looked critically at the old man and took his wrist. The pulse was rapid and weak, but his temperature felt normal.

'I have brought you some laudanum.'

The captain nodded slowly.

'Have you had much pain?'

'A little. The rum helps.'

Richard diluted three drops of laudanum with water. The captain drained the tumbler eagerly, and Richard suspected he was in more pain than he admitted.

'Clutterbuck sent his clerk and took my instruction. He expects a draft will should be ready next week.'

'Good news indeed.'

Captain Tremayne relaxed as the laudanum began to take effect. 'Yes,' he said quietly almost to himself. His mind was on other matters.

'I brought you a book that you might find amusing.'

'Oh?'

'*Tom Jones* by Henry Fielding – have you read it?'

'Umm?'

'*Tom Jones* – Henry Fielding,' Richard raised his voice.

'Oh yes,' he replied vaguely. 'Is it good?'

Richard would not have a sensible conversation, until he

flushed into the open, whatever was on Tremayne's mind.

'Is something bothering you, sir?'

The old man stirred, and looked directly at him. A finger of doubt went to his mouth, and quivered there. Then he looked away, the question weighing heavier than his resolve, had tipped the balance.

'Come, sir. Is it about your ailment?'

He smiled, and then chuckled quietly. 'No, not my ailment. No, this is a favour and one I feel I have no right to ask.'

Richard spread his hands wide. 'If I can help, I will.'

Tremayne paused, and picked at a thread in the blanket, covering his legs. 'That laudanum works well – I feel up to a tot; how about yourself, Doctor?' and he winked slyly.

'Why not? Is the sun over the yard arm?'

'Don't know; haven't seen the sun in days. I think the bugger's not coming back. It's been so cold these last days, don't you think?'

While he was talking, Richard poured a tot into each of two tumblers, and added water.

Tremayne took a swig immediately he got the glass.

'Ha! Grog!'

'Grog?'

'Equal part water, I guess.'

Richard laughed. 'Sorry, laudanum and rum may not mix.'

The captain sighed, and looked into the glass. 'Better make it last in that case. I've drunk rum by the barrel all over the world. It's good in the hot climes, and especially good in the cold. A nor'easter off the French coast in winter is an ill wind.' He lapsed into silence as he remembered those far off days. 'What was I saying?'

'A favour.'

'Ah yes. Do you know Peters? Don't like the fella! When I couldn't ride any more he said he would look after my horse. I took him at his word, but found out, by accident, that he lent her to all sorts for hunting and used her over-much. One particular day, I found her covered in mud and altogether in a bad state. Hadn't been groomed for days I shouldn't wonder. I'd have strung the bastard up, and have the bo'sun lay it on with a will, if I'd had my way.'

The rage of that day boiled anew at its remembrance.

'Here,' Richard said, as he handed him a freshly charged glass.

'I tore the bugger off a strip, and told him never to touch the horse again. But Peters is still there, and I don't trust him. I would like to give her to you – and all the tack – there's plenty. Is that a problem?'

'Not at all – it will be a pleasure.' And he immediately began to seek a solution to the stabling problem he had now given himself.

'Excellent fellow! I feared you might refuse – she's called Lady. I know it's a stupid name, but it's exactly how I felt about her from the beginning. She always behaves properly, and never makes a fool of herself.'

Richard glanced at his watch. He would invite Nancy to ride Lady – she would be the right person to look after the mare, but he would not suggest that straight away – it could wait for the right moment.

'Has Nancy changed your dressing today?'

'Oh yes – long before you came.'

Pity, he thought, *I wanted to try the magnesium sulphate; never mind, another time.*

'Do you know where she is?'

'Skylarking with Lucy no doubt – in the kitchen, swapping yarns about who's had their tits out last!' and he laughed.

Richard excused himself and found Nancy exactly where Tremayne had said. The two girls guiltily stopped talking as he entered, which half confirmed the captain was right. He smiled, thinking that perhaps he was the last to – well, accidentally – touch her breasts. They took his smile as a friendly greeting.

'Nancy, a favour. Can you go to the stables and have Lady saddled. I am taking her to Devoran tonight. If you are leaving soon, perhaps you can ride her for me. Are you going home soon, Lucy?'

Lucy bobbed unnecessarily, blushed and said, 'Iss.'

'Good, well you can both ride Lady – tell me when you are ready and I'll accompany you.'

In due course, Richard rode behind Lady and the two women, who giggled and twittered all the away. He assumed they were talking about him from the occasional glances in his direction, but what they could be saying for so long mystified him.

Ruth was not pleased with the extra horse. She grumbled, quietly, all evening about too much work, and "two 'osses" frequently punctuated her mutterings. Richard allowed her to vent her spleen without offering any explanation.

After the meal, when he was sitting in his drawing room with a glass of brandy, she came to the door to ask if he wanted anything else before retiring. She didn't actually come into the room, which meant she was unhappy.

'Ruth, I have made a decision with regard to the horses and the work outside the house.'

She listened intently.

'I shall take on a man to help out.'

Still she said nothing, but advanced beyond the architrave.

'I am thinking of engaging a local man.'

'Oo?' she hooted finally, unable to bear the tension.

'Edward Trezise.'

Chapter 7

April came and with it spring at last. The air was suddenly warm. The promise of longer days and summer sun persuaded mankind to smile at their fellows, linger when exchanging greetings, and seek out the ways forsaken in the frosts and hoars. The warmth penetrated winter-chilled bodies and tempted the foolhardy to shed clothes, bare backs and till the soil.

'Not yet, Edward!' Richard warned as he stepped outside and breathed in the invigorating air. 'I know it feels good, but your lungs need more proof of lasting sun. You know the old saying.'

Edward smiled and tucked his smock back into his breeches. His new employment and kindly master had already transformed him, but most of the improvement was a result of better meals, less exposure to the elements and reduced hard labour. The fundamental reasons for his poor health remained.

'Iss I know. Don't cast a clout till the May be out.'

'That's it, Edward. Have you left your sample?'

Edward nodded; he disliked performing what he thought was an indignity to Richard. That a man of the doctor's learning and means should have to deal with the phlegm he spat contemptuously into the ground didn't seem right. The doctor had performed other, even more undignified, examinations of his body. Richard's reputation grew and further proof was running between Edward's legs at the very moment. Molly was dressed in rough, but clean clothes; a bonnet covered a good growth of fine, short blonde hair. Richard picked her up and made a fuss of her.

'If it stays fine, Edward, the garden is the place to be. How are you getting on with the lane?'

'Nearly finished. These light evenings make some difference. Why, we was out till near dark last night and nearly done it. It's some different indoors already, even with all the wet we had – dry and handsome.'

'Good. If it should come to rain or cold will you do some more to the privies?'

A man at the gate attracted Richard's attention before Edward could answer.

'Someone coming to see me, Edward.'

Edward turned and recognised the stout man approaching.

''Tiss Cappen Ross.'

The man walked with bowed head so as not to miss his footing on the cobbled path. He glanced up from time to time assessing his approach and when just a few feet away he stopped and removed his hat. Edward was the first to speak.

'Cappen Ross!'

The man looked at Edward, but did not recognise him.

'Specy, Cappen Ross!'

The man addressed as Ross stood back a little. ''Tiss never you is it Specy? Well I'm blessed! You'm looking well, boy. I shouldn't have recognised you.'

Ross was of average height and well built. His nose and chin were his most striking features; they darted towards each other at every word but never met. A short beard, just showing signs of greying, hid most of his face. His deep bass voice had a natural vibrato.

Edward laughed. 'All thanks to the doctor here.'

Ross realised he had been rude and not introduced himself properly.

'Begging your pardon, sir – I didn't mean to be so rude. 'Tiss Ross Hitchens, sir, I'm Cappen up to the mines in Poldice. I'm here to see you, sir.'

'Glad to meet you, Captain Ross.'

Although surprised by the use of his first name and the proffered hand, Hitchens shook it.

'Is it personal matter, Captain?'

'No, sir, it isn't. I be good in meself, thank you. 'Tiss a matter of the mines, sir.' The meaning was not clear and Hitchens was hesitating to go on.

'I'll be about the stable, Doctor, if you need me – I'll take Molly...'

'Molly will be all right with me, Edward.' As Edward turned away, he called him back with a question. 'Is Lady in the stable?'

Edward smiled knowingly. 'Maid Nancy was here a hour ago, Doctor,' he replied softly.

Richard nodded and spoke to Ross. 'Shall we go inside or can we talk here?'

'This'll be fine, sir, if it pleases you – can't waste the sunshine.'

'No indeed!'

'Well now, 'tiss like this. Do you know the scheme that the miners have when there's a accident or sickness?'

'I think so, but you'd better explain.'

Ross Hitchens would have been rehearsing his speech every step of the way, but now he hesitated and looked to the ground to collect himself.

'All the miners pay tuppence a month to the clerk – 'tiss called the "doctor's pence". Now, if any one of them gets hurted, or sick, they are paid out of the savings.'

He looked at Richard to see if everything was going all right. Richard nodded and he continued.

'If a surgeon is wanted then he gets paid as well. Now, several of the miners aren't all that pleased with the one we got.'

'Surgeon?'

'Iss.'

'Ah,' Richard's tone conveyed a difficulty but, to his surprise, Ross had anticipated this reaction.

'Iss, now I know that's a problem, but Mr Carthew, who is a owner, has asked you to call on him. He would have come his self but he can't, begging his pardon. Now tomorrow, he'll be at Wheal Andrew, and he'll be waiting for you to call.'

'What time would be convenient?'

'Tomorrow is the end of the month – well, 'tiss the nearest to it – and the owners have a bit of feast, dinner time – that's noon – and they would like you to join them in the Count House.'

Richard was secretly delighted at this invitation. Not only would it afford him experience of the miners but also of the work they did. An opportunity would surely present itself to go down a mine to see them at work.

'Please tell Mr Carthew I shall be delighted to speak with him, and I shall join him, and the other owners, in their feasting.'

Captain Hitchens, well pleased, had nothing more to say.

'How do I find the Count House, Captain Ross?'

'Ahh! Well now. The best to do is follow the Carnon Stream,' and he turned indicating the whereabouts of the stream in the creek. 'Go so far as Bissa, then keep going until a bridge crosses the stream. Don't go over the bridge, but keep the stream on the portside,' and he shook his left arm. 'You'm then in the mining country.' He pronounced those last words expressively and, unaccountably, a shiver of foreboding ran down Richard's spine. 'Just follow the stream and you'll get there.'

'How far is it?'

'Why, 'tiss no more than five or six mile – I just walked it and I got to walk back!' He laughed. 'On a morning like this it isn't hard, Doctor. Good day to you!'

Richard took Molly to the stables where Edward was making alterations to accommodate Lady. Jake snorted gently as Edward worked and spoke quietly around him.

'Edward,' Richard asked softly. 'Is the *Sweet Union* in the docks today?'

Edward could not resist a wry smile. He rose with the sun and could not understand why Richard missed the best part of the day.

'Iss. Come up on the tide at first light.'

'Did Nancy say when she would be back?'

Yet another smile. 'No.' He did not volunteer any more information.

'Are tides spring?'

'Iss. Early morning tides are always spring – neaps is dinner time.'

Richard smiled at this. 'Ah, she'll be back early then – she doesn't cross the stream when the tides are full.'

'Aw, 'tiss different now she got a 'oss.'

Richard realised he was being teased, very gently, and let the subject drop.

'Come along, Molly, let's go down to see Lij.'

He told Molly of each interesting feature they passed but she had her own interests at her level. Closer to the ground, primroses, wild garlic and early buttercups attracted her. He gave the names and she repeated them as best she could. She held a primrose to her nose, and the scent embedded itself in her mind and would become a cherished, childhood, memory. The short walk to the quays took a long time – time not wasted, but drawn out; time slowed to a child's pace.

The sunlight sparkled on the water dazzling the eyes and hands went up to shade the glare. The *Sweet Union* was further down the quays where men were busy unloading timber and coals. Mules had their burden of tin ore removed from their backs; twenty already stood quietly feeding from nosebags, and more were arriving.

They sat on the wooden planks of the quay and watched. Molly pointed and asked in her own language and Richard explained.

This was a time to think. Nancy would not reject his advances; on the contrary, she would embrace them enthusiastically. But what then? Where would it lead? Not immediately – he knew where that would lead – but in the longer term.

'Morning, Doctor.'

Richard looked up and saw Nicholas Parker removing his hat and smiling a friendly greeting, 'I hope I'm not disturbing you.'

'Not at all, Mr Parker. As you see, I am entertaining a young lady whose mind is full of nothing and who is determined to fill it to the brim this very morning.'

Parker nodded. 'This must be Miss Trezise?'

'The very one – and doesn't she look well?'

'She does indeed, and all thanks to you, I understand.'

Richard smiled indulgently. 'There is an expression "*vis medicatrix naturae*": the healing power of nature. There is often no better treatment – and more often than not – no other treatment.'

'Nature may lend a hand, Doctor, but I believe your skills count for the most part.'

Mr Parker was not alone in having a misplaced faith in his ability and there was no point in dissuading him or his other patients from their reasoned, and hopeful, faith in their physician.

'You're very kind, Mr Parker.'

'Please call me Nicholas, Doctor.'

They talked about the best way of travelling to London but were interrupted by someone halloing and waving, at the entrance to the quays.

'Somebody for you, Doctor, by the look of it. I think it's Mr Jennings from the wink.'

They both shielded their eyes to get a better view.

'I've not met the man, so I do not recognise him.' Richard got up, and waited as Mr Jennings ran towards them.

'Ah, Doctor – found you at last. The baby's coming this last five hours and 'tiss all wrong, sir.'

'Calm yourself – Mr Jennings is it?'

'Iss, from the inn, sir.'

'Is anyone attending your wife?'

'Iss, the midwife, Mildred Cocking. But 'tiss all wrong see. There's no head.'

It sounded like a breech and no other doctor present. Richard hurried back to his surgery.

Ruth held his leather bag open while he selected several instruments. He dithered a great deal, much to her consternation.

'That seems to be that.'

Ruth looked at him quizzically. 'Mildred won't have nothing more than hot water and her old stool that's a fact.'

A wheelbarrow partially blocked the door at Mr Jennings' and, just inside the door, a well-scrubbed birthing stool almost barred his way.

'This way, Doctor,' an anxious Mr Jennings pointed to a staircase leading steeply to the upper level. Creaks and groans from the stairs and the wooden floorboards announced his arrival. A middle-aged woman of neat and tidy appearance opened the door. She gave Richard a quick bob. 'Morning, Doctor.'

'Good morning. Mrs Cocking?'

'Iss. Mildred.'

No further conversation passed as he took in an unusual scene. The patient, Mrs Jennings, was on all fours, close to the only window, in the low-ceilinged room. Her shift was around her neck, and she was sweating profusely. He turned to look at Mildred, his face aghast. She was quite calm.

''Tiss a breech,' she explained without any of the alarm that was coursing through his head. He positioned himself at the business end of the procedure, and saw two small protruding legs.

Mrs Jennings started a contraction and let out a deep-throated growl.

'Her groans are coming regular,' said Mildred. ''Twint be long now, Mrs Jennings,' she raised her voice to be heard and encourage.

'Not long now, Mrs Jennings – you're doing very well.' Richard repeated Mildred's words, as he felt in her neck for a pulse, and noted it was very rapid. His actions were designed, to calm the patient with a show of masterly experience but inwardly he was close to panic.

'Have you had breech presentations before, Mildred?' he whispered.

'Scores,' she said and he smiled at her, relieved by her obvious competence.

'And this unusual position is correct?'

''Tiss the only one I know of, Doctor. Get them on their backs, and nothing happens – try the stool and 'tiss too painful. This here way is more natural-like as far as I do see. All the weight is proper.' She positioned her hands under the patient, showing how all the bits and pieces hung, allowing gravity to do its work.

'We have to be careful with the head. Make sure nothing is wrong like – get the chin right and the little mouth closed. Only need a finger to do it, that's all and out he'll come.'

Another contraction and Mildred moved to support the little body. 'Not long now,' she encouraged Mrs Jennings. 'Next time.'

As the next contraction started, Richard crouched close by Mildred, to offer his assistance. The upper chest was visible and Mildred expertly felt for the arms. She nodded to indicate the critical time approached. The next contraction, the shoulders were clear, and Mildred gave more support to the tiny torso. She waited, reassuring Mrs Jennings. Richard also waited anxiously but left the task, and the responsibility, totally with Mildred.

'I'm just going to hold the chin and then push the head gently up and back.' As she did so, another contraction started, and the baby was born.

'There 'tiss – all over, Mrs Jennings,' she exclaimed triumphantly, holding the little boy by his heels and giving a sharp slap to the buttocks. Almost instantly, Mr Jennings was at the door with a large kettle.

'What is a? Is a boy or a cheeld?'

'Boy,' Mildred replied officiously, ushering him from the room and closing the door.

'Eight pound four ounces – good-sized baby I'd say. And nothing wrong, Mrs Jennings; healthy boy.' The end of her sentence was in a raised voice as if the mother was slightly deaf.

'And what be your name, Doctor, if you please?' Mrs Jennings asked.

'Richard.'

'And that's what we'll call him – after you.'

'Well thank you, ma'am. I'm very honoured. I think I should have a good look at Master Richard.'

Richard carried out a thorough examination the like of which Mildred had never seen.

'All excellent – a very healthy boy,' he declared. 'And you have come through with flying colours,' he said to Mrs Jennings, now beaming with happiness. 'Take plenty of rest and remain in bed until I visit you in a couple of days. Now I'll wish you all good day.'

Richard was relieved to get out of the tiny room, redolent with the sweet smell of birth, and humid from heat and perspiration of too many bodies. The stairs, he now noticed, were steep and narrow causing him to hold on to the beam over his head to steady his descent. At the bottom, Mr Jennings was waiting with a broad grin.

'Well, Doctor! All over and all done with, thanks to you.' Richard reached the last step and then the slate flooring where he was able to transfer his bag to shake Mr Jennings by the hand. He was conscious of yet another fable-in-the-making for which he could take no credit.

'Thank you, Mr Jennings. You have a fine boy.'

'Sit yourself down here by the window, sir, and I'll bring you a glass of the best stuff.'

The room was small with just one window looking out onto the quays below. A low-beamed ceiling, stained dark brown from tobacco smoke, prevented him from standing upright. An unlit range filled most of one wall on which stood a large black kettle. Two tables and four chairs were the only furniture; more would have lead to congestion. The slate floor was uneven with no other covering. The abiding impression of this bare, sparse room was one of gloom. The farthest corner was inky black where a person could observe, and not be seen. It was a winter's haunt, when the lit fire would give a welcome and the closed door shut off the vilest weather.

And the weather was suddenly vile; the skies had turned liquid grey and sheeted rain.

Mr Jennings poured a large glass of brandy from the kettle on the stove. He stood slightly back to observe the tasting.

'My word! A very good drop, Mr Jennings!'

'Best cognac. Got a anker only last night. Brought in on the morning tide.'

Jennings leaned over the table. 'I can get one for you if you like?'

Richard nodded.

'I'll bring it this evening – after dark.' He turned to go, then came back, and whispered again. 'Doctor, about your fee?'

'Half a guinea, Mr Jennings. How much for the brandy?'

'Why, that's very good of you, sir – that's no more than what Mrs Cocking gets – a London doctor for half a guinea.' He shook his head in disbelief.

Richard laughed heartily. 'Mrs Cocking is worth every penny.'

'So's the brandy, sir. 'Tiss a anker; that's more than seven gallons.'

'Seven gallons, heavens above!'

Jennings laughed at his reaction. 'Taste like heaven as well!' Then he leaned very close and whispered. 'Two guineas. That's all.'

There was a brilliant flash of lightning instantly followed by a crash of thunder and the pelting rain came down even harder. The inn shook as the heavens raged until the rumble faded in the distance. Four youths ran down the path and fell into the doorway laughing. Their clothes ran with water and the washed out mud left an ochre trail; their hair lay plastered to their heads. Three were tinners according to their dress, and the fourth was a sailor in the navy.

Jennings greeted them with a smile, declared it was their lucky day, and treated them all to a large brandy in honour of his new son.

'What's he called?' asked one of the tinners.

'Richard, after the good doctor, there.'

All eyes turned to Richard and they raised their glasses, shyly, in good cheer. With practised art, they sliced and ground tobacco in their palms before packing the clay pipes. A blue-grey smoke began to pervade the room, and despite Richard's aversion to tobacco, he delighted in the aromatic scent in that first instance – before it became over-powering. It was so evocative of inns and taverns throughout the land. Such a place as this, conjured the romance of the smugglers trade – the mix of sail, salt, contraband brandy, tobacco, tea, lace and all bound by the excitement of adventure and danger. Or perhaps, he mused, too much brandy already.

Mrs Cocking descended the steep stairs, and made her way to Mr Jennings, wearing a clean white starched apron. Mr Jennings nodded affably as he counted out the money to pay the midwife. This she tied in a handkerchief and placed in the large pouch at the front of her apron.

'No use going out in this, Mrs Cocking,' Richard said. 'Come, let me buy you a brandy.'

She approached cautiously – professional cooperation was one thing, but fraternising with a doctor was quite another. She seated herself across the table and waited expectantly. Richard signalled Jennings for a brandy that arrived almost immediately and he brushed aside any attempts to pay.

'Well, thank you, Mr Jennings,' he said and then he raised his glass to Mrs Cocking.

'Your good health and a difficult job well done!'

He leant across the small table. 'Where did you learn that

particular technique for dealing with breech presentations?'

She laughed lightly, took another sip, and looked out the window.

'It was a long time ago, Doctor, when I was a young maid – well, just twelve or thirteen I suppose. Old enough for mother to take me along when she was seeing to the women in the houses long the quays in Falmouth.' She did not elucidate further. 'Now, it so happened a slaver was in port on account of her taking water. None of the slaves was allowed off, save two. One was a old nigger women – black as coal she was – I never seen the like afore and I weren't too happy, you might say.' She paused and looked around the room. 'The other was a young girl no older than myself and she was having her baby,' she whispered. 'Mother said she had young girls afore and nothing to be afraid of – she said that to me. Well, what was different was, she was standing up holding onto a pole supporting the ceiling. The old woman was speaking, quietly like – and we watched. Every time she groaned, she'd scoopee down still holding the pole. Then she'd get up and waited. Well, this went on for some time and the maid was sweating but she didn't seem worried. Then all of a sudden, little legs appeared, and the old woman made her get on all fours like Mrs Jennings. Well, mother was in some state really but we couldn't say nothing, so we bit our tongues. But all went well and the baby was born easy and no trouble. And the maid was standing up in no time. No lying abed for that little dear – but it didn't seem to harm her at all.'

'A good story, Mildred, and a lesson I shall remember well.'

Mrs Cocking was now anxious to leave, saying her husband would be expecting his meal on the table when he returned from work. Home was at Perranwell some three miles away. The rain was easing she said, and she'd take her chance. Through the window, Richard saw her pushing her barrow along the muddy lane as the rain poured down in a torrent.

His mind was fuddled, and it was not a time for serious thinking, despite the fact he had only one item on his mind requiring all his mental powers to resolve. He half listened to the conversation in the bar but the vernacular generally defeated him until he heard "Nancy". Then he concentrated hard. The sailor mentioned Billy, his tone was menacing.

'That bastard need seeing to I tell you,' the sailor said vehemently. 'And I be the one to do it. I never forgot what he did to poor Martin. Broke is head in, he did, and left him to die!' The seaman was working himself up into a rage that the tinners were trying to subdue.

'No, I aren't the same man I was before pressed. No! I've boarded three ships with cutlass and run several through. No, if I see the bastard I'd have it out with him.'

Mr Jennings searched under the bar, extracted a concertina, and tossed it to a tinner.

'Here, Janner, give us a tune,' clearly hoping to defuse the situation and restore an atmosphere of celebration that better suited his mood.

As Janner played a few chords there was a sudden loud noise of men's voices and scraping of boots at the door. A large, rowdy influx of tinners invaded the inn, all very wet and steaming from their haste to take cover. Each had something to say to the landlord as he entered. "Entin down", was a frequent expletive; orders shouted for brandy and rum; the need to light the fire to dry clothes, and shouts to make room. Soon, the whole room filled with broad-shouldered, boisterous, cheerful men. Richard felt obliged to stand to make a little more space; as he did so another glass of brandy was discreetly placed on the table. Pipes lit up everywhere, and the pleasant aroma Richard savoured previously, now became a thick, noisome fog.

'Give us a tune Janner – strike up,' one man shouted across the room and a general murmur of encouragement followed. Janner stood on one of the chairs and began to play an introduction. He had a fine tenor voice and the song started prettily enough telling of a summer's day in the fields and the birds singing. The great volume of sound of the chorus, Richard found galvanising; the quality of their voices, and the sincerity with which they sang was uplifting. The tune was simple, and he felt assured he could join the next chorus if the words came.

A sailor and his true love were walking one day
Said the sailor to his true love I'm bound far away
I'm bound for the Indies where the loud cannons roar
I must go and leave my Nancy she's the girl I adore

Richard waited for the chorus line but found the shock of the words left him voiceless.

I must go and leave my Nancy
I must go and leave my Nancy
I must go and leave my Nancy she's the girl I adore

More than one pair of eyes searched and found his.

A ring from her finger she hastily drew
Saying take this dear William my love will be true

The mention of William also drew some cries of "not that bastard" and Richard thought he heard the abbreviation of his own name substituted by some of the singers, with much laughter. The chorus rejoined with even more vigour.

But as she embraced him tears fell from her eyes

Saying may I go along with you, oh no Nancy farewell
Saying may I go along with you
Saying may I go along with you
Saying may I go along with you, oh no Nancy farewell.

So it's goodbye dear Nancy I can no longer stay
For the topsail is blowing the anchor is weighed
The good ship lies waiting for the next flowing tide
And if ever I return again I will make you my bride
And if ever I return again
And if ever I return again
And if ever I return again I will make you my bride.

Then a final rousing chorus, which was a repeat of the first, that Richard remembered and was able to join in.

And the larks they sang melodious
And the larks they sang melodious
And the larks they sang melodious at the dawning of the day.

Richard fought his way to the bar to buy a brandy for all. They cheered him to the echo for his gesture, and there followed an hour of singing local songs and finally Wesleyan hymns.

Early evening saw him discharged from the inn, followed by a blue smoke laden with human perspiration. He staggered along the uneven path in the still pouring rain; his ears rang in the silence. Mostly, what resonated in his head was the song about Nancy. He now had two thoughts struggling for dominance; first to get a piano: the singing had reminded him of how much he was missing music that had previously been a rich part of his life. And the second, what to do about Nancy.

There were many arguments why he shouldn't become entangled with her; foremost was that he was already married – others, like station, class, and intellect, had mostly to do with preserving some part of him, rather than impediments against her. Above all else, in this interminable debate, what reigned supreme was her undoubted beauty – in that, all who knew her, agreed. He straightened himself, as best he could, as he entered his house knowing Ruth would be waiting. He cautiously trod through the hall into the warm kitchen.

Ruth tutted. 'Wetting the cheeld's head is one thing, drowning the dear baby, another.'

'A fine boy, Ruth – Richard Jennings! Mother and son doing well.' He was heading towards the dining room and spoke to her over his shoulder, which would displease her further.

'Nancy says,' she began and he was drawn back to face her. 'Nancy says the Cappen isn't good – failing fast, and he wants to see you.'

'I have to go to the mines...'

'I told her that and she said that the day after will do – he isn't at death's door, she said.'

She delivered the message in a flat impatient monotone and waited.

'Anything else?'

'What do you want for supper? Cold meat is all I got!'

A warm mate was what he needed most, but food he needed desperately and cold meat would do.

'Thank you, Ruth – in the dining room I think.'

Chapter 8

The sun had been up for hours but the low cloud diffused a dim light. It was five miles to the mining country and, even allowing for the unfamiliarity, he should have been there in a couple of hours. The highway ran straight for as far as he could see in this poor light.

A light, and the sound of hooves, were coming towards him. The first beast of a mule train passed. The animals were taking tin ore to the docks at Devoran and he counted fifty mules before the drover drew up. The small man removed a pipe from his mouth and spat. 'Morning, sir. Damp.' His face was the colour of dark stained oak, and weather beaten to a degree Richard had not seen before. Deep fissures ran riot all over his face and any expression it carried was impossible to decipher.

'Morning. Am I in the right way for Bissoe?'

'Bissa! Iss. Mile or more yet.' The man waved his pipe and was gone.

He continued his dismal journey, noting a bad smell was intensifying. He reached a small hamlet of two or three dilapidated cottages and assumed that it was Bissoe. The windows of the cottages were still as black as night; no friendly light of habitation showed. A stack appeared from the gloom, from which a thick smoke lazily drifted; it was the source of the obnoxious smell.

'Arsenic,' a voice proclaimed from the darkness close to the cottages, which startled him and Jake. A short figure was standing close by the wall carrying a heavy staff. The man moved closer; a miserable wretched creature clothed in rags.

'Worse when 'tiss missle, like this here,' and he glanced all round indicating the drizzle.

'I'm looking for the Count House, at Wheal Andrew.'

'Andrew,' the man repeated, with heavy stress on the second

syllable, as he stepped even closer. Richard felt for the butt of his pistol fearing the man may put his staff to use. With laboured breathing, the man turned his face slowly up and to one side. He had one walleye and had to twist his face to allow the good eye to see – his toothless mouth dropping open from the effort.

'Over the river be the mill and follow the road this way,' and he waved his right arm. 'Keep to the path – don't stray off it mind!'

Buildings loomed out of the mist, each noisy with industry. Fires flared, steam hissed and wheels turned. People ghosted in and out of sight.

He kept to the narrow path, as Edward had also warned him, since the area abounded with shafts. Eventually, he arrived at a collection of buildings surrounding an engine house, whose bob was working almost silently. Close to hand, was a large smithy where sparks flew from the glowing hearth. He made for a building where three horses were tethered and a man was waiting.

'Morning, sir,' he said touching his forehead in a salute. 'Doctor Maddern?'

'Yes indeed.'

'Iss,' he said and waited while Richard dismounted, holding the bridle to steady Jake's head.

'All going in the stable dreckley,' he explained, nodding towards the other horses. 'Bit o' meal and a grooming like. Soon as the moyles are gone,' and he pointed to where a train of mules stood ready to move off.

'Good.'

Richard looked at the two pistols wondering what he should do with them.

'They be all right, sir,' the man said anticipating the question in his head. 'Better leave them here in case they think you'm going to rob them,' and he laughed.

Each side of the main door, ranging down the sides of the building, were impressive piles of copper ore, demonstrating the wealth of the operation to the owners inside. He tapped at the slightly ajar door and pushed it open in one movement. Three clerks, on high stools, murmured a greeting. All the wall-spaces of the room had floor to ceiling bookcases filled with ledgers. At the centre stood a large chest of drawers, with a plain polished top that also served as a table; the labels on the two topmost drawers said "maps". A cast iron coal fire protruded several feet into the room, radiating comforting warmth, even to the doorway, on that foggy dank morning. The nearest clerk was dressed in a black frock coat that had seen many years of use. This sparse, tall man, his feet able to rest firmly on the boards even from the high stool, was presentable and tidy. He wiped his quill carefully, before placing it in the groove on his desk cut for that purpose. He stood easily and approached Richard with a warm smile.

'Doctor Maddern?' he asked, in a deep mellifluous voice, coming from the depths of his tall frame.

'Yes.'

'Absalem Bennetts, sir; pusser.'

'I'm very pleased to meet you, Mr Bennetts.'

'Mr Carthew is in the meeting where the accounts are being read – 'tiss unfortunate that this month is also the quarter-end, so there be more to consider, and they be later than usual.' Allowing for the slight lapses in pronunciation, the accent was pleasant and, because he spoke slowly, he was clearly understood.

'Perhaps you could inform Mr Carthew I am here?'

A loud roar of laughter came from the adjoining room. The door opened, and a gentleman emerged. He strode across the room with his hand held out.

'Doctor Maddern – I saw you arrive and the meeting is all but over. Excellent timing.'

They shook hands and Mr Edward Carthew introduced himself. Dressed in a smart frock coat over a white shirt, topped by a loosely tied black neckpiece, Mr Carthew gave the impression of a busy, successful mining adventurer. He was the same height as Richard and about ten years his senior.

'Unpleasant morning. Thank you for coming to see me at such short notice – I'm much obliged. I'm not sure how much Captain Hitchens told you, so I'll start from the beginning. But I forget myself – some refreshment first. A little brandy perhaps, on such a morning?'

Being in a state of recovery from the previous day, brandy was the last thing Richard wanted.

'Ah. Too much of that yesterday, I'm afraid to say – celebrating a new arrival. Tea or coffee would suit me better, Mr Carthew.'

He laughed. 'Congratulations, Doctor – boy or cheeld as they say?'

Richard hastily corrected the assumption. 'A patient presented her husband with a boy.'

Carthew laughed at his mistake. 'Married yourself, Doctor?'

'I live alone, sir.'

'Do we have any coffee, Mr Bennetts?'

Mr Bennetts looked to another of the clerks who nodded and fetched a metal jug from the back of the stove.

'Please take a seat, Doctor, and I'll explain the situation. Then Mr Bennetts will go over the system we operate – which is little different to any other mine – after which he will show you the accounts. They will give you instances of the fees doctors ask for and the various demands made upon them.'

Richard gratefully accepted a steaming mug of coffee, even though it was stewed.

'At present we have two doctors serving the group of mines in this area: Dr Morse from Penryn and Dr Andrew from Ponsanooth. Dr Andrew is wishing to retire. So, if you take up the appointment, I'm sure he will be delighted to relinquish his role.'

'That sounds perfectly acceptable, Mr Carthew, and much better than I was lead to believe.'

'Well that's settled then,' and they shook hands warmly. Carthew then leaned back a little and doubt clouded his brow. 'The message that Captain Hitchens delivered seems to have given some rise for concern, Doctor?'

'Yes, I inferred from what he said there was some hint of dissatisfaction with the present doctor, and a change was being sought.'

Carthew nodded slowly, thinking over what Richard had said. 'I must be frank with you from the outset. There is dissatisfaction, as you say, and the retirement of Dr Andrew does not solve it.'

'Thank you for that explanation, Mr Carthew. It makes it much easier knowing what the problems are.'

Mr Bennetts explained about the sickness benefit scheme. Richard was surprised to learn that, as well as covering the attendance fees of a physician, monies were paid during convalescence, as much as a guinea a month. The adventurers often supplemented these payments, such as the cost of getting an injured person to his home, and a woman to tend the man. Should the injury prove fatal, it was customary for the mine to bear the expense of the funeral. To aid in the recuperation of a miner, the management sent bread and brandy. Mr Bennetts spoke of benefits paid to some of the older men, those worn out and unable to work: 'and a coffin when the time comes for the Lord to take him home.'

'I see the fund stands at close to two hundred and fifty guineas – a tidy sum. Tell me, Mr Bennetts, who administers the money, on the miners' behalf?'

Mr Bennetts gave a short nervous cough. 'I be the pusser of this mine, Doctor, so that's for me to see to.'

'And I'm sure you do a handsome job, Mr Bennetts.'

He nodded his acknowledgement of the compliment. 'Is there something else you'd like to see, Doctor?'

'I think not, Mr Bennetts. This has told me sufficient for the time being. Thank you.'

Mr Bennetts closed the ledger and seemed relieved to do so.

Bennetts preceded him into the adjoining room. It was narrow, its length accentuated by a long board table taking up almost half the space, and set exactly in the middle. A woman and two girls were laying the table for a meal.

'Gentlemen!' Carthew rapped the table and called above the clamour. 'May I introduce you to Dr Maddern who, I am very pleased to say, has agreed to take up a post of bal doctor to these mines. Dr Maddern is a physician who comes highly recommended, an Oxford graduate and one who has spent time, and money for tickets, to walk the wards in London with the best minds in the country.'

There was a murmur of appreciation and some tapped the table in polite applause. The information could have only come from the Chairman of the Board, Sir William Lemon, who

96

began to speak from the head of the table.

'Well, Doctor Maddern, I'm so pleased to meet you again, and under such happy circumstances. Little did I think you would get yourself inculcated so early into the real fabric of our society. Mining is the very life-blood of this county, and a backbone to the defence of our country in these troubled times. You are most welcome.

'Gentlemen! I commend Dr Maddern to you; a valuable addition to our company.'

The ensuing mêlée disrupted the efforts of the women and Carthew held up a halting hand. 'Gentlemen! Gentlemen, there will be ample time to exchange greetings *after* the table is laid.'

White linen covered the table and pewter dishes, stamped with the mine's seal, demonstrated the wealth of the company and showed the place setting of the guests.

Richard was at the middle of the table, next to Dr Andrew and opposite Dr Morse. He knew four people in the room: Sir William, Captain Ross Hitchens, Mr Trethowan the solicitor and Mr Carthew. There was a London adventurer each side of Sir William: Mr Marriott, a barrister of Knightsbridge, and Mr Edington of Chelsea, both significant investors. Another mine's captain, Mr Tonkin; the manager of the Cornish Bank, Mr Williams; two more local investors; a representative of Boulton and Watt, the engine makers; and Mr Bennetts the purser, made up the assembly.

The talk was mostly about the accounts and the general tenor was one of great satisfaction. They were discussing plans to increase production, which met with Richard's approval, but when talk turned to the more efficient shipment of the ores by improving the docks at Devoran, he felt his recently won isolation was under attack.

'Gentlemen!' Sir William thundered across the table talk. 'One of the greatest obstacles to increasing our business, apart from the eternal pumping,' and he gave a wry look to the engine maker, 'is the transportation of the ore to the smelters. Access to South Wales is invariably via the north coast ports – Portreath, for example – and we all know the treacherous nature of that coast. Whereas, the south coast offers well sheltered harbours able to take the largest vessels. Furthermore, the access to smelters in and around Truro is within a day's reach of Devoran. Gentlemen, we must think boldly.'

He had their attention and a murmur of approval rose from the table.

'Look outside this window; you see fifty or more mules loaded with canvas bags of ore – perhaps a couple of hundredweight each. That is a total of about five tons. Five tons! And we are thinking about mining tens of thousands of tons. How many mules must we keep?' They thought about the question, knowing he would provide the answer or at least venture his solution to the problem.

'Imagine a railway!' he said quietly but with great emphasis. Then he repeated his suggestion over the rising murmurs. 'Yes, a railway collecting ore from Camborne continuing onward to Redruth, and to these our mines at Great Consols and Poldice; taking the whole production from this part of the county to Devoran where hutches, much larger than those at present, will hold the stocks until the barges and lighters load from enlarged and improved docks!'

All present slapped the table in approval. ''Tiss but a short distance to Calenick or Carvedras smelters – and, if we were to be truly bold, there is no reason why smelters could not be built at Devoran.'

Calls of, 'Hear him, hear him,' came from everyone with the exception of Richard and his nearest neighbour, Dr Andrew.

'How much would such a scheme cost, Sir William?' asked the manager of the Cornish Bank.

'Ah! That is the question. It will be manageable or it will not float. We need to balance the increased output against the cost of implementing the scheme – less of course the present expense of mules; yes, it bears thinking about. There are thousands of mules at present – all requiring handlers, stabling, fodder and so on. Look at the accounts and you will see the cost.'

Sir William relaxed a little having whetted the interest of the assembly. He would give them time to think about their pockets.

Two women carried in a large platter with a steaming side of beef the size of which Richard could not remember an equal.

'Shall we be able to eat it all?' he asked Dr Andrew.

'Have no fear, sir, it will be demolished and more besides! I invariably get a feeling of guilt whenever I see such abundance when all around me there is hunger and want. There is many a miner labouring heavily beneath our feet, at this very moment, who could not imagine this cornucopia. They exist on short commons, pasties if they are fortunate, hoggins, or if not, a crust. They will go home to a starving family who will have barley bread, a thin gruel of home-grown vegetables, and perhaps a morsel of meat – poor meat at that – mutton or shin. The celebration of wealth these gentlemen enjoy is won by the poorest creatures – our fellows nevertheless. All of us, made in God's image, as the priests so fondly declaim each Sunday, without offering any explanation as to why we sit here and feast with Him at the Canaan wedding, while their inheritance is to be one of the multitude sharing five fishes and five loaves. What do you say, Maddern?'

Richard smiled and leant towards his companion. 'You have read my mind, sir! Those that make capital available deserve to reap the rewards since they also suffer the losses more extremely. Yet the division of wealth ought to be fairer. "To him who hath it shall be given", is truly a blessing from heaven for the rich, but the preachers seem not to relate that to Judaism, which they abhor, but to Christianity – a religion that teaches the entirely opposite view.'

The older man looked with sudden renewed interest. Then he laughed. 'God bless you, sir.' He leant towards Richard and whispered. 'The medical gentleman opposite is relieved to see me going, thinking the thorn in his side is vanquished. Yet you give me hope that this is not the case.'

Richard saw Morse, concentrating intensely, on what was passing between him and Andrew.

'I'll not influence your opinion of Morse – you must find out for yourself. What I can do is to caution you of his deviousness. I live closer to the mining area than he, yet often, when I am called out, he is there before me. The first to arrive takes the case. I never looked upon miners as a source of great income, indeed, not even a good living, but the system is open to – let me say – manipulation, if not abuse.

'There are two underground captains at this table: Ross Hitchens and Mathew Tonkin. Tonkin is not liked. If Ross calls out the bal surgeons, I am usually the first to arrive; when Tonkin makes the call, Morse is always first.'

'I have just looked at the accounts of the Club the miners contribute to, and I noticed there is near two hundred and fifty guineas in the account. Are there any checks, audits even? And is the money invested?'

Before Andrew was able to answer, Morse spoke across the table to Richard.

'Did I hear you say investment? Will you be investing in the mines, Dr Maddern?'

Richard laughed and rose to shake Morse's hand across the table, which gave him time to think of an innocuous reply.

'Not until I know more, sir.'

Morse straightened in his chair, and leaned back; a finger of doubt covered his lips.

They stared at each other for a while, and then Morse said, in a louder voice.

'I suppose the living you have in Devoran is not sufficient for speculation.'

'The living is non-existent.'

The room became silent at this pointed exchange.

'Will you be attending the board meeting, Doctor Maddern, at the end of the month – the 28th April I understand?' asked Sir William.

Sir William was being the parliamentarian and diplomat, giving Richard a way of explaining how his financial interests lay, but he did not intend to disclose his business other than his medical work.

'Yes, Sir William – but what is the best means of getting there?'

'Following your advice, I have bought shares in the East Indian Company, and since the April meeting is the AGM, I have decided to attend. I would welcome your presence at our London address and if the timing is right, perhaps we can travel together. I usually embark in the Packet to Plymouth, tranship to Portsmouth and then take the coach – two days! Travel is quite remarkable nowadays, do you not think gentlemen?'

There was general agreement around the table and Sir William had excelled himself in both defusing the situation, and hinting heavily of Richard's comfortable background, without divulging any confidence. Richard caught his eye and raised his glass in admiration, and Sir William returned the gesture smiling broadly.

Pork followed the beef, it being too early for spring lamb and too late for game. After clearing the table, brandy and port arrived with cigars and pipe tobacco. Sir William called for attention.

'This is the last day Doctor Andrew will attend our meetings as a physician, so I think it behoves us to hear his views on the state of the health of the miners and how it might be improved.'

'Without costing too much,' Morse added gratuitously.

Sir William smiled and nodded in his direction. 'Well, we all know of Dr Andrew's reforming zeal, but we should give heed to what he has to say, remembering that he has the longest service.'

There was polite but genuine applause before Dr Andrew began.

'Thank you, Sir William. I stand here before you at an age of two miners' lives. Yes! Two. The average life span of a miner is 30 years. A life spent at hard labour to which no judge would condemn a criminal. Our brave seamen, defending our dear land, have a better chance to see old age than a Cornish miner! He is married as early as sixteen and, it is usual under such circumstances, to have fathered a child while still barely a child himself. It is a brutish life, often living with his or her parents, who are still producing other children. His chances of seeing a grandchild are slim'

'Like rabbits they are. Can't stop them. You should see them!' Tonkin beamed, nodding enthusiastically at everyone.

Andrew looked at him contemptuously. 'I'm quite sure we can rely on you to do that, Captain Tonkin.'

The barb did not find its mark in so insensitive a skin, but there was general amusement around the table and knowing glances.

'Surely the church should take a lead in these matters,' Carthew, very gently, suggested.

'I don't think we should encourage clerics to skulk the lanes as Tonkin does,' Andrew deliberately deflected the question.

'Many a miner has to walk five or more miles to his work place, and then descend, perhaps in extreme cases, two hundred fathoms on a ladder. In only the light afforded by a candle, he walks or crawls more miles until he reaches the rock face. There he picks at hard rock for hours. A poor meal and cold water is all he has to sustain him. As to his reward, that is not for me to question – you are all better qualified than me to judge.'

'They don't have to work at the mines, Doctor. It is their choice,' Mr Marriott interjected.

'That is true to a point. But take away the mines and what else is there? Precious little. And the mines do offer the chance of making a good living – very good, and that is why the tribute system is favoured. A tributer is an adventurer, such as yourself, but one who risks no capital. The system seems fair and equitable, until you see at first hand, what they risk instead. Under our feet, men work in temperatures of up to seventy degrees and more, dirty water drips, and sometimes pours, over their naked bodies throughout their core – eight hours. The air they breathe is low in oxygen, and after blasting even lower, and full of noxious vapours and black dust. Tuberculosis is rife among miners but the phthisis he suffers is a deadly complication. When their toil is over, they retrace their steps, but this time climbing ladders – imagine climbing possibly a thousand feet. When they come to grass from temperatures we love to experience on a hot summer's day, it is often frost they meet, when their clothes are wet through. The shock to the system is hard to imagine! And they walk to their homes in the cold winds, if the hovels they live in maybe called that, to be greeted by starving children, and a distraught wife, who has little to give them in the way of nourishing food.'

He paused for a few moments to let his words take hold.

'You can't expect the owners to tell them how to spend their earnings, Doctor. If they can't manage better, it's nobody's fault but theirs.' Tonkin attempted to placate the position of those in the room.

Doctor Andrew sighed. 'Be mindful of events across the channel, where the aristocracy are ruing the day – if they still live – when they made the lives of the average Frenchman intolerable. Hunger has led the miners to rebellion just a few years ago.' A rising murmur of disapproval greeted what was seditious talk.

'You are encouraging revolution, Doctor, with such talk!' Mr Marriott exclaimed.

'I am not, sir! Quite the opposite. I am urging you to think about measures to alleviate the miners' situation and avoid a revolution! Remember, most of what they produce goes to industry that makes instruments of war to defend ourselves.' He paused and looked at each in turn.

'More dries are needed, where the men can change their clothes in warmth, a place where hot water is available and soap to cleanse their bodies before going home. A hot drink may be enough to dissuade them from stopping for hours at the nearest kiddleywink.' He sensed nothing he said would make the slightest difference, but he made one last effort.

'Finally gentlemen, for I can see you are rapidly losing patience with my argument, can I give you the benefit of many years of observation of one particular habit which, I believe, has a detrimental affect on health, not just of miners, but they are the ones I am speaking of.'

He looked carefully at those around the table. 'I am talking of smoking tobacco!'

Apart from Andrew and Richard, everyone else had a cigar or pipe and the room clouded with thick smoke.

'Almost the first thing a miner does in the morning, on waking, is to have his first touch of the pipe. Even before breakfast. Immediately after breakfast, he has another pipe, and then on the way to work and when underground after the descent. And so, it continues throughout the day. They smoke rather than eat.'

'I've always believed smoking tobacco improves a man's health, Doctor,' Mr Edington, the quieter of the London adventurers, suggested.

'I offer no proof of what I say, it is just an observation – those that smoke the heaviest find earlier graves than those who do not smoke.'

Several pipes were tapped out and they listened with more interest.

'Furthermore, there are several accidents each year from

smoking next to a powder keg. Loose powder does not explode violently but flashes, and can take a man's sight. It would be a simple expedient to ban smoking while underground.' Above the murmur of disapproval he continued.

'You may scoff at this suggestion but you impose more ridiculous penalties; a miner is fined for swearing and other petty misdemeanours, that have no affect on health or output! Alcohol is banned underground so why not smoking?

'One last thing. In the case of a serious injury, it is not uncommon that many hours pass before a doctor attends. Someone has to fetch a doctor, and the patient is often removed to his home, and finding him delays matters further. Having reached a patient, I have had to prop the talfat to take my weight, before I can examine the man. Clean water is usually not to hand – I have fetched it myself, in a crude vessel that was used as a chamber pot! In my opinion, a room ought to be set aside at the mines – somewhere clean and warm where water is available, where a patient can rest until help arrives.

'Thank you for your indulgence gentlemen. I wish you all well, and that you continue to prosper.'

'Gentlemen, let us thank Dr Andrew for his thoughts and for the many years of service he has given. Your health, Doctor.' Sir William raised his glass, and invited all to raise their glasses, and drink the toast.

As they resumed their seats, Sir William asked, 'And what does our newest doctor have to say about Dr Andrew's valediction?'

Richard looked directly at Sir William. 'It is exactly what I would have wished to hear; the distilled thoughts of an intelligent mind that has had long experience in the mining industry. Plague, cholera, smallpox always occurs among the poor first. Why should this be? One can only agree with Dr Andrew, that the conditions they live and work under must be suspect as contributory causes.'

The room was quiet, and everyone was listening, with interest, as they began to appreciate that the new man was urbane, articulate, and deserving attention. Richard glanced around the table as he spoke, making each one feel as though he spoke to him.

'Dr Andrew has given us a good example. He has observed that smoking tobacco may be a contributing cause of chest illness and suggests banning smoking while down the mines. This is practical medicine at work and ought to be tested.' He tapped the table at each word for emphasis. 'The men will not like the imposition and some small recompense should be offered as encouragement. An on-site medical room is a most excellent idea, and I think should be pursued with haste.'

A silence followed, heads fell forward whether from thinking or the affects of too much alcohol, Richard could not say.

'It all means further expense,' Mr Marriott said, after the long pause. 'And it's always the same people that have to bear it. Providing dries and setting aside rooms for treatment is all expense, all expense I say, and no return on the capital. The new infirmary at Truro is being financed by people like those around this table, for just that purpose, and now you want more before the place is finished!'

Cries of, 'Hear him,' rose from around the table.

'It might be possible to persuade the miners to make a contribution from their own funds. I have learned that the bal doctor's fund stands at near two hundred and fifty guineas. It attracts no interest not being invested, when all around this table are gentlemen who could give sound advice on this matter,' Richard continued to argue.

Mr Bennetts coughed but made no comment.

'It's a very good question – does anyone have a suggestion?' asked Sir William.

'No? More brandy, gentlemen – there's more yet to celebrate before we wind our way homeward.'

Andrew turned to his new ally. 'A valiant effort, Doctor Maddern. You must excuse me, I shall make my way home. All this heavy drinking leaves me dull and I take several days to recover.'

'I think I will follow your lead, sir.'

They made their excuses to Sir William and, as they left, Captain Ross Hitchens chased after them.

'I believe you asked to go down the mine, Doctor?'

'Yes, Captain, would sometime next week be convenient?'

'Iss, whenever you've a mind to – I'll be here somewhere.'

As they waited for their horses, Andrew spoke, 'Dr Maddern, it has been a pleasure meeting you, and I am highly delighted that you will be pressing for reform at the mines. The owners cannot continue to abuse their positions. There are women and children employed here under the most atrocious conditions. As you will see, the mines are dangerous and unhealthy; changes must be put in place.'

Dr Andrew held out his hand and they shook warmly.

'Good day to you, sir.'

Chapter 9

Richard opened the door quietly and saw the old man was in his usual chair. Nancy was reading to him from *Tom Jones*. Nothing she read seemed to disturb her, but she could not have read anything of the like before. Richard knocked at the door and Nancy leapt to her feet and turned in his direction, blushing when she recognised who was there.

'Who's there?' asked Tremayne, his voice was barely audible.

'Doctor Maddern.'

'Ah, Doctor – so good of you to come.'

'Not at all, Captain. I'm glad to be of service.'

Nancy made way, and took the opportunity to excuse herself.

'How do you feel, sir?'

He nodded, the effort of speaking taxed what little strength he had.

'All my affairs are in order as you suggested.' Then another long pause. 'The time has come, Doctor – the struggle is unequal.'

Richard gently squeezed his hand before getting up. He poured a large amount of laudanum into a glass and added some water.

'Here, take this. It will ease your pain.'

The old captain's eyes focused meaningfully, and Richard nodded, reassuringly.

On the 15th of April 1799, Captain Tremayne, passed peacefully away before his great cousin, Sir William Lemon, could tear himself away from business to visit him.

Two days later, in a steady downpour of rain, the funeral took place at St Piran's Church. The church stood on a rise, and broad granite steps gave access into the churchyard, where mouldering mounds of the resting places of former parishioners surrounded the building. Tall pines crowded around the west side, dolorously decorated with wet crows making occasional harsh calls, tolling the knell in the absence of a bell.

Swirls of driving rain and mist enveloped the topmost parts of the Norman tower. Adjoining the church was the Home Farm, and from the nearest barn a figure appeared clad in a large number of layered garments to keep out the wet. He approached Richard, respectfully touching his headgear, and took Jake.

Richard made his way to the lychgate as a coach drew rein. It contained Sir William Lemon and a younger man that the doctor assumed was Charles Lemon, the son.

The priest appeared in the porch, clutching a bible, his surplice flapping in the gusts. He looked anxiously out at the appalling weather. Breaking cover, Richard walked quickly, his head bowed against the wind.

'Good morning, sir. Reverend Nankivil, curate-in-charge of this parish,' and he shook Richard's hand. Mr Bennetts and another man moved past into the church, while a third man, Mr Clutterbuck, stayed.

'The coach – is it Sir William's?' the curate, a man of about forty-five, asked, anxiously trying to peer through the murk.

'Yes.'

'Ah! Good. Thank you,' and he signalled to someone further inside. The church bell began to toll a single melancholy note at a solemn pace.

There were only four others present and already seated. Five minutes passed in uncomfortable silence until a scraping noise at the door signalled the arrival of the cortege. The coffin was borne by six men from the estate, preceded by the undertaker, dressed wholly in black. All were soaked to the skin having walked the mile or so from Carclew. The priest began intoning the service for the burial of the dead. Sir William and Charles Lemon followed the coffin to the end of the nave, and took their family pew.

The priest sawed through the ritual, demonstrably having little affection for a man he never knew or visited to comfort. The hymn, *O Love divine, how sweet thou art* was announced, and Mr Bennetts' fine bass, accompanied by his companion's high tenor and a single fiddler in the gallery, led the

108

congregation in the only serene moment in the dull and lack-lustre service.

The committal was perfunctory and soon over while the rain continued to sheet down in torrents – lords and commoners alike suffered the same drenching, until the curate nodded to the sexton. They made brief exchanges at the conclusion and then the few hastily dispersed.

Clutterbuck accosted Richard by the lychgate.

'The will shall be read at Carclew on Thursday next, in the forenoon. As a beneficiary, I suppose you will attend?'

Richard nodded curtly.

'And could you do me a great service, Doctor, of asking a Miss Nancy Rosewarne and Mrs Lucy Chynoweth to be there, since they are also beneficiaries.'

*

'There are just four beneficiaries of the estate of Captain Arthur William Tremayne who died without issue or other claimants.

'To Mrs Lucy Chynoweth, whom I thank for the many kindnesses she afforded me above that of her duties,' Richard saw Lucy smirk into a handkerchief at this, 'I leave ten guineas and the kitchen utensils that are mine to dispose of.' Clutterbuck glanced at Lucy and saw she was overwhelmed by her good fortune. Clutterbuck coughed gently, and then proceeded.

'To Dr Richard Maddern, for his attendance upon me when his skills were much needed, I leave my mare, Lady. I also leave him fifty shares in Davenport.'

Again, he glanced up from his papers to ensure the beneficiary had understood.

'To Miss Nancy Rosewarne, whom I hold in the greatest esteem and have a great fondness for, as an elder person to a younger, I leave two-hundred-and-fifty shares in Davenport.'

Richard was staring at Sir William's back and noticed a twitch in his shoulders – the experienced politician could not disguise an unexpected and, perhaps, unpleasant surprise.

'It is my dearest wish that Dr Maddern gives instruction and guidance to Miss Rosewarne in the dealing with these shares.'

Nancy looked towards Richard and smiled. She did not realise the value of the gift she had been given.

'And finally, the residue of my entire estate, I bequeath to my relation Sir William Lemon, in grateful recognition of his graciousness and kindness toward me in my last years.

'That concludes the will of Captain Arthur William Tremayne and is duly signed by myself and my clerk, Mr Thrall.'

Sir William was the first to get up. He faced Richard and smiled – a smile of mild irritation, like one who had lost at a gaming table.

'Those shares, I understand my relation thought I coveted,' he said as he approached Richard and Nancy. Nancy bowed and hung her head low.

'Well it is not true,' and he smiled condescendingly. 'I abhor the slave trade and have always supported its abolition.'

Then he took Richard's arm and led him aside.

'How do you propose to deal with the shares?'

'I had no idea Davenport had any connection with the sugar trade in the West Indies. I have no stomach for that business and I will dispose of the shares as soon as I can. But you see the dilemma I have with Miss Rosewarne.'

Sir William nodded, slowly, and looked again at Nancy.

'I shall be happy to give you some assistance there, Doctor, but you will need to wait a while.' He turned to go, and then turned back. 'Are we to sail together on the packet next week?'

'Yes indeed, Sir. I shall be honoured to be your travelling companion.'

'Good! That's settled then. You must visit Lady Lemon who is most anxious to meet you. Good day to you, Miss Rosewarne. It has been a pleasure,' and he bowed very slightly and left.

Nancy audibly sighed. 'He don't seem very happy, Doctor, and I don't know what I've done.'

Richard laughed at her bewilderment. 'What do you think you have been given, Nancy?'

'Shares,' she said, unenthusiastically. 'I'd rather have Lady.'

'Nancy, you shall have Lady. It was always the Captain's wish.' He was about to explain further, but Clutterbuck was suddenly at his side.

'Begging your pardon, Doctor. The share certificates, for you and Miss Rosewarne, are at my office. Do you have any instructions regarding them?'

'Both Miss Rosewarne and I need time to think about what to do with them. I am not acquainted with the company. Do you have any information about them?'

'Umm,' and he looked about the room, although there was only Lucy. 'They are a firm in Liverpool connected with the sugar trade in Jamaica. Trethowan tells me they are selling for more than a guinea a share and are steady.'

Clutterbuck took his leave, which left Richard with a bewildered Nancy.

'What is happening, Doctor?' she asked frowning. 'First everybody is happy and now no.'

He smiled at her and touched her intimately by putting his arm around her shoulder.

'There are things we need to talk about, Nancy. Call to see me before you go home. Let's see what Lucy is up to!'

Later, in his library, he had Nancy to himself. 'I have learned from Mr Clutterbuck that the shares in Davenport are valued at approximately a guinea each.'

'Well that's very nice,' she said without any excitement.

'That's about two-hundred-and-fifty guineas altogether.'

Her expression froze in one of amazement – it remained like that for some time. She tried to swallow but her mouth was too dry. Her eyes widened and, unable to speak, she shook her head in disbelief.

'Two hundred and fifty guineas!' she finally was able to shout.

Richard placed a finger to his lips. 'Shush!' he cautioned in a whisper. 'Ruth!'

Nancy could not contain herself and the need to keep silent was impossible.

'My God! My God. Jesus, Mary and all the angels!'

With that exclamation, Ruth was at the door, rattling cups and teapot on a tray.

'Whatever is it?' she asked, pale-faced and worried. 'What's a matter, maid shouting like that? '

Nancy got up, took the tray, placed it on the table, and then took Ruth by her hands and danced around the room, shrieking and laughing.

'Are us having a wedding?' Ruth exclaimed. This was an unexpected question and one that brought Nancy to a halt. Hands covered her mouth, then her eyes; the ground should open up and save her more embarrassment. Ruth uttered woeful noises and ran from the room in great haste, quickly followed by Nancy. From the kitchen, there were whoops, shrieks and then silence. A soft knock at the door and Nancy walked in very sheepishly.

'Did you tell Ruth?'

'No!'

'Good. Best to keep the news to yourself. What would you like to do with the money?' he asked, trying to emphasis money, rather than shares.

''Tiss no good, Doctor – me head is too flummoxed to think.'

'Nancy, you have enough money to buy your own house – in Truro if you like. Would you like to leave your home and make your own way?' She shook her head vigorously.

'Well in that case, would you like to become the owner of your parent's farm?'

Her mind was quickly on an unimaginable journey. Glazed and distant she took time over this idea. Slowly a smile signalled the acceptance, and then enthusiasm took over.

'Oh, Doctor, you got such ideas. No wonder Cappen Tremayne thought about you to help me. But how to do it?'

'To whom does your father pay rent?'

'Why 'tiss...let me think…Robartes. They got a great house called Lanhydrock somewhere. Daddy pays the money to the Cornish Bank in Truro.'

'You must write a letter to Clutterbuck saying he should make an offer to Robartes for the farm. Can you do that, Nancy?'

'I can do the writing all right, but what to say? If you could tell me what to put down?'

He was surprised she did not baulk at the idea of writing.

'I will draft a letter this very evening. You must speak with your parents and ask them if they have any objection to your plans. If they do not understand I will explain it to them.'

She glowed at the prospect of the adventure ahead. 'Oh, I

112

never thought such a day was possible. What wonders money can bring!'

'And what about yourself, Nancy? You must give yourself a reward also. What would you like to have?'

'Yes,' she said thinking wildly. 'I once saw a dress in Truro that I...'

Richard knew the moment had arrived. This was the propitious time – all things had fallen into place. Now, it all depended on her response. He rose slowly, and holding her by her arms lifted her from the chair.

'Nancy, I shall be going to London next week, and I shall buy you dresses – all colours: yellow, like spring primroses, green, like summer leaves, and blue, the colour of your eyes.'

He kissed her quickly; then again. She stayed close. So again, this time longer and her hands reached to his shoulders. Now a long kiss and she pulled him to her. Her mouth and lips were soft and warm; she moved them sensually, exploring his mouth and lips, opening her mouth slightly, massaging his mind. When they parted, they were both breathless. Hardly pausing, they engaged again.

'Nancy!'

'Yes, Doctor?'

'I think it's time that you called me something else other than Doctor.'

'What?'

He held her away to study the expression on her face. Did she not know his name?

'Oh, I think "sir" will do well enough,'

She slapped him on the chest. 'Sir!'

He kissed her. 'Richard, then.'

Chapter 10

Water spilled from the rim of Captain Ross's hard bowler hat onto his oilskin where it collected in rivulets and streamed to the ground.

'Now a change of clothes, I'm thinking,' he said, bending his head against the driving rain.

'Not necessary, Captain Ross, I come dressed in old clothes.'

'That's proper, Doctor. Give your coat to the boy and we'll be fitty.'

At the shaft-head, Ross produced a bowler treated with tar to make it hard. He demonstrated how to stick a candle into a lump of clay at its front, and then handed it to Richard, along with several more candles, to hang around his neck.

Close to the shaft, the bob of a mighty beam engine was nodding, turning a huge wooden drum – a whim. From this, a thick rope was uncoiling sending it down the shaft.

'There's a kibble going down to load with ore. See that there ladder?' Richard saw the head of a ladder, perilously close to the rope.

'We shall go down there about thirty fathom, and then along an adit. I'll go first and tell you what to look out for. Mind the rope, and don't fall off. The shaft goes down two hundred fathom.' He was cheerful in his warning.

At the ladder, Ross lit two candles; one he stuck into the clay on his hat and the other he gave to Richard to do likewise.

Thus accoutred, sprang to mind and, like Christian, Richard set out on the straight and narrow, knowing it was not the Celestial City waiting below. He placed his foot on the first rung and began the descent. Captain Ross quietly encouraged at each footfall and, when a stave was missing, he called out and Richard felt a firm grip on whichever foot was about to wave in thin air. His knees trembled slightly and when he looked down, beyond Ross's candle, there was only blackness. The noise of the whim faded and the only sounds were that of Ross below him and his own breathing. The first sense assaulted as they descended was that of smell, a damp, mineral smell – sulphurous. Water ran down the shaft walls and in small falls from the shaft head, which was a diminishing bright circle overhead. It seemed an age until Ross called he was at the thirty-fathom level.

'Go easy now! There's a sollar here – boards across the shaft to step on,' he explained.

Richard was grateful to feel strong arms about him ensuring that he stood in the right place. They were in an adit, a level running horizontal from the shaft. A rattling noise of something large coming up the shaft preceded a kibble. It passed the adit in an instant and Richard was thankful he had left the ladder.

'Half a ton a time,' Ross said. 'They come right up the centre of the shaft – most times. This here is a level following a lode of copper. The miners drive the lode as long as the ore is good. Keep your head down and watch me candle,' he warned as he set off again.

After what Richard judged to be a hundred yards, the air became thick enough to taste. The temperature climbed and warm water dripped. The blackness, beyond the glow of the candles, was intense. On they trudged, frequently his head banged against the top of the drive and the caution to keep his head down was hammered home. The next time his hat struck, his candle went out. Now, there was just the glimmer coming from around Ross, ahead of him.

'There's a winze up ahead so be careful.'

'What's a winze, Captain Ross?' No sooner the words were out of his mouth than he ran into the still figure of Ross.

'Candle's out, Doctor,' he said quietly. 'Better light it or you'll go...'

Where he would go was not clear. 'You must tell me if it goes out again. If both candles go out 'tiss a darkness like nothing you've known before. Even an experienced miner is hard put to get to grass safely in the dark. Now, a winze is a shaft going to another level, and if you don't see it, that's the end of you.'

The ground was more uneven now and the going uncertain.

'Here!' and Ross lit another candle and showed a yawning hole, ten feet in diameter.

Three wide boards spanned the gap.

'Look down at the boards and you'll see them better. Take your time, and go steady.'

It was hot; beads of sweat broke out and ran down his face and back. Over he went and Ross took his arm as he reached him. 'Nearly at the end,' he said and marched off.

Eventually they heard the noise of iron tools striking rock, signalling life at the end of a very long tunnel. Then a soft lambent light ahead steadily became stronger.

'Cappen Ross,' someone called.

'Iss. I got the doctor with me.'

'Doctor?' The question was full of meaning.

'Iss, the new doctor.'

'Aw, I thought 'twas that bastard Morse for the minute.'

'Now, Henry, that's enough.'

The striking ceased and Richard saw two naked men glistening in sweat at a rock face and a boy with a shovel and a barrow nearby. The men shifted to see Richard better in the very confined spaces. As they did so, Richard saw a wall of rock, sparkling brilliantly yellow – like a huge wall of gold.

'This here's Henry and his brother John and John's boy Mark. They are the pare that's working this pitch – day core.'

'Doctor Maddern,' Richard introduced himself. 'Glad to meet you.'

'How do, Doctor,' they said and then nothing more.

Ross continued to explain the method of working.

'These are tributers. They bid to work the pitch for a month. They might bid for ten shilling for every pound's worth of stuff raised to grass. Out of that they take all the expenses – candles, the blacksmith for sharpening the borers, dressing the hammers, shovels, hilts and powder. Then they pay for the drawing, that's tramming and hauling, bringing the stuff to grass – to the surface,' he explained.

'Copper is only now making some money. A mine, in a place called Anglesey, has been out doing us. But the copper there is running out, so we're starting up again. This here is the

116

best pitch in the mine and they be picking the eyes of it.'

'Do you find the air poor?' Richard asked.

They laughed. 'No, 'tiss handsome here. We haven't fired for days, the picking is so easy. No, 'tiss good. Not too hot and dry.'

Richard was amazed at this response; in his mind, the exact opposite would have been a more fitting description.

'Well, now we're moving on,' Ross informed. 'If you follow me, Doctor?'

Ross was talking about the tribute system and comparing it with the tutworkers, giving the arguments for and against the two systems of working. Richard was not listening, his mind consumed by the image of the black hole called the winze. Ross stopped close to the top of a ladder protruding from the depths of the abyss.

'Now, Doctor; same as afore. I'll go ahead and guide you down.'

Richard stepped onto the sollar and stared down.

'You all right, Doctor?' Ross asked anxiously, trying to gauge his expression, as he stepped onto the ladder.

'How far shall we descend, Captain Ross?'

'Seventy fathom to the hundred level. A foot isn't no different to a mile, Doctor, if you aren't fitty,' Ross stated the situation plainly.

Richard drew breath, grasped the ladder, wished he could pray to a god for his safekeeping, turned, and went down.

Quite suddenly, into his mind came a vision of Nancy, her face – bright, smiling sweetly as she was when she left him last evening. He remembered kissing her, how she pressed her body against his. She wanted more, but the timing had to be right he reminded himself. But why? If he should fall, he would regret, however briefly, not having consummated their relationship. So why postpone it? There was a little trap he had to spring in order to argue a difficulty away. By accepting the idea to purchase the farm for her parents, she had made a huge stride in the direction he wished for, and her deflowering that she wanted. That was all satisfactory and...

'Doctor? We're almost at the level. If you wait just a second I'll jump onto the sollar and give you a better light.'

There already! What wonders that girl performs! When Richard was safely in the adit, Ross gave more instruction.

'This here is the hundred-fathom level and the first tin lode in the mine. 'Bout twenty fathom along and we take a short cut to the tin lode. 'Tiss a bit cramped in the cut...' and he left the statement alarmingly in the air.

'I shall be all right, Captain Ross – lead on!'

'Good. You're doing well, Doctor,' he encouraged.

It was even hotter and the quality of the air poorer, with the unmistakeable odour of black powder. His breathing was quicker and heavier. Steady walking soon brought them to another adit that was half the height and narrower.

'It gets tighter further in, but don't worry. I have been through here more times than I can remember!'

In he went and Richard followed. The air was even worse and the heat oppressive. He sweated freely, feeling the drips running from his body and saturating his clothes. The roof pressed him down. He was hundreds of feet below ground in a tunnel that touched his head and sides. This was no place to be! His legs trembled and he snatched the air. Panic was beginning to rise in his breast.

Nancy! Think of Nancy.

> *Had we but world enough and time,*
> *This coyness, Lady, were no crime.*

He recited Marvell's poem in his head as he struggled after Ross.

> *An hundred years should go to praise*
> *Thine eyes and on thy forehead gaze*

The heat was unbearable and the confines even closer than before. The rock walls trapped his hips and his hat scraped continuously against the ceiling of the tunnel.

> *Two hundred to adore each breast*

If I survive this ordeal, I shall have them out tonight.

> *But thirty thousand to the rest;*
> *An age at least to every part,*

118

God yes! What unimaginable joy to see the rest. He had that last image in his mind as Ross helped him from the adit.

'Good, Doctor! That's good.'

They were in a much larger drive where they were able to stand nearly upright. The candle had been knocked from Richard's hat and Captain Ross had the only light.

'Can you hear singing, Doctor?'

Richard heard men's voices some way off.

'That's the men on this pare; four all told. They be no more than two hundred paces from here and there's nothing between they and us to cause any harm. Now I got the only lit candle and I want you to know how dark a mine is.'

He snuffed out the candle and Richard felt Ross's hand resting on his arm for reassurance. The darkness was complete. His eyes groped for particles of light but there was not the merest glimmer.

'You'm facing where the miners be and you can hear the singing. If you put your arms out you'll touch each side. Now slowly make your way, feeling all the time. I'm right here.'

Richard was not as afraid as before and began to step out towards the singing: "O For a thousand tongues to sing". What a joyous sound in the depths of hell!

The adit turned slowly in a left-hand bend and, as he rounded it, a small ray of light penetrated the darkness. He walked quicker and the light intensified; quicker, and the words of the hymn became clearer. Around another bend and he saw the men at work. They were entirely naked, hacking at the rock face unaware of their presence.

'Yo!' Ross called. 'Perran James.'

'Yo, Cappen Ross!' came a quick reply. 'Lost your candle?'

'Iss. I got the doctor with me; come to see the workings.'

There followed a lot of banter and cajoling that, for the most part, Richard did not understand. Ross relit the candles and six-candle power did much to illuminate the area and the people. It was rare, even for a doctor, to view fellow humans in their entirety. Here were four, three men and a boy. The men were about five foot three to six, and weighing perhaps eleven stones. Their upper body muscularity was well developed. None carried any excess weight – indeed, some degree of under-nourishment

119

was evident. They all decided the visit warranted a touch of the pipe and, before long, the poor air was thick with tobacco smoke. Richard looked at each man and the scars of injuries were manifest on each of them. The leader had scar tissue from his shoulder down to the elbow of his right arm. He was a rough-looking man, with black curly hair and an aggressive mien, his speech was quick and unfriendly.

'How long ago did that happen?'

'Aw, let me see. Two year ago.'

'Iron bar, Doctor,' Ross explained. 'Iss. Somebody dropped it down a winze.'

Richard turned the man's arm and saw that the flesh had healed over the dirt of the mine giving the scar a black line.

'No one saw to your injury? Did you not think to wash the wound?'

'No time for that, Doctor.'

'Perran was off work for several weeks with that there arm,' Ross said.

Perran nodded and sucked on his pipe, hawked and spat. 'If that bastard Tonkin had his way, I'd be put off for good!'

'Your hand!' Richard said looking at another. 'What happened to you?'

This miner was younger and shyer. He hid his hand and Richard had to take it to examine it properly. It had been crushed and, judging by the general disfigurement, the bones had not been properly reset.

'Hit with a sledge,' Ross answered for him. 'He was holding the boryer and the striker missed.' Ross picked up an iron drill to show what a boryer was.

'Does it give you any pain?'

'Iss it do, sir,' replied the miner who seemed grateful someone was asking about his well-being. 'He still work all right, sir. Nothing I can't do with it!' He gave a defensive explanation, perhaps fearing for his job.

'What is your name?' Richard asked the boy who looked shyly away and then towards the miners for guidance. Perran nodded encouragingly.

'Peter, sir.'

'And how long have you worked down the mine?'

120

'One week, sir.'

'How far did you walk to the mine, Peter?'

'The boy is mine, Doctor. 'Tiss five mile to the mine,' Perran explained.

Richard still gave his attention to Peter. 'What time did you start out?'

'First light I be up. Made tay and had some bread 'fore father was out.'

His father laughed, and shook his head. 'Your ma had to give you a shake to get you up.'

Richard reasoned that to be at the mine by six and walk the five miles must have meant leaving the home between four and five. A hard life for one so young and he could look forward to nothing but unmitigating toil for the rest of his short life. He was still a boy, yet in five years he could be married with a family. Richard took his hands and saw the heavy calluses.

'For someone who has been underground for just one week, your hands are very rough.'

'Aw, he's been working the budel for more than a year since, Doctor, afore going underground.' It was Ross again, who seemed to be alert to Richard's questions.

Richard placed his ear on Peter's chest and heard clear lungs and a steady heart beat. He looked at the boy knowing he had only another twenty to thirty years to live if he stayed underground.

'Your heart and lungs are fine, Peter. Show me what you have brought to eat and drink.'

'Croust was a hour ago,' Perran said. 'Me and the boy shared a pasty.'

Richard looked to the man with a deformed hand.

'Oggin.'

Then the third miner declared that he had had cheese and bread.

'And to drink?'

'Water,' Peter held up a stone jar.

'Where does the water come from?'

'Why 'tiss the water used here in the mine – same as feed the engine,' Ross explained somewhat incredulously. 'Now, the men will show you how to drill and blast.'

The miner, with the damaged hand, picked up a boryer and placed it against the rock face as Perran shaped up with a very heavy sledge. He swung easily and the head crashed against the drill sending it into the rock. A twist of the drill just before the next blow arrived, and the process repeated, rhythmically and precisely. Slowly, it inched into the rock to a depth of about two feet. A swab stick cleaned the hole of dust. Then the third miner took the hammer and Perran held the boryer and another hole drilled above the first; then a third. Perran inserted black powder using a solid rod of iron with a small spoon-like shape at the end. An iron tamping-bar compacted the powder. They then inserted a blasting nail, a tapering rod, into the hole around which they packed clay. After tamping by beating with an iron bar, the nail was withdrawn and a rush, filled with powder, put in its place.

'Ready?' asked Ross.

'Iss.'

'Now, Doctor, we must take cover, back down the drive.'

When safely around the corner of the drive, Ross called out: 'All clear'.

A pause; then Perran joined them and they waited. Not long. They all covered their ears just before the blast happened. A sharp noise before a shock wave hit Richard, which took the air from his lungs and knocked him hard, such that he nearly fell to the ground. The rush of air brought with it a mixture of mineral dust and smoke from the powder. The two other charges fired within seconds; dust and smoke filled the whole volume of the drive. Richard reached into his pocket and placed a handkerchief over his nose and mouth. The air was thick and foul tasting; he retreated further down the drive. Ross followed and grasped Richard by his shoulders.

'Don't go too far – there's a winze to watch for. Stay here a minute.'

So they waited and the noise of falling rock gradually ceased.

'There! That's that.' Perran was satisfied that all went well.

'I've seen enough, Captain Ross,' Richard exclaimed from behind his handkerchief and Ross led him away. Panting, not from exertion, but because of his unwillingness to breathe,

Richard turned to Ross. 'That is the most awful working condition. How often does that happen?'

'Everyday. All over the mine. They might blast several times each core. Depends how the rock falls. Hard rock needs blasting and hard men to work it. It do leave you know what mining is all about, Doctor. It isn't no place for the wisht. You got to stick it or get out.'

Going up was less fearful – the unknown not felt for with trembling foot but seen each time Ross gave a warning. The upward climb was bruising nevertheless and after a hard day's labouring, it must indeed be arduous.

'Rest here, Doctor,' Ross interrupted his thoughts. 'This here's the thirty fathom level that we stopped at on the way down.'

'When there is an accident underground, what happens to the injured miner?'

'Get him out as quick as us can. We send him up with the kibble. If we can't, we manhandle him all the way. If he's badly injured 'tiss a terrible journey. Hours, sometimes, 'fore we get to grass.'

A short rest and then the last climb. The bright ring became larger and more brilliant; the air freshened and sweetened. The air moved over his drenched clothes and gave a welcome cooling. "Coming to grass" was a misnomer – grass was most notable for its absence. Nothing grew in the immediate area around the shaft. Soon the breeze that was welcoming just minutes ago was chilling.

'Best get into the dry, Doctor. This wind is cold.'

The dry was a lean-to shed attached to the side of the engine house. It had neither doors nor windows and the draft was worse than the free wind. Rows of miners' clothes hung on pegs, out of the wet but scarcely a place deserving the name of a dry. The atmosphere hung with mist that swirled beyond its wall. Richard found his riding coat and sought any comfort its heavy material would afford.

'Not much of a place to dry ones clothes, Captain Ross. Is there nothing better than this?'

Ross was smiling as he answered, 'Iss. On the boiler of the engine if you be venturesome.'

'Why venturesome?'

He laughed. 'Sometimes the clothes get scorched or blown up if a pipe burst. Most times the clothes are dry and handsome to put on.'

'The man Perran is an angry person, I think?'

Ross considered his answer carefully – he delayed matters by whistling through the window space at the old man who looked after the horses and mules. He eyed Richard.

'Us Cornish are able to bear grudges better than most, but Perran is a master. See, his arm was bad and Cappen Tonkin spoke out against him having money out of the club and Dr Morse said 'twas right. If it wasn't for Dr Andrew and Mr Carthew, he would have got nothing. Why, Perran didn't take to that kindly and Cappen Tonkin do keep clear of him – just in case.'

'The next time a man is badly injured, leave him in the mine and I'll tend him there. If that is not possible or he is in more danger from staying where he is, take him to the Count House and keep him there until I arrive.' He mounted Jake and then leant down towards Ross. 'If anyone should object to that, Captain Ross, inform me at once.'

*

'Edward, here are two samples from the hundred fathom level Perran asked me to give to you.'

Edward examined the two black rocks flecked with gold and then snorted his disgust. 'Nobody will buy these! No good 'tall.'

They manhandled the heavy bath from the stables into the kitchen, much to Ruth's annoyance, and the demand for hot water increased her irritation.

'As much as you can, as quickly as you can, Ruth, please; and towels.'

He returned to the stables, lit the fire beneath the copper and put his discarded clothes into it. He removed the majority of the grime using the pump in the open air.

Ruth was pouring water from a large kettle into the bath as he walked in naked and cold.

'Ooh my dear soul,' she screamed but she could not escape until the kettle was empty. Then she rushed out with her hands

124

about her ears when Richard thought they should be over her eyes if the sight so offended her.

'There's another kittle on the stove – you must see to it yourself if you're going round like that!' she called from beyond the door.

The second large kettle of boiling water, followed by cold water, gave a sufficient depth for the time being. After filling the two kettles again and adding coals to the fire, he got into the bath, sighing with the ecstasy the warm water brought. Shutting his eyes, he thought of nothing but the gradual return of warmth. He should do this more often – once a month he resolved. Twenty minutes later he poured more water from the singing kettles washed with soap and again soaked in the warmth.

A knock at the door disturbed his reverie. 'Nancy here to see you,' Ruth shouted.

He leapt from the bath and grabbed a large towel.

'Wait!' he cried, and was sure he heard a snigger at the door. She had found some keyhole or crack to spy on him!

'I shall go to my room to dress. Show Nancy into the drawing room,' he shouted instruction at the door and hastily retreated. As he dried himself, he smiled and wondered whether she did spy on him – a second time perhaps. In clean breeches and white shirt, his damp hair swept behind his head, he was ready to see her. She rose as he entered the drawing room and curtsied!

Richard bowed and showed a leg. 'Miss Nancy.'

She meant her greeting to be a mock of formality but she now blushed at her own parody.

'Afternoon, Doctor'

He approached close. 'Doctor?'

She blushed even more and he thought her lovelier than ever. He took her hand.

'Doctor?' he asked again.

She looked up shyly into his eyes, smiling. 'Sir?'

He pulled her into his arms and kissed her. Only when he heard her breathing heavier did he stop.

'Richard.'

As they parted, he fingered the bow at the front of her dress; that was the only barrier to her charms.

'I've been thinking about you all day,' he said.

Nancy stepped back and he lost his hold on the bow.

'And me you,' she exclaimed. 'I spoke to Mummy and Daddy. They didn't like it at first – me using my money – but they seen the sense of it and said "Yes!"'

Richard had a pang of guilt. He was selfishly thinking of how to undo her dress and she of course was bursting with news.

'So all we got to do is to compose the letter.' She remembered the phrase he used. Her face glowed with joy and he knew he had to postpone his plans and gazed at the bow fondly as it retreated another step.

'Sorry, Nancy,' he apologised for his thoughts of which she was unaware. 'I wrote the letter last evening.' He went to the bureau, fetched a single page, and placed it on the table in front of her. She seated herself and began to read.

'I hope you can read my terrible hand, Nancy! All my acquaintances remark I write like a drunken spider,' he said anxiously trying to divine from her expression whether she was reading the letter.

She didn't look up and continued to read. 'Iss, I can read it, Richard. 'Tiss not as bad as you say.'

'Good.'

She seemed to take as much time to read the letter as it took him to write it. Just as he was about to offer help she looked up and smiled.

'I understand it all, Richard. Thank you.'

'I suggest you sign the letter and I'll get it posted tonight.' Then a thought occurred to him. 'No, your parents need to see the letter before it goes.'

'By the time they see it another day's gone. Best to post it tonight like you said.'

'We could make a fair copy and show that to your parents,' he suggested.

'Iss,' she cried, delighting in the way he was able to surmount obstacles. 'If you get a quill and ink I'll copy it while you eat the rabbit stew Ruth has made for you.'

Richard was astonished at her taking on what he expected to be a difficult task.

126

Having finished a large plate of stew and drunk a glass of claret, he realised how hungry he had been. He poured another glass, and rose to rejoin Nancy. He hesitated, and then poured another glass, for her, smiling at what he believed was a good notion.

Nancy was looking out of the window across the creek to Carclew woods and the deer park, bathed in warm colours of a beautiful sunset. She turned her head to the door and smiled as he walked towards her.

'A glass of wine, my sweet. Have you finished copying?'

'Yes,' she replied softly and took the glass he offered. 'It's on the table.'

He was relieved she made the half suggestion to look at it but he was astonished when he saw a bold, even, copperplate hand and an error-free copy. He took it up for closer inspection. It was perfect.

'Who taught you to write like this?'

She joined him at the table, standing close enough to touch. 'Mummy and me write a diary every night since I was small. And she made me write it. All of it. She showed me how to do writing that way. Copperplate. Spelling is difficult. She often wished we had a dictionary.'

He kissed her lightly on the lips. 'I shall bring one back from London for you.'

She laughed. 'You're going to bring back some stuff from London!'

'What do you write in the diary?'

'Not so much now. What I want to write I don't want Mummy to read.'

The meaning was clear and it pleased him.

'I think you should sign your letter and post that to Clutterbuck and keep my scrawl to show your parents.'

She hugged him closer and reached up to kiss him. He pulled her close, kissed her, and fingered the bow again. She moved very slightly allowing better access and the small cord undid. He unlaced the front of her dress and, as he began to realise his dreams, a huge clatter came from the kitchen. Nancy instinctively pulled the cord tight and tied the bow. He stepped smartly away from her and both stared at the door expectantly.

More noises and hurried footsteps before the door burst open.

'You'll have to shift that there thing, Doctor. I can't put nothing away proper. Every time I open the cupboard doors, the pots come out to meet me!'

Chapter 11

The AGM of the British East India Company was held at its headquarters in Leadenhall Street, London. Richard sat with Sir William Lemon in the body of the meeting and was gratified to hear that the profits of the company continued to improve steadily. The Dutch East India Company was bankrupt, which cleared the way for expansion.

'Clutterbuck tells me you wish to exchange the shares you have in Davenport for any shares I care to nominate?' Sir William broached a topic he could have opened days before.

'Yes.'

Sir William nodded. 'Very well. I propose shares to the same value in Wheal Kitty. You don't know it, but I am being unaccustomedly generous,' and he gently prodded Richard in his ribs. 'By the by, does that pretty little thing you were given charge of by my cousin wish to sell her shares in Davenport?'

'Miss Rosewarne is hoping to use the shares to purchase the farm her parents lease. She thinks Robartes owns the land and has asked Clutterbuck to make enquiries. I am certain that any help from you would see the transfer of the Davenport shares to yourself by way of payment.'

Sir William became thoughtful. 'Robartes does own the land, but I fear he may not part with it easily since he will be looking forward to the dues from the tin streaming works as they progress further down the creek.'

He thought again. 'However, if the mining rights remain with him, including the streaming operation, then perhaps...Would you allow me to make my own enquiries?'

Richard was almost beside himself at his good fortune. 'I am sure Miss Rosewarne would be delighted at your intervention.'

The chairman called for order to make an announcement of great importance.

'Gentlemen, a ship has just arrived at the port of London with news that Colonel Arthur Wellesley will mount a major effort to overthrow Tipu at Seringapatam. This would mean the entire region of Southern India would be secured by the British and the end to French interests in India.'

The news was months out of date but the room resounded with cheering an event that might well have gone the other way.

'Your company is taking on the role of government even more, Dr Maddern – a dangerous prospect don't you think?' Sir William leant closer. 'Nothing to fear for the moment. The Government is pleased to have the company's and its interests exactly parallel; the Government's main concern is Europe. Had Napoleon succeeded in Egypt he would have marched on India. When you have India in your grasp, then is the time to assess your future. Best to wait.'

*

Shopping was a hugely important task and he called upon the Lemons for assistance in obtaining the dresses for Nancy and the other, necessary, feminine accessories. Lady Lemon appointed Lady Penelope, one of her London circle of friends, to assist Richard in this matter.

On the 5th May he was booked on a packet ship out of Portsmouth. The next day he would be home and Nancy would be there to meet him.

And so it proved. Nancy saw him on the *Sweet Union* and was outside his house when he arrived. At first, she was shy as she waited in the lane, glancing up and down several times as he approached. Richard seized her into his arms the instant he was close enough and kissed her.

'How I've missed you, Nancy.'

She slowly enclosed him in her arms, thankful he was home and wanting her.

'No young women stole your heart from me in that there place?'

'My heart never left.'

130

Chapter 12

It was still dark as he mounted Jake. Ruth had the day off, so no breakfast! His brain would not make contact with any of his vital organs for some time – his stomach had an empty, unattached feeling, giving rise to a deep-seated gloom and a desire to crawl back to the comfort of his bed. He did not equate vigorous ebullient life with early morning darkness.

'Is Nancy here yet, Edward?' She had been so insistent, pleading with him, to take her to Helston for the Furry dance. The new dresses had completely driven all sense from her mind. She had to wear one of them somewhere. So, it was to Helston he must go to witness a spring rite. And to do this properly he had to be there before sunrise because greeting the sun was the purpose of the dance.

'Waiting over yonder,' Edward whispered, so as not to wake the day. Richard just made out the outline of a horse and rider against a vast starlit sky.

He moved Jake over to her side and gave her a light kiss. The aroma of fresh bread smote his senses when he desired an early-morning, warm, bed-redolent smell of a female body.

'Bread, Nancy?' he asked in disbelief.

'Morning, Richard,' she whispered. 'Fancy bread more than Nancy?' she teased.

They skirted Poldice Valley and its mines, and headed out onto rough moorland where she paused at a high point.

'We shall go cross-country heading for the coast.' She turned and, even in the darkness, he saw her smile. ''Tiss rougher but quicker. You'll have to get use to a bit of rough.' At first, he did not understand her meaning; he couldn't believe she would say such a thing – then he too smiled.

On the uplands, there was a breeze carrying the scent of moors, but not yet of the sea. The path was a track cutting a straight course. Another hour passed before they descended onto the highway to Helston.

Nancy reined in. 'Eight miles and an hour till sunrise. The sea is over there.'

Well it might be, for all he knew, but one of the immediate benefits of the highway was that he could ride beside Nancy. A grey light glimmered over the land presaging the sun's arrival. They passed through hamlets and farmyards where lights at windows signified life was stirring. Cocks crowed and were answered by others in the distance – dogs barked at their passing. The curfew imposed by the darkness was being breached – the perils and dangers of the night were over. Another valley, then a steep rise, and they found themselves on high ground where the entire area and the sea spread out before them, calm and quiet. First light – that magical time of day when the brushes of dawn gloriously fill the sky from an orange and yellow pallet. Clouds that had passed the night, dark and sombre across the moon's face, glowed like mantles in a gas flame. The air stirred and freshened; birds offered their aubade in a chorus fit for the lords of the heavens. He brought Jake beside Lady and put his arm around Nancy and they both stared at the advancing sun over the sea. The breezes lifted her hair from her face and the early sunlight made her flesh glow.

'Tell me what you think, looking at this. Say it!' she sighed.

Placing both his arms about her waist and holding her as close as he could, he whispered:

> *'Oft listening how the hounds and horn*
> *Cheerly rouse the slumbering morn,*
> *From the side of some hoar hill,*
> *Through the high wood echoing shrill:*
> *Sometime walking, not unseen,*
> *By hedgerow elms, on hillocks green,*
> *Right against the eastern gate*
> *Where the great Sun begins his state,*
> *Robed in flames and amber light,*
> *The clouds in thousand liveries dight;*

'Is it possible to have too much happiness?' She lifted her face to his and they kissed.

A gang of boisterous youths in a valley still cast in night, witnessed this rapturous moment and shattered their bliss with raucous calls, shouts, and whistles. Nancy broke away with a short cry. They both peered towards the noise and saw the youths waving billhooks, axes, and saws in their direction. Richard reached for his pistols. One of the youths shouted something and Nancy laughed and covered her mouth with her hands.

'What did he say?'

She blushed and shook her head. 'What are you doing?' she shouted back.

A long answer came and she waited patiently.

'They are cutting branches from the trees and gorse to decorate the town. The girls are picking bluebells and any other flowers they can. They say we should follow them to the town. The first dance is at seven.'

The light strengthened with each stride, and their long shadows merged to form one and he wished it were so in the flesh. Another mile and they fell into the company carrying branches and flowers. Stables and rooms were to be had at the Angel or the Blue Anchor Inns they were told. More walkers swelled the numbers heading to Helston. At the beginnings of the town, a band was waiting. As they drew level, it struck-up to the cheers of the crowds. Richard and Nancy headed the procession following the band. As they entered the main part of the town, the street widened considerably and the paved areas were crowded with people waving and cheering. They were thrust reluctantly into the roles of honoured guests. Richard was reticent and nodded to the people, whereas Nancy waved wildly to each side. The band halted in the middle of the wide street, played one more resounding rendering of the tune, and the populace sang. When it ended, the crowds dispersed to decorate the buildings. The Angel Inn was close by and they led the horses to the stables at the back. There the landlord greeted them as "sir" and "madam". While Richard would have expected none other, Nancy was flattered by what she mistakenly took as gallantry.

'We wish to hire a room to use during the day – if that is possible?'

The landlord hesitated just long enough for Richard to sum him up as an opportunist – one able to make a shilling even in the most unpromising situation.

'If you follow me, sir.'

A narrow passageway opened onto the main reception area where barrels ranged down one wall. It was dark and stank of stale ale and tobacco smoke. The landlord went behind the bar and examined a book and, as he did so, a woman appeared at his side. She smiled grimly at Nancy, and more pleasantly to Richard.

'Now a room for the day,' he appeared to speak to himself but was informing the woman. Richard was well acquainted with this ritual and irritated by it.

'If you have nothing to offer we shall go to the Blue Anchor straight!'

The woman nudged the landlord and smiled more earnestly at the couple.

'Well, we do have a room, sir, but 'tiss unusual to let it be the day,' and he glanced from the book in a knowing manner.

'We need somewhere to change from our riding habits into something more suitable – surely you can manage that!'

Richard's brusque tone changed their demeanour instantly. The woman answered directly.

'Of course, sir. And we have a room you can use for your convenience like.' She nodded all the while as she spoke.

'Breakfast?' Richard demanded. 'Is it available at this time?'

The woman gave a short nod of her head and bobbed quickly.

'Eggs, bacon? Coffee! What else?' Richard was showing a different side of his nature; masterful and demanding.

The landlord quit the bar, touching his forelock as he went, leaving the situation to his wife.

'Iss, sir. I'll make breakfast right away, sir,' she said.

'First, show the lady to the room and have her belongings brought up. I shall wait in the lounge – do you have a lounge?'

All was now fluster. The landlady rushed from the bar calling out for assistance. A maid arrived and was given hasty instructions to show Nancy up. A boy received a cuff around the ears, and told to fetch the lady's things. Richard looked to Nancy and smiled as she began to mount the stairs. He waited and took coffee. He waited a long time. The landlady appeared and, most apologetically, informed him the meal was ready and would the lady be down soon?

'The lady will take as much time as it requires! Send your maid up to enquire and render any assistance if she needs it.'

The maid soon returned, smiling and nodding towards Richard. 'Me lady is ready, sir!' Then her hands went to her mouth. 'Oh! And she's looking something handsome, sir. A princess I do believe, sir,' and rushed away embarrassed.

Richard rose to a rustle at the stairs. She had chosen the yellow dress and she stood tall and proud waiting his approval. Being the latest fashion, it displayed her décolletage then gathered beneath her bust before descending to her ankles in flowing material, which fitted where it touched her and that changed with her every movement as she walked towards him.

'A princess indeed, Nancy.'

They seated themselves at a table and after they had eaten, the landlady approached proffering the visitor's book, inviting him to sign. Richard glanced at the latest entry, dated December 1798, and before that, October 1798. It was yet another ruse to discover who they were.

The band began to play again in the street. The maid, clearing the dishes, said it was the start of the first dance of the day.

'Shall we watch, my love,' he asked but to his surprise, she shook her head. 'No. You must change first. Mummy says the midday dance is the main one.'

Richard hurried into his change of clothes, reappearing in a dark frock coat, opened to display a waistcoat of many colours that gave mainly a blue impression. A white shirt, buttoned high at the throat, buff breeches fastened at the knee, and black leather boots topped with brown.

'As handsome as can be,' she whispered when he appeared, and kissed him quickly.

Clinging to him tightly, they stepped into the street, just as the band re-entered near the Coinage Hall, preceding the dancers. Ordinary folk made way as they walked slowly towards the Hall, and the better off raised their hats, in greeting. No sooner was the early morning dance over than the mummer's play, *hal-an-tow,* commenced.

At a large house with a splendid garden, filled with many guests, they were invited to take tea, where they were gently quizzed. For Richard, the answers were straightforward. Nancy said very little using well-chosen words.

'I aren't letting you down?' she asked after a rather persistent enquirer finally took leave.

He kissed her lightly. 'Not in the least bit, my love. With you at my side I am floating.'

The main event, the noonday dance, began. Richard prided himself that he danced tolerably well, whereas Nancy moved with rustic enthusiasm. Here, in the wide spaces there was room for her wild steps, but in a ballroom, where he suspected she had never been, her movements would be excessive. The most interesting aspect of this dance was the way it weaved in and out of the houses and civic buildings. They danced for ages, never changing partners, but involving other couples regularly in a wheel of four holding hands high in the air. She noticed his dance steps were smooth and economical of space, and she modified her own. He noted the change, and that she smiled less, and became more serious. Her eyes stared at his absorbedly, then with intensity, until they seemed to meld with his. When the dance was over, they knew each wanted to leave to be alone together.

It was the hottest time of the hot day. All sounds were muffled and distant. The birds sang short solos, and answering calls were faint. The horses snorted, tossing their heads to rid the flies plaguing them. Richard had already discarded his coats and necktie and loosened his shirt. She glimpsed dark hairs surrounding each nipple, thickening slightly towards the breastbone. She found herself seeking the glimpses more and more; the hair formed a black cord that ran down and out of sight.

'Look!' she said. 'A cool stream for Lady to drink.'

A path led to a shallow stream, which divided a small beech copse from a field of hay ready for the scythe. He dismounted

136

and lifted Nancy from the saddle. She kicked off her shoes, lifted her skirts and paddled in the cool water. At the bank, Richard took off his shirt and threw water over his head and chest. Now she saw more of what had teased her. He took off his boots and joined her in the stream. The new beech leaves dappled the sunlight and veiled her face like lace. She smiled, and they kissed for a long time. He fumbled at her breasts and she screamed, 'No!', and ran across the brook into the tall grass. There she turned, and waited, smiling. He followed.

'Unlace me,' she spoke in a whisper.

The yellow dress barely bent the tall grasses. She turned and slipped out of her petticoat. She had nothing else to remove.

He saw everything he had dreamed of and more.

She saw where the black cord ended.

Crushed meadowsweet, and late primroses, perfumed their bed while the leafy beeches sheltered them from the scorching sun. She lay anticipating, wondering, and waiting. He was urgent and lacked finesse, half-expecting to be refused at the last moment. It was over too soon. He began to apologise but she closed his mouth with hers. Her hands enclosed him and allowed no release. The enlightenment, to the mystery that had eluded her since a girl, had begun and she became a woman.

In the early evening in his bedroom, he washed her. The warm water quickly evaporated, cooling and tightening her flesh. She washed the dust of the journey from his brow, the rank maleness from his arms, smoothed his chest and anointed her new pleasure. Richard no longer expected to be disturbed nor refused. Now, tenderly, unhurried and with skill, he began anew. She learned quickly as in all things. She asked for more, then begged, then demanded until spent.

When he awoke with a start, the room was filled with sunlight, but the space beside him was empty and cold. Nancy was gone.

Chapter 13

'This one, Mr Heard. I shall take this one.' Richard had played several instruments before deciding on the Broadwood, which cost twenty guineas.

'Very well, Dr Maddern. A good choice.'

'Now, delivery Mr Heard?'

'Devoran you say?'

'Yes.' Richard waited while Mr Heard thought how much more he could extract from the deal.

'Yes. Rather out-of-the-way,' and he grinned. 'One guinea is the usual fee to a town address but...'

Richard's good humour had increased his patience, but the frown on his brow was automatic as he still awaited the decision.

'Two guineas.'

'When?'

The deal seemed acceptable, so now it was a matter of arrangement.

'Ah! I know the approximate location,' Heard continued, going over the difficulties. 'Five miles you say?'

Richard got up from the stool quickly. 'Yes.'

'Now let me see, today's Thursday. Certainly by tomorrow.'

Friday would normally be perfectly reasonable but today it was not.

'Five guineas if you can deliver it today, Mr Heard. Two, if it's tomorrow,' Richard laid down the challenge.

Heard called out, 'Thomas!' A small boy appeared. 'Fly to the quay, boy, and ask about barges to Devoran.' As the boy sped on his mission, he shouted after him. 'A piano to Devoran today!'

Then he turned smiling towards Richard. 'Perhaps you could call back in a little while when I hope I shall be able to give you

138

more information.'

Richard called on Clutterbuck and made enquiries about the farm purchase.

'Well, Dr Maddern, the matter is one for Miss Rosewarne,' he began, reciting a lawyer's confidentiality to a client. 'But,' he said, his demeanour lightening, 'since you are known to be acting on her behalf, I can tell you of the good news.' He went to his desk and picked up a letter. 'This is from Robartes' lawyer agreeing, in principle, to the sale of the farm leased by Mr and Mrs Rosewarne.'

'Bravo, Mr Clutterbuck. The details of course...'

'The mineral rights, both on the land itself and in the river bed adjacent to the property, remains with Robartes.' He looked over his spectacles with an unspoken question hanging on his brow.

'That is what we expected, Mr Clutterbuck. Are there any other conditions?'

'None. And so to the price...' Clutterbuck knew the amount Nancy inherited from Captain Tremayne, and smiled. 'Seventy guineas.'

'Excellent! What next?'

Since Richard had declined to be seated, Clutterbuck assumed a matching briskness. While still studying the letter he spoke into the desk.

'After formal acceptance of the offer from Miss Rosewarne the purchase can proceed,' he waved a hand in the air dismissing the details for now. 'So,' he said looking up, 'I will write a letter to Miss Rosewarne setting out our terms of the sale to which she must agree in writing.'

'Can I deliver the letter to hasten the process?'

Clutterbuck hesitated, but then nodded. 'I shall prepare an abstract with my advice on how to proceed. If you call back in an hour I shall have it for you. I shall have the letter sealed of course.'

At the bank, he withdrew sufficient money to pay Heard and more besides. He had in mind to buy Nancy jewellery, not a ring – that would be too precipitous. Pearls. A jeweller's shop, Carkeet's, was close to High Cross and he made his way there quickly. Mr Carkeet was a nimble little man who attended to his business in a straightforward manner. 'I've got a limited stock,' he said, which turned out to be just one string.

'I'll take it.'

It was now an hour since he was in Heard's, so he called upon him again.

'Ah! Dr Maddern. The piano is in a wooden frame and is, this very moment, boarding a barge leaving immediately on the last of the ebbing tide. I am assured it will be at Devoran docks this very evening.'

As Richard was leaving, Heard handed him a scroll of brown paper.

'This is a gift, Dr Maddern. I would not venture to give it to many of my clients but I think someone of your ability might appreciate it. Have you heard of a composer called Beethoven?'

Richard shook his head.

'No, not many have. A young German who I think will have a prodigious future. A friend has just come back from a tour of the continent. He heard Beethoven play and learned he had published three sonatas. This,' he tapped the scroll, 'is the first sonata. I would be pleased to have your opinion.' Fortune seemed to smile on Richard from every quarter – a day like this had few equals – except for yesterday.

*

'Richard how good to see you!' Hector exclaimed with genuine warmth. 'I have some extraordinarily good news. I am to become engaged! Yes!' He leapt from his chair.

'My heartiest congratulations! And who is the lucky lady?'

'Miss Elizabeth Warrick. Good local family with excellent connections. She's a wonderful person. You must meet her, Richard. I'm absolutely thrilled I can tell you; thrilled!'

Richard knew Hector would be very conventional in courtship: an acceptably long engagement and then marriage. The thrill he spoke of, would not match Richard's of yesterday for many a day. No spontaneous loving in a sweet-scented meadow in the warm sun – Richard's mind lingered again.

'What are you thinking about?' Hector asked, after observing his friend in a study for some time.

'Oh! Nothing!'

140

'Pity you can't meet someone to be happy with, Richard,' he said gravely. 'God knows you deserve it.'

Richard sat back in his chair, steepled his hands and spoke from behind them.

'I have, Hector.'

Hector's brow creased. 'Be careful, Richard,' he said with obvious concern.

'Hector, do not worry so. Let's drink a toast to Miss Elizabeth and her good health – and yours also!'

Hector nodded sagely. 'Yes, indeed. Good health is what we should cherish most.'

Hector was clearly remembering his own first marriage that had ended so disastrously in his wife's early death. This was a time for celebration and Richard quickly sought to lighten the mood.

'Medicinal brandy will do, Hector, if you have nothing else, or what about dinner?'

Hector shook off the bad thoughts, reached into a cupboard and withdrew two glasses and a bottle.

'Can't dine today, Richard, unfortunately, but we shall drink a toast.' He poured a generous amount into each glass, passed one to Richard and then raised his own.

'To happiness, health and a long, comfortable life.'

Poor Hector! There was not the slightest hint of passion, no desire expressed for an enthusiastic sexual partner, no description of the woman in terms of her figure, face, colour of hair – but she was from a well-connected family!

'And I am hopeful she will be the matron of this splendid hospital.'

This interrupted Richard's thoughts; he looked at his friend, anew. He was beaming with pleasure at the thought of Elizabeth being his working partner, which was unusual even in that changing age.

'She will probably be unpaid; still the reward will be in the knowledge of serving the poor and tending those in dire need.' Hector fell silent for a moment. 'That's reward enough, don't you agree, Richard?'

It would be insufficient for me, thought Richard*; a poor life if bereft of pleasure outside of work. There would be entertaining* *and being entertained no doubt, but all associated with the position Hector held. He would be unable to express himself freely – to tell those who lord it over him that the matron should be paid a salary, and that the chaplain should give his services pro bono.*

'Yes indeed, Hector. What better rewards are there?'

Doubt clouded Hector's mind as he played with the glass.

'And what is the name of the lady that has captured your heart?' he asked tentatively.

Richard smiled, knowing how difficult the question was for his friend.

'Miss Nancy Rosewarne. And she feels she is unworthy of me – what women wouldn't!' he joked.

Hector looked glumly into an out-of-focus distance. 'Well, in some ways you are very fortunate, Richard.'

'No! In all ways, I am very fortunate. She is quite the most beautiful woman I have ever met. And beyond that, she is modest, amiable, sweet, charming and completely unaffected. Natural and most adorable!'

Hector did not react to what he thought was a high-flown, emotional and probably unbalanced outburst brought on by Richard's natural inclination to lust after any good-looking woman. He again managed to refrain from mentioning Richard's wife.

'Elizabeth and I plan to get married next year – August looks to be the most propitious time.'

*

They were within a mile of Devoran when Jake's ears pricked and he unexpectedly stopped, nervous. It shook Richard from his reverie and immediately his thoughts went to the pistols. There was a faint groan from the other side of the high hedge. He drew a pistol.

'Who's there?'

There was no answer. He dismounted and led Jake to a small gap in the hedge. A boy lay on the ground a little distance away holding his breeches in his hands.

'Don't be afraid, I am a doctor. What is your name?'

'Jamie, sir.'

142

'Jamie what?'

'Uddy.'

He looked closely at the boy and saw the strong build and tight blond curls.

'What's wrong with you?'

'Got the skats.'

The boy griped with pain and he evacuated a jet of diarrhoea.

Richard made a mental note of "skats"; the boy's brow was hot from a fever.

'Where do you live?'

'Farm. Over yonder,' and he looked in the direction where it lay.

Richard gave Jamie some water and helped him to his feet.

'Are you able to walk if you lean against me?'

The boy nodded and they set off, Richard with one arm around the boy, leading Jake with the other. It took a while to cross the field and enter onto a beaten path. They stopped frequently, while Jamie dealt with the spasms, as best he was able.

'How old are you, Jamie?' he asked when the boy recovered slightly.

'Nine, sir,' he replied not looking at Richard as he spoke. 'Ten come 21st of August.'

A well-built boy for that age and the resemblance to Billy Uddy was striking.

They entered a cobbled farmyard and a distraught woman whom Jamie called "Mother" rushed from the farmhouse. She bent to her son and hugged him closely asking what the matter was.

'Morning, ma'am. My name is Dr Maddern. I found Jamie near the highway. He has a fever and should go to bed at once.'

She was about to reply when a gruff voice roared from the pigsty.

'That bugger's got work to do. He's been missing all morning.' The voice came from a short, broad-shouldered man with tight grey curly hair who emerged from the low granite building. He strode quickly over to the group carrying a pitchfork in a menacing manner.

'This here's a doctor and if he says to bed that's where he's going!' Jamie's mother spat out. Her resistance was met with the back of a clenched fist across her cheek that knocked her to the ground unconscious. It was an act of unwonted brutality, which shocked Richard who, for a second, was torn between avenging the brutality and helping the woman to recover. The latter won out and he lifted her head onto his bent knees. She regained consciousness quickly, but was dizzy and confused.

'Can you open your mouth?' Richard asked and when she did so he found a cut on the inside of her cheek bleeding profusely but no teeth were missing. As he helped her to her feet, the pitchfork loomed large and close.

'Don't you answer me, m'lady! Do as you are bleddy well told. Now, get inside and leave the boy here.'

Jamie glared angrily towards the man. Richard touched Jamie on his shoulder and the boy faced him with a quick movement, still full of anger.

'Wait until you can be sure to beat him!' he whispered. Jamie understood instantly and looked to his mother who had still not quite recovered.

Richard placed the woman and Jamie behind him and confronted the ugly tempered man.

'Who are you, sir?' he demanded.

'William Uddy. I own this here farm. Who the hell are you?'

'Doctor Maddern and I'm telling you the boy is sick. He is to rest and take nourishment. If you do not do as I say I shall have the constable at Truro arrest you!' It was an idle threat but it had an effect. Uddy lowered the fork and glared but did nothing more. Richard turned his back on him and ushered the pair towards the house. Standing in the doorway was an older woman, thin and frail, whose face wore a grey expression beneath her grey hair. She placed an arm around Jamie's mother and shepherded her inside.

'He must go to bed and be kept warm. Give him as much water as he can take, and hot broth or stew. Do you have any?'

The older woman spoke quietly. 'Iss we got broth, Doctor, and thank you for bringing the boy home.'

'If his condition is not improved by nightfall, send for me in Devoran. I want to see him tomorrow, at my surgery, even if he is feeling better.'

He turned to the boy's mother, 'You also, Mrs...'

'Jane Prior, sir,' she informed him with a short bob.

'Are you feeling better?'

'Iss, thank you, sir,' she managed a smile, but clearly had not recovered.

William Uddy was still in the yard as he walked briskly to Jake and mounted. This was not going to be the end of the confrontation.

'There is no money for you. If I see you here again you'll get the fork.'

Richard surveyed the angry man and knew he was looking at Billy Uddy's father; the same handsome face that never had a smile and the same bad temper.

Richard drew one of his pistols.

'This seems to be the only language you Uddys recognise. Let me warn you. If I come again to see the boy and you stand in my way, this ball will find lodging in your skull. Move aside, now!'

*

He swept through the kitchen; the episode with Uddy had blown away all his good humour. Ruth, sensing his bad mood followed him as far as the door to the drawing room before asking what he would like for supper.

'What do we have, Ruth?'

'A nice piece a pork.'

'Well, in that case, as soon as you are able.'

Ruth retreated further behind the door before asking another question. 'And how many shall us cook for?' she asked timidly.

Richard looked up, and saw only her face around the edge of the door, and could not but smile. He glanced at his watch and saw it was nearly four o'clock.

'I don't know if Nancy will be coming. Set a place for her anyway.'

Small things gradually dispelled his gloomy thoughts. The letter he had collected for Nancy would surely make her lovely face light up and give him a kiss: a second kiss, perhaps warmer, for the present in the blue box. He got up and walked to the window to do nothing more than admire the view, and saw at the gate four men carefully carrying his piano.

'It's arrived!' he called to Ruth and rushed to the front door. It was not a large piano and they quickly brought it up the path. Heard's two men had been joined by two tinners. A window was removed and the four men manoeuvred the piano carefully through the space. Richard had to play something, for this was an unusual event. He opened the lid and played an arpeggio, to gauge the tuning. It was playable, and he sat on the stool. One of the tinners was Janner, who was in the inn at the time of Mrs Jennings confinement. Richard picked out the tune he remembered about Nancy.

'Is this right?' he asked, above the music, and they all nodded and the singing began.

As if summoned by the music, Nancy appeared at the door, and took one pace into the room. Her face was a picture of wonderment; amazed by the sight of a piano, something that graced so very few homes, and then by Richard's playing. She realised what the men were singing, and her hands covered her face from embarrassment.

Nancy's presence redoubled their efforts, increasing the volume of sound and emphasising the words alluding to the song's heroine. Ruth's head came around the door and pushed Nancy further into the room. Then Edward arrived with Molly and her three brothers, all wearing clean breeches and smocks with bare feet. Nancy approached the piano closely and stood nearest to Richard who smiled encouragement.

The singing of a hymn ended the recital. Heard's men may have arrived by sailing barge, but they had to walk back to Truro and were anxious to leave.

When they were gone, Richard asked Ruth to take the children into the kitchen for something to drink and eat. As the door closed, they leapt into each other's arms. Her eyes were moist with happiness and she held him tight.

'You ran away from me last night!'

She nodded, but said nothing.

'What time did you go?'

'Oh about...I don't know. Early, still dark save for the moon.'

He was still looking into her face as he spoke. 'I don't like the idea of you being abroad at that time.'

She laughed. 'Only the foxes and the badgers about after dark and they don't bother me.'

He wanted to caution her, but equally he didn't want to frighten her, but always at the back of his mind was Uddy.

'Someone saw you because Ruth knows you spent the night here.'

'Must be Horace. He would have brought something early this morning for Ruth.'

'See! You think you are alone but others watch you.'

She pushed him away. 'Stop that! If I listen to you I shouldn't do nothing!'

Richard pulled her back into his arms and kissed her again.

'So you've got your piano. How did you get it so soon?'

'Money! Money always makes things happen. Do you like it?'

She walked around the instrument trailing her fingers across the smooth polished surface until it was between her and him.

'It's wonderful. I've never seen such a thing before. And you play handsome. All they boys singing about me. I went crimson,' and she blushed again.

'Was your mother waiting for you last night?' he asked quietly, as if the gentle asking made it permissible.

She nodded coyly.

'What did she say?'

She shook her head. 'Nothing much.'

He waited knowing there was more to come. 'Daddy is pleased but I know disappointed as well.' She looked directly into his eyes. 'But it is my choice.'

Richard went to the table and picked up the letter. 'This will make Daddy happier, if I'm not mistaken.'

She took the letter and examined it.

'Miss N. Rosewarne,' she read. She looked to Richard in some amazement; perhaps she had never had a letter before. She broke the seal and began to read the contents.

She dropped the letter onto the table, ran to him, and embraced him vigorously.

'Oh, for seventy guineas I can buy the farm! Tell him, Yes! What do us do?' She was beside herself with joy.

'Whoa!' he cried and she released him and looked into his eyes for help.

'First, we should talk to your parents, and then write to Clutterbuck.' He held her away from him to observe the effect of his words. Before she could answer, he asked another question. 'What did your mother say?'

'We had a long talk. I told her not to expect a wedding and she cried a bit but got over it.'

This was what Richard feared most. He knew he would have to explain his way out of the dilemma. He could not admit to being married without risking losing Nancy, but he had a plan.

'Tomorrow I will see your parents, speak with them and explain.'

'What's to explain?'

'You'll see. Now I have something else for you. Come here.'

He led her to the blue box and gave it to her.

'Open it.'

She gasped and glanced at him before returning her gaze to the pearls. 'Mine?'

'Yours. Turn around.' He put the pearls about her neck and then kissed her. She sighed ecstatically and leant back against him. 'Oh, Richard! How can I thank you? They are beautiful.'

'You can thank me by telling me that you love me. That's all I want.'

She kissed him softly and warmly. 'I love you, Richard.'

This rapturous moment was interrupted, as Richard was becoming accustomed to, by Ruth opening the door.

'Aw,' she said and retreated again.

'Ruth,' Richard called and she poked her head around the door.

'Only 'tiss ready, see,' she said, which was as near to an apology as they were likely to get.

Nancy laughed and wriggled free. 'I must help her,' she said, running after Ruth.

They seated themselves at one end of the large table. Nancy observed his every move, and copied, while he took pains not to notice and smiled to himself. *There's nothing wrong with your manners, Miss Rosewarne.*

'Was it Horace?' he asked.

She smiled. 'Yes. He told Ruth this morning, early, when he came with some bass. Bass be about in the creek,' she added disarmingly.

'They belong to Sir William. '

She stared in amazement. 'Fish! Old bugger can't have all the fish! They do think they own everything...' Then she stopped, thinking she was over-reacting.

Richard laughed loudly. How he wished even he could respond to Sir William in like manner!

'Do you know a Jane Prior?'

'Jane Prior!' she sounded alarmed. 'Iss, I know Jane – lives at Carnon Crease Farm. Uddy's farm. What of her?' Nancy's face was full of concern.

He gave an account of the happenings at the farm and she listened intently.

'Poor Jane, she's had an awful life with that lot.'

'How came she to the farm?'

Nancy shuffled in her chair in preparation to telling a long tale.

'Well, it all began when Billy's two older brothers left the farm. They hated the old man – William. One went to sea and the other joined the army – never set eyes on either one since. Billy's sisters all left home long afore: married.' She paused to take stock.

'Mr Prior was a widower and his daughter, Jane, was just thirteen. William Uddy got him to come to work as the farm hand. Well, it wasn't long 'fore there was talk. Billy and his father, both of them, was shagging the poor maid.' She stopped abruptly, her eyes wide open and staring at Richard. 'That wasn't right was it?' She was not embarrassed but confused. 'Mummy and I never talked about such things so I use the common talk.'

'Was she agreeing to their, umm...demands?'

'She didn't want any of it!'

'Ah! In that case the two men were raping her, which is against the law, of course.'

'Law! What good is that?' she snorted. 'Raping – that's what they were doing. Billy was fifteen then, and he got to bragging about it.'

'What did her father do?'

'One night he was found hanging from a beam in the cattle shed. Took 'is own life they said and nobody could say different. They said Jamie was her father's baby.' She stopped, remembering how it all happened.

'Law!' she said dismissively. 'What did they do? Mr Prior was killed by they two and nothing was done! The Parish was worse! They said the best place for the boy and Jane was on the farm where they could be looked after. They still went on raping her, and she was expecting again, a couple of months after Jamie was born. Course now they couldn't say it was her father.'

She rested her elbows on the table, holding her head between her hands.

'They took her to somebody and she nearly died. No more babies.' Nancy's eyes were moist as she reached the end of her tale. He needed to know, but seeing the pain it brought, he wished he had asked Ruth.

'Come,' he said, taking her hand and leading her into the drawing room. He played the second movement of Mozart's 21st piano concerto. A lovely, soothing melody, he imagined written for a woman in love. She listened to the rapturous music, her eyes never leaving his face.

'Will you stay tonight?'

She smiled but did not answer until he stopped playing.

'Yes,' she said quietly. 'Last night changed everything. I cannot undo what was done and I shall not deny myself the pleasure of loving you.'

Chapter 14

'Well, you are both of an age to know your own minds.' Mrs Rosewarne was the first to speak after Richard announced their decision to live together. She smiled, but not warmly. Mr Rosewarne looked glumly at his hands.

'Let me explain the reason for this decision. Nancy intends to purchase the farm. You have made it clear that you will not accept the farm as a gift, so Nancy will be the owner, which is all well and good until she marries.' He shifted uneasily in his chair and felt Nancy squeeze his hand.

'English law is unfair but very clear. As soon as Nancy marries me, I take full possession of all she has. The farm will become mine. So, from a situation where your home is in the hands of someone you trust and love, it passes to someone you do not know well.'

Mr Rosewarne unclasped his hands and looked at Richard with more interest.

'Worse, if I meet with an unfortunate accident and die, then all my property will not go to Nancy but to my nearest male relative. My nearest male relation is someone I neither like nor trust. I would not want your future, or Nancy's, to be in his hands.'

He relied on their not grasping this distortion.

He paused for a while and they all remained silent. Mrs Rosewarne was the first to react.

'We aren't used to such things, Doctor.' She said, turning to her husband for support.

'No,' he agreed. 'I see the quandary we are in. You must understand that I can't take something from me cheeld – I just can't do it. I know it would make things easy but there 'tiss.' He shook his head in frustration.

'Never mind, Daddy,' Nancy said to comfort him. 'I know

you want a proper churching for us but...'

'Iss,' he said. 'And so do Mummy.'

Mrs Rosewarne nodded agreement. His explanation had not had the desired effect so he had to go further.

'I would like to propose something that will allay any suspicion you might have as to my good intentions. First, it is my dearest wish that Nancy and I have children. They will bear my name and the first male child will be my successor and claim inheritance of my fortune.' This was the first time he had alluded to his wealth and it was intentional. 'Then marriage will be possible.' The lie escaped easily but it did produce a more positive effect and smiles began to appear on their faces.

'Meanwhile, I am minded to implant the idea that we are married to anyone who might be interested. I shall purchase a licence to marry in London. As a token of my affection and natural love of Nancy, and to assure her future well-being, I will deposit in her bank account one thousand guineas before the week is out.' This drew a gasp from everybody, such a vast sum was difficult to grasp by people who dealt in pennies.

'I can never have any claim to this and it is hers to do with as she pleases.'

The smiles around the table were warmer but Richard could see that they were not completely genuine.

''Tiss a lot of money I must say, and it will see Nancy in good stead, no doubt about it.' Mr Rosewarne said, looking at Mrs Rosewarne as he spoke. 'You must know that we are, both of us...' and he struggled for words so Mrs Rosewarne came to his aid.

'What Bob is saying is that we love Nancy dearly and will not stand by to see her come to harm, Doctor.'

'I shall do my utmost to make Nancy happy and you proud of me. Oh, and I think you should call me Richard, please. Doctor is just a title, Richard is my name.'

Mrs Rosewarne broke the ensuing, slightly embarrassing, silence by making tea. Bob Rosewarne rose, his bulk filling the room, to shake Richard's hand.

'Do you like a spot of fishing, Richard?'

*

As they strolled back to Devoran, Nancy was not entirely herself; a shadow of sadness had fallen over her usually happy disposition.

'Are you sad at leaving your home?'

'Umm...' she replied.

'What disturbs my Nancy?' he asked, pulling her close, and kissing her gently. 'You're still not smiling as you used to – if this is the affect of living with me, then I want the old Nancy back and we should live apart.' He was teasing, but her mood was so sensitive that she heard more than was meant, and saw more than was intended.

'No!' she cried violently. 'No!' and tears welled in her eyes and she clung to him tightly.

'Nancy, Nancy my love. I'm teasing you. Please forgive me. Please!'

For a time she buried her face in his chest, crying and inconsolable. Gradually the crying stopped and he eased her gently away to see her face.

'Whatever is the matter?'

She sniffed and he gave her his handkerchief.

'Tell me!'

''Tiss all that talk about money, Richard. I felt like a whore!' She was never one to mince words.

Richard had not allowed for a generous gift being held against him. Poor the Rosewarnes might be, but pride they had in abundance.

'Nancy, more than anything else I love you dearly – more than I have ever loved anyone. Your future happiness is my greatest concern and I will do anything to ensure that. Giving you money is not to buy your affection and love – I have that, but to safeguard you should anything happen to me.'

Chapter 15

'Cappen Ross sent me.'

A youth with a lantern raised above his shoulder waited in darkness and heavy driving rain. ''Tiss a accident, sir. Wheal Andrew. A man fell and broke his head.'

He packed all he thought he might need in a large leather bag and added more. In the stable, Nancy was in her riding habit with Lady and Jake saddled.

'You might need me.'

There was no time to argue.

'We must make haste!'

Captain Ross and a few others gathered at the head of a shaft with grim expressions.

'How long?'

'Nigh on two hour ago, Doctor.'

'Nancy, go to the Count House at Wheal Andrew and prepare the large table there to receive the patient. I shall need plenty of hot water and something warm and clean to wrap him in.' She nodded but remained at the shaft's edge, worried by what might be in store for Richard.

'The best way down is by the kibble. 'Tiss quick and that's what us need. Put your feet in and we'll lash you to the rope from the whim.' Ross Hitchens paused. 'Two hundred fathom. Right to the bottom of the shaft.' Ross did not spare his words. 'Best to think about the man you're going to help and nothing more. Take this here lantern.'

Richard nodded and looked to Nancy who smiled from a pale worried face.

When lashed in place, Ross gave him one last look of encouragement, and the kibble started to descend twelve hundred feet. The descent gathered speed and the temperature rose quickly. The now familiar mineral smell greeted his nostrils as all light vanished. By some unknown means, the whim slowed and stopped when he was opposite the lowest level. Here, there was a blaze of light, from many candles. The atmosphere was humid, the temperature unbelievably high, and the air poor, making breathing harder.

'Take your time, Doctor,' a miner closest to him advised, as he pulled the kibble close enough for Richard to step into the level. Strong hands and arms undid the rope that tied him and pulled him to the safety of firm ground.

'Where is the patient?'

'Just here,' and hats with candles turned to illuminate the ground a few feet away. 'We had to move him out of the sump where he fell for the water was making – the pump stopped, see.'

'Bring as many candles as you have – I need light.'

He began to examine the unconscious miner carefully feeling around the neck before turning him to lie on his side. The miner was nearly bald and there was a large scalp wound. The skull was visible, but little of the scalp was removed. The man's smock looked to be saturated in blood but the normal ochre colour confused the issue. Scalp wounds bleed profusely but for now, it had, substantially, stopped. There was no sign of a depressed fracture of the skull. He wrapped a bandage over the wound and around the jaw, keeping pressure on the wound in the hope the bleeding would not start again.

'I need a large board or plank to strap him to – and ropes?'

There was no answer but he saw several men dispatched to search out the items.

'How long has it been since he lost consciousness – knocked out?'

They turned to each other to consider and agreed that it was, perhaps, two hours.

'He fell from here to the sump – I heard a shout then nothing. When I got to him he was out like a candle.'

'How old is he? And what is his name?'

'Why, Nathan Chegwin is nearly forty.'

He listened to the chest and heard the usual rattles and gurgles of a miner with consumption. The heartbeat was faint but steady. He suspected a greenstick fracture of the right ulna and applied a splint. There were no further injuries so he worked quickly to get the patient to the surface. It took precious time to secure Nathan to the board and then lash it to the main rope of the whim. Nathan lay horizontally just above the kibble and swinging in the middle of the shaft. Richard climbed into the kibble and they tied him to the rope. He could look down on Nathan and hold the board.

'Up. Very steadily.'

It took an interminable time. He ached and his arms were tired from the strain of hanging on and keeping his burden from the sides of the shaft. Heads peered down from the side of the shaft and called out. When the grey sky filled his view, Ross pulled the rope closer to the side and other hands, eager to help, made it fast.

The rain was still sheeting down, driven by the wind, and among the waiting group Richard spied Nancy. She was soaked right through her clothes. Richard grasped willing hands to help him out of the kibble and a party bore the patient to the Count House and placed Nathan on the large map table.

It was blood that coloured the smock and Nathan's face had the ashen pallor of a dead man. Fearing the worst, Richard bent over his chest and thankfully heard the beating heart. The body was chilled. He took a hand and felt it was cold.

'Get some stone jars and fill them with hot water – quickly. Nancy, help me remove all his clothes. Now, Captain Ross, perhaps the rest of the gentlemen can leave us to our task.'

The cold had penetrated Nathan's whole body and increasing his temperature was paramount. Richard covered the body with a blanket then packed hot stone jars around him as best he could, then wrapped heavy dry coats and other warming materials over everything. When satisfied he stepped back approvingly. Now he would clean and suture the head wound. There was a scraping at the door and Dr Morse appeared. He strode into the room eyeing the patient, and placed his bag of instruments at the head of the table.

'Who the devil are you?' he asked Nancy, with a disdainful and angry look. 'I don't approve of women tending my patients.' Richard was instantly furious.

'This is my patient, Morse, and I'll thank you to behave

156

properly towards my fiancée.'

Morse looked aghast and muttered. 'Beg pardon, miss.'

Morse was now on the horns of a dilemma; to stay and endure the wrath of Richard or leave and not witness the treatment of Chegwin. Richard continued to clean the scalp wound and, when satisfied, asked Nancy for the threaded needle and commenced suturing the long wound. Morse came closer and looked on. When he was finished, Richard glanced at Nancy, and saw her shivering.

'Nancy, take Lady, go home, get out of those wet clothes and rest before the fire in the kitchen. Ask Edward to make up the fire in the drawing room. I'll be as quick as I can but it will be several hours yet.'

Morse was inspecting the scalp wound when Richard again approached the patient and brushed him to one side.

'It's customary to ask for a second opinion under these circumstances.'

Richard looked angrily towards Morse. 'If you hadn't been so bloody rude I would have done!'

Ross, standing in the background, watching everything, spluttered and stifled a smile. Morse turned on him.

'What are you doing here? Have you no work to attend to!'

'Captain Ross is here at my invitation and will remain here, as long as he wishes, or until I ask him to leave.'

Morse snorted angrily but he would adhere to the code of practice in the mining areas.

'May I examine the patient?'

Richard recited the injuries and the treatment given. He stopped and bent to look more closely at Nathan.

'No other treatment so far?'

'None.'

'The usual practise would be to bleed the man about the ears to reduce the…'

'Your recommendation is to bleed!' Richard shouted in astonishment. He picked up the discarded smock and threw it hard at Morse.

'The smock is saturated in blood from the head wound. What blood he has left in his veins remains there – recovery will be delayed by bleeding.'

Morse sensed a weakness and struck home. 'You are defying conventional medical practice – you are not doing the best for the patient...'

'I'll decide that.' Richard's face was inches from Morse's.

Morse was not done, even though he picked up his bag, and was preparing to leave.

'I shall let it be known that you saw fit not to take notice of my advice, and did not carry out common medical procedures any medical assistant would recognise as necessary.'

He left without another word. Silence ensued for what seemed a long time. Captain Ross was white with fury and stood with his fists clenched tightly. His deep voice boomed about the room.

'He wouldn't go down the shaft to bring Nathan to grass so gentle. He would wait 'till Nathan was in his house and then – only then – have a look. I know the bastard from old, Doctor. One day he'll meet his Maker...unexpected like.'

Richard appreciated the sentiments but refrained from commenting on the last words. He walked about the room thinking hard about what more he might be able to do. Minutes passed, and neither man spoke. The clerks, who had vacated their room for the patient, now hovered at the door speaking quietly, but making their presence known. An hour passed during which time Richard made frequent examinations of Nathan while Captain Ross maintained an unwavering vigil.

Richard sighed, and then approached the body again. He bent over Nathan and felt for a hand. It was warmer. The cheeks had the merest blush of pink; the back of his hand on Nathan's brow registered some warmth. The pulse felt stronger. He pulled down the lower eyelid of the right eye and saw it had some colour again. Pushing the upper lid, the eye suddenly blinked open.

'Nathan?' Richard reached for his left hand, unable to disguise his excitement. 'If you can hear me, squeeze my hand.'

Nathan gripped his hand. 'Excellent! Can you see my fingers, Nathan? My fingers!' and he moved a forefinger across his line of sight. He saw the miner's eyes follow for a while then they fixed on Richard and would not leave him.

'Captain Ross – come close. Tell him that I am a doctor.

158

Where can I get some tea and sugar?'

'Now, Doctor, one at a time.' Ross was not going to be rushed at a time when calm was required. 'Mrs Tonkin who lives in this here house can be found behind that there door – she's listening right now. She has the key to the tea caddy and the sugar. She won't give you either is my thinking.' Then he turned to Nathan. 'Well my boy, you'm in some pickle that's for sure. How are you feeling? Iss, that's the doctor who got you to grass.'

Richard heard Nathan's whispered response and left the two to rap on the door behind which Mrs Tonkin was lurking.

'Who's there?' came a shriek.

'Doctor Maddern, Mrs Tonkin. I need the tea caddy and sugar.'

'Mister Bennuts got the key.'

Mr Bennetts presented Richard with a wooden box, beautifully made with a fine marquetry finish. Inside were two smaller boxes, one containing tea and the other sugar. When Richard returned to Nathan, Ross was still talking to him and getting some response.

Richard leant over Nathan who attempted to smile.

'Are you in any pain?'

Nathan nodded and raised his left arm to his head.

'You'll have an ache there for some time – you shouldn't fall on it!' he joked. 'I have something that will make you feel better,' and he propped Nathan up, and offered the cup. 'Just sip a little – not too much at first.'

Richard feared he would vomit the liquid back, but if he could keep some tea down it would help. With frequent rests, he managed to drink the whole cup, and then lay back.

'Where does he live?'

'Over to Pons'nooth – about a couple of mile.'

'Is there a houseful of children?'

Ross removed his hat, smiled and scratched his head. 'No. Most of Nathan's boys are gone and the maids as well. I do believe there is one girl still home.'

'And Missus Chegwin? Would she be able to nurse Nathan?'

'As I see it, Doctor, we haven't got no choice but to take him home along. Whatever we find is all he's got and that's that. We can't improve it one bit and there's nowhere else, as far as I'm thinking.'

Bells rang signalling the end of the morning core – it was two in the afternoon. Four miners coming off core volunteered to carry Nathan the few miles to his home.

The house was a low, rough building set in a small field where a pig rutted and a few hens pecked at whatever they could find. Mrs Chegwin was stolid, not coming to meet her husband, but waited until he was actually at the entrance to the house, before inspecting the parcelled injured man. She said something in a whisper and then went inside. Captain Ross spoke to her and introduced Richard. Inside was the daughter Ross spoke of, who shyly stepped away and merged with the dark interior. The talfat being right under the roof was warm even on this cool May day.

'Do you think it would be better, ma'am, if Nathan should stay here where the air is fresher?' Richard enquired.

She replied to Ross and the answer was no – it was better that he was taken above, out of harms way.

'I have a screw of tea and another of sugar. Make some tea as soon as we leave and give it to Nathan. If he gets sick, never mind – wait a while and try again. It is important that he drinks as much as he is able.'

Captain Ross discreetly palmed money to Mrs Chegwin.

'This is from the mine for you to buy some meat and vegetables to speed his recovery,' Richard explained. 'He is to receive no strong drink – some ale but nothing else. And he is not to smoke until I say he can. Do you understand, Mrs Chegwin?'

She gave a short curtsy. 'Iss Doctor – no drink and no touch of the pipe.'

Richard leant over Nathan and saw he was listening.

'No drink and no baccy!' Richard reminded him. 'I shall be out to see you tomorrow.' He turned to Mrs Chegwin again. 'I have asked that you receive money from the miners' sick fund to tide you over until Nathan can start work again. Mr Bennetts will bring it to you.'

*

'Nancy's poorly,' Ruth greeted him in the kitchen without ceremony. 'She's in the drawing room. I've got a pie ready as soon as you like.'

In the drawing room he saw Nancy fast asleep on the couch near a warm fire. She had a high colour, but nothing else was of any concern. He washed in the cold surgery, cleansing the staining ochre from his hair and body, calling for more water that Ruth placed outside the door before retreating hastily. The altercation with Morse continued to rankle even though he dismissed it as trivial every time it entered his head. The accusation of not adhering to accepted medical practice was a cause for concern especially if Nathan Chegwin did not improve or, worse, died. He consulted his medical books and slammed them shut out of frustration, poured a brandy and thought about playing the piano. He would look in on Nancy first. She was sleeping and the high colour was still in her cheeks. He touched her brow and noted she had a temperature but his touch woke her and she smiled.

'How are you feeling?'

'Hot,' she replied. 'I've got a cold – it will be gone by tomorrow.'

'Umm...' he murmured and felt her pulse; she was right – all the symptoms of a cold.

'A hot drink – I'll make some tea and then into bed with you.'

After she had drunk the tea, she reminded him that she had to return to the farm early in the morning to help her mother. 'There's things I still have to do – leaving suddenly is too...'

'Will cause an upheaval?'

'Yes.' Then, not sure, she said. 'I expect so. Anyway, I have to get some eggs to Lucy. I haven't seen her for...well, I don't remember the last time,' she had a far away look trying to recall.

His attempt at the Beethoven was speculative and unsatisfactory. He then played with more determination, feeling for the music and found it an entirely new experience. By the time he got to bed, Nancy was in a deep sleep and he was careful not to disturb her.

When he awoke, she was gone. The anxiety of last evening returned and his thoughts turned towards Nathan Chegwin. Less than half an hour later, Mrs Chegwin opened the door to him. Barely waiting for an invitation to enter, Richard was quickly at Nathan's side, and relieved to see he was awake and bright.

'Did you have a good night, Nathan?'

Nathan winked and smiled and he took that as a positive reply.

'Any aches or pains?'

Nathan pointed to his head but said nothing. Richard took his pulse and inserted a thermometer into his mouth. This surprised the miner and his eyes widened and tried to focus on the long glass rod. Mrs Chegwin gasped and turned to her daughter who had come to witness the scene.

'Has he lost the power of speech? Can he talk?'

The daughter bobbed. 'He's been talking all night, Doctor. He wants his pipe and we won't give it to him. Then he said his head is aching something terrible and a glass o' brandy would fit him up proper – but we didn't let him have any. Course, he's teasy then, and won't say nothing more.'

The head wound was healing nicely and the arm would take its course. Temperature was normal.

'Do not disturb anything, and keep away from strong drink and baccy. If you do not do as I say, I will stop the money,' he smiled as he said it, but the horror in Nathan's face was clear to see.

'If you feel able, you can sit up but no more! Do you understand, Nathan?' Nathan said nothing. 'Do you understand, Nathan?'

'Iss,' came a defiant reply.

'I shall see you tomorrow.'

Chapter 16

At the door were Jane Prior and Jamie. She smiled and bobbed while Jamie kept his eyes firmly to the ground. Jane wore a clean white apron covering her from neck to knees, suitable dress for a rare visit to see the doctor.

He took them into the surgery and, when comfortable, he asked Jamie if he was feeling better. The boy was very shy and Jane had to prompt him.

'Iss, thank you, Doctor.'

'Good. Keep drinking as much as you are able and take warm nourishing foods. Now, if you go into the kitchen, Mrs Endean will have something for you.'

'And what of you, Jane? Can I look at your mouth?'

The cut was healing, but must have caused her difficulty in eating. He could do nothing to speed the healing process so he spoke the usual comforting words. He took the opportunity to practise his dentistry skills, and probed with a pointed instrument where residues had hardened and teeth needed scraping.

'That's fine, Jane,' he said when he finished. Then more quietly, he added.

'There are two teeth that would be better out but we'll wait until your mouth has healed properly.'

She nodded but he doubted she would be back. He led her to the kitchen where Jamie was enjoying some sweets. At the door, she slowly unclasped her fingers to show six large pennies. Her head was bowed slightly and her eyes looked up deferentially. Richard took her hand and refolded her fingers onto the coins.

'Nothing to pay, Jane. Buy something for yourself.'

Jamie noticed and there was no doubt that this small act of kindness pleased him more than the sugar sweets. His eyes didn't leave Richard as they both turned to make their way home. He was still looking toward Richard when he collided with Nancy. Nancy made a fuss over Jamie but Jane gave her a cool stare and merely wished Nancy good day.

Little wonder that Jane had no time for Nancy, Richard thought. *If she believes what Billy Uddy has no doubt been telling her, Nancy is the future mistress of the farm.*

Nancy gained his side and he kissed her lightly on the lips. Jamie shook his mother's arm until she turned, and witnessed for herself that Nancy was firmly and happily in the arms of the doctor. Jane stopped and looked hard. Richard waved an arm and hesitantly Jane returned the wave and smiled.

'You still look unwell, my love.'

Nancy's face was flushed but it was not the usual healthy glow that sat on her cheeks.

'You should go to bed this instant.'

She smiled at the attention he gave her. 'If you had your way I'd never be out of the bed!' Richard's smile was indulgent so she half agreed to his advice.

'As soon as I give the eggs to Lucy.'

'Edward shall take them for you,' he insisted.

'No,' she shook her head. 'I must see Lucy.'

'Ten minutes!'

Less than ten minutes later Nancy came into the drawing room. 'Well this is good,' he teased. 'Obedience...'

He stopped, seeing she was pale and trembling. He rushed to her side and took a firm hold about her waist. 'What's wrong darling?'

'You'd better look in on Lucy – be careful!'

He barged the cottage door open and there, in front of a long-extinguished fire, was Lucy lying on the bare floor wrapped in bundles of clothes. There was the smell of death in the house. As he approached more closely, he saw two other bundled figures lying close by. He lifted the blanket from Lucy's face and was horrified to see the black pockmarked face – smallpox. Next door, he found Everlidia, seated in a chair, dead.

He went straight into the Heard's next door without knocking.

'Why, Doctor!' Mrs Heard said indignantly.

164

'Beg pardon, Mrs Heard. Urgent matter. Are all in the house well? Any fevers?'

Mrs Heard was instantly serious. 'No. No, all of us are fitty.'

'Let me see the children!'

'There's only the little ones here, the rest are out.'

The little children gathered around and he looked at each carefully. There was no fever. They all were dirty but free of blisters.

'Mrs Heard you must get all the children home and they must stay indoors.'

She was alarmed. 'What is it?'

'Lucy, her two children, and Everlidia are dead from the smallpox. Do not go into those houses – stay here. Do you understand?'

Mrs Heard nodded and looked fearful.

'Have you or anyone had the cowpox?'

She shook her head.

'I will get some vaccine as soon as I can. You should all be vaccinated.'

She wiped her forehead on her apron while thinking. 'Me husband...'

'Yes of course. Ask him now. Go to the stream and ask him. I need to know.'

He knew the Trezises were well, having just seen them, but he gave the same warning to Mrs Trezise.

Everyone in the Hoopers' household was well. Mrs Hooper heeded the warning and agreed to vaccination without having to wait to consult with her husband.

Horace Gay was the only man at home, sleeping off a hard night's work. He roused quickly as Richard came in, sensitive to the slightest changes around him. He gave the dire message but Horace was unperturbed.

'Iss iss iss, Doctor! Seen it all afore. I had cowpox when a boy and I made sure my boys had it as well. We're all right. Course, I'm sorry for they little cheelds – 'tiss awful when it come, mind.'

Richard sensed a haven of calm and tried to emulate Horace. After all, the disease died with the body, so there was no fear of infection from the dead. More important was to protect the living and find out where the disease may have come from.

'Horace, tell me have you...when was the last time you...ah...saw Lucy?'

Horace grinned. 'Well I seed her last more than a week past, but the last time I saw to her was more than that! Seem like she come into some money and found other gentry!'

'Who?'

He grinned again. Little escaped Horace even, or especially, in the dead of night.

'I heard tell,' he began 'that she was onboard a ship down in Falmouth. Homeward bound from Jamakee. Called in for orders and Lucy was put aboard – quiet like,' and he tapped the side of his nose.

'The name?'

'Merrymaid.'

Chapter 17

'We must act at once!' Hector said. 'I have the vaccines here – it is agreed I should hold a significant amount for such an emergency.' He got up, opened a safe in the wall, extracted several glass vials and placed them in a cardboard box. Then he took up his bag, selected some instruments and was ready.

'Come! I'll get my horse saddled and we must be away.'

Richard had been gone a little over one hour when he dismounted back at his own stables. He took the reins of Hector's horse and assisted him to dismount with the precious parcel.

They settled in the surgery, laid out the instruments and set the vials in an ordered row.

'Hector, would you care to look at Nancy for me. She has a fever – a cold, influenza perhaps.' Then more darkly, he added. 'I am worried about the affects of the vaccine in her present state. Some patients have a violent reaction. Should Nancy react on top of a fever, then I fear the worse may happen.'

Hector saw the apprehension in his friend and touched him on his arm to reassure him.

'Let me have a look at Miss Rosewarne and I will make the decision. You are best not involved.'

At the bedside Richard introduced Hector to Nancy and her mother. Nancy was in good spirits although not feeling well.

'She has not had the cow pox Mrs Rosewarne?' Hector asked.

'No, sir, nor I or my husband either.'

Hector took Richard out of hearing.

'To spoil that very pretty face with pockmarks would be worse than death, Richard. We cannot take the chance with an outbreak of smallpox in the immediate vicinity and my advice is to vaccinate immediately. The fever I judge is no more than a cold that she would get over in a few days.' He smiled. 'Do you agree?'

Richard saw that Mrs Rosewarne had overheard the discussion.

'Mrs Rosewarne, you know the problem we face. How do you say?'

She bowed her head. 'I know you love Nancy as dearly as we do. You two gentlemen must do your duty as best you can.'

'I shall do it, Richard.'

He placed a small amount of the liquid from a vial on Nancy's upper arm forming a bead, through which, a sharp needle punctured her skin releasing a stain of blood.

'That is all, Miss Rosewarne! You may get a reaction to the vaccination that will make you feel uncomfortable but no more. Now you must rest.'

Richard was determined to record all he could, and the first step was to take her temperature, which was 102 degrees.

It took most of the afternoon to vaccinate everyone in the Row and, when finished, Richard poured two large brandies.

'Your good health, Hector, and I mean that sincerely. Thank you for your invaluable help – a good friend indeed.'

Hector raised his glass in acknowledgement. 'It's good to be back doing some real work instead of seeing to builders and other merchants. Now it is not finished yet! We must trace the source of the disease. What do we know?'

Richard repeated Horace's tale.

'Excellent! If that is true then we must inform the authorities and track the vessel down. The Admiralty must be informed.' Then more circumspectly, he asked how they should best do that.

'We should send a messenger to Falmouth. Pendennis has a system of semaphores that can send signals to London in a few hours if the visibility is good.'

'A few hours?' Hector was incredulous.

'Yes. I'll ask Edward to see if there is a boat in the docks that can take the message to Falmouth. If not then I shall ride.'

Hector remained silent then gave some more advice. 'You have more to do here yet. You must notify the Parish that they have smallpox; they will have to dispose of the dead in the prescribed manner. The disease must be contained. I must inform the authorities in Truro.'

*

The day had turned sultry, the room was hot and humid; Nancy was uncomfortable. Again, his thoughts were at odds with the usual medical practice; someone with a fever must be kept as warm as possible – treat like with like, even if it meant a hot airless room. He went to the window and opened it wide admitting a cool early evening breeze.

Nancy sighed. 'That is better. I can't breathe in that stifling heat. Come and sit by me.'

He sat on the edge of the bed and took her hand that felt warm, hot even.

'Have you taken any nourishment, my love?'

She shook her head. 'Just some water.'

'Could you drink some soup Ruth has made?' Nancy nodded but not convincingly.

'I'll fetch some soup,' Mrs Rosewarne said quietly.

Her temperature was slowly increasing; her pulse was strong although a little quicker. They talked for some time mainly about the smallpox and he comforted her over the loss of her friend Lucy. When Mrs Rosewarne returned he went to the kitchen.

'All well, Ruth? No reaction from the vaccination?' Ruth stared wide-eyed and shook her head.

'Ruth, I need to get a message to the Parish council urgently.'

Ruth stirred a large pot so as not to seem too interested.

'Is there someone you know who might take a letter now?'

She faced him with a worried look. 'I can't go. I got supper half made.'

'No. No, I didn't mean you. Of course you are too busy.'

'You could ask one of Horace's boys. Give him something for the wink and I 'spect they'd go.'

The cottage door opened in response to his knock.

'Wesley! Is your father at home?'

The youth looked at Richard with a preoccupied stare before giving a reply. 'Father gone feeshun. Shutin' a net off P'narra.'

Richard did not understand a word. The best approach was to instruct the young man to take the letter rather than to ask.

'Iss, I'll take it for you,' he readily agreed in a good-natured manner.

'On your way back take a drink,' and he handed him sixpence. 'On the way back mind,' he added with a cautionary smile.

When he regained his home, he tried the newly-acquired phrase on Ruth.

'Horace is gone feeshun. Shutin' a net off P'narra.'

'Aw,' she said comprehending the message completely and turned her attention back to the preparation of the meal. 'Who's gone with the letter then?'

'Wesley!'

'Umm...let's hope he gets there all right,' she added, expressing little confidence. 'He likes his wink.'

He dined alone not wanting to disturb Nancy while her mother was trying to get her to take food. Thoughts tumbled one after the other into his head: smallpox, Nathan and Morse. He needed some distraction, so he resorted to Beethoven where the concentration required to master the piece banished all other thoughts. The light faded and he continued by candle light until he was overcome by tiredness. When he opened the door to the bedroom, he saw Mrs Rosewarne, uncomfortably asleep in a chair. She woke as he came in and he whispered that he would take over.

Nancy tossed, turned, and cried out as her fever increased. There was just a slight redness on her arm; no undue reaction yet. He opened a book and settled as best he could for the night's vigil. He awoke hours later when Mrs Rosewarne came in. It was still dark outside. She walked quietly to the bedside and looked carefully at Nancy.

'How is she?' she asked.

'She slept most of the time since you left. Her temperature is still increasing,' qualifying it with, 'slightly.'

'She doesn't look well,' she appraised quietly. 'You best get some rest, Richard.'

He went to the kitchen where a kettle was always singing and made some coffee. It restored his flagging spirits and he began to function again. He glanced at his watch and saw the hour was approaching five. If he saddled Jake now he could see Nathan Chegwin and be back before seven.

Nathan's wound was improving and his temper deteriorating. Richard still insisted on the no smoking and no drinking regime, much to the open amusement of his wife. The broken arm would take more time to heal.

'I'll hold me pipe in t'other hand,' he complained. 'It won't put no strain on it,' he pleaded, but Richard was unrelenting.

On his way home, he met Dr Andrew who heard with keen interest about Nathan's accident and injuries. Richard also told him about the smallpox outbreak.

'Would it be of help to you, Dr Maddern, if I were to look in on Chegwin for you?'

Richard immediately accepted the offer and Andrew beamed pleasantly.

It was nearly eight in the morning when he arrived back home and straightaway he saw to Nancy. Her temperature was 104 degrees. She smiled but he noticed her eyes were dull and her face a brighter red: her nightclothes wet with sweat. Her mouth and tongue were coated and her throat spotted with sores. Smallpox could take seven days to develop the dreaded pustules. His hopes hung on the small fact that, during the incubation period, patients with smallpox did not have a fever. In the kitchen, he gave some instruction to Mrs Rosewarne while they both ate breakfast.

'A change of nightwear and a wash with warm water will revive her spirits. I will prepare a mouthwash to ease the pain in her throat. She must be given some hot soup or broth,' and he included Ruth, who was listening to the discussion.

'Try not to worry, Mrs Rosewarne. There are no signs of the smallpox. Concentrate on feeding her and keeping her cool with bathing.'

Mrs Rosewarne was not impressed with these measures and began to ask about pills and other usual methods of treating the sick.

Richard shook his head. 'No, not bleeding nor leeches nor blistering. Nourishment, liquids and sleep will cure her.'

He spent the morning nursing Nancy, and playing the piano

as a distraction. Nancy's condition slowly deteriorated as the Beethoven improved. At noon, two men from the Parish arrived at the docks in a large rowing boat. On the thwarts were two large, rough elm coffins and two smaller ones. The men had a grotesque appearance, dressed in layers of sacking that enlarged their girth to an alarming degree. Scarves masked their faces, and they had covered their heads with wide brimmed hats shielding their napes. They worked quickly, and soon two coffins were standing outside the houses with the lids firmly nailed. On one of the larger coffins was a rough scrawl: "Lucy Chenoweth and 2 infants". They fumigated the houses with brimstone and boarded the doors and windows.

That evening Nancy's temperature still measured 104 and she was visibly worsening. Richard noticed an increasing anxiety in the house. They were expecting some miracle from him or at least a treatment they could witness. There had been a nagging thought in his head about a treatment to reduce the temperature of a patient with a fever and it had to do with the bark of trees. The bark of the cinchona from South America had found favour among several practitioners but he had never tested its use. He found the bark in his medicine chest and ground it in a mortar with a pestle to a fine dust. This he infused in boiling water, and strained it through muslin. Mrs Rosewarne dipped a finger and then applied it to her tongue. Ruth was at her elbow, wide-eyed, following the motion and screwing up her face in anticipation of the revolting taste that good and effective medicines should have. Mrs Rosewarne's reaction to the bitterness was almost applauded by Ruth.

Her mother administered the cinchona extract from a spoon. Nancy took three spoonfuls, gagged over the fourth and Richard cried enough. She did not speak a word the whole time and Richard's concern deepened. He slept fitfully on a chair and, just as he fell asleep, the rattle of a window disturbed him. The moon was full, shedding a soft, green light, sufficient to see all the familiar details of the garden below and the creek. Dark clouds scudded across the moon's face plunging all into darkness and, once passed, the light appeared again. The scene changed from moment to moment giving a surreal, nightmarish ambience. He turned to view the room behind him where the effect of light and dark shadows coming and going made the furniture, seemingly, move of its own accord. The only constant light came from a single guttering candle. It extinguished and, as he prepared to light another, he glanced at Nancy. In this light, she presented a hellish picture. She was delirious, tossing and turning, moving in an uncoordinated and disjointed manner. Her lovely face contorted and became an image that could be a prescience of her death. He lit the candle to banish this masquerade of death. He approached nearer and the image became reality. Nancy was enveloped in a cloud of vapour of her own making. The fever was at its height and the full impact of the seriousness of her condition hit home. Her temperature was 105. He paced the floor until dawn and still there was no indication of an improvement in her condition. She sweated copiously and took no water; the last food she ate was hours ago; she was battling on her reserves. Her appearance visibly shocked Mrs Rosewarne. She said nothing, tacitly acknowledging the seriousness of Nancy's condition. She sat at the bedside and Richard took his leave.

He walked to the wharves with no particular aim in mind. It was a bright brisk sunny morning with a stiff easterly wind. Passing folk wished him the time of day and he greeted them, little comprehending what they were saying. Others passed snippets of news; too much rain was hindering the tinners; wind that caused ships to take shelter in the harbour; the press gangs of naval ships were looking for crew. He stayed out not wanting to go to his home. But he could not put it off forever. When he was again standing at her bedside, he saw she was calmer and she was sweating less. Perhaps she had finally given up with no more resistance. Her pulse was still rapid and her temperature was just below 105. Still at the back of his mind was the notion of a curing bark extract – the cinchona had had no effect, but he knew there was something else!

He went downstairs, poured hot water into a wash bowl and added some fragrant oils. Ruth gave him a clean and freshly ironed nightgown and a towel. He washed Nancy from head to toe. She slowly roused and opened her eyes for the first time in hours. She smiled and then closed her eyes but remained cognisant of all that went on. When he finished he lifted her up and tried to put her nightdress on. Just as it became too difficult, Nancy raised her arms and slipped into the garment. As Richard pulled it down over her face, she smiled again.

'Are you feeling any better, my love?'

She nodded and placed her arms about him and held him close.

In the late afternoon, coming from his surgery, he entered the small hall when there was a loud rapping at the door. His mind was still on Nancy, as he opened the door, without looking to see who was there. He was immediately and abruptly, borne bodily across the hall and rammed hard into the oak panelling, knocking his breath away. Billy Uddy was holding him off the floor with a hand at his throat. Unable to take another breath he began to suffocate. Uddy's strength was irresistible and he could do nothing to defend himself. He placed his knife at Richard's throat, swearing and cursing him. His voice was becoming distant as Richard slowly lost consciousness. As quickly as the assault began, it stopped and Richard was on the floor gasping for air. He needed to act quickly. He staggered to his feet, saw Mrs Rosewarne holding the muzzle of a pistol to the back of Uddy's neck, and heard the clatter of the knife on the floor.

'Move to the door Billy,' she said in a firm voice. 'Stand very still!' she commanded and then looked to Richard.

'I'm all right,' he assured her, but it took a few more moments to fully recover.

'What is the meaning of this, Uddy?' Richard asked, as he drew his other pistol from its holster. He cocked it, and stepped toward Uddy. Uddy was defiant and snarled at Richard.

'You're killing the maid I shall marry! I want to take her to a proper doctor who will treat her right. You and your fancy ideas is killing of her!' he shouted, and spittle showered from his mouth, such was the vehemence of his words. With two pistols trained on him, any attack would be suicidal but this might not bother him.

'Nancy stays here. This is where she is being cared for best, surrounded by those who love her.'

'I love her!' Uddy shouted and his face contorted to a grimace. 'I loved her long before you came, you bastard. You stole her from me and I want her back. You hear me?'

174

In his rough way, he was trying to save her. Another, less confronting, approach was required to defuse the situation. Richard lowered his pistol.

'Would you like to see her?'

Uddy had not entertained this idea, the offer left him speechless, and in the pause for thinking, his anger abated a little.

'See her?'

'Yes. In her bedroom.'

'Is she dying'?' Uddy asked quietly.

'She is very sick.'

Richard waved the pistol towards the staircase.

'You go first, Mrs Rosewarne.' Then he spoke to Uddy. 'When she is at the top of the stairs you may follow slowly. Remember my pistol is at your back.'

Billy Uddy entered the room reverentially, removing his cap, and creeping across the wooden floors until he stood by Nancy. He went to his knees, and looked upon her calm and quiescent face. He stayed in this position for some time. This was as close as he could be to fulfilling his dreams.

Mrs Rosewarne looked to Richard and mouthed, it was time Uddy should leave.

'Come, you have seen enough.'

Uddy got to his feet, and with one final look, turned and left the room.

'You will stay bound in the stable until the constable from Truro can be summoned.'

He seemed to acquiesce to this or perhaps did not understand. Suddenly, in these exceptional circumstances, Richard called aloud, 'Willow bark!'

Turning to Mrs Rosewarne, he exclaimed again. 'Willow bark! That is what I have been trying to remember all this time. Nancy needs willow bark.' Other thoughts now rushed into his mind. 'Do you want to do something useful to help Nancy recover?' he asked Uddy.

Uddy nodded but not enthusiastically.

'Good. Do this one thing, I shall not inform the constable.'

Uddy gave a nodding consent and waited while Richard wrote two letters.

'Here is a letter for an apothecary called Williams who lives in Falmouth. I am not certain of his address but you should enquire at any of the local inns or taverns. It is an order to purchase some willow bark.'

He handed the letter to Uddy who shook his head. He could not read as Richard suspected.

'Give this other note to someone who can read when you get there – it asks for direction to Mr Williams' shop. I believe it is near the docks. Here is half a guinea, that is more than enough and you may take what remains for refreshment. You must be quick! Nancy's life may depend upon it.'

Uddy took the two unsealed letters and the half guinea.

'I'll take me boat to Weir on this coming tide and walk to Flushing and catch the ferry to Falmouth. If I do find the gent easy I shall be back here on the same tide.'

Richard showed Uddy out of the door and then barred it.

'He can't be trusted, Richard! You let him off too lightly, I fear. Bodmin gaol or the noose would be a more fitting end to the likes of him. He nearly strangled you!' Mrs Rosewarne admonished him.

Richard held up a cautionary finger. 'Come, Mrs Rosewarne.'

She followed him to the surgery where he extracted from his medicine chest a sheet of crumpled paper wrapped around some dark wood-like matter.

'Willow bark, Mrs Rosewarne. '

He repeated the procedure of the previous day that he had followed with the cinchona bark. Mrs Rosewarne watched and listened but thought on Uddy's mission. As they gave the bitter liquid to Nancy, a kernel of an idea formed in her head. As she walked home to the farm, she smiled and marvelled at Richard's quick mind and ingenuity. As she got to the gate leading to her home she paused, beset with doubt; the facility of such easy deception could be a double-edged sword.

When he took up his bedside vigil much later, after practising the sonata for many hours, Nancy was awake and brighter.

'Are you feeling better, my love?'

'Yes,' she replied, the first words she had spoken for days.

'My head is clear and doesn't ache anymore.'

Her temperature was 100 exactly! It had fallen by four degrees in as many hours. Her pulse was now almost normal.

Richard was astonished as he watched Nancy sitting up in bed eating a light breakfast.

'Lucy and her children have been taken away,' he said in answer to her questions. 'As was Everlidia. Everyone else is fine and no signs of smallpox.'

He knew she was struggling with the loss of her friend and the children, but it was her nature to shrug off the consequences of events she and the world had no control over. Life and death were close relatives.

'When can I get out of bed?'

He laughed. 'As soon as I think you are able.'

'Able? To do what?' she teased.

'Are you comfortable – would you like something?'

She stretched languorously. 'Oo, you do ask a girl such questions. What I would like is...to wash. I feel so sticky in these clothes.'

'How would you like a bath?' he asked with unmistakeable enthusiasm.

'A bath! Like you had before the fire in the kitchen?'

'You *did* spy on me,' he chided playfully.

'I did not!' she strongly denied the accusation. 'Ruth wouldn't let me,' she sniggered.

'Edward and I will bring it into the bedroom and you can bathe in privacy.'

'You will have to show me. I don't know how,' she teased again. 'You will stay in case I come to some harm.'

Later in the morning, Mrs Rosewarne learned of Nancy's rapid recovery. On the stairs, she stopped and turned to Richard. 'Billy's boat is still over to Weir. He hasn't come back from Falmouth.' She began mounting the stairs again. 'The gangs were about all week long.'

Richard nodded. 'I haven't told Nancy what occurred with Uddy. Best to leave it until later I think.'

He wrote a letter to Hector, informing him of the state of affairs. In another letter, he instructed his bank to transfer 1000 guineas to the account of Miss Nancy Rosewarne. It was with infinite satisfaction that he sealed that letter. He posted both at Perran-ar-Worthal and made his way to Ponsanooth where he was pleased to see that Nathan was well enough to be irascible.

'One more week, Nathan, and then, perhaps, you can take a small brandy – nothing more, you understand?'

'I never known s'much doctoring in all me life. That there Doctor Andrew is a stickler, I tell you! He was here every bloody day!'

'You should be grateful, you wicked old man,' Mrs Chegwin chastised him. 'Oo, he's such a miserable bugger, Doctor – s'cuse me talk!'

'If you are able to work in the garden or take a short walk you can do so.'

'Iss, but when can I go down the mine? That's what I do want, see.'

'When I say so and not before. When your head and your temper is improved.'

*

In the late afternoon Richard and Edward struggled getting the bath into the bedroom.

'Would you like to bathe before or after supper?' She thought for a long time about this before deciding she would have supper downstairs and bathe afterward. She bathed in water he had perfumed with some exotic oils. With Richard's help, she washed her long hair. She persuaded Richard to bathe also. Then he learned Nancy's recovery was complete.

'Can we do that more often?' she asked in the early morning.

'We can do it now,' he whispered. 'But I have to advise you on over exertion.'

'I was speaking of the bath!'

Chapter 18

It was the beginning of July and a fresh southerly breeze filled the sails of the *Sir Francis Drake* taking them to Plymouth on the first stage of their journey to London. The low sun burnished the few clouds hanging on the distant horizon, auguring a fine day to come. Nancy, thrilled at her first sea voyage revelled in the salt laden air, letting the breeze take her hair. The ship lifted on the waves and plunged in the troughs, smashing into the shorter seas and sending spray over the decks. Richard would sooner have been in the cabin but the penalty of having to stand with his arms around Nancy was a light one to bear. From his pocket, he produced a small box containing a wedding ring. He turned Nancy and took her left hand.

'With this ring I thee wed, with my body I thee worship. From this day forward Nancy you are Mrs Maddern, my loving wife, and I forbid anyone to say otherwise.'

Nancy kissed him and looked at the ring. Then she turned away.

'Nancy?' he asked taking her by her shoulders and turning her to face him. Her eyes were moist and tears not far away.

'I know you long for a real marriage and I promise, as soon as I can, I will marry you in church for all to see. You are the dearest person I have ever loved. I will always be true to you; I am bound to you by love, more tightly than any priest's words could.'

At Plymouth, they transferred to the *Brunswick* bound for Portsmouth. As they approached that port activity on board increased. Hundreds of ships of all sizes crowded the docks as the *Brunswick* made for her berth. Men-of-war bristled smartly, showing their black and white chequered sides; sailors clambered aloft and let go sails; others at a capstan weighed anchor to the sound of a fiddle and the singing of shanties.

Nancy watched with growing interest and gripped Richard more firmly.

'Do you think Billy could be on one of those?'

This was the first time she had alluded to that night that he had never mentioned to her. He wondered who had told her of Billy being taken by a pressgang in Falmouth.

'Possibly. If he is he will not get off for some time yet, if ever – never fear, Nancy.'

She fingered her ring knowing it would prevent nothing in Billy's eyes and she shivered.

They arrived, late, at their London apartment: Lincoln's Inn Fields – number 32. She could not believe that the rooms were not part of a palace. Fine furniture filled the rooms: highly polished tables made from dark imported wood and graceful chairs covered in gold brocade with golden legs. She could not resist looking into the mirrors on the walls. Many candles illuminated the interior, bringing out the colours of the floor-coverings that Richard called 'Turkey'. At first, she avoided walking on such magnificence until Richard stood in the middle, in his boots and held out his hands for her to join him.

'You must see the bedroom,' and he led her to white double doors decorated with gold filigree that opened revealing a splendid room. The décor was mainly green: green floor coverings, white linen on the large four-poster where the heavy green drapes were pulled back; green velvet curtains at the windows, edged in white and tied with golden sashes. Nancy's mouth fell open at the opulent splendour.

'We are to stay here?' she asked in amazement.

'Yes, until the end of July.'

The honeymoon was both the biggest adventure ever, and the most romantic experience of her entire life. It was their last evening. Nancy was writing and reading her diary.

They had seen and experienced all manner of things. Oxford Street, a street so long it took half an hour or more to walk its length, so rich and full of every kind of shop imaginable: the milliners, Tyers and Edwards and the Crown and Sceptre; New Bond Street, where her blue dress was waiting; the Theatre Royal Drury Lane, where they saw *Much ado about Nothing* by William Shakespeare; the Ranelagh Gardens; Sadler's Wells;

180

the Theatre Royal at the Haymarket close to St Martin-in-the Fields; St Paul's, a truly wonderful place; the magnificence of Greenwich with its fine hospital and observatory. While dining at the Crown and Sceptre in Greenwich they had been amazed to see the Prince of Wales entertaining guests.

Nancy had dancing lessons and Richard consulted a tutor on the technicalities of the Beethoven sonata.

When Richard asked her if she would like to live in London, she answered carefully, trying not to give offence considering all the attention and expense lavished on her.

'No.'

'No?'

She shook her head; it was easier than giving a fuller explanation. But her eyes gave her away.

'You want to go home?'

She nodded and awaited his reaction.

'So do I. I long to be back, especially this time of year.'

She smiled, clasped her hands around his neck and kissed him. The closeness of her in her thin nightdress aroused him, but she went back to her diary. There was silence with just the turning of pages and the occasional sigh. She glimpsed over her book again; then looked longer.

'What are you reading?'

It was a translation from the German of the latest medical researches. It had not engaged his mind for the last quarter of an hour.

'It's about ancient Roman customs.'

'Oh,' she said. 'That sounds boring.'

'It's about the way they feasted.'

'Oh?'

'Oh yes. Anyway after they had eaten there is a discussion about cunnilingus.'

'What?'

'Cunnilingus.'

She laughed. 'Whatever is that?'

Richard took her diary, shut it and then lifted her nightdress over her head.

'Let me show you.'

Early next morning she had a question.

181

'Is there anything else in that book that...?'

'Plenty. Fellatio is something you ought to be introduced to – soon I think.' He spoke in the voice he used when giving instruction, although his smile betrayed his teasing mood.

'Fellatio?' she said screwing up her nose. 'That sounds painful.'

'Well it can be – it depends on a certain level of skill.'

'Oh,' and she had a look of uncertainty.

He smiled as he pulled her deeper into the bed.

Chapter 19

Monday, the 12th August 1799: the dedication of the General Hospital was to be held in St Mary's Church. It was also the birthday of the patron of the hospital, the Prince of Wales. Several subscribers gathered in the hospital grounds including: Lord and Lady de Dunstanville; Sir William and Lady Lemon; the Duke of Leeds; the Earl of Mount Edgcumbe; the Duke of Bedford; Sir William Molesworthy; Sir John St Aubyn and Sir John Moorhead. These personages would ride in their coaches to the church, whereas Richard and Nancy, Hector and Elizabeth walked the short distance across town. Nancy clung with enthusiasm to Richard while Elizabeth behaved with proper decorum.

'You actually met the Prince?' Elizabeth asked.

'Yes.' Richard emphasised, detecting the disbelief in her voice. 'He stopped by us, helped Nancy to her feet when she curtseyed, and spoke to her most kindly.'

'What was he like?'

'Fat,' Nancy replied flatly, 'but charming,' she added with a smile.

Inside St Mary's it was cool and the light, diffusing through the gothic windows, illuminated the nave but did not pale the many candles that cast a mellow orange glow, lending the right level of serenity to that holy place. As Nancy and Richard entered, the organ began a Bach fugue that overwhelmed the low murmur of the congregation. The darkly-clad ladies and gentlemen complemented the dim interior, but the sobriety was punctuated throughout the body of the church by the scarlet and gold uniforms of soldiers, and the golden epaulettes on the smart naval uniforms of visiting seamen. Young, admiring and gaily-dressed young ladies accompanied almost all of these gentlemen.

Reverend Cornelius Cardew, the hospital chaplain, gave the sermon.

After reminding the congregation, 'To the poor we are indebted for all the elegancies, all the accommodations, which improved and polished life affords us.' He went on.

'For, it is the power of language, in adequate terms, to describe, or rather can any imagine…a more afflicting scene of human misery, than that which too often presents itself in the wretched hovel of some indigent creature, who lies languishing on the hard and uneasy pallet of sickness, and drags on his wearisome life, either wasted by slow and intermittent fevers, or racked by excruciating pains, or writhing under the anguish of festering wounds…Destitute of all medical skill and assistance, wanting frequently even the necessaries of life, much more the comforts, which their sad case requires; unfriended, unaided, they feel the pinching gripe of poverty under its most frightful form, and at last expire, with the heartrending reflection, perhaps, that a wife and helpless children, now robbed of their only prop, are left heirs to their misery, destined under similar misfortunes to endure similar afflictions! And will justice, will gratitude, will any consideration that ought to influence social beings, suffer us to be careless spectators of such pitiable distress.'

Cardew eloquently expressed what Richard felt so passionately and he determined to speak more with him.

The Board of the hospital dined at the Red Lion at 3.30pm; Hector had a table at Pearce's Hotel. The meal, so Nancy described to Richard later, was dull and the company stiff. Elizabeth's attitude did not lend itself to amiable and light conversation, always bent on obtaining, or maintaining a good position in society. When the meal ended Hector made his excuses saying there were patients to attend to, after he had seen Miss Elizabeth home.

Richard and Nancy walked about the busy town purchasing cottons and ribbons. They called on Mr Heard where Richard bought some sheet music. Mr Heard was pleased to learn that Richard was attending the function at the Assembly Room later in the evening and was gratified to learn he had obtained a good degree of proficiency with the Beethoven sonata.

'The entertainment is largely local amateurs – so perhaps?' he questioned knowingly and Richard agreed.

Nancy changed into her blue dress and wore a little oil that Richard had obtained while they were in London, scented with frangipani, a flower neither had ever seen nor knew of its home. Sedan chairs took them to the Assembly Room at High Cross. The room was of a good size and decorated tastefully. They both agreed it was as fine as any they saw in London.

The Reverend Cardew chanced to pass. He was trying to attract the attention of Lord de Dunstanville who was in conversation with Sir William Lemon.

'Reverend Cardew, may I introduce myself.'

Cardew was momentarily distracted from his quarry, and looked at Richard sharply.

'Doctor Richard Maddern.'

'Please to meet you I am sure. Reverend Cornelius Cardew DD.' As he spoke, he glanced toward his prey, but was disappointed to see it moving further from him. He sighed heavily and turned his eyes to Richard.

'Are you a visitor on this splendid day?' His manner was brusque and he spoke quickly – he was a busy person with much to do.

'I live in a small place, Devoran. I have been in residence since earlier this year.'

Cardew was still looking after Dunstanville as he spoke.

'Devoran? Barely heard of the place. What sort of living do you get there?'

Richard chose to ignore his question. 'I was impressed by your sermon, sir, that so eloquently put the case for the poor of the county. I understand you were instrumental in launching the appeal for the building of the hospital.'

'Yes,' came a distracted reply. Then he focused his full attention on Richard.

'The Board of Governors has requested that I suffer it to be published and the income, 1/6d each, will go the hospital...'

'I shall make a point of seeking a copy out, sir,' said Richard. 'I am much interested to learn of your ideas of what else might be done? Looking after the sick in a hospital, however small in numbers, is an admirable...'

185

'Admirable? Admirable indeed! The small number, you seem to disparage, is a great leap forward and let us not forget for an instant the effort involved in building that noble edifice.'

Cardew was still not fully attending to Richard who nevertheless went on.

'Beg pardon, sir, I am not demeaning the building nor the efforts of those such as yourself. What I am inadequately trying to say is that we can do much more to improve the miners' conditions. They are poor, as you said, and our comfortable lives are made through their hard work...'

'You are paraphrasing, Doctor erm...'

'It made an impression, sir. We should not just wait until they are sick before helping them. There are some simple measures that can be taken that might sustain them better and prevent sickness.' Cardew was looking intently at Richard which he took as a sign of interest. 'With so much interest gathered here, perhaps this is the time to state further aims and...' Richard stopped. Cardew had his head to one side with a look of irritability.

'Do you really think that at the opening ceremony we should ask for more funds to build more hospitals or feed the poor or even furnish their hovels? Let me tell you, Doctor Maddern, of the arguments and discords I have endured to build this one hospital in Truro! There are many in the county would have it elsewhere, if at all. Good day to you, sir!' He was standing on tiptoe, head bobbing from side to side, gauging the distance between him and the noble gentlemen like a heron about to strike.

A professional group started the entertainment with Handel and moved on to Mozart; Mr Heard played the piano. Later the entertainment was from members of the audience. There were clearly favourites among those who stood by the piano and received loud applause. During the recital of a poem, Mr Heard tiptoed to Richard's side and asked if he would play as the finale to the entertainment. Richard took Nancy's hand. 'I would like to play the Beethoven Sonata you gave me, especially for my wife, but alas I did not come prepared.'

Mr Heard beamed a broad smile. 'How very fortunate that I have a fair copy of that piece. May I turn for you?'

186

They reached the piano as the clapping for the poetry recital died. Mr Heard announced the next and final item.

'My Lords, Ladies and gentlemen I have great pleasure in introducing a gifted amateur musician who is living among us – Doctor Richard Maddern – who has agreed to play for us a very new piece by a composer who is, for the moment, not well known is this country. Doctor Maddern will play Beethoven's First Piano Sonata.'

Richard stood by the piano and bowed to the Lords and Ladies at the top table, then a lower longer bow to Nancy.

The usual faint murmur of the uninterested stilled as he played the lively first movement. Nancy was always enthralled by the way his fingers massaged her mind – their movement across the keys changed her mood from minute to minute, toying with her emotions. When he played for her, he glanced to see the effect it was having. The same fingers played on her body producing a different and more exquisite sensation – he watched her then also as she was overcome and abandoned herself to the pleasure. The second movement was slower and serene. The audience was hushed and attentive with the realisation this was something special. The warm room was without a breath of air from the large opened windows. The candle flames stood tall, almost motionless, as if not to disturb the mood Richard was creating. The third movement had a memorable melody and it built to a powerful finale.

Richard finished, exhausted, and leant forward to recover. Mr Heard rose to his feet and began to applaud the performance. Lemon leapt to his feet, quickly followed by Sir Francis Basset, Lord de Dunstanville, both vigorously clapping and slowly approaching the piano.

'Excellent, Dr Maddern! Bravo! You are a man of many talents,' Lemon said and shook his hand. 'Allow me to introduce Lord de Dunstanville.'

Sir Francis Basset was positively glowing with pleasure.

'Well done indeed, sir. I have heard no better in town. A pleasure.'

The applause continued and Richard was unable to reply; he saw Lemon talking rapidly to Basset. The clapping and shouting finally abated and Basset had something else to say to Richard.

'Sir William has been telling me of your heroic rescue from a mine and I am lead to believe you have certain ideas concerning the improvement of the miners' conditions. I shall be very happy to hear them at another time. Perhaps you and your lovely wife,' and he glanced to where Nancy sat and bowed slightly, 'will dine with us one evening at Tehidy?'

'It will be a great pleasure, my Lord,' and Richard bowed again and the great men retreated.

Nancy was bursting with pride and kissed Richard openly which raised an ironic cheer.

As Richard left the crowd of admirers, he caught the eye of Cardew. He was clearly perplexed, his mouth alternating between forming smiles that instantly retracted into grimness. Richard passed him closely with no recognition.

They lay on the bed in their room at the Red Lion letting the faint breeze waft over their naked bodies. Richard poured some of Nancy's perfume onto her back and massaged the oils into her warm flesh. She moaned sensually and manoeuvred her body, inviting the fingers to explore. 'I've been waiting for this all evening,' she said.

Richard was in no hurry and declined the invitation. Nancy had learned this was a very special trait. He delayed gratification for as long as he could while she enticed him to engage.

'Lord de Dunstanville has invited us to dine at Tehidy. Would that be an ordeal for you?'

'Umm?' she purred.

Moonlight from the window cast Nancy in silhouette but highlighted the parts of her that fell into the pale light. He watched the teasing show as she moved under his fingers.

'What did you and Elizabeth talk about?'

She started up, half rising on an elbow.

'She's strange that one. Doesn't want to tell me anything about herself or Dr Bull, but keeps asking about being married. I didn't...'

'You didn't understand what she wanted to learn?'

Nancy moved closer and he could feel her body glowing.

'She's terrified. She wants to know how Hector will appear on her wedding night.'

'She's never seen?'

188

'No. She knows nothing and fears the worst. That is what she has been asking.'

'Oh! Is that all?'

'Mummy told me very little mind. Poor Lucy told me most – well told me everything!' and she laughed. 'Except for you of course. You know more than she did.' She moved closer. 'You know more than anybody. You read about it in dirty books. You know lots,' she whispered into his ear breathily.

'They are not dirty books – they are classics,' he said swallowing hard.

'Mmm?' She kissed his neck and dug her fingers into his chest. 'Are we a bit unusual?'

'Yes. Free and uninhibited.'

'What?' she sniggered.

She was now sitting on his chest. 'You know they there Latin words you told me?'

'Umm.'

'Well,' and she wriggled higher onto his chest and bent towards him even closer. 'I've been thinking and I know a way of doing both together – at the same time...'

'Simultaneously,' he sighed.

'Mmm,' she sighed and turned slowly away. 'Let me see what...Oh! You haven't been listening to a word I been saying.'

Chapter 20

The last days of August were sunny and warm and they were to visit the Ferris family about a boat for her father. Dressed in a shirt and breeches, Nancy pulled the rowing boat while Richard sat in the stern sheets.

'Pill Creek?' he said.

'Yes.'

'How far?'

'Two mile.'

'Two miles! You must let me help you out.'

She laughed. 'We must get there afore dark, Richard!'

Richard took out his watch – nine o'clock.

'Us'll git pressed,' he said, more from want of something to say than anything else.

She stopped and looked about. The water was flat calm and not another soul was upon it.

'You mustn't speak like that!' she said.

'I only do it so that you understand,' he mocked.

'No! I mean about pressing,' and then she laughed. 'Mind, you'm larnin t'spake proper!'

Out of the creek, they hugged the shore passing the farmhouse at Porthgwidden. Another half mile and they passed Loe Beach where a few small boats were riding at their anchors. The steeply descending wooded shores almost concealed the entrance to Pill Creek, which was small and quite narrow for all its half-mile length. Two barges and a schooner were loading ore at the dock just inside the entrance.

They rowed together, side-by-side, right to the head of the creek where a rough shed leaned against the side of the cliff. The boat grated softly on the shingle beach and stopped. A young man with his back to them was using an adze on a large piece of oak. He hacked at the timber removing large chunks of stock and, having achieved the desired shape, he began to finish the timber with the same tool. He stretched his back from a crouched position for a moment of relief as Nancy's shadow fell across his work.

'Why 'tiss our maid Nancy!' he said in a familiar way. 'I heard tell you was married...'

His voice faded when he saw Richard.

'Father!' he shouted.

'What now?' came an irritated voice.

'Out here!' he called and said nothing more until his father peered round the door.

'Why 'tiss Nancy!' He smiled cheerfully.

'Morning, Mr Ferris, Peter,' she added, nodding to the son. 'This is my husband, Richard.'

'How do,' they both said in unison and then, standing shoulder to shoulder, they stared smiling at the couple. They had the same facial features; thin with high cheekbones, blue eyes peered through almost closed lids but sparkled mischievously, a small but firm jaw line and smiling mouths. They were of the same short stature and spare build, the elder slightly bent and slower in his movements: the younger, upright and wiry. Their arms seemed longer, their hands larger and more muscular than normal, developed by the use of hand tools day in and day out.

'We've come about a boat,' Nancy said cautiously.

'A boat!' John, the father answered and Peter nodded. 'What sort of boat have you in mind?'

'Something for father – a lug and mizzen!' she lapsed into the vernacular laughingly.

'Iss. How is father?'

'Proper, thank you. And you?'

'Ow, just as you see me. Not so good as I was but better than I can 'spect. How long do you want it?'

'Fourteen feet.'

Father and son looked at each other swiftly and then back to Nancy.

'Too short for lug and mizzen. Sixteen feet is what you want. Clinker or carvel?'

'Clinker.'

They both shook their heads. 'Carvel's best,' Peter said.

Nancy looked to Richard who gave a helpless shrug.

'All right, carvel,' she agreed.

'Drop keel?'

She nodded.

'Five shilling a foot,' John replied quickly.

Nancy stood firm.

'Paddles thrown in, mind!' the pitch of his voice rose for emphasis.

'And all the spars and sails,' Nancy insisted.

Both the men sniggered. 'You drive a hard bargain, maid Nancy. Aw – twelve pound, altogether!'

'Good!' Nancy struck the deal. 'Now, when will it be ready?'

'What colour do you want?'

'Colour? Blue!'

'White be best.'

Nancy did not understand what was going on, but to speed matters along, she agreed.

'White then!'

John and his son smiled more intensely.

'Would you like to have it now, Nancy – take it with you?'

John walked to the inner part of the shed and beckoned with a hand for her to follow. They followed a narrow track, through mounds of wood chips, sawdust and shavings littering the floor. Around the edge of an upright dividing board was a new boat, beautifully made with every line pleasing to the eye. A pair of paddles lay across the thwarts together with the spars and sails.

'We made the boat for a Coombe caffer, but he died. Anyhow, his widow didn't want it. So there 'tiss. Fine boat, mind. Best material – red deal on grown oak frames. Last a lifetime.'

'It's a lovely boat, Mr Ferris. Just what Daddy wants. But how to get it back?'

'Well, sail! Mister here can row t'other and you sail this one,' a simple and obvious solution. Nancy glanced to Richard and then shook her head. After a short consideration, John said. 'Well now, let's see.'

He walked to the beach and they followed and watched him looking at the creek's mouth and then the sky.

'Wind is getting up,' he declared. ''Tiss southerly. Could be enough – will you chance it or no, maid?' he asked Nancy.

'I didn't bring any money.'

'Pay next time,' John said, and they fetched rollers and moved the boat out of the shed to the water's edge where they stepped the mast and bent on the sail.

Peter fetched the pulling boat they came in.

'Billy's boat isn't it?'

'Yes,' said Nancy much to Richard's surprise.

'Pressed! Mind he was a silly bugger...oh, scuse my language,' he said to Richard. 'But to go to Falmouth that late was asking for trouble.'

Peter moved around Billy's boat prodding with a knife.

'Two frames gone and a plank,' he said as he prised wet wood.

His father looked closely and found more. 'Best leave it here, Nancy, and we'll fix it. Come back in a week with a extra ten shilling.'

Nancy rowed while Richard steered, but as soon as she felt the breeze on her cheeks, she took the tiller and sheeted the sail. They reached across to St Just and the whole of Carrick roads opened up and, in the far distance, they saw several ships at anchor.

The little boat heeled over and Nancy laughed with joy at the sensation while Richard considered if he was able to swim to the nearest shore. She tacked and settled on the new direction – Restronguet Creek. Nancy sat out on the gunwales and encouraged Richard to join her. She revelled in the wind and handled the boat with such skill that he relaxed.

'What shall we call her?' she asked.

'Maid Nancy.'

Chapter 21

In September the kitchen garden yielded an abundance of fruit and vegetables: carrots, parsnips and potatoes in clamps; apples and pears rested in the vain hope of surviving until Christmas. Edward tilled the soil, spread manure and planted beans, shallots and onions; the cycle of sowing and harvest was never ending.

Mackerel shoals were abundant and Bob Rosewarne was able to do a bit of fishing in the *Maid Nancy*, and all enjoyed the feast of grilled fresh fish.

Flies were numerous and invaded the houses; they had become lazy and bit. Wasps, tired from a long summer's work and drunk with too much nectar, stung without reason. The air was heady and wanted a fresher breeze to make the spirit livelier.

Richard visited the mines on a weekly basis. While the men were comfortable with his presence, the bal maidens were not. He was determined to tackle them and rode Jake up the steep path to where the women were working under a rough shelter, open on all sides to the elements. There were about fifteen on one side of a table facing him. On their heads they wore large bonnets – gooks – consisting of a cardboard shape covered with white cotton that hung down to their shoulders. When working they tucked their bodices into heavy skirts that reached to the ground and rough hessian aprons – towsers – replaced their usual white versions. Each woman used a hammer that had an unusually large flat head to beat stones on an anvil to release the metal ore from the dross. The noise of the hammering on the anvils hurt the ears. As he walked to and fro, the women became curious. His presence disturbed them and they became more agitated with each passing minute. They began speaking to each other over the noise of the hammering, directing the questions to one robust woman of about twenty.

'Escuse me, Doctor,' she shouted. 'We want to know what you'm doing here.'

'Looking at the work you do.' He replied firmly with no hint of friendliness.

'Well bugger off!' someone said behind his back and laughter began.

'Who said that?' he asked briskly and with authority.

Heads bowed and the chatter ceased. He addressed the one who spoke first.

'What is your name?'

She remained defiant, concentrating on her work, so Richard stood immediately in front of her and close – waiting.

'Lizzy Larken.'

'And how old are you, Lizzy?' he asked in a friendlier voice.

'Eighteen come Michaelmas, sir.'

'What do you call this work, Lizzy?'

'Buckun. I do eight barras for a shilling.'

He looked at a full handbarrow and went to feel its weight. He could barely lift a side.

'Hundred and half,' she called.

Richard could scarcely believe what she said; more than half a ton of stone to break a day.

'What time do you go home?'

'Ow, four in the afternoon, when I'm finished. I walk home to St Day.'

Richard asked Lizzy to come to one side away from the din.

'I can't spare much time, Doctor,' she said apologetically while busily wiping her hands.

'I shan't keep you long, Lizzy. I would like to speak with each of you in turn to see if you have any problems. Do you understand?'

'Iss,' she said and waited.

'Is there any among you who is sick?'

Lizzy stared at the girls. 'Iss, Martha yonder is sickly,' she said, keeping her head low, and wiping her fingers nervously.

He did not hurry and looked at each bal maiden as he passed until he arrived opposite Martha. She was a slight girl of about ten or twelve. Her face was pinched and her skin sallow and tightly-drawn giving an allusion of transparency. Black shadows surrounded each deep-set eye and sores covered her small mouth. When he asked her for her name, she looked up from her work startled and turned her back to him. Lizzy, who had been following what was happening, threw down her hammer in irritation, marched to Martha, and began to rail against her. She took the girl by her shoulders and forcibly turned her around to face Richard. Martha's small face was still downcast and he was finding it difficult to speak above the din. He had to draw her away from the table and remembered he had an apple in his saddlebag. He beckoned her to follow and eventually Martha put her hammer down and walked toward Richard looking to the ground. When she finally stood in front of him, he lowered the apple into her vision. She tentatively raised an arm and, after what seemed an agonisingly long time, took hold of the tempting fruit. She placed it behind her back and stood quite still knowing this treasure had to be paid for one way or another.

'How old are you, Martha?'

'Eleven,' she said in a barely audible voice.

'And how long have you been working here?'

'Since six.'

Richard smiled. 'I mean, how many years have you been working here?'

Martha remained serious. 'Two year.'

'How many barras do you buck?'

She held up three fingers.

'And how much do you get paid for that?'

She held up her hand indicating five pence.

'Would you like to give Jake a carrot?'

She looked at Jake, and with child-like enthusiasm, she nodded more vigorously. He gave her the carrot and to his amazement, she began to eat it.

'Would you like to sit on Jake,' he asked her. For the first time she looked fully into his face not sure what to do. He held out his hands and she nodded. Still clinging to her apple and carrot, he put his hands about her waist and lifted her into the saddle. She was dreadfully thin and much under weight. He felt her ribs stark with little flesh coverage. As she sat on the saddle, he felt down her legs – spare and stick like. He smiled but she did not smile back. He led Jake down the short steep track to the

196

lower path. He did not wander far, always keeping the group of bal maidens in sight and ensuring they could see him. Suddenly, the clanging din stopped and the girls gathered for croust. It was too good an opportunity to miss so he rounded Jake and returned. He removed from his saddlebag a small linen parcel, containing some cold meat. He carefully opened the folds and showed Martha small portions of duck, pigeon and mutton.

'Martha, fetch your croust and come back here to me and we can share some of this meat. Would you like some?'

It was a cruel game; she looked longingly at it and then her eyes met his with wordless questioning. He knew she was wrestling with not giving up the offer of so much to eat against showing him her poor fare. Still she hesitated so he tempted her with a piece of duck breast. She ate slowly chewing to get the maximum benefit.

'Fetch your croust, Martha, and you shall have more.' Reluctantly she returned to the table, picked up a paper parcel and slowly came to Richard again. All she had was a single piece of bread.

*

'If things don't improve for her she will perish before the year is out. I mean starve,' he said to Nancy. He strode about the room to rid the frustrations he felt. 'I must learn more about their condition then I can shame the shareholders into making improvements. But I know I will not win the bal maidens' confidence – at least not for a long time. I think you could have more success.'

She brightened at this idea. 'I could try.'

*

Michaelmas, quarter day, and the Count House was full of shareholders with Sir William in the chair. Rain had set in with a vengeance during the last week and everyone declared the year had been exceptionally wet. The figures brightened the dull day and radiated the warmth that wealth brought. Good figures meant a short meeting and Richard thought there would be time for the shareholders to listen to his plea and be indulgent, but they were not. At the banquet, Richard refused a plate and

197

unwrapped a cloth, exposing a few morsels of food; a cold pasty corner, and a hoggin. A glass of water was all he had asked to drink. His actions dampened the festive spirits of the noisy guests. A quiet descended about the groaning table.

'A week or so ago I saw what a bal maiden had for her croust' He picked out a small crust of bread. 'She is just eleven years and thin – very thin. This was all she had to sustain her all day. Each day she had to stand at a table, and crush – buck – five hundredweight of rocks to earn five pence.' He broke the bread and began to eat. A faint murmur started then faded quickly.

Sir William was impatiently looking over his plate.

'Really, Dr Maddern, could you save this for another time?'

'What girl was that, Dr Maddern?' Morse enquired and Richard noticed his usual cynicism was absent.

'Martha, Martha Clode.'

Morse nodded slowly his eyes narrowed and he looked to the tablecloth. 'She passed away two days ago.'

Another murmur from the diners filled the room but this time one of sympathy.

'What did you record as the cause of her death, Dr Morse?' Richard asked.

Morse looked uncomfortable and evasive. 'I had trouble with that having not seen her previously as you did. She was very much neglected I have to say and to spare her parents I recorded her death as due to a visitation by God.' He turned to look directly at Sir William. 'The real cause was starvation. There are twelve in the family and the father is not in good health – miner's phthisis.'

A solemn stillness filled the room when Morse stopped speaking. Richard had intended to give a minor scratch to goad them into action but Morse had delivered a deep wound.

'Tonkin, would you ask Mr Bennetts to come through,' Sir William's expression was grave. A scrape of a chair across the floor and a slight cough preceded the tall Bennetts' appearance.

'Mr Bennetts, be so kind as to amend the Minutes of the Meeting to say that the examination and treatment room Dr Maddern requested was approved and will be available in the shortest possible time.'

Bennetts gave a short bow and left.

'I think the grace today should reflect the sad loss of such a young child who was in our employ. Perhaps we could have done better, perhaps the measures we have now put into place will go some way to prevent another occurrence. Reverend Jose.'

*

Richard was confused and angry. He talked the whole matter over with Nancy, putting his special interpretation on the details, making this one more evil and that one more saintly. It was cathartic.

'They confessed their sins and were given absolution all in the space of a few minutes. The Kingdom of God is ruled and regulated by proxy, presumably, with the consent of the Almighty. God does not need to look on such as those. Martha's death meant nothing to them other than it ruined their appetites – only for a short while, mind you. A quick prayer and they were off like the start of a race, eating and drinking to excess in celebration of yet another highly profitable period of business.'

Nancy was saddened to hear of Martha's death but she had a more ready acceptance of the dreadful events visited on the poor and needy.

'It is nothing new, Richard. William Lemon can't live in a grand house and not eat well. If each miner had a share of all that food it would be no more than a mouthful – it would do no good. The treatment room is what we planned for and got. Now we must plan again and get a bit more.'

She was learning his ways well, Richard acknowledged. Too well.

Chapter 22

October: the month brought shorter days, gales and excessively high tides.

Nancy was at the window overlooking the creek, watching the leaves fly as the gale stripped the trees bare. She tried to stop the sashes rattling with bits of card in the small gaps. But mostly she stared out at the autumnal rages, enjoying the rising tempest from the sanctuary of her home; safe within the thick walls and warmed by the fire in the grate. She turned as she heard Richard enter the drawing room.

'Come here,' she called and as he joined her she clutched at his arm and leant her head on his shoulder. 'I love to watch a gathering storm.'

The logs cracked in the fire and threw a red glow around the room casting moving pictures on the walls, mirroring the outside drama, but in a softer, friendlier manner. The door opened again and their latest acquisition entered, licking lips and heading for the fire.

'Puss,' he said.

'Cornelius,' she said derisorily and Richard laughed. They were comfortable and thankful that they were inside and not out there.

'My God it's dark for just four in the afternoon.'

Above the woods of Carclew a murder of crows whirled and wheeled. The skies were lowering and a great darkness filled the river valley. The wind gusted strongly taking the tops off the waves in the creek

'A squall coming!' she said with apprehension in her voice as though she were at sea.

The blast shook the windows and boomed against the side of the house. Simultaneously a bolt of lightning forked down from the heavens, striking some point in the creek not far from the house, and they instinctively clung to each other as the thunder exploded instantly, shaking the house. Two more bolts in quick succession and the roars of thunder merged to a continuous, close growl. Ruth came in with the sempstress, both deeply distressed and clinging to each other. They made a circuit of the room and then exited, shrieking all the while. Nancy and Richard laughed at their superstitious behaviour but jumped into each other's arms at another thunderous roar directly overhead.

Rain; at first a few heavy drops, then gathering in numbers and momentum until it lashed at the panes so heavily that the view of the world disappeared. The storm raged for half an hour before it moved slowly away, still lighting the skies with flashes of a brilliant blue whiteness.

'I must see to Ruth.' Richard left the room and headed towards the kitchen. She was not there so he called out. 'Ruth! Ruth, where are you?'

'I'm in here,' her muffled voice came from the cupboard under the stairs. 'And I aren't coming out.'

He laughed and, as he was about to return to Nancy, there was a loud insistent knocking at the door. A tinner was at the doorstep; the rain hitting his shoulders with such force it bounced and formed a wet halo about his head. The lightning struck again behind the man and cast the rising water into a bright shroud.

'There's been a accident. A man's trapped. Two baulks of timber got him. He can't move.' The tinner placed his hands about his waist. 'Here!' and the meaning was plain.

Richard collected instruments and, most importantly, laudanum. He left in just his shirt and breeches.

The scene was one of utter devastation. So much rain had fallen and continued to fall that a foaming river now poured down the central part of the diggings where there was usually no more than a trickle. The valley above the working was sending down torrents of thick, muddy water threatening the whole volume of the works. Most of the tinners stood on the embankment looking anxiously across the expanse of the forming lake to where a dozen or so of their fellows gathered around a fallen pump.

'Over there. The pump was struck be the lightning and

brought it all down,' the tinner shouted above the storm.

They ran along the embankment towards the seaward end and then turned at right angles to cross the creek. The tide lapped against this part of the embankment and was within inches of the top.

'Is the tide full?'

'No,' the tinner said. He stopped and faced Richard. 'No. Another hour yet and the wind is in the sou'east. 'Twill drive it up more. Never seen it so high.'

Captain James was at the foot of the ladder and took him firmly by the arm and led him to the trapped man.

'Doctor's here, Joshua,' Captain James spoke kindly and with confidence.

Joshua! The boy that helped him on his first day. His body emerged from between two huge pieces of timber a foot square. The upper ends were resting against the embankment some six feet from the floor of the workings and the other ends were beneath the water. His lips were bloodless and his face ashen from the shock. Richard felt beneath the water trying to understand where his body was in relation to the wood. The gap between the timber and the body was no larger than his clenched fist. He felt lower; the pelvis was crushed to half its normal size. He withdrew his hands and smiled at Joshua.

'Nothing to worry about, Joshua. We'll have you out of there in no time. I'll give you something to make you feel better then we'll get the timber shifted.'

He waded away and took James with him.

'He's a goner,' Captain James said quietly looking intently at Richard.

'Yes,' Richard agreed. 'I'll give him a large dose of laudanum that will...will ease the situation.' He nodded deliberately, his intention was clear.

Richard cradled Joshua's head and helped him to drink the draught. Joshua's eyes looked into his and he shook his head almost imperceptibly. He knew. Richard talked to him for a few minutes until his eyes became heavy. Then he gave the word to Captain James. Crowbars plunged into the water and strong arms heaved. No movement. It needed more hands. A thin curtain of water was running down the whole length of the

202

seaward wall. The men would not leave without their comrade. Richard saw Bob Rosewarne running across the embankment to help and others joined in the rush.

About twenty men stood-by on the bars waiting the order.

'Now!' came the call and the crowbars levered and movement was made.

'Again!'

And the downward pressure of ten crowbars now made their weight felt – the wood moved and Joshua fell forward into Richard's arms.

They laid him on a wood beam and Richard began to wind a large bandage around the body, binding it tightly, to keep it in one piece. It took time, and in those conditions of impending doom, it seemed endless. But none of the tinners moved until Joshua was able to leave with them.

'Quickly!' Richard shouted above the roar of the storm. 'Everybody must get out of here. Joshua is beyond help – carry him as best you can. No more lives to be lost this day. Hurry!'

No second bidding was necessary; they made straight for the far shore, wading in water above their waists. Directly above the point where the new river smashed into the seawall, the breach was widening, and water was pouring into the bowl at an alarming rate. The two forces were acting together and collapse was imminent.

He urged the men forward and more were coming in the opposite direction to help. As they began to wade out of the deepest part of the river, the sea wall collapsed with a roar, behind them and the unstoppable surge of the tide filled the whole volume rapidly. Hands reached out and pulled them to the embankment, up the side to safety.

'All safe?' Richard cried.

Captain James nodded.

A large lake was now forming, swirling with the different currents, destroying years of work and the source of livelihood of a hundred men. They stared in silence at nature doing her worst. Most of the dirty grim faces wore fatigue and sorrow. They were not angry; they accepted what was happening.

*

'A young life gone Nancy, and nothing we could do to help him.
'This truly was an act of God. But what sort of God?'

Chapter 23

Brother was standing on the embankment as Richard approached. Smoke flew from a pipe clamped in his teeth. The sky was dull but lifted higher than during the storm; the sun was just a brighter patch in the dullness. The air had calmed but occasional angry gusts came from any, and all, directions. The workings were deserted and a river continued to run through them, but with less volume; banks now kept the flow within bounds. Where the sea had broken through a gap had been cut through which the river ran and large timbers ensured the integrity of the soft edges.

'Morning, Brother.'

Brother removed his pipe. 'Morning, Doctor.'

He spoke with a detachment that told his thoughts were not here and now but elsewhere.

'Where is everybody?'

Brother shifted his ground. 'Why, they be gone up the valley a ways,' and he looked over the workings again, his head and lips making small movements as he mused.

'Sad day, I call it. He was a nice boy, Josh,' and he wiped his eye. 'Sad.'

'Yes.'

Brother shook his head. 'I know his father too. He had the devil in him sometimes,' and he laughed. 'I mind the time when...' As he spoke, he could not hold the smile on his face, his lips trembled and the story would not be told that day.

'Who did all this?'

'Aw, they worked when the tide was out...'

'What in the night?'

'Iss. Cut the bank straight and rigged up the timber. When the tide is out the boards are taken away to let the river run. And, afore the tide comes back, they'll board it up again.

'We've had so much rain this year that the ground is saturated. When that cloud burst there was nowhere for the water to go. This here river – the one behind us where the barges are – should have taken the flood from the valley.'

He spat and relit his pipe. 'Well, the river carried so much muck and stuff that the bridge up by the causeway got jammed. The water had nowhere to go, so it broke through the causeway and into the workings here.'

'What happens now?'

'They've gone up to the bridge to clear it. Then they'll stop up the breach and be back here in time to board up that there gap,' and he pointed to the seaward breach. 'God willing, the tide will be kept back and the river flow in his proper place.'

It was more of a prayer than an explanation.

'Will the work start again?'

Brother nodded and sucked strongly on his pipe. 'I hope so! I truly hope so. Most of them will try; the old men especially. Some of the young ones will leave I spec.'

'Where will they go?'

Brother gave a short cynical laugh. 'My bet is they end up in America. If it weren't for that bloody mad George we'd still have it. But they'll find a way – that's where I'd go.'

Richard sensed the bitterness, thought it better to leave matters lie, and bade Brother good day. He walked disconsolately along the embankment and was upon the tinners almost before he realised it; there were neither raised voices nor even the murmur of conversation; only the scrape of a shovel or the squeak of a wheel needing oil.

Captain James spotted him and waved a hand. As Richard waited, faces turned and smiled briefly and more arms raised in greeting.

'Morning, Doctor.'

'Morning, Captain James. You were hard at it all night I hear from Brother.'

James looked weary and wiped his brow with the back of his arm. More than weary, his whole being had the heavy burden of sadness pressing down on it.

'Iss. All night. Half are gone home to rest up a bit. We shall be leaving shortly.' He dug his shovel into the ground so it

206

could take his weight. 'Just have to fit the boards in the sluice and then home.'

They stared at each other. 'Did you get him home?'

James' eyes cast down. 'Iss,' he said heavily. 'Carried him on the board. He was too slack...you know...wouldn't hold together like. His mother was in some way.'

'I should have gone with you.'

'No, no. You done your bit, Doctor, and all of us here would like to thank you for what you did. The money will...'

'No! No money, Captain James,' Richard also felt the grief that shrouded the tinners. 'I wish I could have done more.'

They both stood in silence and only the whispering wind filled the void, lifting their hair and blowing through their clothes. There was a bond between those who have battled together and a comradeship rises from a loss, grievously felt.

'When is the funeral?'

'Friday at Mylor; ten in the morning.'

*

'Sir William's man came while you were at the funeral.' Nancy waited as he broke the seal and read the letter. He gave it to her without revealing its contents.

'An invitation to dinner! To meet Lord and Lady de Dunstanville. Friday at four. PS,' she read. 'Lady Lemon has had the piano tuned at great expense. Need I say more!'

Richard smiled at her alarmed expression.

'Oh my God! Oh my God!' and she hid her face in her hands. 'Oh no! I shall die! 'Tiss disrespectful, Richard, to go when that poor boy is...' She didn't finish, realising the disrespect was in using Joshua's death as an excuse not to attend the dinner. 'Who are Lord and Lady de Dunstanville?'

'Lord de Dunstanville is Sir Francis Basset. Sir William introduced us at the Hospital function.'

*

They descended from the baronet's carriage and were lead by a liveried footman up the stone steps to the grand entrance of Carclew mansion. Nancy was in her green dress and as Richard took her arm, he felt her trembling. Otherwise, she was looking radiant: bathed and scented with perfume, her hair lustrous and shining, held in place by a string of pearls matching those around her neck. The butler announced the arrival of Dr and Mrs Maddern. Lady Lemon was already on her feet and came forward to greet her guests warmly, inviting them into the room where only one other woman was present. Richard bowed to Lady Lemon and Nancy curtsied low and held her head down, an act she had been practising for hours. Lady Lemon helped her up and was clearly very pleased to see her again.

'Now, my dears, may I introduce you to Lady Frances de Dunstanville, the wife of Sir Francis Basset?'

Lady Frances was about forty and she walked toward Richard and Nancy, smiling gracefully and full of confidence. Richard bowed. 'M'Lady. May I introduce my wife, Mrs Nancy Maddern.'

Nancy repeated the curtsy and rose slowly until her eyes were level with those of Lady Frances.

'Charmed to meet you, Mrs Maddern,' she said and her eyes approved of what she saw.

'The gentlemen are...' Lady Lemon began but before she could finish the door opened and Sir William and Sir Francis Basset entered. All turned in their direction. Basset was a small man, sharp-cut and energetic. Nancy noticed Sir Francis look to her immediately and she ventured a timid smile.

'Sorry Doctor – Mrs Maddern. Saw you coming and made haste,' Sir William explained.

'Mrs Maddern!' Basset exclaimed. 'I remember the night at the Assembly Rooms where you made as much an impression as your talented husband. How nice to see you again. And you Doctor – more heroics we are lead to believe.'

'Sit down and tell us more,' Lady Lemon addressed them all and directed the places they should occupy.

Richard described the events and did not avoid telling of the awful conditions. He believed these people should know and, in knowing, act.

'That must have been dreadful to behold!' exclaimed Lady Frances. 'I feel quite faint just hearing of it.'

'Should I continue, your Ladyship?' Richard asked.

'Pray do, Doctor, but perhaps not so much detail.'

208

They all sighed when the tale concluded and relaxed into their seats.

'And the funeral was this morning at St Melloris?' asked Sir William.

'Yes, Sir. There were about fifty tinners present – mainly Methodists, who made certain suggestions about the service that the vicar did not readily acquiesce to.'

'The Reverend Whitehead,' Sir William said wearily. 'But he did, I'll warrant, faced with that lot!' he added and smiled in amusement.

'Yes. Indeed.'

'Will the works arise again do you think?' asked Sir Francis.

'I thought not, but miraculously they worked overnight and made unbelievable progress by morning. The fortitude of these people is truly amazing. Even so, their livelihood is severely reduced and I cannot guess when they will be selling tin ore again – and what will they live on until then?'

'That is something we shall think about,' Sir William said gravely. 'Certainly some relief must be obtained if they cannot recover tin ore soon.'

'This is all too glum. I think we should have a glass of Madeira to lift our spirits,' Lady Lemon declared.

They wished each other good health and sipped the wine together. Lady Frances had been discreetly, but closely, examining Nancy. While she approved of her dress and grooming, she was uncertain of Nancy's background and she had a long-standing opinion of who should mix with the aristocracy.

Over dinner, Sir William did most of the talking and used the opportunity to give more information about Basset. He made frequent interpretations, usually prefacing it with, 'Of course Lord de Dunstanville...was made Baron in 1779 after leading a large group of miners to Plymouth to improve the earthwork batteries...MP for Penryn for many years until 1796 when he was elevated to the peerage, joining Lord North's party...Harrow and Eton of course, and King's College Cambridge.'

By this means, Nancy and Richard learned that they were in the presence of one of the most powerful men in the county, vying with Boscawen. Basset was a confident figure and, taking into account his age, his achievements were considerable. He was slim by the day's standard for a wealthy person. His face had a soft countenance with a gentle mouth. His eyes were wide set and in them Richard detected a steeliness and imagined he did not suffer fools gladly.

They started with fish. 'Bass,' Sir William declared, 'out of my river.'

The meat was on a large platter and the lid removed for Sir William's approval.

'Venison from our own park. Killed and hung for three weeks to the peak of perfection. A haunch, roasted for most of the morning.' The butler and under butler took the large platter to the dresser for carving. Nancy took just a little – the less she had to eat the less chance of committing a faux pas. She was astonished to see how much Lady Frances was prepared to tackle.

'No theatre today, Doctor, please,' Sir William pleaded. He crooked a finger at Basset for his attention even though he had it.

'At our latest monthly accounts meeting, the good doctor chose to bring a hoggin and a corner of pasty. Put us off our feast I can tell you,' and he laughed at the remembrance.

'And why did you do that, Doctor?' asked Lady de Dunstanville.

'To draw attention to the plight of some of the young girls that work in the mines – bal maidens. One little girl in particular had almost nothing to sustain her through a very hard working day. She was severely undernourished.'

'One cannot expect the mine owners and shareholders to look to the welfare of every one of its employees, Doctor, surely? They must manage their household accounts and not expect the owners to interfere.' Basset seemed sensitive to this area of discussion. 'In 1785 there was a food riot. With fifty constables, I arrested the leaders. Some were hanged and others transported. That is the only way of dealing with that sort – anarchy reigns otherwise!'

Richard's riposte was immediate. 'I know nothing of that and therefore cannot comment. My immediate thoughts are, however, if faced with starvation, I would not die quietly.' Richard's colour rose slightly. 'Martha Code died a few days later, eleven years old. The attending doctor stated the cause of death as a visitation from God, but to his credit he openly acknowledged it was from starvation.'

The diners continued eating but now listened more attentively.

'Should we acknowledge there are men, women and children working at the mines close to death from malnutrition while we pass on the other side? Or that God lurks among the poor and needy and "suffer the little children to come unto me" takes on another meaning.'

'You go too far, Doctor,' Basset fiercely interjected.

'Ah! I did warn you, Basset,' Sir William played the role of Speaker. 'The upshot was he got what he wanted – a clean, warm, treatment and examination room at the mine.'

Lemon thought the topic needed to be changed and with a, 'What is the latest news on Bony?' opened the conversation to a wide-ranging discussion, mainly self-interested, but occasionally demonstrating that Lemon and Basset had a statesman's view of the wider implications.

'No chance of young gentlemen engaging on the Grand Tour nowadays, eh?'

'Less,' Basset replied. 'Italy is safe for the time with Nelson in the Med, although he's playing a dangerous game with Hamilton and God knows where that might lead.'

'What?' Lady Lemon interjected, sensing more news of the scandal.

'Yes, yes. Same old story. A man's entitled to some...'

'No, he's not!' she insisted, interrupting her husband. 'Do you know, my dear,' she said to Nancy. 'Nelson is cuckolding Lord Hamilton right under his nose.' Nancy shook her head not knowing exactly what she was alluding to, but Lady Lemon took it as disapproval.

'Quite right, my dear. I should think not.'

'Let us not forget that our future lies in the hands of this man,' Sir William stressed trying to uphold Nelson's position.

'That's not a reason for philandering,' his wife maintained.

'Yes, my dear, but should the navy fail then Napoleon will

come looking for our heads. Does that modify your opinion a little?' he teased.

Lady de Dunstanville continued to take much interest in Nancy and noted her small hesitations and was coming to the conclusion that she was little more than a peasant. The girl was attractive, certainly, and still had that wonderful bloom of youth. Beauty was able at times to break social barriers where money, sometimes, could not.

Lemon asked the guests to take more. Nancy and Richard refused politely.

'Venison not to your liking, Doctor?' Basset asked, as he watched his plate being replenished.

'Excellent meat, my Lord, but too hearty a feast I fear.'

'And you, Mrs Maddern?' followed up Lady de Dunstanville.

Nancy puffed from the exertions. 'I admire your appetite, my Lady, but it is one I cannot match.'

'Perhaps I do eat too much,' she said and Nancy was not sure if this was an admonition.

The claret decanter made its rounds but Nancy refused to take any.

The talk diverted to plans for a rail line linking Portreath on the north coast to Devoran on the south.

'It will be a long time in coming, William,' Basset said, trying to play down Lemon's enthusiasm. The great men discussed the pros and cons until the chatter died, and they ate until knives and forks came to a clattering finish on the ceramics.

'Pineapples, Mrs Maddern. Have you seen the like before?' and Lemon handled two large fruit.

Nancy looked hard and wondered what sort of challenge eating it would bring.

'These are especially grown in hot frames that I have heated all the year round – at great expense.'

The butler took the fruit to the sideboard and Nancy watched intently as he carved it to reveal the yellow insides. Each person had a portion and Nancy waited, not knowing what to do. Lemon saw her dilemma and immediately helped.

'Here, let me show you how to eat it.' And he cut smaller

morsels with a knife and fork.

'Try it!'

'Umm...' she exclaimed. 'Delicious!' Richard tried and agreed while the de Dunstanvilles looked condescendingly on.

'I think the gentlemen should withdraw for a short time,' Lady Lemon announced, stressing short. 'Then we shall hear Dr Maddern play for us,' and she smiled in Richard's direction.

Lemon and Basset filled pipes from a bowl of tobacco, already reduced to a manageable size – not like the pricks and coils that the miners had to deal with.

'You don't smoke, Doctor?' Basset asked, as his pipe began to draw satisfactorily.

'Tobacco and I do not get on, my Lord. I have tried on several occasions and the result is always the same – light-headedness followed by sickness.'

Both men laughed. 'The smoke doesn't bother you though?'

'Oddly not – I even enjoy the smell until it becomes concentrated and then I have to seek fresh air.'

'Sir William tells me you have suggested banning smoking in the mines.'

Richard shifted in his chair realising he was under interrogation and related Dr Andrew's advice.

'Umm,' grunted Lemon. 'A glass of port?' and the decanter began its round.

'You seem to have the welfare of the miner particularly in mind, Doctor. Do you have any other firm ideas to improve their lot?' Basset returned to the touchy subject but in a more conciliatory tone, perhaps realising he had a more formidable opponent than he first thought.

'None that would please a mine owner, of course. Any improvement has to come from those who have the means.'

'All from us and nothing in return as usual!' Basset called from behind a screen where he was using a chamber pot. Richard smirked behind his glass. 'It depends how you see it. Any investment takes a while before a return can be realised.'

'You know about investment?' Basset laid a trap, as he emerged adjusting his breeches.

'Ah! I forgot to mention; Dr Maddern is a member of the Court of Proprietors of the British East India Company and his father before him was a Board Member.' Lemon seemed to be savouring the encounter.

'Well! Pray continue. The floor is yours,' and Basset displayed an open hand, palm up.

'I don't have a solution – improving the conditions would require the input of engineers as well as doctors and anyone else in a position to give a knowledgeable opinion. What I should like to see, my Lord, is twofold. Before starting down the ladders, each man, each worker has a bowl of soup or broth. And the dries should live up to that name. Much heat from the engines is wasted and could be utilised at little expense. You asked where is the return for your investment. Compare the miner, if you like, to that of your grand engines. Starve the engine of coal and it has little energy to work. I contend that a miner with a full belly will work that much better!'

'Bravo, Doctor!' cried Lemon. 'Worthwhile considering, eh, Basset? And now the Doctor must play for his supper,' he chuckled.

*

Lady Lemon called for more candles as the light was getting dim. This was the time Nancy dreaded most, in the more intimate surroundings where the ladies were freer to talk.

'Where did you say you lived, Mrs Maddern?' Lady Frances asked.

'Devoran, my Lady.'

'Devoran?' she repeated airily. 'Can't say I've heard of it. Is that far from here?'

Nancy squirmed and thought quickly. 'Not far – just across the creek. Near the tinner's workings.'

'Oh!' Lady Frances said quietly with that air of surprise. 'Is there a living for the doctor there?'

'My husband came to Devoran to give himself more time to think and write.'

'A gentleman's existence?'

Nancy nodded.

'How long have you been married?' Lady de Dunstanville changed the subject to one that might now be raised.

'Earlier this year,' Nancy replied and smiled. 'July. We were

214

married in St John Zachary in London. Richard wanted us to marry there.'

'They honeymooned in London for a month during the season,' Lady Lemon added.

'And they graciously paid us a visit at our apartment in St James'.'

'Grand indeed,' Lady Frances acknowledged. 'Did you attend the theatre?'

'Oh yes. We sought entertainment every night – we saw the Prince on one occasion and he spoke with us. We also saw several of the...what Richard calls the Ton. But I never fully understood who they were.'

'Not worth the effort, my dear,' Lady Lemon said scornfully. 'Wasters and pleasure-seekers of the worse sort. Don't you agree, Frances?'

Lady Frances did not immediately agree, but nodded slowly and in Nancy's mind, unconvincingly.

'Yes, the Slyph does not paint a pretty picture of their morals,' Nancy agreed and Lady Frances's eyes noticeably arched.

She again observed how much care had gone into Nancy's grooming and even in the close atmosphere of the parlour, she remained cool and her perfume gave off a heady intoxicating scent. Perhaps she was worth some care in cultivating.

'Our first child came almost exactly twelve months after we were married.'

The intended question was obvious and, even though Nancy knew it was coming, she could not hide a look of disappointment. Because she was not able to formulate a reply quickly, the assumption was that she had nothing to say on the matter.

Lady Lemon deciphered the pause and fussed with her napkin. 'Their daughter, she is also called Frances,' she informed Nancy, 'is now – what? Nineteen?'

'Yes.'

'Getting ready to come out and leave home no doubt?'

'No,' Lady Frances replied, in a far-away voice where her thoughts had temporarily gone. 'She is, regrettably, our only child...' her voice faded away.

'Don't fret about children my dear – the more you fret the longer you'll wait,' Lady Lemon spoke to Nancy. 'My advice is to enjoy yourselves – once you start there's no stopping unless you send your man to sea – there's much to be said for a good long sea voyage!'

Their laughter was interrupted by the return of the gentlemen.

'A sea voyage? Who's going on a sea voyage?' asked Lemon.

*

Richard began with a favourite of Nancy's; the middle movement of Mozart's Piano Concerto 21. He moved to a minuet from Mozart's London Notebook and then a Bach transcription of a short fugue for piano, before he played tunes that could be sung: Where ere you walk followed by the Ash Grove and Early one morning which Lady Lemon found irresistible, and softly sang while trying to encourage Nancy to join in.

The evening grew late. Sir William thanked Richard and warmly praised Nancy whose appearance, so he said, brightened a dull autumnal day.

'Your carriage awaits,' he said theatrically, as he accompanied them to the main doors.

Lord de Dunstanville bowed smoothly and graciously and Lady de Dunstanville held out a gloved hand. Nancy curtseyed to both ladies and the men.

'Oh!' Nancy sighed, as the carriage rolled away.

'Didn't you enjoy it? Richard teased.

'Enjoy it! I'd rather watch a sow having a litter.' As she spoke, he could hear Nancy being busy but, in the darkness, he was unable to discern what she was doing.

'Nancy?'

She fell into his arms without her dress.

'Come on,' she said as she undid his breeches. 'Not many have done it in a baronet's carriage. Quickly!' He felt her warm flesh against his own.

'If we are lucky we'll call him Francis or her Frances. It must be confusing.'

216

'Why? Ah!'
'Both called Francis...oh!'
'Oh! Yes!'
'And the daughter. She's called Frances as well!'
'Good God!'

Chapter 24

Christmas Eve: they gathered greenery in the lanes and came home with rosy cheeks and smiles. Christmas morning they attended the early service at St Piran's with her parents. The long walk to and from church in the clear frosty air made the cup of warming brandy on their return most welcome.

Christmas dinner started with a fine bass, progressed to a goose from the farm, and finally pork from their own pig. Richard provided some rare spices – cinnamon, cloves, nutmeg, mace and black peppercorns to flavour and season the food handsomely. Mountains of fresh vegetables steamed on the table and cool yellow cider gently fizzed. Later, Mr Rosewarne slept in the drawing room in front of the blazing fire while the womenfolk were in the kitchen washing and cleaning. Richard had eaten too much and decided he would benefit from a walk.

The afternoon was dull and the leaden skies hinted of snow. The garden immediately at the front of the house showed just brown earth. The cold east wind briskly took the smoke from the chimneys of the cottages in the Row. It was with some satisfaction that he saw the back lane was clean and the bright, white spar stones clearly visible.

There were only two men in the stream workings engaged in replacing the boards that held back the tide. The rest were taking the time off to celebrate Christmas. Tomorrow they would be at it again and every day for the rest of the year except Sundays and a few feast days: Paul's Tide in January, Friday in Lide close to St Piran's day in March and Chewidden, Thursday before Christmas and the special feast days associated with a village or town.

The wind chilled after the comfort of the fire and he pulled his coat closer. Flocks of teal and widgeon arrived but, finding no water, banked high over the woods then turned into the bitter wind now spitting sleet. It was after four and dusk approached as he turned homeward. Lights from his house glowed orange and yellow beckoning him to the warmth within. On the quay, a small boy anxiously looked in his direction. The boy doffed a ragged cap.

'There be a accident – at the mines. Cappen Tonkun is dead.'

*

Richard looked at the body on the table in the treatment room.

'He been here since the morning core came off at six,' Captain Ross was standing close to the body, his hat removed. He looked tired and frowned a good deal, his thick eyebrows arched from deep thought. 'He was found in the eighty fathom level about five hour ago.'

Richard moved around the body and saw a wound to the head. He turned the head towards the light Ross held and saw a deep crater in the skull.

'He was dead when they found him.'

'No evidence of a fall?'

'No.'

'If an obstacle – a stone for example, fell eighty fathom it would inflict such a wound?'

'Or a iron tool falling from such a way,' Ross suggested.

More likely an iron tool from close too, Richard thought.

'Who else was down the mine at the time?'

Ross paused too long. 'Now then, let me see,' his deep voice boomed even when *sotto voce*. 'Well, there's a list in the office.' Although it was Christmas Day some essential maintenance was necessary to ensure the mines remained operational. The pumping never stopped. A minimal number of selected miners and surface workers had this task and an unfortunate captain had to oversee the work. Tonkin was that man.

'Who found him?'

'Missus said to the boy that Cappen Tonkun oughter be in be now and sent him looking. Well, he couldn't find him nowhere and, asking around, he learned that Cappen Tonkun had gone down the shaft to see if the water was making. Now, boys are always looking to get down the mine – any excuse – so down he went and found him.'

'Whom do you suspect, Captain Ross?'

He coughed. 'Now, suspect? Why, I don't suspect nobody – no, neery a one.'

'Morse? Has Morse been informed?'

'No.'

Richard nodded slowly.

'Best someone informs Morse that Tonkin has met with an accident and is dead. Tell him that...'

Ross cleared his throat once more. 'It isn't as easy as that, Doctor. See, Dr Morse is gone away. Back in a couple of days.'

'Is he gone far?'

Ross shook his head. 'Don't know.'

The set-up was near perfect but it placed Richard in a most vulnerable position – collaborator would be an obvious accusation.

'Send someone for Dr Andrew.'

Andrew confirmed Richard's suspicions. 'A blow above the right temple. Not from a fall. More like a hammer, a blunt instrument at least.'

'What shall we do?' Richard asked.

'My advice? Bury him as quickly as possible. We can make out the certificate as accidental death from a fall at the eighty-fathom level.' Andrew looked to Richard. 'The alternative is to report it to the constable and let an unintelligent man carry out a pointless and futile investigation. The name of the murderer will not appear on the list of people officially working today.'

Richard made out the certificate and they both signed it. Richard handed it to Ross and instructed him to take it to the parish priest for registration.

'Accidental death,' he said to Ross. 'Get him into a coffin. After Mrs Tonkin has seen him, fasten the lid.'

*

Richard fretted during the next days. He feared Morse would return before the interment and open an investigation. Any examination would throw doubt on the cause of death. It was not until Ross called on the afternoon, 29th December, to inform him the burial took place earlier, that he sighed with relief, vowing never to do anything of the like again.

220

'A good crowd turned out to see him off and we sung the burying tune as us walked to the church.'

'Burying tune?'

'Iss!'

'Is Dr Morse back?' Richard asked.

'Iss. He went to the funeral.'

'He didn't look at the body?' Richard asked anxiously.

Ross rubbed his chin. 'Well iss he did. Made us take off the lid and all.'

Richard blanched and the foreboding returned. 'And?'

'He didn't make nothing of it. Didn't more than look at his face. Said he was looking well enough in death. So he was mind; peaceful, like what he just gone a sleep. Purty like. Let's hope us'll all go the same.'

Ross was preaching having forgotten the 'peaceful' way Tonkin went.

*

On New Year's Eve, as the arm of the clock swept into the New Year, Richard and Nancy stared out of the window.

It was a clear, frosty, bright starlit night enhanced by a full moon.

'A new year and a new century!' Richard marvelled at the happy coincidence. 'Not often do people witness the death of one century and the birth of another. You must make a wish.'

She took his arm and rested her head on his shoulder. 'Is a wish any different to a prayer?'

He felt troubled by her response.

'Are your prayers answered?'

'Not yet.'

He sensed darkness in her reply, as if he were in the shadow of her mind.

'Oh I wish! I wish for a...'

'No, you mustn't say – it has to be a secret or it will not come true.'

'All right,' she said defiantly, 'I wish...' and her voice trailed to nothing.

'Now you,' she said.

He put his arm around her and hugged her tightly.

'I have everything I want right here.'

For a while they were silent, but Nancy was not satisfied with that answer.

'You haven't,' she said softly.

Chapter 25

January and February were bitterly cold months. Frost lay on the ground for days. Icicles at the eaves hung like daggers, grew into swords and fell, too heavy to be borne. The kitchen garden was lifeless and needed little attention but unless Nancy was busy, she was not contented. Even when frosts had turned the ground to iron and covered the bare black branches of the trees in hoary rime, she dragged him from his fire and book, wrapped him in warm clothes and walked the lanes or rode the horses further afield.

'How did you discover places so far from your home?'

'When we were children, which is the best time.'

'We?'

'Billy and me.' There was a fondness when she pronounced his name. 'Before he took to drink,' she added with bitterness and tossed her head.

Then home, on those cold winter days when their breath issued like steam and fingers tingled with cold, to a treat Nancy had introduced him to – pilchards roasted on the gridiron over hot coals. The smell at first was wonderful, but it pervaded and lingered too long.

Winter had taken its toll. Many miners added colds and coughs to their already damaged chests and those tough men succumbed easily. Nathan was among those who did not survive the winter. The opencast tinners suffered much less, even though they were out in all winds and weathers. They had colds, coughs and occasionally pneumonia, but mostly they came to him with injuries to their hands and fingers that lost their feeling in the cold and made common actions clumsy.

One evening Nancy was not happy and came to his side in the surgery where he was trying more experiments with willow.

'Oh, this is hopeless,' he declared and put his arm around her waist. 'Why so glum?' he asked with over-cheerfulness. She did not respond and leaned against his arm, her head lowered, and her face turned slightly away. A warm tear fell onto his hand and instantly he put the problem into the most serious category. He turned her face towards him and saw tears running down her face and her sad expression overwhelmed him.

'Here, here, sweetheart, whatever is the matter? Why so many tears?'

She did not answer but buried her face in his chest and sobbed. Her softness melted into him, her sorrow suffused his body.

'I'm still not expecting,' she said, looking into his eyes.

'Did you think you were?'

'No,' she said, spoken quietly. Then angrily she shouted. 'But I should be!'

He smiled to himself at her typical reaction to unsolvable problems.

'Shush, we'll have none of that. Remember what Lady Lemon said about wanting it too much...'

'Bugger Lady Lemon! I want a baby now!' she screamed full of anger and disappointment. 'You're a doctor – you should know what to do.'

How often he had heard that and most times, as now, the appeal was unanswerable. Doctors knew so little about the body and the functions of its many organs. The cloak of absolute knowledge many professed to wear, did not fit on his shoulders. He was more apt to tell the truth and reveal the concealed ignorance. But he also knew this would lead so many to despair; while the doctor assured help, the patient received hope.

'I will help you and we will get to the problem and solve it.'

Some days later after visiting her mother, she came to him again seeking some explanation. Late evening when she was dressed for bed, she walked around his chair slowly, trailing her hand on his shoulders. He folded his book to give her his total attention.

'I had a talk with Mummy today but it didn't help. She didn't really want to talk about it, which was strange, normally she is only too ready to sit and talk. You said you would help me...'

'Us. It is us, Nancy. Both of us want to have a child. Sit here and I will do my best to explain.' He took a book from the large bookcase on the wall.

'In the last century, William Harvey believed all life begins from an egg. Well think about a chicken's egg that develops into a chick.' She nodded and he continued. 'There are two ideas about the way conception takes place. One is that humans are preformed in the egg – and the other, that the sperm carries a small human that is nourished and grows in the egg.'

Richard sighed. 'None of this really helps you does it? All I am doing is showing you that we know nothing.'

'Why do women bleed?' she asked despondently.

Richard lifted his hands in the air in exasperation. 'I don't know. Now you understand the frustrations of being a doctor – too much is a mystery. The belief is there is a human egg somewhere inside the belly of a woman. A woman has two ovaries, where the human eggs are, although the eggs have never been seen. They are about here.' Richard placed both hands about and below her waist and pressed with each thumb the approximate location.

'Oh!'

'Now the assumption is that the eggs travel down a tube, called the fallopian tube, into the uterus.' And he traced the path. 'Here!' he exclaimed. 'The mons veneris – or as some say "fanny hill"!' He laughed, but Nancy did not respond.

'The sperm have the appearance of tadpoles. They are tiny, so small you cannot see them except under a microscope.'

'Oh!'

'Yes. Countless numbers.'

'You've seen them? '

He had a flush of embarrassment. 'Yes. It's all part of a doctor's training,' he made the excuse.

'Yours! You looked at yours?'

'No!' he exclaimed. Then more quietly. 'No.' His mind travelled back to his student days and he recalled vividly the occasions.

'The fellows who attended the great schools of England were always the most eager. The ones that Basset and his like attended.'

'What?' she smirked. 'They toss each other off just like the boys in the lanes do.'

'Do they?' It was his turn to be surprised.

'You are always asking me what the boys are shouting. "Come here and hold me dick!" they say. Or "give us a starter, Nancy". Some of them are doing it!'

He was stunned, but before he could collect his thoughts Nancy was at his breeches.

'Let's see what yours look like.'

The sample was transferred to a glass slide. Richard hastened to the microscope and adjusted the focus using a hair from his head. Nancy stood at his shoulder waiting to see.

'Strange,' he said and pulled another hair. A longer silence ensued and Nancy was restless.

'Well?'

Richard pulled back from his crouch. 'Nothing. There are no sperm.'

'What!'

His gaze into her eyes was serious. 'Nothing. You are not the barren one...I am.'

'What do you mean?'

He got up and sought out his breeches to cover his infertility.

'I am not producing any sperm. I cannot father a child...' He paused and dredged from his past.

''Tiss a spell, Richard! Somebody has put a spell on you. We must find out who!'

He looked at her in disbelief. 'You mean a witch or something?'

She nodded vigorously. Superstition was still rife among the uneducated and in this part of the country the folklore was redolent with such stupidity.

'Nancy don't be ridiculous. There is no one and there are no such things as witches. That is superstitious nonsense!' He raised his voice, his face white. Nancy took this to be anger and fled from the room already sobbing. This was the first time in their relationship that dissent had arisen between them. Richard stared at the closing door thinking of the conflict of emotions that had spilled into the room. He had just made a mind-numbing discovery about himself that changed his life completely and Nancy blamed it on witches and spells! Here, then, was a widening gap in their union that he never considered previously – this difference in their education could drive a wedge to separate them. He sat before the fire and looked into the glowing embers. More time passed and each minute meant the chasm between them widened and, with a slight sense of reluctance, he finally decided to climb the stairs to their room. He opened the door quietly and saw her stretched on the bed, face down, crying. A great emptiness had entered into their lives and he had no way of filling it. She sensed his presence and turned to see Richard standing over her with glasses of brandy.

'Here,' he said in a whisper. 'The doctor prescribes it.'

*

Richard withdrew into a brooding melancholy and Nancy allowed him time and privacy to come to terms with his life-changing discovery. They had not talked about it since and it lay heavily within her like a bad meal. The air was fragile and a wrong word or gesture could shatter their world into sharp shards destroying what they had created. Days later, at dinner, she plucked up courage.

'How would you have treated me if you discovered I was barren? You must have thought about it?'

He toyed with a knife looking at the cloth and not her. Then with a quick movement, he pushed the knife away.

'In my experience when a couple comes to a doctor complaining of childlessness the fault is invariably laid at the door of the woman. Her role is so much more complicated. It's a facile diagnosis to blame her – who would argue? I am beginning to understand how a woman feels. I am the one who cannot complete a marriage – I am the one who brings sadness and emptiness to the marriage bed...'

'Richard, please.'

He raised an arm. 'No, we must face the truth. You will not have a baby because of me. Any one of the boys and men that shout after you could give you what you want – '

'Richard!' she shouted and he stopped. Through her tears, she pleaded with him. 'It's you I love – even more...'

'Out of pity?'

'No! From pure and natural love.' She went to him and they embraced and stayed together for a long time.

'Nancy, I am going to Bristol.'

She tried to decipher what lay in his face. 'You are leaving me?'

He smiled briefly. 'Only for a few days.'

'Because of...'

'Partly.'

Chapter 26

Nancy watched the boat leave from the cliff tops overlooking Portreath. She watched until it was just a small patch of white on the wide sea. Then she turned Lady to retrace her sad path homeward. Where was home now? She harboured grave doubts that he would ever return. He had suddenly appeared in her life and could just as easily leave – evaporate like the morning mist. He had not spoken any more about his reason for going to Bristol – all she knew of that place was that he had a house there; perhaps a home, another place to stay. She bitterly regretted speaking of spells and witches but it was all that entered her mind to rid the crisis. She had none of his learning to bring to the problem. The look in his eyes burned into her soul – belittling, robbing her of self-esteem, and making her feel unwanted.

Nothing in the ensuing days had been said or acted out between them to afford any amelioration. Tears glistened on her cheeks that she wiped away angrily in frustration.

Ruth was unaware of the reason for Richard's departure. She did not ask but her expressions questioned continually so that Nancy avoided her, which made matters worse. A week passed and she left for the farm. There she knew, for sure, was a home where she would be welcomed. She stayed and her mother sensed a difficulty and was not reticent to ask why Richard had gone. Business, she said, but in truth Nancy did not know herself and introspection clouded her mind more. Unable to give clear expression to her feelings she railed against the unfairness of her dilemma – if she were barren, the matter would have been closed. Because it was Richard, a male, the world – her world – was to be turned upside down.

When her mother's tacit assumption that Richard would not return became clear, she decided to return to Devoran, worn down and more deeply depressed. She would wait, hope and pray.

*

Richard stood before a house in Bristol that lay close enough to the city centre to enjoy the benefits of a wealthy city, but not be intimate with its busy commercial life. The day was raw and a cold wind raced off the sea. Black wrought iron railings embraced the three steps to the front door, following their elegant converging curve. Grasping the lion's head, he rapped twice and waited.

A maid peered around the door and, recognising Richard, opened it wide and greeted him with a short bob.

'Good morning, sir.'

'Good morning, Mary,' he said as he entered the hall. Her eyes seemed pleased to see him, but there was no smile on her lips.

'And how are you, Mary?' he asked, handing her his hat and gloves.

'Very well, sir,' she answered now with a smile.

'I am not expected, Mary, but if your mistress is at home I will attend her in the drawing room.'

'Very good, sir.'

The large room had high ceilings decorated with plaster mouldings of a simple design. Dark red embossed paper covered the walls giving a heavy gloominess when the large windows clamoured for a lighter interior. The room was musty and smelled of dampness. The bookshelves no longer bulged with books and a film of dust covered the fashionable mahogany table.

'Richard! You should have warned me of your visit. This is most ungallant of you.'

The speaker was a tall woman who gave a brief curtsey. Her hair was the colour of raven's feathers. She wore it up at the back, caught with a large tortoiseshell clip.

He returned a short bow and looked at her intently. Her brown eyes pierced and penetrated whom she observed. She had a proud, confident countenance; her aquiline features were becoming stronger as she grew older turning hawkish that more suited her personality he thought. She had aged, he noticed, but she was four years older than he.

'To what do I owe this visit?'

He declined to answer her question; he must lead the conversation.

'Are you well, Kathrine, and the boys?'

She seated herself beside the cold grate and indicated that he should do likewise but he remained standing.

'I am as you see me – well enough, but I don't suppose for one moment my well-being is of interest to you.'

'And the boys?'

'At school; where else should they be?' her eyes never left him.

'William is now nearly ten?'

'Well, you should remember his age, Richard – he is your son!'

'Is he?' he asked with deliberation and paused. 'And Jonathan?'

'Eight. Both at boarding school as you know – you pay their fees!' her voice rose with irritation and impatience.

Despite now knowing they were not his children, he could not dismiss the love he felt for them, having brought them up as his own from their birth.

'And what of Lieutenant Bidgood?'

She smirked knowing the criticism that laced his question. '*Captain* Bidgood of the Dragoons is stationed here in Bristol.' There was a note of triumph in her voice.

'Wherever you were so was he shortly after. We left London to rid ourselves of the fellow and within months he found his way here!'

She laughed scornfully. He collected himself by walking around the room.

'Kathrine, I am experiencing some difficulty in being here and the reason makes it more so.' He paused to look at her directly. She sat impassive and cool. She could command a presence so easily it unnerved him. He hesitated and she lost patience.

'For goodness sake, Richard!'

'Y-yes,' he stammered. 'The fact is I have good reason to

believe that neither William nor Jonathan is my child.'

Her mood changed immediately. She looked vacantly at Richard and then clapped her hands almost silently.

'Bravo, Richard! What young maiden is complaining of your inability that has brought this revelation to light?'

She had that skill of finding a raw spot and rubbing it. She continued.

'We married while you were still at college, if you remember. You were handsome, intelligent and above all very rich – all that I needed.' She looked away towards the bare boards of the floor. 'But you were, and still are, so naive! Three years we were married and went at it like rabbits but no heir to your vast fortune that I might manage! What a dilemma! I thought at first it was I! I needed someone else to fill the gap – if you will excuse the pun. Lawrence Bidgood comes into the scene – yet another pun – and lo! Pregnant...And in a short while another son. No escape!'

Richard listened to the extent of the deception.

'After that I could begin the grand scheme, but Lawrence unfortunately plays the game as well as I.'

'Meaning?

'Lawrence wasn't to be left out. He had contributed handsomely, but your leaving wrecked both our plans. Neither of us expected that. So we sit here in cold penury until a solution arises and my guess is you are about to offer something.'

Richard nodded thoughtfully. The scheme was laid years ago and her impatience had lead to this admission. Impatience was the fatal flaw in her make-up.

'Divorce is what I want.'

She laughed scornfully. 'And divorce is not what you will get! It takes an act of Parliament to divorce. Will you foot the bill and suffer the ignominy? I think not.'

Richard smiled. 'As you say.'

She smirked. 'Are you married to the little hussy who has won your heart, Richard? Are you a bigamist?'

He turned white at the mention of Nancy as a hussy. That this schemer should insult her was very offensive. He turned on her with newfound resolution.

'You will leave the country. Our association is to be expunged – forgotten, obliterated.'

She laughed loudly. 'You are unbelievable, Richard! Where had you in mind?'

'A captain ought to be able to choose where to serve. India, for example, or Canada; I would prefer Australia.'

She continued to laugh at the absurd proposition until Richard delivered the blow that would make these suggestions seem reasonable.

'Your amusement does not help your cause, Kathrine. I have this very morning instructed my lawyers to sell this property. You will be served notice to quit immediately. You should seek alternative accommodation as of today. The allowance I give you will cease from tomorrow.'

The severe ultimatum removed her smile and an ashen pallor took its place. The cold meal of revenge had been devoured. He turned the screw.

'My lawyers inform me there are several buyers waiting for a property like this so the expectation is you will be evicted within a short time if you chose to stay.'

'How long?' she asked, now subdued, her head trembled slightly and she held her hands tightly to control them.

'One month at most.'

She had trouble containing herself but, to her credit, she did. To rage at him would do no good. She got up, walked to the fireplace and held on to the mantelpiece.

'How much would you give me to obtain my riddance?'

He had not anticipated her quickness of thought.

'Where would you go?'

'That is no concern of yours – all you need to know is that I have quit the country,' she snapped, her confidence was returning. She rightly guessed he would make an offer since he continued the line of questioning rather than refuse to entertain the idea she threw at him.

'How would I know that you had? You could take up residence in some country district and remain in this country until you choose to again interfere in my affairs.'

'Yes,' she smiled, 'your affairs.' She now walked around with a slight swagger. 'Well let me suggest the allowance continues and is forwarded to a foreign address – to yet another lawyer to whom I would present myself in person.'

The table turned, Richard now found himself on the defensive. His immediate thoughts were that it was a good compromise but the very fact she had suggested it put him on his guard.

'I want a clean break. If I pay an allowance it could be misinterpreted.'

'Well?'

He was thinking as fast as he was able but wanted time.

'Come on, Richard. You hold all the aces.'

He took a turn around the room.

'When you are elsewhere of your choosing and my approval I will send you the proceeds of the sale of this house and its contents.'

She considered this, a finger pressed at her lips. 'Not good enough. I have to get abroad and find somewhere to live before getting the money. Will you fund my removal?'

'Captain Bidgood?'

She laughed scornfully. Perhaps all was not well between them.

'Captain Bidgood would accompany you?' he persisted.

Again, a scornful laugh but he sensed she was thinking hard.

'That is something I have to deal with – it's not your business.'

Richard decided to press ahead. 'Tell me where you are bound and I will purchase the ticket.'

She nodded. 'What reassurances will you give that the proceeds from the sale of the house and contents will be sent to me? I could be left bereft!'

Richard felt he was within a whisker of getting what he set out to achieve but he did not want to make further concessions. He wanted time to bring his thoughts to a tidy conclusion.

'I shall call upon you tomorrow when I shall expect to learn where you intend to go. On the other matters, you will have to trust me that I will carry out what I promise. I take my promises seriously. What time would suit you best?'

His abruptness surprised her and she tried to re-engage the conversation, but she had to follow him as he made his way out.

At the door he faced her again. He felt nothing for her except contempt. From her expression, the feeling was mutual.

'Well?'

'Ten in the morning.'

The walk to his lodgings, in the face of a strong breeze, refreshed him and a solution came to mind almost immediately. He would transfer the house into the name of Miss Nancy Rosewarne and make the money instantly available. That way Kathrine could have no qualms or excuses to stay longer. He knew she had already made up her mind where she would go and that money was the only obstacle to her leaving. This way he could decide how much he would give. He called in at his lawyers and told Mr Lamb what he intended and asked them to draw up the transfer documents.

*

'Jamaica,' she announced and waited for the news to take effect. 'My brother, Tom, is in sugar on the island,' she explained.

He had forgotten about Tom. The two were much alike in temperament, volatile and reckless but with an acute sense of self-preservation.

'I have already had an offer on the property and contents for nine hundred and fifty guineas and I have agreed to settle on that. I will fund the passage to Jamaica in addition.'

She mused on the sum. 'Not a great deal to set up with.'

'It's enough. You must make your own way from now on.'

'A small allowance of one hundred guineas would hasten my departure.'

'Fifty and no more.'

She accepted this with a wilful twist on her mouth.

'The ticket will be given to you when on board, together with the allowance. You must write to my lawyer when you arrive informing him where the sales proceeds should be sent. It will only be paid to you in person at that address. All correspondence will be in your maiden name, Miss Brompton. There is to be no Mrs Maddern in Jamaica. Is that understood?'

She nodded curtly.

'When you have booked passage, see Mr Lamb,' and he handed her a card. 'He will arrange the rest.'

Contact between him and Lamb would be through Clutterbuck.

He stayed two more days to allow the completion of the transfer of the title of the house to Nancy. Thereafter the property would be rented and the money sent to her bank account.

As he waited, he trawled the shops looking for a suitable present for her. In his heart, he knew she wanted the one thing he could not give. No matter what he bought, it would be an empty gesture. Nancy would accept with obvious pleasure whatever it was he settled on but would she act the part or be genuinely pleased? This was the cross he had to bear from now on. He regretted bitterly the manner in which he dealt with the problem. How would she have been during those days since he left her – wondering, perhaps, if he might just disappear from her life as suddenly as he had appeared? He stared with a glazed look at the gift he had for her.

*

Falmouth was cloudy and the winds in the Roads blustery as he sought a boatman to take him to Devoran. At the quays he recognised Tensy, the boatman he had seen on his first day and he agreed to ferry Richard home. Huddled in the stern sheet, Richard's anxiety returned, his mood darkened in sympathy with the growing evening gloom.

Even in March the evenings still crowded in early, and on days like today the cold breath of winter could still be felt. At the deserted docks, he picked up his burden, took a deep breath and set out on the last stage of the journey. His heart grew heavier with each step, fearing the worst – that Nancy was no longer at home waiting for him. He hesitated at the door, listening for any familiar noises but all was quiet.

Ruth was at the kitchen table, her chin in one hand, dozing. She stirred and saw him holding a finger to his lips as she was about to say something, or more likely scream.

'Is Nancy in?'

'Iss. In the drawing room,' Ruth smiled and nodded enthusiastically.

A good sign he thought.

236

'Whatever have you got there?' she asked.

'A present for Nancy.'

'Aw,' she beamed.

'Take it, Ruth, and bring it to the door and wait.'

He placed his hand on the doorknob and paused. Ruth was right behind him and she waved her arm with a forward motion.

Nancy was sewing at the table, facing him. She did not look up as the door swung open.

'Nancy,' Richard said softly.

She looked and her mouth fell open and she rushed to his side and they embraced and kissed each other time after time. Tears ran down their faces, which they wiped away for each other. They both declared how much they had missed the other until, still hugging tightly, they calmed and looked each other in the eyes and found truth.

'I have a present for you,' and he gave her a large envelope. 'It is the title deeds of my house in Bristol that I have made over to you.' She looked bewildered. 'I was determined to sell it and rather than wait for a buyer I decided that you should have it.'

She was almost dumbstruck, the smile gone from her face.

'Thank you, Richard,' she said but with no real enthusiasm.

'Ah, I knew you would react like this,' he began but she interrupted him hastily.

'It's wonderful, Richard, any woman...'

'So I have something else,' and he walked to the door and opened it a little, just wide enough for a King Charles puppy to bounce warily into the room followed by Ruth.

Nancy's shrieks of delight were suitably subdued so as not to frighten the puppy. She fell to her knees and patted the floor encouraging it to come to her and he dutifully obeyed. She swept him into her arms and smothered the soft head with kisses and more tears.

'Oh he's wonderful, Richard. Thank you, thank you, thank you. Look Ruth!'

Ruth approached and smoothed its head.

'Better than a thousand houses?' he asked.

'Much.'

*

Later Richard insisted that the puppy could not be taken to bed since it piddled at every step. Nancy was still overwhelmed and pondering over the name.

'There must be something Greek or Latin that means something clever?'

'Probably, but he is an English dog and ought to have an English name – or Cornish.'

'Umm...' she mused.

The toing and froing of names went on for sometime before Richard ominously said, 'Nancy.'

She immediately knew, using those fine sensitivities that women have, what the subject matter was going to be.

'Shuush. I'm thinking about my puppy.'

'Nancy.'

'No! Please, Richard. I haven't seen you in nearly three weeks. Three weeks! I have been entirely on my own with only Ruth for comfort.'

She woke early, went to the kitchen to see her latest possession and returned with him in her arms. 'Oh look! Look how happy Prinny is!'

'Who?'

'Prinny!'

'What an excellent choice. Prinny! Yes! Don't let him get as fat as his namesake!'

Chapter 27

Spring, almost imperceptibly, drifted into summer. The world burst into activity with fresh new colours, awakening from the drear of winter. Nancy revelled in the kindlier air and, with Molly, they introduced their new companion to the wider world. Wild flowers were given names; she showed them where the small animals lived and uncovered the hidden birds' nests with their colourful eggs.

Molly was always responsive but Prinny had difficulty with her instruction and just turned his large lugubrious eyes upon her.

One afternoon of increasing warmth, Nancy and Prinny interrupted Richard doing very little.

'Busy?' she asked.

'Yes.'

She smiled indulgently and, as she sat at the window, Cornelius sprung onto her lap and purred loudly.

'What have you seen or heard on your travels this morning?'

'Mrs Trezise is pregnant.'

Richard started in his chair. 'What!'

'You heard me.'

He looked at her critically.

'It's all right, Richard, I'm not going to become clucky.'

Richard nodded knowingly. 'Well Edward's health has vastly improved,' he said, relaxing back into his chair.

'Missus is not happy about it, or Edward, so she says.'

'Oh.' Richard hoped the direction of the conversation would quickly come to a dead stop. He said nothing more but waited.

'Well 'tiss nothing but Edward's fault.'

'True,' he agreed, but inwardly thought Mrs Trezise might have been a willing partner.

'Mildred is seeing to her.'

Those words could cloak many activities and the conversation took on a different tone.

'Ah, Mildred. An excellent midwife.'

'Umm...' She got up. 'Time to get some tea.'

'Oh stay with me. Ruth will get the tea!'

Nancy continued towards the door. 'Ruth is with Mildred,' she said with that tone that brooked no further inquiry, but increased his uneasiness.

Tea was a simple affair and throughout Nancy was distracted. To enquire might well invite a tart reply or it may not – she might be hoping he would ask. *Such are the complexities of the feminine mind,* Richard thought.

'Ruth is a long time with Mildred?'

Nancy drank her tea with studied deliberation and gave the impression of not hearing.

He smiled to himself. 'Her eyes were with her thoughts, and they were far away.'

Nancy looked up and a fleeting smile crossed her mouth.

'Oh, you always know what to say,' she said with more than a hint of exasperation.

'Well, are you going to tell me what is bothering you?'

She placed her teacup on the table and then looked at him squarely, for dramatic effect.

'Sometimes, Richard, you are...'

'What,' he smiled at her struggle to choose the right word.

'Oh!' she exclaimed in exasperation. 'You don't understand what everybody else does. You seem as simple as a donkey but you know full well.'

'Ah. I have been often called naïve.'

'What does that mean?'

'It means I'm easily fooled.'

His downcast expression softened her mood.

'No, I don't mean that. You are the last person I would call that.' She came to his side. 'Something is going on and it worries me.'

'Ruth?'

She nodded. 'She has done it before but she is only helping today.'

'Today? Now?'

'This minute,' she said grimly.

'Oh my god!'

They both looked at each other in silence.

'Did you, or perhaps, do you, expect me to do something? I could not except under exceptional circumstances. If the woman had been the victim of rape or incest then I *might.*'

She shook her head. 'Missus isn't good anyway. Not looking well.'

'Nancy, the law in this country does not look upon abortion as illegal unless there is quickening. The church takes the lead, and the state follows, arguing that until a quickening is felt, ensoulment hasn't taken place.'

'What does that mean?'

Richard thought for a while before going on. 'When life can be felt, then God must have given the foetus a soul – ensoulment – before that, what is in the womb is not a person. But an abortion after that time is murder.'

Nancy followed the explanation. 'Yes. What can we do? When people love each other and...The wrong ones always end up with too many children. What to do to stop them except...' her voice trailed off.

'Who would advocate contraception? Neither the aristocracy nor the church – preventing conception is an anathema to the church.'

Chapter 28

Mr Williams, the manager of the Cornish Bank, was in the chair for the midsummer meeting while Sir William was attending the season in London. He was precise and sharp and sped through the matters of the day. The profits were good and the orders well ahead of supply. When the meeting and the feasting was over Williams sought Richard out and accompanied him to the stables.

'I congratulate you, Mr Williams, on the way you handled the meeting.'

The banker nodded acknowledgement and placed the silver handle of his riding crop against his lips.

'I have to confess I enjoy it. It is quite different from ordinary customer-banker relationships. Here one has to deal with a livelier animal; business with people who are looking for advantage – now! It's exciting stuff, I admit.'

They walked on together and Richard sensed there was something else.

'I am glad of the opportunity to speak with you alone – as banker now – so I have to be more obsequious,' he smiled and looked to Richard. 'When I say you, I actually mean your wife.'

Richard became more attentive.

'Of course I cannot discuss her affairs except in general terms and as long as you agree that I should.'

'There are no secrets between us.'

'Lucky man. Now your wife, in her maiden name, has one of the larger and more interesting accounts and I have not had the pleasure of meeting her. She owns a farm and collects rent from it, and a house in Bristol with rental income; shares in a tin mine and a deposit that would be the envy of most of our citizens.' He paused. 'This is all known to you of course.'

'Yes.'

'I should like to meet your wife to discuss her accounts and to inform her of the services that we offer; would that be something you could perhaps suggest to her?'

'That is very kind of you, Mr Williams. I am sure my wife will willingly come to see you. You may have noticed that my wife, Miss Rosewarne, makes small withdrawals from time to time. This is to fund some small charitable works she does for our more needy neighbours.'

Mr Williams' face lit up. 'Indeed! Might I then make another suggestion? My wife also has a penchant for helping those in need and is forever trying to cajole our friends and acquaintances to make small donations. They should meet! Would you accept an invitation to dine with us?'

'We should be delighted, Mr Williams. Thank you.'

They gained the stables where the ostler had their mounts ready.

'By the by, your own investments of late are yielding a handsome return.'

'The railways?'

'Indeed. I have followed your lead – one of the advantages of being a banker is to see how others do and benefit from it.'

Richard laughed. 'And next?' he challenged.

'What is it to be?'

'Iron.'

Mr Williams smiled knowingly as he took the reins of his horse. 'A pleasure, Dr Maddern, and I look forward to seeing you and your wife very soon. Good day, sir.'

*

Richard wrote to Mr Williams suggesting that they meet on the 7th August when he would arrange for the banker to speak privately with Nancy, and he invited Williams and his wife to dine with Richard and Nancy as they would stay overnight at the Red Lion since the following day Hector and Elizabeth would celebrate their marriage.

Mrs Williams was a short, heavy woman with an ample bosom whose décolletage exposed more as she pushed herself against the table's edge when adding emphasis to a point. She was compelling, however, and held her audience with her lugubrious expression, exaggerated by large bulging eyes. Nancy's fears of having to contribute to the evening's conversation evaporated in the presence of the loquacious Mrs Williams.

Richard expounded on the miners' situation. 'Poor sanitation and too many children. The answer lies in subjects never discussed – forbidden even! Who would crush the love of a husband and wife by forbidding intercourse unless it is only to procreate, as the Catholics do? Not by our church – but no-one advises how to control the number of pregnancies.'

Mrs Williams' colour increased. She had never heard these ideas discussed openly.

'You see the enormity of it all, my dear,' said Mr Williams. 'The good doctor plainly speaks the truth. State and Church have to recognise the problem before change is possible. You ladies must continue in your own ways, and we must bring pressure, gentle pressure, to bear in higher places.'

*

'I don't like the way Mr Williams is so...' Nancy floundered for the right word. 'I mean the way he...what did he say? Something about leaving the important things to men.'

'Ah yes – we men must bring pressure to bear in higher places.'

'Yes,' she agreed. 'What are you doing?'

'I'm bringing gentle pressure to bear in higher places.'

The night was long on passion and short on rest and the morning of the wedding saw them tired and late, with no time for breakfast. Nancy was in high spirits nevertheless, and was giggling and whispering to Richard as they approached the carriage. There a man, slightly older than Richard, was waiting, clearly irritated. He stood aside as they drew near and he signalled, by raising his arm, that they should get aboard – quickly. But Richard was having none of this and stopped.

'Good morning, sir. May I introduce my wife, Mrs Maddern?'

The gentleman, bowed slightly. 'Good morning, ma'am. Dr Luke. Happy to make your acquaintance,' he said, unsmilingly.

Nancy grinned in disbelief at his stiffness. Inside the carriage was a lady and, as Nancy boarded, Dr Luke introduced her curtly. 'My wife, Mrs Luke,' he said waving an arm in her direction.

'Good morning, ma'am,' Richard spoke with exaggerated enthusiasm. 'Haven't kept you, I hope?'

Mrs Luke, in contrast to her husband, seemed happy to meet them.

'Yes, you have!' she smiled. 'I hope that whatever detained you was worthwhile.'

Nancy and Richard settled opposite Mrs Luke and Dr Luke clambered into the carriage, said nothing more, and stared vacantly through the open window to avoid conversation.

'You are looking charming, my dear.' Mrs Luke seemed eager to begin an acquaintance.

'Thank you, ma'am,' Nancy replied and the two women continued to look at each other with interest.

'You are acquaintances of the groom?'

'Yes. My husband and Dr Bull met while they were studying in London.'

Dr Luke coughed but continued to disregard his fellow passengers. It was, nevertheless, a message Mrs Luke understood, and dismissed with a quick glance in his direction before continuing.

'I can tell by your accent, my dear, that you are from these parts, as am I,' she addressed Nancy. 'But you are from elsewhere I would guess,' she said to Richard.

'I am not of this county, ma'am, but have taken up residence in Devoran – not far from here.'

'Yes, I know of it. Not a large settlement, I recall, and close to Sir William Lemon's place. And are you from Devoran?' she asked Nancy.

'Yes, ma'am. My parents have a farm close by.'

'Oh how splendid! And that is how you met?'

Nancy nodded.

'Not much in the way of clients,' Dr Luke interjected sharply.

'No, sir. That is why I set up there to do some research and think about our profession. But I seem to gather patients.'

'One can always gather the poor,' he cynically replied.

'Like our saviour.'

Luke cleared his throat loudly and prolongedly, indicating that he had summed Richard up and returned his attention to the window.

Mrs Luke seemed unimpressed by her husband's behaviour and was determined not to be silenced.

'Dr Luke is a physician attached to the hospital and has a private practice in the town.' Luke added nothing and a short awkward silence developed.

The carriage headed east over a small stream and then up a steep hill.

'St Clement's Hill,' Mrs Luke informed them. Then she saw behind them another carriage. 'Ah, the bride follows close behind.'

'I'm not surprised,' Luke commented. 'We could have taken them.'

'Oh, I'm sure she will look lovely and her father, Dr Warrick, is so proud.' As Mrs Luke and Nancy talked together, Richard looked more carefully at Mrs Luke. Her looks, mannerisms and even her speech seemed familiar, but try as he might he could not recall where he could have met her. Perhaps it was in the Assembly Room when he played.

St Clements church was about three miles from the town, but the hill and rutted lanes ensured the journey was long and arduous. The carriage stopped beside a small row of thatched cottages, the line of which led directly to a lychgate, itself adjoining another cottage. Dr Luke got out first and shook hands with the vicar, the Reverend Francis Jenkins. He was in his sixties and wore a cheerful expression that was undisturbed by Luke making his excuses for being late in a loud voice. As they alighted, the bridal carriage pulled up hastening the four into the church. Once through the lychgate, the Norman tower of the church, encrusted with ancient lichen, reared up in front of them. The short step to the main door was enough to realise it was a small church. The layout of the nave was familiar; the pews were huddled closely together and those of the central aisle awkwardly disrupted by granite columns supporting arches running down the length of the church. Its provenance was embedded in the stones and wood of its construction; a place of

246

peacefulness and tranquillity, which it owed to time.

Elizabeth, the bride processed towards where Hector stood, clearly shaking. *Poor Hector,* Richard thought*, the ordeal was nearly over. Finita iam sunt praetia.*

The service, with just one hymn and a short address by the vicar, was soon over and the newly-weds rode back to the Red Lion followed by the guests.

'Such a long way for so short a service,' Mrs Luke mildly complained, which was enough to set the two ladies discussing the bride, her dress and how she looked.

'You're a bal surgeon, I hear.' Luke had obviously been able to glean something of Richard while in the church.

'Yes.'

'Ah!' Luke exclaimed, his eyebrows rising. 'Rough lot!'

'The miners? Oh, hard work and poverty is what makes them seem rough. I wrack my brains trying to find ways of improving their estate.'

'Waste of effort if you ask me.'

*

Having not eaten breakfast, the effects of the wine loosened their inhibitions long before the other guests arrived. Nancy flushed noticeably, became more animated and engaged all who came close. Her joy was infectious and Elizabeth sought her out rather than remain with some of the more staid guests.

Richard felt a hand grip his arm and turned to see Hector at his side with another glass of champagne. Richard raised his glass in the direction of the bride.

'Elizabeth is looking wonderful, Hector. You must be very happy.'

'Indeed I am. Perhaps the happiest man alive.'

'And where will you honeymoon?'

'Ah. We leave,' and he looked around as if being overheard, 'as soon as possible. Dr Luke has arranged a cottage on Lord Vyvyan's estate for a few days and his carriage will take us there. Just three days in fact – all the board will allow.'

'Lord Vyvyan?'

'Yes. I've told you before, but you seldom listen.'

'To gossip?'

Hector laughed. 'Fact – Dr Luke married one of Lord Vyvyan's daughters.'

*

The bride and groom left the instant an opportunity arose.

Mrs Luke especially sought out Nancy to say goodbye and then whispered something in addition. The other guests quickly dispersed leaving Nancy and Richard alone.

It was early evening and both needed fresh air so they took a turn about town until the twilight began and then returned to the Red Lion. Richard took a bottle of champagne and two glasses to their room.

'I like this hotel,' Nancy said as she undressed in the candlelight. 'It is almost a year since the last time we were here,' she said. 'Remember?'

He did, and he poured the champagne carefully, as buttons were undone and clothes fell to the wooden boards.

'The moon was up, I remember,' he said absently and she sniggered.

'Did you like Mrs Luke?'

'He was a miserable old bugger,' she said ignoring his question.

He laughed. 'But what about her?'

Nancy did not answer but proffered her glass.

'Well?'

'She is a lovely lady. Very friendly and easy to talk with.'

'Hmm...'

'Why are you so interested?' she was becoming bored.

'Well...her maiden name...'

Nancy was busy.

'Never mind – it's not important.'

Chapter 29

April 1805

'Gentlemen, I am obliged to you for postponing this meeting until today.' Sir William Lemon paused in his address to the quarterly accounts meeting at Wheal Andrew. Richard looked upon Sir William with admiration. Past middle age he was still very active in business and Parliament; the latter had delayed the meeting.

'These are parlous times for our country. Bonaparte, *Emperor* Napoleon,' he scoffed, 'has massed the largest invasion force ever known in Texel, Holland and elsewhere along the channel – perhaps one hundred thousand troops and thousands of barges. Be under no illusion – he intends to invade.'

'Do we have any idea as to when, Sir William?' Mr Carthew asked.

'Ha!' and the baronet's face lit up. 'He has a problem to sort first; Admiral Lord Nelson in the Med and the Home Fleet, under Admiral Cornwallis, off Brest blockading the channel ports. Admiral Calder is off Ferrol with a further fourteen ships and Collingwood off Cadiz with four. Only England stands against Bonaparte; we are alone. Let us drink a toast to our sailors and those that command the ships. Rule Britannia!'

Everyone rose, held their glasses aloft, and roared: 'Rule Britannia!'

Richard resumed his seat and listened to Sir William continuing.

'Impressment is a despicable and deplorable practice but...'

He seemed to suddenly realise that the only effect this didactic speech was having on the assembly was to delay the start on the feast spread before them.

'Gentlemen, please!' he yielded the floor at last and invited them to eat.

Richard was the senior bal surgeon, not as a reward for his medical work at the mines, but as a result of his funding the heating of the dries. He had heeded Sir William's warning about the British East India Company becoming too powerful and the threat of state intervention, but he did not intend to lose his position there – indeed, he took more interest in the Company and regularly attended meetings and took Nancy to town.

The feast over, Richard wandered to find Jake and heard someone coming up behind. 'Sir William!'

'Ha! Doctor,' he puffed from the exertion. He drew alongside and slowed to Richard's strolling pace.

'I imagine you think there is more to my being delayed in the House than the explanation I gave in there. The situation is much worse.' He glanced around. 'We have lately learned that Bonaparte's plan is for ships to break out of the channel ports and the Med and make a dash towards the West Indies. This is a feint to get Nelson to follow. The French ships will rendezvous and return *en masse* to the channel and the invasion is free to start. All efforts are being made to acquaint Nelson with this news. The fastest frigates are searching the high seas. The Channel Fleet of twenty ships of the line is being reinforced, but the French could have up to forty battleships and more from Spain – thirty perhaps.'

He shook his head despondently. 'We must prepare ourselves for the worst and be ready to fight to the last man. The question is where will they make landfall? Ireland may be discounted following the failed rebellion.' Sir William wagged a finger. 'Here, right here. Our coast is most vulnerable – too much coastline to defend. The Almighty helps those who help themselves. So we must look to our bright swords and brave hearts.'

*

At home, Richard was greeted with children's laughter and Prinny's barking before he set foot in the kitchen. Nancy refused to adopt but fostered any child in need of care. She rented one of

Mr Lanyon's Almshouses at Playing Place when the numbers were more than she could cope with at home. Today there was just Molly, Nancy's constant companion, who, now aged nearly eight, and grown much taller, was well proportioned and had long brown hair. Molly was always full of fun and high spirits as she demonstrated by calling out, 'Uncle Richard,' and running into his outstretched arms.

Later that evening, after supper, Richard played Beethoven's piano sonata number 14, opus 27 no. 2 – gentle, lilting music that had become a firm favourite. Nancy sat on the couch by the fire sewing, with Prinny in her lap. Those simple things he cherished most and, if it became necessary, were what he would die defending.

*

Two days later, on a dull spring day with a brisk wind, there was an urgent knocking at the door. Elijah stood there, panting, almost unable to speak.

'Bob's been taken! Pressed.'

'When, Lij?'

'We was getting in the creek when I see a ship's boat rowing up the harbour, hard. Bob was fishing and not taking notice.' He paused to get his breath. 'They was on him afore he knew anything. Put up some fight mind, but they had him in the end.'

Nancy hurried to the door. 'Who's got him, Lij?' she asked urgently.

'A frigate in the harbour – one of the Impressment Service!'

'Ready for sea?'

'No. He's windbound – wind is right in the harbour and getting heavy. He can't weather the point until the wind changes; tomorrow earliest.' Another pause but this time it was to think. 'Funny thing though. One of the crew hops into the *Maid Nancy,* but instead of taking the prize to the frigate, he hoist sail and run away. He sailed up the creek and went ashore at Daniells Quay. I'd bet my *Sweet Union* that it was Billy Uddy in that boat.'

Nancy grabbed Richard's arm. 'We must get my father back tonight!'

'Yes. For sure!' The words were easy but the how was far

from clear. A captain had the right to impress; no law had been broken.

'What is the easiest way to get to see her captain?'

Elijah's head dropped. 'Speak with Ginger. He might know what to do.'

Ginger appeared from behind Elijah. 'I'm here, Doctor. The only possible solution is to offer quota money for Bob's release. The captain may accept it, but I would suspect that he is not happy at taking one man and losing another. If you could recover Uddy as well that might help your cause.'

Elijah took Richard by the arm and whispered fiercely into his face.

'The *Sweet Union* will be at Custom House Quay in two hours.'

Richard and Nancy arrived at Custom House Quay in Falmouth consumed with desperate desire, but with no plan. They saw the frigate anchored far out, displaying a single lanthorn at the stern. It was after six in the evening and dusk was gathering, hurried on by lowering clouds and a southwesterly gale. The quays were deserted.

Nancy sighed heavily and fingered Lady's rein. 'It's hopeless isn't it? We have no chance even if we could get out there.'

As they waited, the *Sweet Union* arrived with more than Ginger and Elijah on board. When safely secured, Richard and Nancy stepped onto the deck and looked around.

'Tinners!' Richard said quietly.

'Yes,' Ginger replied. 'Twenty all told.'

Elijah came to Richard's side and scanned the frigate through a glass.

'Thought so,' he said. 'There's a boat being lowered and coming ashore.' Richard raised his own telescope and dimly saw a small shape leaving the side of the vessel. It made slow way against the short seas and wicked wind.

'A woman and two children I'd say,' Richard observed.

'Iss. Captain's wife and his cheelds,' Elijah confirmed. 'Two sailors pulling and one in the stern sheets.'

'Where are they heading?'

'I should say the family will be staying in that hotel for the night,' Ginger said indicating the nearest building. 'There is no conveyance out of Falmouth at this hour.'

Richard was immediately alive with a plan.

'Nancy you must follow them into the hotel and learn their names and obtain some articles from them that I can show the Captain.'

They watched the passengers cautiously disembark in the disturbed waters. It was beginning to rain and the three made haste up the steep slope from the quays. Nancy set off, taking as she went a pistol from the holster on Jake's saddle. She followed the group into the hotel in time to see a skirt disappear around a bend in the staircase. Nancy moved quickly to follow them. On the first landing, they had stopped while the mother opened the door. The children entered first and, as their mother turned to shut the door, Nancy thrust the pistol in her face.

'Be quiet,' Nancy hissed and pushed the woman back into the room. 'Light the candle – quickly!' she commanded. The candle glowed and the woman shielded her children in her skirts.

'Do as I say and no harm will come to you. What is your name?'

'Mrs Fortescue.'

'You are the wife of the captain commanding the frigate in the harbour?'

She nodded.

'First name?'

'Mary.'

'The children?'

Mrs Fortescue held them closer. 'What do you want with them?'

'Just their names. Quickly!'

She jumped at the imperative. 'George, aged six and Anne, who is just four.'

'A man was pressed this afternoon. You and your children are hostages until he is safely ashore. Do you understand?'

Mrs Fortescue nodded.

'You will write a letter saying you are held captive and will only be released unharmed when the man is ashore.'

Nancy motioned she should start and while she wrote the

children stared at Nancy. Her heart cried out to comfort them. Nancy snatched up the letter when it was finished.

'Now, some articles from each of you that your husband would recognise. That brooch you are wearing.'

Mrs Fortescue unpinned a cameo brooch and handed it to Nancy.

'What of the children?'

'They have toys – but they will not sleep without them.'

Nancy held out her hand and the children yielded their favourite toys – a small wooden cockhorse belonging to George and Anne's rag doll. Out of the window, overlooking the quay, she saw a shadowy figure sheltering from the drizzle. She brought the candle to show her face and waved. The figure detached from the shadows and ran towards the hotel. A soft tap at the door and Ginger was standing there holding a finger to his lips. Nancy handed him the note which he read quickly and murmured his approval. He took the toys and brooch and went without another word. Nancy breathed a sigh of relief and looked to Mrs Fortescue.

'Get the children to bed and make yourself comfortable. It's going to be a long night.'

The tinners and Elijah had commandeered two pilot gigs, each able to carry eight men, and two smaller rowing boats. The four boats set off, but did not head directly for the frigate. They gave it a wide berth and lay waiting some distance below its stern and high on the larboard side. Ginger and Richard in the tender off the *Sweet Union* then made slow progress rowing to the frigate, keeping close to the shore on the Bar beach side of the harbour where they cheated the wind and avoided most of the short seas.

'The ship is not a frigate but one of His Majesty's sloops: the *Agnes*. Fourteen guns arranged on the gun-deck; all twelve pounders and probably some six pounders on the main deck,' Ginger said. 'The master will be a commander. His orders are to impress as many men as possible by visiting ports and inspecting commercial shipping. The men are either held in a guard boat – there, over there,' he pointed to a large vessel moored close to the shore, 'or on board the *Agnes*. When he can he will take them to the fleet – to Admiral Cornwallis probably.'

254

Ginger stopped rowing in the shelter of an old hulk, allowing Richard to regain his breath.

'They are supposed not to take anyone under the age of eighteen or over the age of fifty-five but who's to tell? More than half the crews of British ships are pressed men. From here on, I shall do the rowing and you must sit in the stern sheets. I shall come alongside on starboard – that is the official side, which the captain and higher officers use. On a night like this, in a homeport, the watch will be huddled somewhere out of the weather.'

They got within twenty yards of the *Agnes* without being challenged.

'Just as I thought.' Ginger looked over his left shoulder and hailed.

'On deck!' once, and immediately again, 'On deck!'

Then more insistently and louder, 'On deck there! Look alive!'

A scarlet-clad marine sentry, bobbed up over the rail.

'Who goes there!' he shouted and brought his rifle up. An officer appeared at his side and stared into the darkness.

'Mr de Tour with an urgent message for Commander Fortescue,' Richard called.

There was a short pause as the boat came alongside and the painter thrown to a seaman. Several sailors were at the ship's side trying to penetrate the gloom.

'What business...'

The officer's question was not finished and a scuffle broke out on the deck. Only a few grunts and groans punctuated the capture of the watch.

The tinners and Elijah appeared at the rail. 'All clear,' he whispered. Richard and Ginger clambered up the side and through the open gangway. Elijah was beaming with pleasure. 'Does my old heart good to give these buggers a bit of roughing.'

Richard felt bound to see to the injured officer, but his eyes focussed and there was no trickle of blood to betray them.

'Don't worry bout him. Just a little kiss – that's all,' Elijah said and brandished the belaying pin that administered the loving touch.

'Now, sir, you will conduct us to your commander and introduce us. I am Mr de Tour and this is Mr Annear. You will say we are on His Majesty's business and have urgent messages. There is a pistol at your back – beware! You will make no mention of the others aboard or that the watch is taken.'

There being no quarterdeck on the sloop; they gained the cabin by descending the companionway on a short ladder, passing lockers containing weapons. The officer hesitated at the door and received a dig in the back from Ginger. He knocked and opened the door with one movement interrupting the commander's bark.

'Come!'

'Visitors, sir, on the King's business with urgent messages.' He then retired smartly into the company of three tinners.

'What!' Fortescue uttered as he stood in the low cabin. He was short and heavily built, of aggressive appearance, with an almost shaven head and a face charred by heavy growth. His face wore a frown and judging by the deep furrowed lines, this was not an unusual expression. Richard and Ginger entered into the confined space and arranged themselves so each had a view of the commander.

'This is most unexpected gentlemen. What business do you have at this late hour? The King's business you say?'

Richard cleared his throat before attempting to speak and hoped his voice would be firm. He placed his bag on the table separating him from the Commander and opened it as if to extract papers. But he just left it open.

'It is a matter of an impressed man taken this afternoon I want released.'

A look of astonishment greeted this demand and Fortescue fell back into his chair. Slowly he repeated what Richard said. 'You want an impressed man released! And who are you to make such a request?' His voice rose with anger.

'I am Mr de Tour, a King's Ordinary Agent who is about to leave with dispatches for Admiral Cornwallis.'

Fortescue smiled evilly. 'A spy! You must give me some proof. I cannot hand over a prime seaman without proof. I know the man you speak of; he was the only one taken today and he cost me dearly. Three of my men were badly beaten – laid-up in the sickbay and one bastard took the opportunity to make off with a prize.'

Richard hesitated. 'I have no papers with me. We left in haste fearing that you would be weighing before nightfall.'

The smile turned to a snarl. 'No papers?'

Richard shook his head. 'Except those for Admiral Cornwallis – it is vital not to delay.'

Fortescue looked out of the stern window although there was only blackness to see.

'I cannot weather the harbour entrance and I am surprised that you think you might.'

'Our vessel is a small cutter, sir,' Ginger explained.

'Important papers are being delayed because of an impressed man – one man?' Fortescue spoke to himself. 'I think not. Now, tell me plain or I'll call the guard and have you both clapped. I might impress you both if a better explanation is not forthcoming.'

'That is as much as I am able to tell you about the man – you must be the judge. What you will possibly know is that Lord Nelson is, at this moment, scouring the West Indies to find Villeneuve. Villeneuve is acting under a plan devised by Bonaparte himself. Villeneuve will meet up with Rear Admiral Missiessy, returning from the Indies, and the combined fleets will then sail directly for the channel where only Cornwallis is on station. The defeat of the Channel fleet will leave the way clear for the invasion to begin. This is what Cornwallis has to learn.'

Fortescue turned half away from them thinking hard about this information. He came to a decision and faced them with his arms firmly on the table.

'That Lord Nelson has left the Mediterranean station is known throughout the fleet. The rest of what you tell me I cannot verify but I don't believe a word of it! Something so important would have the Port Admiral here demanding the man's release. Furthermore, apart from Lord Nelson, I cannot believe that one man is so vital to the success of your mission.' He rose to his feet and yelled. 'Guard!'

The door opened. A large marine sergeant, trussed and gagged, fell into the small space onto the floor. A tinner, whose shoulders were too broad to fit in the opening, grinned at the commander.

'What in hell's name is the meaning of this?' Fortescue demanded.

Ginger seized the moment. 'Having your ship seized while in a homeport will do less for your prospects than being short of the quota of pressed men. A court-martial and then hanged from the yardarm is your bleak future.'

'Watch overcome?' he asked in disbelief.

'Yes,' said Richard.

Ginger pressed home the attack. 'We will assume the man in question is one of the quota from this parish. Eighty pounds should buy his release.'

Stunned by the knowledge that he was in danger of losing his ship, Fortescue defended his position.

'Impressment is legal and any judge will uphold my right! I hold the King's Commission! I'd rather die...'

'What if your wife and children should die instead?' Richard asked quietly reaching into his bag and placing the toys and brooch on the table. Fortescue now looked bewildered. He picked up the cockhorse and looked upon it fondly then the doll and finally his wife's brooch.

'What have you done with them?'

Richard didn't answer but threw the note from Mrs Fortescue onto the table. Her husband read it carefully and then placed it squarely back onto the table.

'You are despicable. Hiding behind innocent women and children is an act of cowardice.' He sighed resigned to his fate. 'What now?'

'Send the sergeant for the man and bring him here directly. There are two swivel guns pointing into the fo'c'sle should any attempt be made to resist. The lockers have been forced and our men have rifles and pistols.' Ginger made the situation very plain.

Fortescue briefed the unarmed sergeant fully before ordering him below. Minutes passed with the slowness of hours. All on deck stared in the direction of the companionway from the fo'c'sle. Bob Rosewarne was not able to walk unaided and the sergeant had problems getting him up the ladder.

'Bear a hand you bloody lubbers,' he growled and two tinners rushed to help.

When they dragged him into the cabin any sympathies Richard retained about the commander's position evaporated. Rosewarne was barely recognisable. His face was a mass of contusions, cuts and bruises. The left eye was closed completely and the other black and swollen. Blood had trickled from his mouth and dried but more worrying was the blood that had seeped from his ears; his white hair, matted with blood, had the appearance of a darkly coloured wig. He clutched his right side where the main source of his discomfort lay.

'Get the commander out of here,' Richard ordered. As Fortescue passed he whispered fiercely into his face. 'You have no right to accuse others of cowardice.'

Richard filled the washbasin and began to clean the blood from Bob's face.

'I'm going to bind your ribs very tightly which will support you and ease the pain when you move.'

Bob nodded.

Richard tore the cot sheets into wide, long strips and began to bind his chest. As he pulled tightly, Bob gasped and a painful grimace set on his face. Richard continued winding and pulling hard all the way to his armpits. Then working his way down again, covering the hard stomach muscles.

Richard brought a candle closer and examined Bob's face. A hard blow had probably fractured the right cheekbone. Elijah interrupted him at the open door.

'Much longer, Mr de Tour?' A smile came and went quickly. 'Bob's looking bad. All right is he?'

'Yes, he's all right. Most of the damage is down his right side.'

'Iss. I see that,' Elijah said quickly and closed the door.

With Bob patched up they considered their next move. The *Sweet Union* was the only sensible mode of transporting Bob. Richard and Nancy must go with him.

'Will they give chase?'

'Only in the ship's boats and an axe through the garboards will put paid to that,' Ginger said.

'Do you know the formal wording that discharges a quota

man on payment of the fee?'

'I've written a few in my time,' he said bitterly. At the table, he began to write as Richard counted out eighty guineas.

Elijah was at the door again, agitated.

'Take Bob out carefully and get him into one of the gigs. Get him flat if you can – if not, support him in a sitting position. He'll go back with you in *Sweet Union*.'

A tinner came to bear a hand and Richard followed them a short distance until he was close to the commander.

'Bring him into the cabin,' he ordered.

Fortescue was scowling fiercely and stood resolute and defiantly waiting.

'You'll hang for this!' he hissed with rage.

'Sign this document.'

He smiled. 'This is not the correct format,' and threw the note back onto the table.

'It is exactly correct.' Ginger was incensed. 'Sign it or be damned. For you will be damned for this day's work if word gets out of your ship being taken!'

Richard dropped the heavy pouch with the money onto the table.

Fortescue's eyebrows rose and he calmly spilled the coins and counted. He faced Ginger. 'You must have been at sea sometime to have learned all this.'

Ginger pointed to the quill.

Fortescue dipped the quill into the inkwell and signed his name 'Under duress,' he said.

'Who will know?' Richard gave a sharp reply. 'Left-handed I see, commander.'

'What of it?'

Richard said nothing more but deduced that a left-handed person would find it more natural to strike someone facing him on their right side. Richard collected the coins and put them in the pouch and then into his bag. Ginger smiled at this and nodded his approval.

'Out!' Richard ordered, and the tinner grabbed Fortescue roughly and threw him onto the deck.

'Lower away, handsomely,' Elijah called and Bob disappeared below the bulwarks.

'Now we shall batten these boys below and leave four of our men to make sure they stay quiet like.'

As they herded the watch below, Richard made for the gangway and whispered to Elijah 'He's left handed – the commander. He did it.'

'You'd better get in the boat,' he said, his voice full of meaning. 'I'll come in the tender – later.'

*

Nancy was still at the window trying to penetrate the darkness. The only light was from a torch on the wall of a building overlooking the quay. She had seen no one in the hours since Richard left for the ship. The two children were asleep but Mrs Fortescue was wide-awake and watchful.

From the corner of her eye, Nancy saw Ginger standing by the torch and waving to her to come down.

'I must go now,' Nancy said as she got up. 'They are come ashore.'

As she was about to close the door Mrs Fortescue asked for the toys.

'I shall do my best.'

Ginger waited, just out of the umbra of the torchlight, and called softly as she approached.

'This way, Nancy.'

'Is father alive? Have you got him? Do you have the toys?'

Ginger laughed quietly. 'Yes to all three.' Then he placed his hand on her arm – a cautionary gesture. 'Be prepared to see him in a bad state, however. The doctor is caring for him on board the *Sweet Union*. You are to sail back.' He anticipated her next question. 'The horses will be taken back by a tinner and he will have the toys.'

Chapter 30

The sun was a brilliant orange ball that shone directly into Nancy's eyes as she walked at a slow pace to her childhood home. The low angle made it difficult to see where she was going and she kept her eyes to the ground. They had all reached Devoran safely. At first light, Bob asked Nancy to inform her mother he was free. Free! She did not expect it – not against the might of the navy. There was still the worry that Fortescue could raise a hue-and-cry to search out the perpetrators of the treason. She sighed and wished with all her might that this would not happen. She was desperately tired, more than she had ever felt in her life.

She did not see Billy Uddy standing a short distance from the farm gate waiting for her. At first, she saw boots. Shielding her eyes with a hand, she recognised him, although he had changed a lot. He had grown thicker about the waist and heavier in his face such that his jaw line was lost in folds of tightly expanded flesh. The blond hair was close-cropped resembling stubble more than the fine curls he once displayed.

'Billy?'

'Who else, my sweetheart?' he said without warmth.

'What do you want?'

'You,' and his strong arms were about her shoulders forcing her to the ground. 'Father isn't coming to help you this time!'

She pummelled him with her fists and screamed until he punched her face very hard. She was helpless until the buzzing in her head and the dizziness passed.

'Please, Billy,' she pleaded.

'Certainly, Nancy, right now,' he laughed.

'Billy, I'm a married woman.'

'I know that you bitch. Couldn't wait for Billy could you. Well now, you'll get what you deserved all they years ago when

Billy didn't touch you. Treated you like a lady, I did. And for what?'

He was lying on top of her and his weight pressed so she could barely breathe as he fumbled with his breeches. She had to think about a way of stopping him but his strength and her tiredness made it nigh impossible. Billy was going to kill her, of that she was in no doubt. She had to direct all her mind and body to saving herself. She remembered where he kept his knife. Being behind his shoulders, she could not reach it until he was closer. It was an unenviable predicament but in those few seconds, she resigned herself and relaxed.

'That's better, my sweetheart.'

Nancy put her arms around his back and felt the sheath and the handle of the rigid blade. As she withdrew it, Billy made the opposing motion and she gasped. He grunted with pleasure. His humped and rounded shoulders in movement and his tight grip did not present any vulnerable part of his body in which to thrust the blade. It waved harmlessly about his shoulder – she had to endure and wait for an opportunity. Uddy's movements became more urgent and she opened her eyes to see his face grimace. He screamed with pleasure and then collapsed, panting.

This was her moment and she gripped the knife firmly. But he didn't stop moving and gradually he resumed.

'You thought Billy was done. No, my handsome, I waited too long for this. You're going to be fucked like never before. That prick you married isn't up to Billy. I am going to fill you up with Billy! Come next year you'll drop Billy's boy.'

What he said did not register, her mind consumed with survival. He was taking revenge – hateful and prolonged. Gradually he became more passionate again and worked harder. He grunted, spoke encouraging words to himself in foul language and spat into her face as his moment approached again. She made herself ready gripping the knife firmly. But another hand snatched it from her. Someone else stood behind Billy who she could not see against the bright light.

Billy reared up, crying in his extreme ecstasy that instantly changed into screams of agony. He stood roaring in pain and anger. Billy's assumed ally had plunged the knife into his back.

'You!' he shouted in disbelief. 'My bastard!'

Jamie glanced at Nancy who was regaining her feet.

'Go!' he called to her. 'He won't come after you.'

She looked toward Billy, who staggered and fell to the ground, unable to reach behind to remove the knife.

Home! She must go to her mother. It was a short distance to the farm gate and as she opened it, she saw her mother was at the door looking worried. Seeing Nancy, she ran to meet her.

'Whatever is the matter, Nancy?' she said staring at the folds of dress clutched tightly between her legs.

'Billy!' Nancy replied quietly and nodded in the direction where he last was.

'Billy?'

'He raped me! Jamie has stabbed him.'

Her mother mouthed 'rape' and looked again at where Nancy was holding herself. Placing an arm about her waist, she assisted her towards the house.

'Are you in pain, my love?' she asked. Nancy shook her head.

'Daddy is at our house. Safe.'

The emotional strain on Mrs Rosewarne was almost unbearable. Joy and outrage, relief and distress vied for predominance in her mind. The concentration of effort to bring the outraged Nancy to safety in her home took over and it was not until Nancy was in the parlour that she cried into her apron. She sunk to her knees and they hugged each other in a comforting embrace.

'Where's Billy?'

'By the path that leads to the Downs.'

'Will he come here?'

Nancy shook her head. 'No. He might already be dead.'

'Oh!' her mother softly sighed. 'What trouble this day has brought. Are you hurt my love?'

Nancy's only physical hurt was from the punch to her face and her hand went to that spot where there an angry violet bruise was already forming. As she examined her feelings, her mother guided her with gentle words to her old bedroom. A depression settled on her as she thought about her situation and her future. Through no fault of hers, she would become an

264

object of pity, scorn and then a social pariah. Her first thoughts were how Richard would react.

'Lie on the bed, my sweet, and I will bring a basin of warm water. Don't worry about what Richard may think – he will be very understanding and forgiving I am sure.'

In her old room, weariness overcame her as her mind flooded with memories. This was where she made her childhood dreams: handsome men came to pay suit by the dozen and fat cherub babies arrived by the score. By the time her mother brought the water Nancy was sound asleep.

Mrs Rosewarne considered each course of action open to her. The blunderbuss over the mantle was always loaded; she took it down and checked it. She could leave it with Nancy or take it with her. If she met Billy, she would use it and in many ways that would be the preferred option. After leaving a note, she hefted the heavy gun and with grim determination set out on the short journey to Devoran.

Blood marked the spot and she paused to imagine the scene. A thin trail of blood was just distinguishable leading to the path to the Downs. Bringing the gun into a firing position, she tentatively entered the tree-lined footpath. The crowded trees arched over and cast a dark shadow and she feared going too far into that tunnel.

She listened and heard nothing unusual.

'Wasting time,' she said to herself and retreated to the main path.

At Nancy's home, all was quiet. She trembled at the door before pushing it open, calling: 'Hello!'

Ruth came in a rush. 'Aw Missus,' she blew the words from her mouth in agitation.

'Bob is upstairs,' and she pointed with rapid repeated motions to the ceiling of the kitchen.

'How is he?'

'Aw,' she moaned, her hands going to her ears. Then she brightened, quickly, not wishing to convey the awful state. 'He's better than he was,' and she nodded emphatically. 'Doctor fit him up proper. He's sleeping now,' she cautioned.

In the bedroom, Richard slept in a chair close to the bed where Bob lay. She crept in, looked at her husband and wept.

Even that small noise awoke Richard and he got up and saw the blunderbuss.

'There's more bad news, Richard.'

He waited fearing the worse.

'Nancy.' She looked into his face fearing greatly what affect the news will have.

'She ran into Billy.'

'Uddy! Is she all right?'

She nodded. 'Alive, but he raped her!'

Richard fell back into the chair and buried his head in his hands. His tired brain was having difficulty functioning so Mrs Rosewarne helped to shape his thoughts.

'She is not damaged, Richard. Fortunately, Jamie, his son, was there and stabbed him.'

'Is he dead?'

'I don't know. There is a trail of blood on the path to the Downs but I didn't venture too far.'

'I must see Nancy,' and he began to stir from his stupor standing in readiness.

'She's sleeping, poor dear. Exhausted.' She laid a hand on his arm. 'Be gentle with her, Richard – she is still Nancy.'

Richard kissed her on her forehead and left.

*

He made loud clumping noises as he ascended the stairs and called out. He peered around the door, smiling, against his real feeling. She rose onto an elbow and burst into tears. Choked with emotion she could not speak. He held her away and touched the bruise on her cheek. She recoiled. 'Sorry. Any other injuries?'

She didn't answer. He had to ask questions that will bring back the horror.

'Shall I have a look?'

He fetched hot water from the constantly simmering kettle in the parlour, and filled the basin in the bedroom and washed her carefully.

'No damage.'

'Will you still love me, Richard?' she asked plaintively.

He kissed her. 'Why "will"? I do and have done so since the

first time I set eyes upon you not far from this spot. Remember?'

She smiled. 'Yes. I do.'

*

Mainly foxes and badgers used the water-rutted path. Few people came this way and the going was rough and uneven. It was close to noon but the sunlight did not penetrate enough to make tracking easy. The signs were there; the occasional spot of blood and mud-skids where Uddy had dragged himself over the more difficult areas.

The path broadened and Richard stood upright. He listened, and heard only the rustle of the breeze in the trees: then, a soft moan, not far away. He put his bag down and crept a few yards further, pistol in hand. Uddy lay, eyes shut, against a rocky outcrop from which a spring issued.

'Uddy!'

His eyes opened but they did not know where to look.

'Aye, sir,' he called and his hand went to his head. But it did not reach his brow because the movement caused pain and he groaned.

'Uddy!'

He opened his eyes with a start.

'You! Come to finish me off? I'm done for – I'm a gonner. My own boy,' he cried in disbelief.

Richard saw the knife still in Uddy's back. It had entered in a poor place. Close to the spine but angled such that it might well have damaged the kidney. He moved Uddy's shoulder and he shrieked.

'I can't remove the blade.'

'Nor can I,' Uddy rejoined and tried to laugh.

Richard fetched his bag and measured a large dose of laudanum. There was no hope for the man. He had lost a lot of blood and removing the knife would certainly kill him. Because of his unusual circumstances, killing Uddy could easily be misconstrued; a heavy dose of laudanum would bring about the desired end.

'Drink this, it will ease your pain.'

'Why are you doing this?' Uddy asked after swallowing the

draught. 'I just had your woman. If you was a man you would put the knife in again.'

I would with joy, Richard thought.

'I am a doctor and I have sworn to help those in need – even you.'

'Nancy put up a fight mind,' he said more to himself than Richard. 'Should have done it years ago. Got guts though. Got her father in the end. That old bugger's gone to sea and won't be back. He had some hammering.'

That he rejoiced in the ill-treatment of Bob Rosewarne was loathsome and Richard did not want him to go to hell with even that small gratification embedded in his damned soul.

'We rescued him last night. He's safe and well in Devoran. Twenty tinners came to his aid and we took the ship. Fortescue was punished for his miss-deeds.'

Uddy snorted. 'He's another bastard! He deserves it as well.'

Chapter 31

'Morning, Doctor,' Ginger said, fidgeting with his hat. 'Sorry to hear about Nancy.'

Richard nodded.

'It's true then! I hoped it was just a rumour.' They both stood quite still and silent for a short while.

'I came to say that *Agnes* sailed yesterday, so I guess Fortescue will not report the matter. It's...just something I thought you might want to know...'

'Thank you, Ginger – you're very kind.'

*

'You have a worried look, sir! Come, this is where problems are aired and overcome.'

'Grave business brings me here, Mr Clutterbuck,' and he related his terrible story.

Clutterbuck listened and gradually his expression matched that of Richard's.

'Grave indeed, Doctor,' he said when Richard finished. 'Some refreshment is required, I think.' He tinkled a bell, a clerk opened the door and Clutterbuck asked for brandy. 'And Mrs Maddern, how is she?'

'Remarkably resilient and philosophical.'

Clutterbuck leant on his forearms and pushed against them slightly for emphasis. 'Rape is thankfully uncommon – leastways reported rape. I daresay there are many instances not reported, but those that are often involve violence.'

'He hit her once which almost rendered her unconscious and after that she ceased to struggle. He is – was – a very strong, heavy man, which I know from personal experience.'

Clutterbuck's eyebrows rose and he made a note but let it pass for the time. He sucked in a deep breath. 'The first rule,

Doctor, is that a client should have complete trust in his lawyer and tell all there is to know. There will be a Coroner's Inquest into Uddy's death and we do not want to hear something there that might surprise us. It is my job to probe, turn over stones to reveal things concealed, innocently or deliberately. I must know all if we are to proceed and be successful.'

Richard nodded.

'Good,' and Clutterbuck sat back into his chair. 'Now, firstly your wife and the deceased were friends from childhood that extended beyond the age of puberty. Yes?' He glanced to the desktop. 'I should rightly ask your wife this question and I shall when the time comes, but do you know if they were ever intimate?'

Richard shook his head.

'You were, of course, a rival in love. Was Uddy upset by this?'

Richard cleared his throat and swallowed hard. 'He was indeed. At first all I knew was that Nancy – Mrs Maddern – had made it known to him that he was not wanted, sometime before I arrived.'

'I see,' and he made a note.

'That did not stop him. Moreover, he assaulted me.' Richard told of the whipping incident and the time he fired his pistol at Uddy.

'So you were in danger of your life! Did you report this?'

'No, I felt it unnecessary; I could deal with the matter.'

'You said earlier you experienced the physicality of Uddy personally. What did you mean by that?'

He told of the evening Uddy burst into his house when Nancy was gravely ill.

'He was drunk you say and still he overpowered you. What stopped him using the knife?'

'Mrs Rosewarne held a pistol to his head.'

'Yes, I imagine that would be very persuasive. Why did you not report this to the constabulary?'

'Between client and legal advisor?'

Clutterbuck smiled. 'Of course. When I have all the known facts, I then have to navigate that treacherous course of declaiming all that I want known while hiding that which is

270

better not declared, but not obstructing the course of justice. Not something for the uninitiated.'

Richard related the happenings of that time and his deliberate deception that led to Uddy being impressed.

Clutterbuck listened with growing interest. 'A pretty story, Doctor. Uddy couldn't read of course?'

'No.'

'But if the note survives then...'

'I doubt that it does, otherwise some wily person would, by now, have tried to extract money for its return.'

'Did anyone else read it?'

'No.'

Clutterbuck's quill scratched some notes and then after re-reading them he began again.

'Let us go over the scene of the rape. Sometime during the dreadful ordeal a person, not recognised, stabs Uddy with his own knife?'

'The light was directly behind Uddy and she could not see properly anyhow. It was a combination if you see what I mean.'

'Yes,' Clutterbuck drew out the word indicating a doubt or difficulty he had. 'The next person, as far as we are aware, to see Uddy was yourself?'

'Yes.'

'Close to death?' Clutterbuck added. 'Well a doctor would know and not ordinarily be challenged,' and his voice trailed off.

'Meaning?'

Clutterbuck gave a nervous coughed. 'You had good reason to kill him. He had just raped your wife.'

Richard felt a door had opened to questions he needed to ask.

'Would a coroner or a jury sympathise with a person accused of that?'

'If you had caught him in *flagrante delicto* and stabbed in the heat of the moment, then I think, yes. Defending your wife, whom the law regards as your property, even to the point of killing someone, would probably be justified. However, later, when the man is defenceless, they may not view it in the same light.'

'What about a passer-by?'

'Anyone coming to the aid of someone being attacked would not be guilty of murder, in my opinion.'

'A lesser crime?'

'Perhaps no crime at all! But why are you taking this line?' He went on quickly. 'Let us take another tack a prosecutor might explore. You and your wife find Uddy and stab him to death. The excuse offered is rape but no other doctor examined the lady. Why was your wife abroad so early in the morning? Moreover, there is Uddy in exactly the spot!' He paused and looked earnestly at Richard. 'However, a third party giving evidence of the rape would lend great weight. But we are considering only you in this instance. No-one else is involved. That is correct?'

Clutterbuck had taken the scent and Richard knew he would worry at it, like a terrier does a fox, until he put it up. He was less uncertain of speaking of Jamie's role now that he had smoked out half an answer.

'You have a gentleman's notion of what early to work means. Nancy is a farmer's daughter and getting up before light is a way of life. She has resisted a life of gentler occupation. Your point about how Uddy should know she was walking that path at that time, I agree, is unexplainable. I didn't extract the knife for fear of putting myself in that hazardous situation you have alluded to, although as a doctor, I am honour bound to go to his assistance.'

Clutterbuck nodded. 'You are protecting someone – the third party that did stab Uddy!'

Richard paused before answering.

'Yes. That passer-by came to the rescue of my wife and probably saved her life as a result.'

'Who?'

'I will tell you but on the understanding that if we decide not to call him as a witness, you will honour that.'

'I will not feign from pressing very hard should I feel it necessary.'

'Agreed. It may amaze you if I tell you it was Uddy's, or Uddy's father's, illegitimate son. Still a boy or a youth; fourteen or fifteen.'

Clutterbuck's face lit up to Richard's amazement.

'Delicious. Life is so much more unpredictable and extraordinary than any novelist can imagine, don't you think? Why would he have done it?'

'He hates both Uddy and Uddy's father for the way they treat his mother whom he adores.'

Clutterbuck picked up his papers, tapped the edges repeatedly onto the desk until they were tidy, watching Richard all the while.

'You, and your wife, must not speak to anyone on this matter. Should the constable press for a statement you should refer him to me. I must speak with your wife and James Uddy. Since they are two, and living in close proximity, Mohammed shall come to the mountain – tomorrow in the forenoon.'

*

'I shall ask you some questions you may find distressing and difficult to answer, but please bear in mind that I need the information to present the best possible case for you. If there are some parts of your story that put you in a bad light, we will find a form of words to explain to a prosecutor, who might ask the same awkward question. I hope you understand and are prepared for that, Mrs Maddern?'

Nancy sat at ease and looked undisturbed by Clutterbuck's direct brusque manner. She had spent a good deal of the night lying awake, thinking, and placing ideas and thoughts into compartments, mentally labelling those that could be freely spoken of and those that needed to be treated cautiously. One compartment was to stay firmly shut: her father's rescue. She was anxious for Jamie even though his testimony might be vital if she and Richard were suspected of colluding in Billy's death. She had the fond hope that Clutterbuck would obviate the difficulties; after all, that was why they were paying him – to protect them from the law.

'Yes,' she replied. 'And I prefer to be called Nancy.' She smiled and Clutterbuck saw how beguiling she was.

'We need to speak about the violent assault on your person...'

'Rape.'

Clutterbuck cleared his throat noisily.

'Just so, the rape. As clearly as you can remember.'

She began to describe the morning walk to the farm.

'Incidentally, Nancy, please forgive me for interrupting you, but we have heard nothing of your father?'

'Daddy had an accident and had broken several ribs and had cuts to his eyes. He spent the night in our house where Richard was attending him. Mummy had returned to the farm the previous evening and I was on my way to help with the morning chores.'

'Thank you, Nancy,' Clutterbuck said with that particular tone and drawing out of the syllables informing of a problem or a difficulty solved. He leant back in his chair, looking at her, holding the feather tip of his quill to his mouth.

'What were you thinking about that morning?'

Nancy knew full well what was in her mind that day and everyday. Why was the Almighty so perverse in joining her to a handsome, rich man who loved her dearly but denied them the precious gift of children? She had long since come to the conclusion that the words of love and care sung every Sunday were biased; the unfortunate, the ill-treated and the cheated ought to write other hymns of condemnation and sing those as lustily.

'You're a long time answering, Nancy,' Clutterbuck said quietly and ended her reverie.

She laughed lightly. 'I'm not answering.'

'Why?'

'Women's thoughts – unsuitable for men.'

Clutterbuck threw a lasting stare. The woman he first categorised as just pretty was transforming before his eyes.

'You have been married for more than five years but no children?'

Her smile faded and her colour rose as the lawyer found her Achilles' heel.

'That is unforgivable and I beg your pardon. I do not mean to pry where I shouldn't.'

The damage done, she looked to her dress with downcast eyes and sad expression. He was at a loss how to continue and coughed nervously, but at last she answered.

'It's a natural enough question and one I have to contend

with from my friends, showing concern, and enemies, being cruel.'

Clutterbuck sighed. 'All I hope is you have enough confidence in my abilities to co-operate fully, but I fear I have dented that through carelessness and being too clumsy.'

'What would you like to ask me?'

'Well, women's thoughts apart, what else were you thinking?' He smiled trying to lighten the mood.

Nancy went over the events again and concluded saying, 'Jamie, took it from me and stabbed Billy. Billy stood, despite his pain and yelled at the boy who backed away. This allowed me to get up and flee.'

Nancy's voice faded and there was silence except for the scratching of Clutterbuck's quill. He viewed his efforts and then grunted.

'Just one more question, Nancy. How often do you see Jamie, ordinarily – around this house and close by for example?'

'Not often.'

At Uddy's farm in the afternoon, in the parlour, Clutterbuck met Mrs Uddy, Jane Prior and then Jamie Uddy. Clutterbuck was surprised to see a sturdy youth rather than the boy he was expecting. He wore clothes better described as rags; breeches that were indescribably dirty, stiff with dried filth from the yard and greased over from the wiping of his hands. He had no shoes and his feet carried the muck of the yard wherever he went, even into the house. Clutterbuck explained why he was there, stressing it was not to find a guilty person, but to gather evidence to present to the coroner who would hold an inquest into the cause of the death of William Uddy.

Jamie showed signs of nervousness when he was alone with the lawyer. His eyes darted about the familiar room as though for the first time. They seemed not to settle and they avoided Clutterbuck to the extent that his whole face turned from side to side like a ship tacking, never looking dead ahead at Clutterbuck.

'How old are you?'

'Fifteen come June.'

'You live here with your mother, whom I have just met, and your grandmother, Mrs Uddy.'

'And the old bastard!'

'Who?'

'Old man Uddy. Granny's old man. He lives in the barn.'

'He doesn't live in the house?'

Jamie shook his head. 'I kicked him out when Billy was pressed. Showed him the eevil. I'd a stuck the bugger if mother didn't stop me!'

'Evil?'

'Dung fork.'

'He helps around the farm still?'

He laughed scornfully. 'No. Old bugger's too tired to lift his ass off the seat never mind work!'

'So you do all the work?'

'Mother help – good as gold she be, and Gran, when she can.'

'Can you read, Jamie?'

He scoffed at the suggestion.

'Do you see any other people besides your mother and your granny and her husband?'

He shook his head.

'Tell me what happened the day Billy Uddy died.'

Jamie stirred on the stool, adjusting his posture as another adjustment took place in his mind. He sniffed before starting and wiped his nose on his sleeve.

'It all started the evening afore. He got here late and come in as though he never been away. 'Twass a bad night – raining and cold so'west wind – he was leaking wet. Well, we was all frightened to see him and let him get to the fire before saying nothing. Mother was affrighted the most. "What you doing here?" I said.

'I said, "You'm get out again, we don't want you!' He laughed till I shoved the axe in is face – Ha, then he didn't laugh no more.'

The lawyer wrote, intrigued by the tale, and noticed Jamie looked directly at him now.

'What then?' he encouraged.

'He said, "You'm no match for I boy," but he wasn't sure, I could tell. I said to him, I said, "One good hit and you'd be buggered for good," and he knew what I was saying.'

Jamie relived the scene and was just as angry; his fists clenched and arms waved vigorously.

'He got to the door and he said to Gran; "I haven't had nothing to eat all day". So I said, "get over to the barn and I'll bring a pot for the both of you," and I did, but I pissed in it as well.' Jamie laughed and expected Clutterbuck to join in but he managed only a wry smile. He needed no encouragement to relate his tale and went on at a pace, each little detail embedded in his mind.

'We took turns to watch. We had the loaded gun ready. In the morning, 'fore sun up, he was out, and came to the door asking for a brandy. He had water and nothing more and left. I followed him and I knew where he was going – the doctor's house, after Maid Nancy – Mizz Nancy,' he corrected himself.

'Why?'

'He always said she was promised him, but she never was!'

'Were you armed? Did you have your gun or axe?'

Jamie for the first time looked foolish. 'No! Bleddy fool, I forgot! Anyhow, he waited and so do I. Then Edward came, and then Nancy stepped out. 'Twass just light. She started down the lane going to her place – the farm. He ran in front of her. I had to go other way,' and he waved an arm in a wide arc that Clutterbuck interpreted as a flanking movement.

'Why not just warn Nancy?'

'Iss,' he said, thinking about that. 'I s'pause I wanted to see what he was up to and if I could a catch him, give him a bleddy good hammering. But I should have...'

'Warned her?'

'Iss. Didn't think to,' he said quietly realising his mistake. 'No. He had to...'

'Give you reason to attack him?'

'Iss,' he smiled. 'That's right.'

'You put her life in danger.'

Jamie nodded. 'Never thought.'

Clutterbuck waited and Jamie continued to think about his conduct at that time.

'What happened next?'

'I was too late,' he said absently and then stirred at the telling of the vital acts.

'He was already at her on the ground. Red in his face and grunting, like a...like a fucking boar. Bastard!' he said with venom.

'What did you think about that? '

Jamie had first to clear up a misconception. 'He might be my father or the other old bastard. Don't know which of them is. But I see both have Mother anywhere. Beat her first and then fuck her till she cried; sometimes both of them. I saw it all – right in front of me and Gran. And I could do nothing.' Tears of rage welled in his eyes and Clutterbuck appreciated why he hadn't warned Nancy; he intended to kill Uddy no matter what. Nancy was his excuse.

'Then?'

'I see Nancy had his knife in her hand! I took it and put it right in his ribs. Wha! He screeched like a stuck pig.' Jamie was again reliving the joy of revenge.

'He could hardly stand. He was bollock naked,' he laughed hysterically. 'He tried to get me but he was done for. Nancy got up and ran off. He said to pull it out but I said "No, do it your bleddy self. Die, you bastard, die," I said. I did. And laughed at him.'

'Then you took the small path to the Downs and home?'

Jamie nodded.

'And you didn't go back later?'

'No.'

*

Mid-morning on a bright May day, when all the world ought to be full of joy, those in Clutterbuck's office were glum. He arranged the chairs in a close semi-circle in front of his desk and chattered amiably while they settled. Richard flanked Nancy on one side and Jamie the other, with Jane next to her son.

'Helston flora next week,' he said, attempting to lighten the mood. 'Have you ever been, Doctor?'

Richard glanced at Nancy and took her hand. 'We have indeed, Mr Clutterbuck. Nancy took me there a few years ago. It was a memorable experience for both of us.'

Nancy, for the first time in days smiled and her face brightened briefly.

278

'You are obviously keen dancers.' Clutterbuck's remark brought a snigger but he was already diving into the mound of paper on his desk.

'I will read what I have written, which, if you agree, will be or will form the basis of your statement for the coroner.' He looked up through his glasses and squinted.

'Firstly to Mrs Maddern.' The joy she felt was short-lived and vanished completely as he read the statement. It read fluently but left gaps that an intelligent inquisitor could probe deeply.

'Dr Maddern, your part in this is peripheral, in the sense that your involvement is after the event. The only point of contention might arise from the several assaults Uddy made upon your person. But I am satisfied that you will be judged blameless.'

Clutterbuck shuffled his papers as a prelude to reading Jamie's statement.

'Jamie's statement is of prime importance since it exonerates both Mrs Maddern and the doctor of any complicity in the death of William Uddy. His statement as a third party clears each of you.'

He read the much-shortened version of the events that Jamie gave. It carefully sidestepped any allusion to Jamie's hatred of Uddy and omitted the declarations of wanting Uddy to die from the stabbing.

'Jamie you must always be civil, I mean respectful, to the gentleman who will ask you questions. Do you understand?' Jamie nodded but Clutterbuck knew he did not understand the power of the court. 'You must look the gentleman in his face when he speaks to you and call him "sir" when you speak.' Clutterbuck looked away to his desktop shaping his words in his mind to confront the next difficulty. 'It is important that your language is moderate – I mean the use of oaths and words not used in normal conversation must be avoided.' He turned to Richard. 'Is there any likelihood of giving the lad some guidance in this respect?'

Richard's eyebrows arched in helplessness. 'We can but try. Would it make such a difference? The coroner will quickly realise what his background is and surely take this into account?'

Clutterbuck gave a drawn-out 'Ye-es. And a further point. Perhaps better clothes, more fitting the occasion and...soap?' He said this quietly as if Jane Prior should not hear. 'The date of the inquest has not yet been set. The coroner is to place a notice in the *Mercury* calling for witnesses and any other persons who have knowledge that might bear on the matter. I should think a month perhaps – later in May hopefully.'

*

'Richard, I think it best if you take Jamie to an outfitter. Clothes for working boys are the usual trade for many of the shopkeepers. He needs something a little better than just working clothes – a fustian jacket and hardwearing breeches. Perhaps a new white shirt? A cap as well.' Nancy issued the orders. 'Jane, we must find a dress for you as well.'

For the first time in her life, Nancy faced a dilemma of status. Jane was dressed poorly in a brown threadbare dress that had seen many years of hard work and hard washing. It was patched and ill-fitting. The shopkeeper might think they were acquaintances, equals in someway. On the other hand, Nancy could treat Jane as a servant and herself as her mistress. The struggle in her mind she finally resolved with a strict lesson in humility. Jane was not inferior; in many ways, she was better, determined to bring up her son as best she could under the most appalling circumstances.

*

Richard was having a difficult time with Jamie.

'You must understand, Jamie, that the court listens to what you say and makes a judgement based on your...' He lost his way and decided that Nancy's ability to use the local dialect was required to calm the speech and moderate the language.

At the outfitters specialising in working men's clothing, Richard purchased decent hardwearing items that would be suitable for the coroner's hearing. The biggest difficulty was in persuading Jamie's feet into boots, since they had rarely, perhaps never before, been encased so closely.

*

The four met up after shopping. A slight embarrassment arose about what to do next. Jane was not insensitive to the pause in conversation. 'We must start off walking or us'll be late.'

Nancy and Richard said nothing for sometime, each avoiding the other's eyes, as Jane and Jamie walked away.

'That was badly done. We should at least have offered them refreshment.'

Nancy nodded still not looking into his eyes.

'I feel ashamed.'

'Stop!' she cried. 'Enough.'

They took refreshment in the Red Lion eating in near silence and speaking mainly to be polite at the table. The journey home was as prickly, and Richard fell into a well of despond. The wind in her face had brought a tinge of red to her cheeks but the accustomed smiles were gone along with her happy joy of life.

Nancy's thoughts of late had begun to take an unexpected direction. She should have bled twice since the rape. At first she thought the shock of the rape and subsequent trauma had upset her normally regular cycle. Now she began to think that she might be pregnant. It would be Billy's child. What trouble that might bring. Yet amid all her fears, doubts, and misgivings, she felt an excitement she could barely contain. A child was all she longed for in her marriage and she was not at fault if she should have Billy's boy. But, it was not Richard's – how would he react? She remembered the fateful words he spoke when Mrs Trezise had needed Mildred Cocking; "if a woman has been the victim of rape or incest, I would".

Her mind was in turmoil, unable to come to terms with the conflict of Richard's love and the child in her body – two opposing loves that might destroy each other and her. She would have the child if nature allowed it, but what if she lost Richard as a result? She wanted both but feared the worst. She shook her head to free the thoughts that ran through her mind endlessly and unanswered. But they stuck fast and were driving her to madness. She needed Richard's advice but dared not ask.

They supped in the same cloak of politeness.

'Some wine, Nancy?' Richard asked pleasantly.

'No,' came an unnecessarily sharp reply as though the question had been in her mind before it was asked and rejected.

'Sorry, Richard,' she said, a strained smile following the words.

He smiled back. 'It will do you good.'

'Will it?' another quick reply volleyed down the table.

He laughed. 'You are on edge, my love.' He was about to add more but she burst into tears. He was at her side in an instant with comforting soft words. He was imagining one thing, but she knew the real reason for her tears. She had to continue with the deception even while he tried to kiss her anguish away.

*

Nancy had several conversations with Jamie, as Richard had advised. At first Nancy stuck to the agreed plan to get to know the boy better and gain his confidence. When she realised she was carrying his half-brother it was a disturbing moment and, from that time, she carefully studied the shape of his features, his body, and the exact colour of his hair.

On the Sunday before the inquest, Jamie and all the other members of the household laboriously carried water to the bath. When full, Nancy strode into the room in an ankle-length white apron carrying a long-handled brush, a large bar of soap and a coarse hemp bag. This was her routine when she fostered a child.

'Now, Jamie, take all your clothes off and put them into this bag for burning.'

The instructions were clear but Jamie did not seem to comprehend. Nancy stared at him. 'Clothes!'

Jamie looked to his mother whose face was rigid.

'Come, Jamie!' Nancy called, and she pulled at the smock and his mother stepped forward to help. He wore nothing underneath except years of ingrained dirt. He stood forlorn in his canvas breeches, waiting.

'Come on, Jamie, get the breeches in the bag.'

Nancy saw him as a young boy with nothing to hide. His head dropped and the colour rose in his cheeks.

'Mizz Nancy, I can't do that,' he said solemnly.

Nancy advanced purposefully, tugged at the string about his waist and then pulled the grime-laden, stained breeches down. She watched them all the way to his feet and then dropped the article into the bag.

'In the bath, Jamie,' she cried triumphantly. Jamie, with hunched shoulders, tried unsuccessfully to cover his nakedness with his hands. His shame was overpowered by the force of his maleness and, exposed for all to see, his shame grew.

'Oh!' Nancy said quietly. In addition to her fond hopes of the likeness of her baby to be, she saw what he might grow into. She took him by the arm led him to the bath and forced him, gently, into the warm water.

'Hot, Jamie?' she asked.

'Iss!' he yelped, but getting most of his anatomy underwater and out of sight was the preferred option. Her planned intentions were now in disarray. She handed the soap and brush to Jamie.

'Scrub yourself until every bit of dirt is removed. And wash your hair! We will wait outside until you say you are clean and wrapped in the towel.' Jamie nodded and Nancy gave a quick jerk of her head to Jane and they both left. Once outside they both dissolved into suppressed laughter and rushed downstairs.

'He's a fine boy, Jane. He'll make some girl very happy one day!' Nancy teased.

Jamie washed as best he could and dried himself with the towel before wrapping it around his waist. He saw himself in the pier glass and looked away. Then cautiously, as though spying on someone, he looked again at his own reflection. His hair fell in soft ringlets reaching almost to his shoulders. The colour was a white blond – he touched his hair and seemed pleased. As he did so, the towel slipped from his waist. The first reaction was to retrieve the towel and cover himself, but curiosity got the better of him and he slowly exposed his image again and stared. Nothing he saw displeased him. His muscles were well defined and his belly flat. His penis appeared larger in the mirror. He grasped it and wondered what it would look like if he rubbed it until hard. Then he remembered, and dropped it. No sooner had he wrapped the towel around his waist, Nancy came in followed by Jane, both of whom expressed amazement at his new fresh appearance.

'Look at you, Jamie Uddy! Oh how I wish I had hair like that – such colour and curls.'

He looked away and blushed. Jane beheld her son and beamed with pride but made no comment.

'Now, we have brought your new clothes for you to try on and we shall see if they need to be altered. When you are ready come down.'

As they admired him in his new cotton breeches, white shirt, smock and boots, Molly came into the kitchen. She did not expect to see so many people; Jane she knew, but she did not recognise Jamie and looked coyly in his direction.

'Hello, Molly'

She smiled at Nancy. 'Hello, Nancy. Hello, Uncle Richard,' she replied. 'Mrs Uddy.'

Still looking at Jamie, she suddenly figured out who the young man was.

'Jamie?' she asked cautiously.

'Yes,' said Nancy.

Molly was emboldened and stood close to Jamie. 'You look different, Jamie.'

'You haven't seen I for a while, Molly.'

'No,' she agreed. 'But...' Then she retired to the shelter of Nancy's skirts and looked from a safe distance.

'Now we must all carry water for Jane,' Nancy broke up the gathering that was in danger of becoming petrified with embarrassment.

Chapter 32

Edward had harnessed Jake in the fly to take Nancy and Richard. As Mr and Mrs Rosewarne arrived in the farm cart, Jane and Jamie appeared with Jane wearing her new green dress. There was common agreement she should not ride in the back of the farm cart so Edward saddled Lady. Richard was surprised when Mrs Rosewarne eagerly mounted Lady and sat confidently in control of the horse. Jane rode on the seat of the cart alongside Bob, while Jamie travelled in the back.

The Market House, which also served as the Court House, was at the end of Boscawen Street. It stood on pillars and, in the open space underneath, carcasses of meat, fowl and game hung from hooks while busy shoppers attended the butchers' blocks. Inside the Court House the atmosphere was already stifling and malodorous from the sweating audience compounded by the smell of meat carcasses wafting through the open windows.

Nancy felt sick and Mrs Rosewarne sat with her. The coroner, Mr John Edwards, was short, his rotund body ensured his clothes fitted him snugly at every possible place. His eyes narrowed to see better, and his glasses were essential for reading. Good living had mostly freed his round, full face of features. Tufted greying eyebrows were wild, but beneath his eyes sparkled and creases surrounded them from frequent jocularity. He coughed to draw attention and looked over his spectacles.

'The duty of this inquest is to establish the cause of the death of one William Uddy of Carnon Crease Farm in the Parish of Feock. You will hear that a young married woman had been raped by the said Uddy and in the course of that most vile act was put to death by stabbing by a minor, James Uddy, the supposed son of the said William Uddy.'

He paused and looked to his notes. 'That Uddy died from a

fatal stabbing is not doubted but we must nevertheless examine carefully what facts there are and consider whether there was any foul play in Uddy's death.'

He now addressed the three witnesses. 'Let me emphasise that each witness I shall call will testify under oath. Anyone found guilty of lying or concealing the truth will be guilty of contempt and, as such, can be committed to prison directly from this court.' He weighed these words with a silence and stared at the three main witnesses.

'Now I shall call the first witness. Mrs Nancy Maddern.'

Nancy felt ill and near to fainting. She gripped the wooden rail to control her swaying and her eyes looked to the ground. Prison was no place for a baby to be brought into the world.

'Please state your full name, age and address.'

'Nancy Rosewarne, aged 26 and I live at Devoran.' The last of her statement was lost in loud cries from the public.

'Order!' Mr Edwards called and banged a gavel several times. He looked carefully at Nancy.

'Am I to understand that you are not married to Dr Maddern?'

'Yes,' she replied quietly.

Clutterbuck hid his head in his hands.

'Well,' said Edwards slightly exasperated. He picked up her deposition and amended the document accordingly. He then began to take her through the statement but she broke down early on and the coroner dismissed her, saying that he had no more questions, adding that she had suffered enough distress. Nancy was escorted to the back of the room shielded by the arms of her mother. Richard was called next.

'State your full name, age and address.'

'Richard Baring Nugent Maddern. I am 37 years of age and I live at Devoran.'

'And your profession?'

'Physician with a degree in Medicine from the University of Oxford.'

Richard's voice was unwontedly weak and unsteady.

'Thank you, Dr Maddern.' Then, in a slightly higher pitch, he asked.

'I have to ask you if you are married, Doctor?'

'Yes sir.'

'I see,' and he picked up a letter. 'I have a letter from a Captain Bidgood that at first I found difficult to believe but now...Can you confirm that your wife is residing in Jamaica and that she is there at your insistence?'

'Yes sir.'

A cry of anguish from the back of the court drew his attention and he saw Nancy leaving the Court House. No sooner outside, than she vomited, much to the annoyance of the butchers.

'Please stay where you are, Doctor. I am sure the lady is being well taken care of,' Edwards said firmly. Slowly, he read the deposition, asking questions of Richard whose mind was elsewhere.

'How long after the stabbing was it before you found Uddy?

'More than one hour but less than two.'

'And Uddy was still alive when you found him?'

'Yes – barely in my judgement.'

Edwards nodded. 'And you gave Uddy assistance in the form of medicine?'

'Yes. I gave him laudanum.'

'That you happen to have on your person?'

'Yes. I had my bag of instruments and medicines that I took to my wife...'

Edwards made a note and went on.

'You did not withdraw the knife?'

'No.'

'Why not – would that not seem a reasonable thing to do?'

Richard raised his eyes level with those of Edward's. 'In my judgement, had I done so, it would have hastened his death. Furthermore, I was in a very precarious situation where my...wife's assailant was at my mercy. I was cognisant of the fact that I could be accused of killing Uddy. With these two considerations, I decided to give Uddy something to relieve his pain and no more.'

Edwards picked up another sheet of paper and read it to himself.

'I have a letter from a Dr Morse.'

Richard blanched noticeably with anger.

287

'Dr Morse writes of what he describes as your unusual practises in treating the sick and injured. He cites the case of a miner who fell several fathoms and sustained an injury to his head. He advised bleeding and you disagreed. He then goes on to cite another instance where you and another doctor certified the death of an experienced mine's captain due to a fall when he, after a cursory examination, thought that unnatural causes should have been brought into question.' Edwards looked directly at Richard challengingly.

'Dr Morse writes about two occasions when our medical opinions differed. In the first instance, the miner recovered from his injuries. As to the second case, Morse's opinion could not be solicited at the time, he being absent, so I invited Dr Andrew, a recently retired bal surgeon for a second opinion. We were both of the same opinion that Captain Tonkin had died as a result of an accident in the mine, probably from a falling object.'

Edwards nodded and looked to his papers.

'I have now to inquire about your own relations with William Uddy. Can you elaborate on your statement that you came into conflict with Uddy shortly after making the acquaintance of Miss Rosewarne?'

Richard related the two events where he had to defend himself from Uddy and then the last time when Uddy invaded his house.

'The usual course of action would have been to send for the constable, would it not?'

'My concern was still Miss Rosewarne's condition. I was in need of willow bark and successfully entreated Uddy to do something useful towards saving the woman he professed to love by fetching what I needed from an apothecary in Falmouth.'

'Hmm,' Edwards interrupted. 'Was Falmouth your choice because you knew of a ready supply of the willow bark?'

Edwards was closing in on a sensitive area. Whether he had other letters he had not revealed yet or was merely asking from supposition, could not be discerned.

'It was Uddy that suggested Falmouth.'

'I see. So it was he that suggested Falmouth,' Edwards repeated for emphasis.

'I wrote notes describing the willow bark and asking for directions to the apothecary. I also gave Uddy some money.'

Edwards pursed his lips as he considered this information and picked up another piece of paper. While looking at the paper he put the proposition that Richard dreaded.

'So, Uddy, with two notes he is unable to read and money sets off for Falmouth in the evening, already the worse for drink and encouraged to ask in the local taverns for directions; a town renowned for press gangs. Should he be so taken it would solve your problems at once?'

Edwards still played with the paper as he waited for a reply.

'Not being familiar with the workings of the law, I cannot give an opinion as to what might have happened had I chosen the option you first suggested, that of informing the constabulary. But I can imagine, for such a serious assault, Uddy may well have faced imprisonment or transportation, either of which would also have solved my problem, as you put it.'

'Quite so, Dr Maddern,' Edwards tossed the paper away – it was a bluff. 'You are dismissed for the present but do not leave the court.'

Jamie was next up in the witness box, his bared head bent to avoid the coroner's gaze.

Edwards adopted an avuncular attitude.

'Master Uddy,' he said and smiled, attracting Jamie's attention.

'Iss, sir.'

'Your name is James Uddy and you are fifteen years of age?'

Jamie nodded.

Edwards read from the deposition outlining the background of relationships up to the point when Uddy reappeared on the eve of his death.

'The next day you followed Uddy guessing what his intentions were – to find Miss Rosewarne. When you came upon them Uddy was violating Miss Rosewarne?'

Jamie's jaw was slack and he screwed his new hat in his hands. Edwards had to put the question again.

'When you found William Uddy what was he doing?'

Agitatedly wringing his hat, he still did not answer.

Edwards looked to the deposition and read. 'You found Uddy violating Mrs Maddern? Yes?'

'He was fucking her, sir!'

Edwards looked exasperated and called for order at the mixture of mirth and disapproval from the floor.

'Gentlemen, I must have silence in the court or I shall clear it. The questioning of this young man is vital to obtain the truth even if it means that the language you might hear is that of the street, which you almost certainly are not accustomed to in your homes.'

'Now, Jamie. What did you do next?'

'I sees Mizz Nancy had his knife and I took it and shoved it in his back,' and he pointed to the place in his own back.

'Then?'

'He got up squealing like a stuck...He backed away from Mizz Nancy, so she got up and ran home.'

'And you? What did you do?'

'He said "get this here knife out," but I said, "No. Get it out yourself". He couldn't reach behind, see.'

'Then?'

'Aw, he started moaning and saying he was done for.'

Edwards looked at him carefully and with an air of finality asked. 'Did you feel sorry for what you had done?'

Jamie nodded vigorously and then pronounced the well-rehearsed reply. 'I didn't mean to kill him, sir – only to save Mizz Nancy.'

Over the murmur of approval, Mr Edwards said, 'You are to be commended for your action, James Uddy.'

Then he addressed the court. 'I shall adjourn to consider my verdict,' and he snapped his gavel down.

Richard gained the cleaner air outside and ran into the large hand of Bob Rosewarne.

'They've gone home, Richard,' he informed him quietly. 'Took the fly and Lady.'

Richard, utterly dejected, faced the wall of the building and hung his head against the rough stones. A hand rested on his shoulder. 'She's in a tissy that's all. She'll get over it, my son.'

*

290

Mr Edwards waited until all were seated and quiet.

'Having considered carefully all the facts, I have come to my verdict. Miss Nancy Rosewarne is blameless in the death of William Uddy and she has the sympathy of the court in her great distress that was so evident this morning.

'Dr Richard Maddern gave a clear and truthful explanation of the history of his dealings with Uddy and his actions at the time of his imminent death are commendable. Few, I think, would have behaved as he did.

'Now as to James Uddy the situation is more complicated: there being a history of hatred between the two – William Uddy and himself. I believe James Uddy was waiting for an opportunity to avenge his mother for the ill treatment that William Uddy and William Uddy senior had meted out to her over the years. Yet I have to consider the facts before me and acknowledge that there had been opportunities before, but not taken. I therefore consider that James Uddy acted in the best interests of Miss Rosewarne and had come to her rescue. To that end, I also acquit James Uddy of any criminal act. Death is recorded as resulting from a stabbing when being apprehended in the gross act of rape. The case is closed.'

*

'He lied! He didn't marry me because he is already married!' Nancy threw more clothes into a saddlebag. Then she remembered. She must remain calm or perhaps lose everything.

'Nancy, calm yourself. Richard has already given you more than most husbands would give in a lifetime.'

Nancy wiped her eyes. 'Bought me more like. You know what that makes me!'

'Enough! He has been good to you – you have everything you want and more besides. There are many men in the same position. Divorce is nigh impossible in this country so people in love live together...'

'Why are you defending him, Mother? If he told me he was married, I would have lived with him. But he didn't!'

Mrs Rosewarne fidgeted in her chair. 'He probably thought he could risk losing you by telling the truth. We all keep secrets to protect those we love.'

Nancy scoffed. 'What secrets?' she asked incredulously. '*You* don't have secrets.'

Mrs Rosewarne was silent, but her agitation belied her quietness.

'Sit down, Nancy.'

'No, I shall leave immediately.'

'Where are you going?'

She sighed heavily. 'I must have time on my own.'

'Please, Nancy, sit for just a while. I have something I must tell!' her mother raised her voice, which was so unusual that Nancy was stunned.

'A secret?' she asked quietly and full of wonder.

'Yes. A secret I have kept from you all your life.' She raised an arm to silence Nancy. 'Now is the time to tell you.' She took a handkerchief from the sleeve of her dress.

'I am sorry that I have not told you sooner and what I have to say will shock you. Daddy isn't your real father.' She spoke quietly with her eyes cast down, not looking at Nancy, fearing the worst. Nancy was stunned into silence by the revelation and stood quite still.

'Not my father?' she repeated and her lips began to tremble. 'You...'

'Yes, I am your natural mother,' Mrs Rosewarne anticipated the question. Nancy began to cry and her mother put an arm, tentatively, around her shoulders to comfort her. Nancy did not move away and she was encouraged to go on. 'I hate myself for not telling you when you were a little girl – it would have been easier then.' Tears quickly followed and the two embraced closer.

'I thank God you do not reject me, Nancy! Do you forgive me?'

'Why didn't you tell me?'

They sat down holding hands across the table. 'Oh it's a long story and once I decided not to tell you I foolishly kept silent. It was the only thing Daddy and I quarrelled about. It's best I tell you – now.' Mrs Rosewarne now looked directly into Nancy's eyes before going on.

'I am the daughter of Sir Richard Vyvyan and my mother was an heiress to a large estate in her own right. I grew up in the

292

lap of luxury having all and anything I wanted. All I wanted was horses and my father indulged my every whim. I was only a few years old when I followed the hounds and when just thirteen, demanded a hunter, far too large for me as my father warned, but I created until he agreed. I was never out of the stable unless I was riding. I knew all the stable lads.' Her thoughts for a moment drifted off. 'I grew up and some thought me beautiful. My hair was golden and long and my eyes were like yours! The young men who hunted were always making love to me – no, not actually! That is what we used to say. I didn't care for them. There was a son of a tenant farmer who I used to see when I rode in the mornings early.' She sighed heavily as she remembered. 'He was the most handsome man I had ever seen and still to this day. The work he did built his body wondrous well. Wide shoulders and chest covered in a blond down that I used so to admire. He was tall and graceful, his face strong and adorable. His hair was the lightest colour – far lighter than mine.' She looked to Nancy. 'Like yours. Eyes of deep blue of course.'

Nancy nodded and looked indulgently on her mother, forgetting that time was rushing past.

'Well you can imagine the rest. We fell in love – actually this time. I even forsook my horses to see him. They were just a means to take me into his arms. We loved every minute we could and inevitably I became pregnant with you.'

Mrs Rosewarne smiled happily, as she recalled that time.

'And?' Nancy asked with foreboding.

'My love was banished – his poor father turned him away in order to keep the farm – there were others: brothers and sisters. Even that was a generous gesture from my father, although I didn't see it that way then.'

'Where did he go?'

'America. He would have fought for the colonialists for sure. What else? I don't know what happened to him from the day he left. I hated my father,' and she paused in her narrative and looked away. 'I thought he could have sent me to his farm to live with my dearest love.' She wiped her eyes and then softly resumed.

'I stole all that I could, money, jewellery, silverware and like you today packed all my clothes and belongings. I had more time than you have and amassed a great deal in chests. I bribed one of the stable hands to load a cart and harness my hunter and I was ready to go. Just as I was about to slap the reins he held my arm. "Where was I going?" he asked me and, in truth, I didn't know. I just wanted to leave. I knew the lad well. He was always so attentive. He smiled sweetly and said he knew why I was going but unless I had a plan, he would not let me go. I said, in jest or perhaps desperation, "If you won't let me have his head you'll have to come with me!" And he did! He jumped up beside me and we drove off. He was Bob Rosewarne, and having such a big man with me was all the security I needed, and how I leaned on him since.'

Nancy was entranced but saw the time and knew that her fate was similarly in her hands.

'I have to go, just like you did, to think about my future.'

'No, you mustn't. Richard will not turn you away, I warrant.'

But Nancy finished packing. 'Will you help me carry these bags please? I must go even if it is for a few days. My mind is muddled and you have made it worse!'

Despite her misgivings, her mother helped with the heavy bags and Edward placed them on Lady.

'Please tell me where you are going, Nancy. I must be able to reach you if need be!'

'Mr Lanyon's Almshouse, but you must promise not to tell Daddy or Richard.'

Chapter 33

Richard's first reaction to Nancy's leaving was to wait. Mrs Rosewarne said Nancy needed time on her own to think. After one week he hoped the time for reconciliation was fast approaching. Two weeks; an anxiety set in of a proportion he had not previously experienced. He worked more at the mines during the day but in the evenings and nights the burden of not having his love close by pressed in on him. Late one evening he read from one of Shakespeare's sonnets all that might be said about the loss of a love and the torment it brought.

> *Weary with toil I haste me to my bed*
> *The dear repose for limbs with travel tired:*
> *But then begins a journey in my head*
> *To work my mind when body's work's expired:*
> *Lo, thus by day my limbs, by night my mind,*
> *For thee, and for myself, no quiet find.*

From the note Nancy left he tried to distil hope.

Dear Richard,
Today has been the worst of my life. To confess to living in sin was not earth shattering to me – I have no pretensions of advancement in society. But to learn that you are married was a very great shock. I understand now why you could not marry but not telling me the truth was...
I have to go away on my own.
Wait for me and remember me.
Your dearest love
Nancy.

But by the end of June he despaired.

'Have you heard from her?' he asked Mrs Rosewarne. She shook her head but said nothing. Richard pressed her. 'I mean has she written?'

'Yes.'

Richard was galvanised by the news. 'When?'

Mrs Rosewarne bowed her head. 'I am ashamed for not telling you, Richard. A week ago, but Nancy said that you should not know. If I get any more letters, I shall ignore her instructions and bring them to you. Here is the letter.'

It said just that she was well, no more.

*

News of the momentous events happening on the grand stage filtered down slowly via the weekly papers. Nelson had arrived in the Caribbean. The Admiralty received Nelson's news on 8th July, delivered by a fast brig that Villeneuve, with the French fleet was returning, and heading for the channel ports. Nelson stepped ashore, the first time in two years, at Gibraltar on the 20th July.

A letter arrived in early August from his Bristol lawyers informing Richard that 'Miss Brompton' had died in March. The ship bringing the letter had had to avoid the hazards of the large French fleet. He had been a widower at the time of the inquest and could have truthfully answered that he was not married. He crushed the note and threw it with great anger against the wall.

*

HMS Victory anchored at Spithead on the 18th August and Nelson travelled through the night to be with Emma at their home in Merton Place.

That same afternoon Richard strolled slowly to the quays at Devoran and sat on the warm wood. His usual sharp and decisive thinking had deserted him in a fog of confusion. A large shadow fell over the wooden planks and when he looked up there was Bob Rosewarne.

'Nice morning, Richard.'

'The sun shines, Mr Rosewarne, but it does not warm me as it should.'

296

Bob Rosewarne nodded knowing what he alluded to. He grunted and settled beside Richard and the wood of the quay shifted slightly to accommodate him.

'Any pain?' Richard asked.

'Noooh, nothing to speak of. Ribs still a bit sore but I can work it off.'

They sat in silence each one thinking of the missing Nancy.

'I'm going to sell up, Mr Rosewarne, and move away. It's not something I want to do but I shall go mad if I stay.'

Rosewarne slowly nodded, not of agreement but acknowledgement. 'I shall miss you, Richard, if you leave. Where will you go?'

Richard looked through narrowed eyes against the glare of the sun off the water. He brushed at his breeches in an act of occupation while he thought how to answer. It was a ploy to test whether his threat would get back to Nancy and evoke a reply. He had only just thought of this stratagem and not thoroughly.

Rosewarne sighed. ''Tiss a bad business altogether, if you ask me, when two people in love can't get together again. Sad, I call it.'

Bob Rosewarne paused and it seemed deliberate to Richard to attract his attention. 'I thought wherever can she be? But no answer comes. I don't know what she's a living on either! When she left in a hurry she forgot to take her purse. Still, you made sure she had plenty in the bank. 'Tiss a worry all the same.'

*

The next morning Nelson and Emma drove to London where, while waiting to see Lord Castlereagh, the Secretary of State for War, Nelson met Major General Sir Arthur Wellesley.

*

Two days later Richard received a short note from Nancy – "Wait for me – I love you dearly. All will be made clear soon. Nancy". His patient strategy had borne fruit – he was now convinced that Mrs Rosewarne was in contact with her daughter.

The words Bob Rosewarne spoke came into this head. *I don't know what she's living on.*

She had to be using the bank and the manager would have a record of the transactions.

The next day Richard rode into Truro to see Mr Williams. There was a briskness in the air and the leaves on the trees were over their late summer dense greenness and turning brown at the edges. A bell rang as he entered the bank and a clerk, recognising him, approached.

'Good morning, Dr Maddern. Is there something I can do for you today?'

'I would like to speak with Mr Williams if I may. It is a matter of some urgency.'

Richard waited, still composing his opening gambit that he mentally changed every few seconds.

Mr Williams got up from behind his desk and came forward to shake hands.

'Good to see you, Dr Maddern,' he said formally. They sat opposite each other across the desk. 'How are things with you after your terrible ordeal?'

'As well as can be expected, is, I think, the usual phrase. You may be aware that Nancy went into hiding after the trial and I have had little communication from her since.'

Mr Williams listened attentively. 'I'm ashamed to say that I did not write to you with my condolences. There is gossip, of course, there always is – but I don't listen. I cannot pretend not to know, however, that your circumstances are estranged but no more than that.'

Mr Williams looked to Richard for the next move.

'Nancy has been absent for many weeks and I know she had little or no money with her when she left in a hurry. She has funds in your bank and I would like to know if she has made any withdrawals and where the money was sent.'

Mr Williams coughed, placing his hand in front of his face. 'Well...yes...now,' and he coughed again. 'Frankly it is not possible to give the information you require...supposing there were information to give that is. Umm...of course I should like to help, but...' and his hand rose to the heavens in supplication.

'Yes, I understand. As her husband and I still regard myself as such, I greatly fear for her life and well-being as I am sure you would feel if in my position.'

Mr Williams nodded slowly gazing at his desk. 'I would indeed,' he said softly. He remained in this fixed attitude for a while and then suddenly he slapped the desktop with both hands. 'Let us take a turn around the town, Doctor – this office is not the proper place for our business today.'

He moved purposefully to retrieve his hat and stick from the stand, opened the door to allow Richard to pass and together they emerged into the town. Mr Williams took Richard by the arm and spoke conspiratorially in a hushed voice.

'Here is better, Richard. Here we are friends and not client and bank manager and that is sufficient to salve my conscience. What I am about to say is not a betrayal of a confidence, but a clear and obvious case of simple straightforward common sense. When the report of the inquest was retold by the press, with obvious relish, my wife and I were desolate. The facts of your matrimonial state took priority over the dreadful violation of Nancy. I heard she had left. Imagine my surprise, therefore, when I received from Nancy a request to pay an invoice for services rendered.'

'Services rendered by whom?'

'Dr Luke.'

'She is ill?'

'That I cannot say. There is nothing on the invoice or on two others that followed to say what condition was being treated.'

'Two others you say?'

Mr Williams nodded.

'When was the latest?'

'A week ago.'

Mr Williams stopped and pulled Richard by his coat sleeve.

'My advice would be to see Dr Luke and raise it with him. But I daresay he is as hidebound as I am and will find difficulty in breaching a confidence.'

He pointed with his stick. 'This is his surgery – faint heart and so on.'

'Thank you, Mr Williams. You are a true friend.'

Richard found himself near the bottom of Lemon Street. At the side of the black door was a brass plate proclaiming Dr Luke had his surgery within. A smartly-dressed maid answered the door and gave a short bob.

'I am Dr Maddern and I would like to see Dr Luke, please.'

'Dr Luke is out visiting a patient, sir. May I take your card?'

As Richard searched for his card, a voice called down from an upper level.

'Rose?' and someone descended the stairs. He saw Mrs Luke wearing a light diaphanous dress over a floral patterned underdress. She smiled radiantly as she recognised Richard.

'Ah, Dr Maddern – that will be all, Rose, thank you,' and she took the card. 'Dr Luke is out and may not be back for some time. Is there anything that I might do,' and her voice faded, like her smile, knowing full well there was not.

Richard was downcast and stared at the wooden floor.

'I was hoping to see Dr Luke on a personal matter that involves my wife, Nancy…'

Seeing Richard hesitate she made another suggestion. 'Let us take a turn around the garden. It is so lovely this time of the year, don't you think?'

A narrow path took them to a seat where they sat close together.

'Now, what can I do?' she asked quietly.

'I learned today that your husband has been attending Nancy – for what condition I am unaware and you can imagine I am most anxious to learn from Dr Luke what the matter is.'

'Oh, you poor man,' she said with genuine feeling and touched his arm. Then she fell silent gathering her thoughts.

'Dr Luke is attending her and – you must not repeat what I am about to tell you – she is not ill.'

'Not ill? I don't understand?'

'Not in the normal sense,' she said, searching for a form of words to escape the predicament. Seeing his bewilderment, she tried to explain. 'Nancy is just taking precautions – there is nothing…I can say no more. Rest easy, Dr Maddern. I am absolutely certain you will see Nancy very soon.'

Homeward bound he passed through Playing Place and by the Alms houses that Mr Lanyon had built in 1726. To his surprise he saw Dr Luke mounted and saying farewell to an elderly man. Luke saw him and raised his riding stock in a faraway greeting. Richard reined-in determined to speak with him.

'Dr Luke, how fortunate. I have just called at your surgery in the hope of seeing you and here you are!'

'Good morning, Dr Maddern.' He seemed friendly enough but guarded as on the last time they met.

'I have learned that you are attending my wife – is that correct?

Luke looked to the ground and then back to Richard. 'You know better than to ask me that, Dr Maddern.'

'Yes of course. It's just that...'

'You haven't seen your...in sometime and are anxious about her,' he finished Richard's sentence.

Richard looked up and said nothing. For a while, neither rider said anything, only the fidgeting of their horses disturbed the silence between them. Luke stared steadily at Richard with hardly a blink.

'Sorry. I should not have asked,' Richard pulled Jake's head around and was about leave.

'Wait man!'

'Wait! I've done nothing else for months! Wait? For what?' Richard's voice rose in his anguish.

'I'm not insensitive to the cruel position you are in, but I have to find a middle way if I am to help you and keep the confidence of my patient.'

Richard could almost sense the machination of Luke's mind. Richard was not married to his patient; he was not a relation and had no rights to enquire.

'The best course of action for you right now is to go home. I know that must sound harsh but you must.'

'And wait.'

Luke pulled out a fob watch and consulted it then snapped it shut.

'No. Just go to your home.' He said this with great deliberation. 'Good day to you, Dr Maddern.' He raised his crop to his hat in a short salute and rode away.

Chapter 34

And wilt thou leave me thus?
And have no more pity
Of him that loveth thee?
Alas, thy cruelty
And wilt thou leave me thus?
Say nay! Say nay!

The words crashed through his head: all the bitterness rang true. Yet he could not put the vehemence into the words it needed and it wilted to a plea.

It was past noon; the day was stifling hot with barely a breeze. The heat muffled any sounds. Work on the land was stilled; the harvests were in and no-one was in the fallow fields apart from the occasional gleaner seen far off in the stubble. The fields awaited the plough and swallows gathered before migrating south.

Entering by the postern, he saw Edward emerge from the stable to take the reins while he dismounted. 'Edward.'

'Doctor,' was all that they exchanged.

Richard brushed the dust of the road from his coat and depressed the latch to the door. The kitchen was hot and smells of cooking greeted his empty stomach. Ruth hovered over the stove smiling cheerfully.

'I got a nice pie for dinner, Doctor. I 'spect you haven't had nothing all day?'

'You're very cheerful, Ruth.'

'Iss.'

'I shall be in the library, Ruth.'

'I should go to the drawing room, Doctor. The kettle is singing and I'll make a dish o' tay for you. And there be post,' she said, putting a letter into his hand.

'And it is better taken in the drawing room than the library?' he questioned. Arguing was not something he wanted to do and he made his way to the drawing room. He pushed the door open studying the letter but became aware someone was in the room and looking up he saw Nancy.

'Nancy!' he said softly afraid he might blow the apparition away. She stood hesitantly and nodded with a wary tense expression. Tense she may be, but Richard saw nothing other than she was looking the picture of health. But she was not at ease and paler than she would normally be for late summer.

'Are you ill?'

'No.'

He could not restrain himself longer and with his arms outstretched, he moved towards her.

'Nancy!' he cried but she backed away and held her hands as if to fend him off.

'Nancy! Please!' he pleaded, his hands went to his face and he began to weep.

'Richard,' she said. 'I have something to tell.'

She parted her brown pelisse and he saw the swelling her hands attempted to enclose.

'A baby?'

'Billy's.'

'Uddy's?'

'Billy's,' she repeated gently.

Richard stared at the slight swelling and then started towards her again.

'Richard! I want to have this baby. He will not be like Billy – his nature I mean. We...' and she hesitated, 'he will be as we teach him – good and kind and loving.'

'You think I would prevent you from having the baby?'

'You said so. That day Edward's wife was visited by Mildred Cocking – you said that you would do it in cases of incest or rape.'

'Nancy, I meant if I were asked but even then...'

'Then you said,' she was determined to finish her speech, constructed time and again during her isolation, 'that after the quickening it would be murder. That is what you said. The baby has been moving these last two weeks and Dr Luke confirmed it this morning. You will have to murder us both, Richard.' She followed this with a most courageous question that stung him to his core.

'Do you have murder in your heart, Richard?'

He could hardly believe she was asking him such an awful question.

'There is nothing in my heart, Nancy, since you broke it by leaving me when I needed you most. It is empty and cold.'

Her hands covered her face leaving just her blue eyes to witness the effects of her words. She was devastated and tears welled in her eyes. All she saw was a sad bent person she loved, suffering needlessly.

'Oh, Richard, I didn't mean to...' and she rushed into his arms. The welcome feel of her body in his arms broke all doubts and released all the pent up emotions. They cried and kissed each other saying comforting words and asking for forgiveness as Ruth knocked at the door and then entered with a dish o' tay.

The sight of the embracing lovers overcame her and she placed the tray with the tea on the table to wipe her eyes. She left and as she exited, she banged loudly on the door.

They sat close over their meal and said all the things they should have said months before. They scolded and chastised each other, their eyes glistened and their mouths smiled almost unceasingly.

As evening faded into night, they continued the reconciliation in bed. There the most difficult questions were asked, in the darkness where expressions could not be seen, where the hurt was less obvious and the ambience more conducive.

'Why didn't you tell me that you were married?'

'You might not have come to live with me.'

'You were very devious – taking my parents in on your plan.'

'Yes. I would have done more. Why didn't you tell me you were pregnant?'

'Oh I so wanted to. I was so pleased at the thought, nothing would get in the way of having it.'

'And you didn't trust me.'

'If you didn't want me to have it you would have found a

way of aborting it. Oh, I know you well enough. You would not force it upon me. You would find something in your chest of medicines.

'But the more I thought about it the worse my dilemma became. What if I stayed and then naturally miscarried – I would suspect you and suspicion would eventually turn to hatred and for the rest of my life I would hold it against you. Those were the terrible consequences of staying; thoughts that raced round and round in my mind,' she continued. 'Learning of your marriage, although it hurt, gave me the excuse to leave until such a time the clock could not be put back.'

'And what if that had not come out at the inquest?'

She fell silent for some time. 'That was what was destroying me. I could think of nothing else. I had to leave this house, my home, but needed an excuse. When your secret was uncovered in the court my mother told me hers.'

'Yes. Your father told me.'

'And all the while I had a secret. I didn't tell her even then! What else is there to discover? What other secrets do you have?' she asked not expecting an answer.

'I deliberately lead Billy Uddy into a trap.'

'I guessed that long ago! And I would have done the same.'

*

On the 2nd September, a post chaise arrived at Merton with Captain Blackwood with news that the French and Spanish fleets had left Ferrol and Corunna and entered Cadiz.

Napoleon withdrew from the channel ports and with some 200,000 men marched on Vienna. The threat of invasion had been postponed by about two years.

*

On Sunday 16 September, by special licence, they were married in St Piran's Church, Perranwell. More than fifty tinners and miners and a dozen bal maidens, their neighbours in the Row and the Jennings witnessed the event.

Afterwards they all retired to Mr Jennings' establishment to toast the bride and groom. They stayed until Nancy tired and, as they left, the whole mass of friends sang the song that first persuaded Richard he was in love: *The Larks they sang melodious.*

*

That same day Nelson boarded Victory and sailed from Portsmouth heading for Cape St Vincent.

On the 4th of November, when winter had cast its cold dark shadow over the land, news of a battle fought off Cape Trafalgar arrived by the *Pickle*, in Falmouth. History was at their doorstep and they saw Lieutenant Lapenotiere lean from his carriage.

'A great battle was fought off Cape Trafalgar. Victory is ours. Our dear Lord Nelson perished on the 21st October.' And he was gone, leaving them to digest the bittersweet message.

For the next weeks, the papers gave a fuller account and the immensity of the victory was appreciated. Not only were they safe now but, with the seas ruled by the navy, it ensured that Napoleon would not attempt to invade ever again.

*

Christmas was a quiet affair, the New Year passed uneventfully and with little celebration across a country that was anticipating the funeral of Nelson on Thursday 9th January. The reports of the awesome and sad occasion did not reach them for more than a week. Richard read the report to Nancy in the evening, as she sat as comfortably as her hugely distended body would allow. As he read, she shifted and held her back and he stopped.

'Uncomfortable?'

He watched as she struggled into a new position. 'Cushion?'

'No. Nothing will ease me.'

He read again until she gasped and cried out. Richard dropped the paper and went to her side. 'Starting?'

She recovered her breath and nodded.

'Ruth!' he called and instantly Ruth arrived as though anticipating the summons. 'Send for Mildred and I'll write a note for Dr Luke.'

Mildred dropped her barrow with the birthing stool outside the kitchen door two hours later. On a cold frosty night her breath steamed from her exertions and she sought the warm kitchen urgently.

306

'Struth 'tiss bitter cold, Ruth!' she laughed. ''Tiss just like it!' and her voice rose to a shriek. 'You can depend on it – to start late sure enough.'

'Come in out of it, Mildred. She broke waters a hour ago.'

Mildred shuffled into the heat and stood by the kitchen range to rid the cold that hung around her clothes.

'Will you have a dish o' tay, Mildred?'

'Iss I will,' she agreed spreading her hands in front of the fire. 'Is the doctor with her?' she asked.

'Her man, Richard,' Ruth assured her.

'Aw, that's all right then. I'll have the tay first then see to her.'

Dawn had a hard time coming against the dark forces of winter; the sky overcast with storm clouds too dense for the weak winter sun to penetrate.

Nancy was hours into her labour and the pains were coming stronger. Richard heard her crying out and clenched his hands each time. His inactivity heightened the anxiety.

'I'm going to inform Mrs Rosewarne,' he said to Ruth. 'Time is getting close.'

Mrs Rosewarne went straight to Nancy, followed by Ruth, leaving Richard and Bob alone.

Settling with a glass of cider in the library, they were better friends through the adversities they had faced and the recent marriage had cemented their relations.

'You've been through this before, Mr Rosewarne – almost exactly the same from what I hear.'

The large man sighed heavily as he toyed with his glass.

'Iss I have, Richard. It brings it home to me like 'twas yesterday. We had nobody to turn to. No.' He sipped the cider. 'Well, that's the way we was. Out of it. Nobody knew where we was. So we had to manage. Course I'd tended 'osses and pigs afore but a woman? No.'

'And not your own child, either.'

'Aw, that didn't make no difference. When she ran off like that and nowhere to go, I couldn't let her go on her own. I found this here farm. And that's where we stopped. Iss, all they years ago.' He lapsed into silence.

'Was it an easy birth?'

'I had no money,' Bob Rosewarne resumed, ignoring the question. 'The missus had it all. She had money, jewels and silverware so we had to sell them. I didn't like it one bit, living off her like that, but the rent had to be paid.'

The occasion was bringing back memories he had kept buried for most of his life. What was foremost in his mind was his guilt from that time and not the imminent birth of his grandchild.

'See 'twas the wrong time of the year – the fall. We had to wait 'fore I could provide.'

He spoke the last words with great emphasis. 'We never heard of anybody come looking for us. That's what she was most afraid of – being taken back by her father. Course, I would have been strung up no doubt. We...' and he coughed. 'We wasn't...well umm...living together like, if you understand me meaning. Anyhow, when Nancy starts 'tiss only me. I was...well worried about things if it went wrong. Missus had it all worked out. Money in a purse for my passage to America.' He nodded to emphasize the point. 'All in hand, as you might say. Well, he didn't work out like that. Nancy was a long time in coming and it wasn't easy, I'll tell you. No. But there 'tiss.'

'Was she a big...'

'I loved her as 'twass me own. Handsome little maid she was from the start. Never a minute's trouble.'

'Did she...'

'Course me and the missus wasn't living like a man and woman – not then. Gradual like we come to it.' His eyes looked vacantly to the floor.

'We got married just after Nancy was born which made things different. But Nancy must have...well you know...we never had children. No.' The last syllable was more of a sigh.

Bob Rosewarne was now deep into his story. He would have gone on longer had not a knock at the door disturbed his tale.

'Dr Luke is here,' Ruth announced.

Richard leapt to his feet and noted the time – ten in the morning.

'Dr Luke! Thank you for coming. Please!' and he waved an arm to welcome him into the house.

'Good morning, Dr Maddern. I didn't rush after I got your

message. I knew she was in good hands.'

'Yes. A midwife is here – I thought it a sensible...' he added almost apologetically.

'Midwives are probably far more useful than a pair of qualified physicians.'

Richard thought he had inadvertently insulted Luke but when Luke saw the worry on his face, he expanded his remark.

'No! Truth. I mean it. Now another indulgence, good doctor, at a time I'm sure you can do without it. My wife insisted she came. Never happened before,' and in an aside. 'I hope it never happens again. She's outside in the chaise.'

Richard smiled broadly. 'Please bring her in. She is most welcome.'

Mrs Luke wore a cloak against the rough weather and hurried inside before throwing back the hood. 'Is all going well?' she asked.

'Now, my dear, I should be asking that,' Luke said laughingly.

'Yes.' Richard answered. 'Although I haven't seen her for a while. There are too many women in close attendance just now. Can I offer you some refreshment?'

'Tea, please.'

'And you, Doctor?'

'I'll see the patient first. Hot water is ready I assume?' he asked turning towards Ruth who snorted with a scornful look.

When Richard showed Mrs Luke into the library, a somewhat startled Mr Rosewarne stood to greet her. He was clearly disturbed by her and stuttered his greeting. Richard was bemused, but before he could say anything more a cry from upstairs alerted them all.

'It's here. It has arrived!' and Richard excused himself and ran up the stairs. In the bedroom all was busy. Mrs Cocking had the baby wrapped in a cloth; Dr Luke was at Nancy's side.

''Tiss a boy, Doctor,' Mrs Cocking informed him and held out the baby towards Richard. He took him and gently laid the new arrival on the scales.

'Eight pounds, all but an ounce. A fine fellow!' he said and turned to Nancy. He caught her looking at him anxiously.

Richard wrapped the tiny, fidgeting baby and delivered the

bundle to his wife. He kissed her lightly and smoothed her hair.

'A boy, just what you wanted,' he said.

She nodded and smiled, but he could still detect the anxious look about her eyes.

'And just what I wanted – he'll keep me young,' he laughed lightly, kissing her again.

'I'll leave you now, my sweet,' Mrs Rosewarne said, and moved towards the door.

Luke watched her with curiosity, seemed about to ask a question, then thought better of it and returned to Nancy.

'Yes, Mrs Maddern, a fine boy indeed,' he said. 'Thank you, Mrs Cocking,' Luke acknowledged the midwife. 'As usual, my services were scarcely required. And now I think we'll all leave the proud parents for a while and take up the offer of refreshment.' Luke held open the door for Mildred and Mrs Rosewarne, and they left Richard, Nancy and the baby alone.

'Happy?' he asked.

'Yes. Wonderfully happy…except,' and the anxiety returned. He sensed she still needed reassurance. He drew nearer and spoke softly.

'Nancy I love you more each passing day and our son will make us whole. We shall bring him up lovingly and ensure his future is as best as we can make it.'

Nancy's smile grew broader and her face relaxed. She looked down at the baby in her arms. 'He's got black hair.'

He nodded. 'They all do at this stage – well almost all. He'll probably turn as blonde as you, I expect.'

She examined the tiny face intently. 'He doesn't look like anyone.'

Richard, too, stared at the face that seemed to have a whole range of expressions passing over it. 'Oh, I don't know. He looks like everyone to me,' he said and chuckled.

He kissed her again. 'Have you decided on names?' They had discussed this at length and Richard had said that it would be Nancy's decision. 'Now that we know that we have a son, not a daughter, and you have seen him, has it helped you to decide?'

Nancy nodded, 'Yes, his first name must be Richard.'

'Splendid! And what is to follow Richard?'

She suggested, 'Robert?'

'Equally splendid! And Maddern to finish – unless you want to include Vyvyan?'

She shook her head and smiled. 'Richard Robert Maddern is enough names for any man.'

*

In the privacy of the drawing room, two women faced each other across the table.

They were alike. Mrs Rosewarne was older and more worn; Mrs Luke cool and elegant. It was the older woman who spoke first.

'So, Harriet, you have found me at last.'

'Oh Florrie…' she could say no more, but moved around the table, her arms reaching out to embrace her sister.